The World's Best Short Stories

Anthology & Criticism

Volume I
Short Story Masters
Early 19th Century

THE WORLD'S BEST SERIES

The World's Best Short Stories

I. *Short Story Masters: Early 19th Century*

Forthcoming:
II. *Short Story Masters: Late 19th & Early 20th Centuries*
III. *Famous Stories*
IV. *Fables and Tales*
V, VI. *Genres*
VII. *Characters*
VIII. *Places*
IX. *Cultures*
X. *Research and Reference: Criticism and Indexes*

The World's Best Poetry

Foundation Volumes I-X

Supplements:
I. *Twentieth Century English and American Verse, 1900-1929*
II. *Twentieth Century English and American Verse, 1930-1950*
III. *Critical Companion*
IV. *Minority Poetry of America*
V. *Twentieth Century Women Poets*
VI. *Twentieth Century African and Latin American Verse*
VII. *Twentieth Century Asian Verse*

CoreFiche: *World's Best Drama*
Microfiche with companion reference

The World's Best Short Stories

Anthology & Criticism

Volume I

Short Story Masters Early 19th Century

Hoffmann, Balzac, Merimee, Hawthorne, Poe, Gogol

Prepared by
The Editorial Board

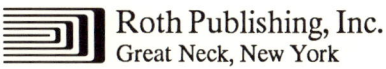 Roth Publishing, Inc.
Great Neck, New York

Copyright © 1989 Roth Publishing, Inc.
All rights reserved

ISBN 0-89609-303-4
ISBN for 10 Volume Set 0-89609-400-6
Library of Congress Catalog Card Number 89-60440

Manufactured in the U.S.A.

Contents

Preface vii
Introduction ix

E.T.A. Hoffmann

Critical Appreciation 3
Councillor Krespel 6
Don Juan 25
The Mines of Falun 38

Honoré de Balzac

Critical Appreciation 61
La Grande Bretèche 66
A Passion in the Desert 83
The Hidden Masterpiece 95

Prosper Mérimée

Critical Appreciation 121
Mateo Falcone 126
The Pearl of Toledo 136
The Game of Backgammon 138
The Etruscan Vase 151

Nathaniel Hawthorne

Critical Appreciation 173
The Ambitious Guest 176
Night Sketches 183
The Prophetic Pictures 188

Young Goodman Brown 200
  The Birthmark 212

Edgar Allan Poe

  Critical Appreciation 229
  MS. Found in a Bottle 232
  William Wilson 241
  Hop-Frog 252
  The Purloined Letter 267

Nikolai Gogol

  Critical Appreciation 287
  Ivan Fyodorovich Shponka and His Aunt..............291
  The Overcoat 313

Preface

The World's Best Short Stories is designed to give both the serious student and the general reader a large selection and broad range of stories from around the world. Its ten volumes organize the stories into seven reader-friendly groupings:

Short Story Masters (Volumes I and II)
Famous Stories (Volume III)
Fables and Tales (Volume IV)
Genres (Volumes V and VI)
Characters (Volume VII)
Places (Volume VIII)
Cultures (Volume IX)

Volume X is a research and reference guide and includes a cumulative index to all the volumes.

The arrangement of the stories suggests the multiple approaches for using these volumes. *Short Story Masters* focuses on the author; it contains stories that demonstrate the development of the short story as a conscious art form. *Famous Stories* is the volume to go to for well-known stories by authors who may or may not themselves be well-known. *Fables and Tales* includes fairy tales and other short non-realistic literature, as well as tales that are ancestors of the short story form. *Genres* is a kind of counterpart to *Short Story Masters*. Whereas *Masters* places the short story in the tradition of an evolving art, *Genres* puts it at the disposal of the general reader and the popular imagination. Included are fixed forms: mysteries, supernatural and ghost stories, detective fiction, science fiction, and other "types" indicative of the wide appeal of short stories.

The later volumes contain stories that are remarkable for a salient feature. The stories in *Characters* are portrait studies: their primary function is to examine the character of the hero or heroine. *Places* compiles stories that evoke a setting in a way that is memorable and important to the being of the story. Finally, *Cultures* uses ethnicity as its backdrop. It carries stories that are informed by their cultural setting.

The organization, variety, and breadth of **The World's Best Short Stories** makes it a unique anthology collection that can be used for study or read for pleasure.

Introduction

Short Story Masters is a two-volume survey that focuses on authors who have significantly contributed to the development of the short story. This first volume, *Early 19th Century*, includes stories by six authors: E.T.A. Hoffmann, Honore de Balzac, Prosper Merimee, Nathaniel Hawthorne, Edgar Allan Poe, and Nikolai Gogol. Volume II, *Late 19th & Early 20th Centuries*, includes stories by eight authors: Henry James, Guy de Maupassant, Anton Chekhov, Stephen Crane, Sherwood Anderson, James Joyce, and Katherine Mansfield. Each author is introduced by a chronology and a critical appreciation; a cumulative index concludes Volume II.

Since the short story as a conscious art form is a nineteenth-century invention, it is no accident that twelve of the fourteen masters in Volumes I and II were born in the nineteenth century (Balzac nearly makes it with a birthdate of 1799; Hoffman was born in 1776). The authors in Volume I (again with the exception of Hoffmann) were all born within a ten year period at the turn of the century. Those in Volume II were born a generation or more later (beginning with James in 1843). Nearly all the stories were written before World War I (only Anderson and Mansfield were actively writing short stories after that). Six of the authors are American, three are French, two British, two Russian, and one German.

What constitutes a "short story master"? For purposes of this anthology, neither abundance nor dedication solely to the short story form. Rather, authors were chosen who helped make the short story evolve from a string of incidents into a fiction having a unified effect. Hawthorne and Poe were the first to be conscious of the short story as a technique, but Hoffmann and Balzac were important predecessors both in their use of short fiction and for struggling with narrative problems associated with short stories. Merimee pioneered the story of detached, dispassionate observation and Mauppassant followed him. Indeed, Mauppassant and O. Henry together are names that are nearly synonymous with *short story*. Gogol and Joyce wrote stories that are among the greatest shorts ("The Overcoat" and "The Dead," respectively), while James continually returned to short fiction to stretch its boundaries. Both Chekhov and Mansfield wrote stories of tone and mood; Crane and Anderson brought the technique home and made their stories idiomatically American.

The survey ends before the short story burgeoned in the twentieth century and became for its practitioners as flexible and varied a vessel for thought and feeling as lyric poetry. It is simply outside the scope of *Short Story Masters* to include those authors here: some of them will be included in later volumes of **The World's Best Short Stories**. The authors that have been included in *Masters* belong on anyone's list of contributors to the short story form; and most would be included on anyone's brief list. The intention has been to present a mix of the familiar and unfamiliar, to please with the reacquaintance of old stories, and to surprise with the discovery of new ones.

Hoffmann

1776	January 24. Ernst Theodor Wilhelm Hoffmann born at Königsberg, East Prussia. (In homage to Mozart he later changes his name from Wilhelm to Amadeus.)
1800	After studying law in Königsberg, Glogau, and Berlin, he is appointed to the Prussian courts of law for the Polish provinces. His first post is in Posen.
1802	Marries the 24 year old Marianna Thekla Michaelina Rorer, who is Polish and two years younger than Hoffmann. Shortly thereafter is discharged from Posen for caricaturing one of his superiors and is transferred to Plozk.
1804–06	Manages a transfer to Warsaw where he cultivates his taste for music and the other arts. Composes music, including a symphony and an opera, and conducts. Meets the romantic dramatist Zacharias Werner and has time to become acquainted with the works of Calderón and German romantics. With the French invasion of 1806, the Prussian government in Poland ends and Hoffmann loses his position.
1808–13	Arrives in Bamberg and works as conductor, musical director, and theatrical designer. Composes the operas *Aurora* and *Undine*; writes music criticism and publishes his first tales. In April 1813 he is engaged as a conductor in Dresden.
1814–21	After a musical falling out, Hoffmann accepts a position at the court of appeals in Berlin, the city in which he lives until his death. Writes many of his best and most famous tales and collects them in *Nachstücke* (1817) and *Die Serapionsbrüder* (4 vol., 1819–21).
1822	Dies on June 25. The tales influence writers in France, England, and America, as well as Russia, Poland, and Sweden. The tales are also influential to composers of ballet (Delibe's *Coppelia*, 1870; Tchaikovsky's *The Nutcracker*, 1892) and opera (Offenbach's *The Tales of Hoffmann*, 1881; Hindemith's *Cardillac*, 1926).

E.T.A. Hoffmann

Theodor Hoffmann was born in Königsberg in 1776, the son of parents whose inharmonious union was soon dissolved. His mother belonged to a painfully well-regulated and conventional family; his father was as eccentric as he was clever, and had irregular habits which were a great affliction to his wife's relations. Theodor lost his mother early, and the pedantic severity with which his uncle brought him up only made the gifted boy's occasional wild outbursts wilder and madder. He found vent for his feelings in peculiar musical compositions and remarkably clever caricatures. He studied law as a profession, but at the same time devoted much attention to music. At an early age he fell in love with a young married woman. Feeling that the violence of this passion was undermining his reason, he cured himself of it by tearing himself away from his native town, at the age of twenty.

Soon after this he received a government appointment in Posen. The wild dissipation which prevailed in Poland in those days carried him completely off his feet and materially altered his character. For caricaturing one of his superiors he was removed to Plozk, where he led a more regular life. In 1804 he was transferred to Warsaw, at that time a Prussian town; and it was the full, varied, and, to a German, quite foreign life of this important city which gave Hoffmann's literary tendencies their decisive, final bent. Much that is mad and strange in his writings may be attributed to the wild, reckless joviality of the Warsaw days. In Warsaw he met Zacharias Werner, another author who was distinctly influenced by the social life of Poland in the beginning of the century. And here, whilst conscientiously fulfilling the duties of his appointment, he not only found time to cultivate his favorite art, music, and to frequent the society of other musical devotees, but also managed to decorate several halls with frescoes, to ornament a library with alto-reliefs executed in bronze, and to paint a room in the Egyptian style, adroitly introducing amongst the extraordinary representations of Egyptian gods, caricatures of his acquaintances, whom he provided with tails and wings. It was in Warsaw too that he conducted concerts for the first time.

In 1806, as every one knows, Prussian rule in Warsaw came to an end. Hoffmann saw the streets of the town crowded, first with the vanguard of the Russian army—Tartars, Cossacks, and Bashkirs—then with Murat's troops, watched the migrations of the races set in motion by Napoleon's campaign, and at last saw Napoleon himself, whom he, the good German, abhorred as a tyrant. In Dresden, in 1813, he was eyewitness of several small skirmishes and one battle; he walked over a battlefield, lived through a famine and a species of plague which followed in the train of the war—in short, his imagination was fertilized by all the horrors of the period, the first result being, characteristically enough, merely a set of funny caricatures of the French.

When still quite a young man, he had married a beautiful Polish lady, who made him a devoted and patient wife; it was probably thanks to her that, in spite of his overstrained nerves, he lived as long as he did. His marriage by no means precluded many passionate attachments to other women, but all these seem to have had their root rather in imagination than in any real feeling. Three days after a young lady with whom he was madly in love had engaged herself to another, he was perfectly happy, having cured himself of his passion by satirizing it. He was helped to bear his woe by the pleasure of caricaturing it.

After figuring as a theatrical architect in Bamberg and conductor of an orchestra in Dresden, he went to Berlin, where he spent the last years of his life as a member of the Kammergericht (one of the principal courts of justice). As was natural, the astonishingly gifted man who could write books, improvise on the piano, compose operas, draw caricatures, and scintillate wit when he was in the humor, became a lion in social circles and a fêted frequenter of the taverns. He devoted a great share of his energy and talent to the observation of his own moods, which he watched closely and described day by day in a kind of diary.

Wine, which he only regarded as an exciting stimulant, was in reality much more than this to him. To it he owed much of his inspiration, his visions, those hallucinations which at first were fanciful, but became ever more serious. In his case intoxication actually produced a new kind of fantastic poetry. When under the influence of alcohol, he saw the darkness suddenly illuminated by phosphorescent light, or saw a gnome rise through the floor, or saw himself surrounded by specters and terrible grimacing figures, which went on disappearing and reappearing in all kinds of grotesque disguises.

It was almost inevitable that this painstaking observer of his own moods and of the external peculiarities, more especially the oddities, of other men, should care little about nature. If he took a walk in summer, it was only to reach some place or other where he would be certain to meet human beings; and he seldom passed a pastry cook's or a tavern without dropping in to see what kind of people frequented it. This explains the striking want of any feeling for fresh, open-air nature in his books. His mind was at home in a tavern, not in forest solitudes. But if his sense of the beauties of nature was weak, his enthusiasm for art was so much the more intense; genuine Romanticist that he is, half of his productions treat of art.

The peculiar, Romantic theory of human personality held by a poet of this temperament and this development was a product of over-impressionable and over-strained nerves and of irregular living. In his diary I find the following memoranda:

1804. — Drank Bischof at the new club from 4 to 10. Frightfully agitated in the evening. Nerves excited by the spiced wine. Possessed by thoughts of death and Doppelgänger.

1809. — Seized by a strange fancy at the ball on the 6th; I imagine myself looking at my Ego through a kaleidoscope — all the forms moving round me are Egos, and annoy me by what they do and leave undone.

1810. — Why do I think so much, sleeping and waking, about madness?

It was a settled conviction with Hoffmann that when anything good befalls a man, an evil power is always lurking in the background to paralyze the action of the good power. As he expresses it: "The devil thrusts his tail into everything." He was haunted, says his biographer, Hitzig, by a fear of mysterious horrors, of "Doppelgänger" and spectral apparitions of every kind. He used to look anxiously round while writing about them; and if it was at night, he would often wake his wife and beg her to keep him company till he had finished. He imparted his own fear of ghosts to the characters he created; he drew them "as he himself was drawn in the great book of creation." It does not surprise us to learn that of his own works, he preferred those which contain the most gruesome pictures of madness or the weirdest caricatures.

He relies for effect, in a manner which soon becomes mannerism, upon the sharp contrasts with which he ushers in his terrific or comical scenes. From the commonest, most prosaic everyday life we are suddenly transported into a perfectly distorted world, where miracles and juggling tricks of every kind so bewilder us that in the end no relation, no species of life, no personality, seems definite and certain. We are always in doubt as to whether we are dealing with a real person, with his specter, with his essence in another form or other power, or with his fantastic "Doppelgänger."

—*from* Main Currents in Nineteenth Century Literature, Vol. 2, *by George Morris Cohen Brandes*

Councillor Krespel

The man (Theodore Began) whom I propose to tell you about as none other than Councillor Krespel, of H—.

This Councillor Krespel was, in point of fact, among the strangest characters I have ever encountered. Going to H — for a prolonged stay, I found the whole town talking about him: one of his craziest performances was in full swing.

Krespel was known as a learned and skillful lawyer and an able diplomat. A rather insignificant German prince had employed him to draw up a memorial for submission to the imperial court, presenting his legal claims to a certain piece of territory.

The claim was prosecuted most successfully; and, as Krespel had once complained that he could never seem to find a house that suited him, the prince, as a recompense for drawing up the memorial, offered to pay for a house built exactly as Krespel wanted it. The prince was also ready to buy any piece of ground Krespel might choose.

This, however, Krespel declined. He insisted that the house should be built in his own garden, which was agreeably situated outside the town gate. He next bought every imaginable kind of building material, and had it delivered on the spot. Then for days on end he was to be seen in his strange costume (which incidentally he had created for himself on lines of his own), slaking the lime, screening sand, and piling up building stone in uniform piles. He had not talked to any architect, nor considered any plans.

But one fine day he asked a capable master mason in H— to report at daybreak the following day with all his journeymen, apprentices, and a number of helpers, to start building the house.

Naturally the mason inquired about the plans. He was not a little surprised when Krespel told him that none were needed, that everything would come right of itself.

When the master mason arrived with his men the following morning, he found a ditch dug in a perfect rectangle. Krespel said to him, "This is where the foundation of my house is to go. Will you kindly run up the four walls until I tell you they are high enough?"

"No windows or doors? No partitions?" objected the mason, as if horrified at Krespel's lunacy.

"Just what I am telling you, my dear man," replied Krespel nonchalantly. "Everything will appear in due course."

Only the promise of generous payment could induce the mason to undertake this insane task. But never was a job more merrily done. The workmen did not quit the grounds, for there was plenty to eat and drink. Amid steady laughter, the four walls rose with incredible speed, until one day Krespel shouted, "Stop!"

Trowel and hammer were silenced. The workmen came down from the scaffoldings. As they surrounded Krespel, each laughing face seemed to say, "What next?"

"Make room!" cried Krespel. He hastened to one end of the garden, then slowly turned and marched toward his rectangle. Near the wall he shook his head in dissatisfaction. He went back to the other end of the garden, paced toward the rectangle again, and stopped as before.

This he repeated several times, and then, finally, running his sharp nose hard into the wall, shouted loudly, "Here, come on, you lads; cut me the door, cut me a door here."

He indicated the width and height in feet and inches, and saw his instructions carried out. Marching in, he smiled complacently as the master mason observed that the walls were just high enough for a sizable two-story house. Krespel walked deliberately up and down inside, while at his heels the masons were working with hammer and pick. He would cry out, "Here a window, six feet high and four feet wide! There a little one, three by two!" They would be broken through forthwith.

During this very performance I arrived in H—. It was thrilling to watch hundreds of people standing agape outside the garden, cheering loudly whenever the stones popped out to make a new window where none had been expected.

Krespel proceeded with the rest of the building in the same way, giving instructions for everything on the spot. The whimsicality of the whole proceeding, the general conviction that everything was turning out better than could have been expected, and particularly Krespel's openhandedness (though this cost him nothing), put everyone in high good humor. Thus the difficulties involved in his eccentric method of building were overcome.

Very soon a completely furnished house greeted the beholder. From the outside it was quite mad-looking—no one window, for instance, was like any other. But indoors it had a special coziness of its own. Everyone who saw the inside was of this opinion, and I could feel it myself when Krespel received me there after we became better acquainted.

So far I had never seen the man to speak to him. He was so much taken up with his building that he did not even come to dinner on Tuesday at Professor M—'s, as was his custom. Receiving a particular invitation, he sent back word to the professor that he would not set foot outside the door until after the housewarming.

All his friends and acquaintances were anticipating a great banquet; but Krespel invited no one except the master mechanics, journeymen, apprentices, and helpers who had built his house. He served the finest delicacies. Apprentice masons grimly gobbled partridge pie, carpenters' lads sawed away happily at roast pheasant, and hungry helpers now helped themselves to the finest bits of the truffle fricassee.

In the evening the wives and daughters arrived for a great ball. First treading out a waltz or two with the masters' wives, Krespel joined the city band, took a fiddle, and led the music for dancing until broad daylight.

On the Tuesday after this feast, which presented Councillor Krespel in the light of a friend to the common people, I was not a little pleased to meet him finally at Professor M—'s.

Anything more extraordinary than Krespel's manner would be impossible to imagine. His movements were so abrupt and uncouth that one momentarily expected him to bump into or break something; but he never did. This was obviously taken for granted, since the lady of the house never flickered an eye as he swung himself with heavy strides around a table set with the most fragile of china teacups and maneuvered his way toward the pier glass, or even when he grabbed a flowerpot of superbly painted china and brandished it about as if to let the light play on the colors.

In fact, before dinner, Krespel minutely inspected everything in the professor's drawing room. Mounting on an upholstered chair, he would take a picture off the wall, then hang it up again. At the same time he kept talking in a steady, violent stream. It became noticeable at dinner that first he would skip quickly from one subject to another, then he would seem tied to a single idea, picking it up again and again, following the oddest convolutions, and not recovering himself until some new thought took hold of him. His tone of voice was now rough, violent and rasping, then soft, drawling, singsong. But it never matched what Krespel was saying.

The talk was about music, and someone praised a new composer. Krespel smiled, and said in a soft, singing voice, "How I wish sable-plumed Satan might send that accursed tone-twister ten thousand million fathoms into the nether pit of hell!"

Then he would burst out in savage tones: "She is an angel from heaven, divine melody, pure and simple! The very sun and firmament of song!" And his eyes would fill with tears as he spoke. One had to recollect that a famous songstress had been talked of perhaps an hour before.

A roast hare was served. I noticed that Krespel carefully cleaned all the meat off the bones on his plate, and asked particularly for the paws, which the professor's five-year-old daughter brought to him with a tender smile. In fact all through dinner the children had been watching the councillor expectantly. They now got up from the table, and went over to him, but maintained a respectful distance of three paces.

What next? I wondered.

Dessert came on. At this point the councillor took from his pocket a small box containing a little steel lathe, which he forthwith clamped to the table. On it, with incredible skill and speed, he turned all sorts of tiny boxes, balls, and the like out of the rabbit bones. The children welcomed these presents with great glee.

Just as everyone was leaving the table, the professor's niece asked, "And how does our Antonia, my dear councillor?"

Krespel made a face like someone biting into a sour orange and trying to look as if it were sweet. But in a moment his countenance was distorted into a horrid mask, wearing an expression of scornful laughter that was bitter, savage, and, it seemed to me, truly diabolical.

"Our? Our dear Antonia?" he asked in a drawling, disagreeably singsong voice.

The professor hastily came up. The reproving glance that he cast at his niece told me she had touched some chord in Krespel's breast that was sure to jar harshly.

"How are the violins?" the professor inquired cheerfully, clasping both of the councillor's hands.

At this, Krespel's face cleared, and he answered in his strong voice, "Oh, excellent, professor. Only this morning I cut open that splendid Amati instrument. I was telling you recently by what stroke of luck it came into my hands. I hope Antonia has finished taking it carefully apart by now."

"Antonia is a good child," said the professor.

"Indeed she is!" yelled the councillor, spinning around, making one grab for his hat and cane, and rushing out of the door. I could see in the mirror that his eyes were bright with tears.

The moment the councillor was gone, I importuned the professor to tell me the story of the violins, and particularly of Antonia.

"Well," said the professor, "the councillor is a very queer character, generally, and he builds violins in a mad way, too."

"Builds violins?" I asked in amazement.

"Yes," the professor returned. "In the opinion of good judges, Krespel makes the most magnificent violins anywhere to be found at the present day. Sometimes, when one of them was particularly successful, he used to let other people play it; but lately he has given that up. Once Krespel has made a violin, he plays it himself for an hour or two, with tremendous power and irresistible expressiveness; then he hangs it up beside the others, and never touches it again, or lets anyone else touch it. Whenever a violin from some old master is to be found, the councillor buys it at any price that may be asked of him. But just as he does with his own instruments, he plays it only once; then he takes it apart to study the inner structure. If he does not find what he thinks he is looking for, he morosely throws the pieces into a big box, which is already piled with the ruins of dissected violins."

"But what about Antonia?" I asked impatiently.

"That is an affair," the professor returned, "which might make me utterly abhor the councillor if I were not convinced—knowing his character, which at bottom is kindly almost to the point of softness— that there must be some obscure explanation. When the councillor first moved to H— some years ago, he lived like a hermit in a gloomy house in—Street, with an old housekeeper to look after him. His eccentricities soon aroused the curiosity of the neighbors. The moment he noticed this, he went out of his way to make acquaintances. Just as at my house, people everywhere grew so accustomed to him that he became indispensably attached to them. Children loved him despite his crusty exterior. But they never annoyed him, for, though he was always kind, he inspired a certain shyness and respect that forbade all impertinence. This afternoon he showed how he can make friends with children by the many arts of which he is master.

"We all took him for a crotchety old bachelor, and he never contradicted the impression. After he had been here for a time, he went away, nobody knew where. Then a few months later, he was back. The evening after his return, Krespel's windows were lit up with unusual brilliance. This in itself attracted the attention of the neighbors, and very soon they began to hear a perfectly magnificent female voice accompanied by a pianoforte. Then the notes of a violin joined in, vying keenly with the voice. The councillor was evidently the violinist.

"I myself joined the large crowd that had gathered outside the councillor's house to hear this marvelous concert, and I must confess that the most celebrated songstresses I had ever heard were feeble and wooden by comparison with the voice and the special, deeply moving expression of the unknown. I had never dreamed of such long-sustained notes, such nightingale warbling, such rolling waves of melody, such swelling to the force of an organ, such fading to a mere whisper. Not a single listener but stood rapt under the sweet spell. Only gentle sighs went up in the profound hush as the songstress fell silent.

"It must have been about midnight when the councillor was heard talking in violent tones. Judging by the sounds, another masculine voice, interrupted by the broken plaints of a girl, was upbraiding him. The councillor shouted louder and louder, until finally he fell into his familiar drawling, singsong tone. A piercing scream from the girl interrupted him; then came deathly silence.

"Suddenly there was a clattering on the stairs, and a young man rushed out, sobbing, flung himself into a post chaise that was standing near, and drove off at a rapid pace.

"The following morning the councillor seemed very cheerful, and no one dared question him about the events of the night before. The housekeeper, however, reported that the councillor had brought home a young girl, as pretty as a picture, whom he called Antonia. She was the one who had sung so divinely. A young man had also arrived, who had treated Antonia most tenderly, and was no doubt her betrothed. But she said, he had had to depart in haste because the councillor had absolutely insisted upon it.

"Antonia's relationship to the councillor remains a mystery, but this much is certain; he tyrannizes over the poor girl in the most abominable fashion. He watches over her as Doctor Bartholo in the *Barber of Seville* watched over his wards. She scarcely dares let herself be seen at the window. If he does yield to people's entreaties, and brings her out in company, he follows her with Argus eyes. He will not suffer the slightest musical note to be heard, let alone allow Antonia to go on singing at home. So, in the minds of the townspeople, Antonia's singing that night became an exciting and fascinating fairy tale, a great marvel. Even those who never heard her at all would often say, when some singer tries her luck in town, 'What vile squeaking is this? Only Antonia can really sing.' "

I have always had a passion for this fantastic sort of thing, and you can imagine how determined I was to make Antonia's acquaintance. I had often heard the townspeople speak of her singing, but I had had no idea that the magnificent creature was in this very town, actually in the madman Krespel's power, as if under the spell of some tyrannical wizard.

Naturally I heard Antonia's superb singing in my dreams that very night. She beseeched me most movingly to save her in a wonderful adagio (ridiculously enough, it seemed as if I had composed it myself); and I soon resolved to force my way into Krespel's enchanted castle, and rescue the queen of song from durance vile.

It all turned out otherwise than I had expected; for I had seen the councillor no more than two or three times, and avidly discussed with him the best ways of building violins before he invited me of his own accord to call on him at home.

I accepted. He showed me his violin treasures. There must have been thirty hanging in a cabinet. One of them was distinguished by every sign of extreme antiquity—carved lion head, and all the rest of it. Hanging above the others, with a wreath of flowers above, it seemed to reign as queen over its fellows.

"This violin," said Krespel, when I asked him about it, "this violin is a superb and remarkable piece by an unknown master, probably from the time of Tartini. I am fully convinced that there is some special peculiarity in its inner construction, that if I were to take it apart, I should uncover a secret that I have long been pursuing. But—you may laugh at me if you like—that inanimate object, to which I must give life and expression by my own skill, often speaks to me in some strange fashion. The first time I played it, I had a feeling that I was merely the hypnotist stirring the sleepwalker to put her inner vision into words of her own. You must not suppose that I am silly enough to have any belief in such fantastic nonsense. Still it is odd that I could never bring myself to cut up that foolish lifeless thing over there. But I am glad I did not. Now that Antonia is here, I sometimes play for her on this violin. Antonia delights in it—she does, indeed."

As he spoke these words, the councillor was visibly moved. This encouraged me to say, "Ah, my dear Mr. Councillor, will you not play while I am here?"

Krespel, however, made one of his sweet-and-sour grimaces, and said, in his drawling, singsong inflection, "No, my dear young sir!"

With this, the matter was dropped. I now had to inspect various curiosities, some of them quite childish. Finally, reaching into a small casket, he took out a folded piece of paper.

He handed it to me, saying very solemnly, "You are a lover of the arts. Accept this gift as a precious memento, and let it remain forever dear to you above all things." So saying, he pushed me by both shoulders very gently toward the door, and embraced me on the threshold. As a matter of fact, in symbolic fashion he was really throwing me out. When I opened the paper, I found inside a piece of E string about an eighth of an inch long. Written on the paper was: "From the E string that the sainted Stamitz had on his violin when he played his last concert."

The rude rebuff which I received when I mentioned Antonia led me to think I should probably never see her. But such was not the case, for, the second time I called on the councillor, I found Antonia in his room, helping him assemble a violin.

Antonia created no very great impression at first glance, but before long one was quite fascinated by her blue eyes and exquisite rosebud lips. She was an uncommonly sweet and dainty creature. She was very pale, but when anything gay or witty was said, she would smile sweetly, and a fiery crimson would flush her cheeks, paling quickly to a breath of rose.

I talked with Antonia quite freely, and saw nothing in Krespel to indicate the Argus eyes of which the professor had accused him. On the contrary, he was quite his usual self, and indeed seemed to favor my conversation with Antonia. So it came about that I was a frequent caller at the councillor's. The growing familiarity among the three of us was wonderfully pleasant, and a source of deep delight to us all. The councillor's utterly antic ways continued to entertain me, yet I suppose it was really Antonia who drew me with irresistible fascination, and led me to accept a good deal that I would otherwise have fled from in my youthful impatience. For all too often there was an element of the absurd and the tedious mingled with the councillor's strange and peculiar nature. It annoyed me particularly that, whenever I steered the conversation toward music, and especially toward singing, he would intervene with his diabolically smiling face and his disgusting singsong intonation, making some irrelevant and, frequently, low remark. From the deep unhappiness in Antonia's eyes at such moments, I could see plainly enough that he did this simply to make sure I should not ask her to sing.

I stuck to it. As the obstacles put in my way by the councillor increased, so did my determination to surmount them. I must hear Antonia's song, lest I should become obsessed with dreams and imaginings of her voice.

One evening Krespel was in particularly good humor. He had just taken apart an old Cremona violin in which he found the sound post at an angle half a line greater than usual. This was an important and enlightening discovery.

I managed to get him excited about truly fine violin playing. Krespel dilated upon the style of the old masters, copied from the great and genuine singers, and I submitted that the very reverse was now the case—song was being distorted to follow the artificial runs and somersaults of the instrumentalists.

"What could be more nonsensical," I cried, jumping from my chair, rushing over to the piano, and quickly opening it, "what could be more nonsensical than these confounded mannerisms? They are not music. They sound like the noise of peas being spilled across the floor." I sang several of the modern sustained notes that run hither and thither, humming like well-spun tops, and at the same time accompanied myself with a few sour chords.

Laughing immoderately, Krespel cried, "Ha! Ha! I seem to hear our German-Italians or our Italian-Germans straining at an aria by Pucitta, Portogallo or some other *maestro di capella*."

Now, I thought, the moment has come. "Surely," said I, turning to Antonia, "surely Antonia knows nothing of this sad apology for singing?" I instantly began to intone a magnificently soulful melody by old Leonardo Leo.

Antonia's cheeks glowed; her eyes flashed with new fire, and seemed to shine like heaven itself. She ran to the piano.

She opened her lips—but at that moment Krespel thrust her away, seized me by the shoulders, and yelled in a grating tenor. "My lad, my lad, my lad!" Then he went on, chanting very softly, clasping my hands in a posture of ceremonious obeisance, "Indeed, most highly honored young sir, indeed, it would be a violation of all good manners and propriety if I were to express the loud and lively desire that the infernal Satan with red-hot talons might gently break your neck on this spot, thus more or less hastily dispatching you. But this aside, my valued friend; you must admit that it is growing quite dark and, since there is no lantern lit tonight, even though I were not to throw you straight downstairs, your valued limbs might come to some harm. Go home like a good fellow, and have the kindness to remember your true friend if by chance you should never—you understand?—never again find him at home!"

So saying, he embraced me, and turned slowly toward the door, holding on to me and turning me with him so that I could not give Antonia another glance.

You will admit that in my situation it was impossible to thrash the councillor, which would really have been the only thing to do. The professor laughed at me heartily, assuring me that I had now forever fallen from grace with the councillor.

I thought Antonia was too fine, I might almost say too holy, for me to play the infatuated adventurer, the languishing lover gazing up at her window. Shaken to the depth of my being, I departed from H—. But as such things usually happen, the vivid hues gradually faded in my imagination, and Antonia—nay, even Antonia's song, which I had never heard—would often light up the recesses of my spirit with a gentle, consoling, roseate glow.

Two years later, having taken a position in B—, I went on a trip to South Germany. The towers of H— stood out in the scented dusk. As I drew closer, I began to have an indescribable sense of apprehension; a crushing load seemed to weigh on my chest. I could not breathe. I felt I must get out of the carriage into the open air. My distress increased to the point of physical anguish.

Soon I seemed to hear the sounds of a solemn chorale wafted on the breeze. The notes grew plainer, and I could make out male voices chanting a church chorale.

"What's that? What's that?" I cried, a veritable red-hot dagger piercing my heart.

"Can't you see," said the postilion riding beside me, "can't you see? They're burying somebody in the churchyard yonder."

We were, in fact, close to the burial ground, and I saw a circle of black-clad figures around a grave that was being filled in. Tears came to my eyes; it seemed as if those spadefuls of earth were falling on the joy, the very light, of my life.

Striding swiftly on down the hill, I no longer had a view of the churchyard. The chorale stopped, and not far from the city gate I saw people dressed in black returning from the funeral. The professor, with his niece on his arm, both in deep mourning, walked quite close by without noticing me. The niece was pressing her handkerchief to her eyes and sobbing bitterly.

I was simply incapable of going into the town. I sent my man with the carriage to the usual inn, and rushed out into the familiar countryside, hoping to shake my mood, which might perhaps be entirely the result of physical causes, such as growing overheated on the journey. When I reached the avenue that led to the pleasure grounds, an extraordinary spectacle took place before my eyes.

Councillor Krespel was being led by two mourners from whom he was apparently trying to escape by the oddest leaping and skipping. He was dressed as usual in his strange, home-designed gray coat, but a long band of mourning crape fluttered from his small cocked hat which he wore rakishly over one ear. A black sword belt was buckled around his middle, but instead of a sword, he had put in a long violin bow. Icy shivers went down my spine. He must be quite mad, I thought, following at a distance.

The men led the councillor to the door of his house, where he embraced them with loud laughter. When they left him, his eyes fell on me as I stood close beside him. He stared at me fixedly for some time, then cried, hollowly, "Welcome, young sir! Ah, you understand, too." So saying, he seized my arm and snatched me into the house,

and up the stairs to the room where the violins hung. They were all festooned with black crape. The violin made by the old master was gone, and in its place hung a cypress wreath.
I knew what had happened. "Antonia! Oh, Antonia!" I moaned disconsolately.
The councillor stood with folded arms beside me as if turned to stone.
I pointed to the cypress wreath.
"When she died," said the councillor in his hollow, solemn tones "when she died, the sound post in that violin shattered with an echoing crack and the soundboard split. The faithful instrument could not live except with her and in her. It lies in the coffin, and it was buried with her."
Utterly stricken, I sank into a chair. The councillor began to sing a merry ditty in a harsh voice. It was a ghastly sight to see him hopping on one foot the while, with the crape (he had his hat on) swirling around the room and brushing the violins on the wall. Indeed, I could not keep from uttering a loud cry when the crape whipped over me as the councillor made a quick turn. I felt as if he were trying to shroud me and drag me down into the black, awful abyss of madness.
At this the councillor suddenly stood still and said in his singsong voice, "My lad? My lad? What are you screeching about? Did you see the Angel of Death? That always precedes the ceremony!"
He now stepped to the middle of the room, snatched the violin bow from his sword belt, held it over his head with both hands, and snapped it so that it flew into bits. Laughing loudly, Krespel cried, "So you think the staff is broken over me, my lad, and I am condemned to die, hey? Not at all, not at all! Now I am free — free — free — huzza, free! Now I'll stop building violins — no violins — huzza, I'll stop building violins!" The councillor sang this to a horribly vivacious tune, dancing on one foot again.
Horror-stricken, I was about to flee when the councillor checked me, saying, quite calmly, "Please remain, young sir. Do not think that these outbursts of anguish, which rend me with mortal pangs, are mere madness. It is all simply because some time ago I made myself a dressing gown in which I proposed to look like Destiny or God."
The councillor went on talking spine-chilling nonsense. Finally, he collapsed in exhaustion. The old housekeeper came in answer to my call, and I was glad to get outdoors.

I did not doubt for a moment that Krespel had become deranged; but the professor stoutly maintained the opposite.

"Nature or a malignant fate," said he, "has snatched away from some people the screen behind which the rest of us live our mad lives unobserved. They are like thin-skinned insects, which seem malformed as their muscles move, although they soon return to their natural shape. What we merely think, Krespel does. No doubt the spirit inherent in all earthly striving often breeds bitter mockery. This, Krespel vents in crazy antics and agile skipping. That is his lightning rod. That which is the earth's, he gives back to the earth; but that which is divine, he keeps. No doubt Antonia's sudden death weighs heavily upon him, but I would like to bet that no later than tomorrow the councillor will be jogging along again at his usual donkey trot."

The outcome was almost as the professor had predicted. Next day the councillor appeared entirely his old self, except that he said he would never build another violin, nor would he ever play one. He kept his word, as I heard later.

The professor's hints strengthened my conviction that the close and carefully hidden relationship between Antonia and the councillor, and indeed her very death, might be weighing him down with some inexpiable burden of guilt. I did not intend to leave H— without holding up to him the crime I suspected. I meant to shake him to the depths, thus forcing an open confession of his awful deed. The more I considered the matter, the surer I grew that Krespel must be a villain, and the more fiery and pungent was the speech that took shape in my mind, almost of its own accord — a veritable masterpiece of rhetoric. Thus forearmed and wrought up, I hurried to call on the councillor.

I found him turning toys on a lathe, and wearing a placid, smiling expression.

"How can there," I exhorted him, "how can there be so much as a moment's peace of soul for you when the thought of your abominable deed must be piercing you like a serpent's fang?"

Laying down his chisel, the councillor looked at me blankly.

"How so, my dear man?" he asked. "Do have the goodness to sit down in that chair."

But I went eagerly on, growing more and more indignant, to accuse him outright of having murdered Antonia, and to threaten him with the vengeance of the eternal power. In fact, as a recently appointed officer of justice, wrapped up in my profession, I went so far as to assure him that I would use every effort to uncover the matter delivering him into the hands of the temporal judge here below, and not waiting upon the hereafter. And at the end of my grandiose diatribe, I was rather taken aback when the councillor looked at me quietly without saying a word, as if he expected me to go on. I tried but my words seemed so wry, nay, so silly, that I gave up.

Krespel reveled in my embarrassment. An ironical, malicious smile crossed his face. But then he turned very grave, and said to me in solemn tones, "Young man! You may think me a fool, a madman I forgive you that, since we are both shut up in the same madhouse and you only blame me for thinking I am God the Father because you regard yourself as God the Son. But how can you dare to intrude upon a life, clutching at its most secret threads, that never was and never could be any concern of yours? She is gone, and the mystery has ceased to exist!" Krespel stopped, got up, and paced two or three times the length of the room.

I ventured to ask for enlightenment.

Looking at me fixedly, he took me by the hand and led me to the window where he opened both casements. He leaned out on his elbows, and there, looking down into the garden, he told me the story of his life.

When he was finished I took my leave, touched and deeply abashed.

The story of Antonia was briefly as follows:

Some twenty years previously, the councillor's fancy for collecting the best violins made by old masters, already amounting to a passion, had taken him to Italy. He was not yet building them himself, and accordingly he did not take the old ones apart. In Venice he heard the famous singer, Angela—i, who was then shining in the leading roles at the Teatro di S. Benedetto. His raptures were not inspired by art alone, though Signora Angela was a superb mistress of this, but by her angelic beauty as well.

The councillor sought out Angela's acquaintance and, despite his brusque exterior, succeeded in winning her affections, largely by his dashing yet highly expressive performance on the violin. An intimate relationship led within a few weeks to marriage, which was kept secret because Angela did not wish to give up the theater nor the name under which she had become famous as a singer. Neither did she care to append to it the harsh sound of "Krespel."

With the most extravagant irony, Krespel described Signora Angela's special ways of plaguing and tormenting him the moment she had become his wife. All the self-will and caprice of all the leading ladies in the world, Krespel thought, had been concentrated in Angela's tiny figure. If he did try to stand on his rights, Angela would unleash upon him a whole army of *abbates, maestros* and *academicos* who, not knowing his actual status, abused him roundly as the most intolerable and discourteous of lovers, a man incapable of yielding to the amiable whims of the Signora.

After one of these tempestuous scenes, Krespel fled to Angela's country house. Improvising on his Cremona violin, he forgot the troubles of the day. But it was not long before the Signora, who had hastily come after the councillor by carriage, entered the room. She was just in the humor for tenderness. She embraced the councillor with sweet, languishing glances, and put her little head on his shoulder. The councillor, however, absorbed in the world of his own harmonies, went on playing until the walls rang; and his arm and bow chanced to touch the Signora rather ungently.

She leaped back, ablaze with fury. She screamed, "*Bestia tedesca!*" snatched the violin from the councillor's hands, and smashed it into a thousand pieces on the marble table top. The councillor stood facing her for a moment like a graven image; then, awaking from his dream, he seized the Signora with gigantic strength, hurled her through the window of her own country house, and fled to Venice and then back to Germany, paying no heed to anything that might ensue.

It was only some time afterward that he realized what he had done. Although the window, he knew, was scarcely five feet above the ground, and he could well appreciate the necessity of throwing the Signora out of it under the above-mentioned circumstances still he was painfully uneasy, the more so since the Signora had given him quite plainly to understand that she was with child.

He scarcely dared to make inquiries, and was not a little surprised some eight months later to get a most affectionate letter from his beloved spouse in which not a word was said about the occurrence at the country house. She reported that she had been delivered of a ravishing little daughter, and warmly begged her *marito amato e padre felicissimo* to come to Venice at once.

This Krespel did not do, but inquired into the circumstances through a familiar friend. He found that the Signora had dropped as lightly as a bird into the soft grass, and that the fall had had no effect except on her soul. For after Krespel's heroic deed, the Signora had been like one transformed. Not a trace of caprices, silly notions, or other vexatiousness. The maestro, writing music for the next carnival, was reported to be the happiest man on earth because the Signora was ready to sing his arias without the hundred thousand alterations he ordinarily had to put up with. Incidentally, the friend added, there was every reason to keep strictly secret the method of Angela's cure, or otherwise singers would be whizzing through windows every day in the week.

The councillor was not a little excited. He ordered horses, and got into his coach.

"Wait!" he cried suddenly. "Come, now," he murmured to himself, "is it not certain that the moment I show my face the evil spirit will regain its hold over Angela? Now that I have thrown her out of the window, what can I do next time? What else is left?"

He got out of the coach, wrote a loving letter to his cured wife, courteously remarking what a sweet thought it was of her to be so pleased at the little mole their daughter had behind the ear, just like the kind he had—and stayed in Germany.

The correspondence went on quite briskly. Protestations of love, invitations, complaints of the beloved's absence, disappointments, hopes, etc., passed back and forth from Venice to H—, from H— to Venice. Finally Angela came to Germany, where, as everyone knows, she shone as the prima donna at the big theater in F—. Although now by no means young, she carried everyone away with the irresistible magic of her superb melody. Her voice was as good as it had ever been.

Antonia had grown up meanwhile, and her mother never tired of writing to her father about the truly great singer that Antonia was going to be. Indeed, this was confirmed by Krespel's friends in F—, who entreated him to come and admire the rare phenomenon of two utterly sublime songstresses. They had no idea of the close relationship between the two and the councillor. Krespel wished desperately that he might have seen his daughter, who was dear to his heart, and often appeared to him in dreams, with his own eyes; but whenever he thought of his wife, he had dark forebodings, and finally stayed at home with his cut-up violins.

You have probably heard of the promising young composer B— in F—, a composer, who suddenly dropped out of sight, no one knew how (or did you by any chance know him yourselves?). He fell madly in love with Antonia, who cordially returned his feelings, and so he importuned her mother for immediate consent to a union consecrated by art. Angela made no objection, and the councillor agreed the more readily because the young master's compositions had found favor before his own august tribunal.

Krespel was expecting word of the wedding, when instead he had a letter sealed with black, addressed in a strange hand. A Doctor R— informed the councillor that Angela had fallen violently ill of a cold caught at the theater, and had died the very night before Antonia's intended wedding day. Angela had revealed to the doctor that she was Krespel's wife and that Antonia was his daughter, and let Krespel therefore make all haste to look after the bereaved one.

Deeply as the councillor was distressed by Angela's death, he soon came to feel that some uncanny and hostile principle had gone out of his life, allowing him to breathe freely for the first time. That very day he set out for F—.

You cannot imagine how heart-rending was the councillor's description of the moment when he first set eyes on Antonia. The depth of his feeling carried powerful and manifest conviction. I cannot even hint at its emotional force.

All of Angela's charm and grace had fallen to Antonia's lot, but she was quite without her mother's darker side. There was no tiny cloven hoof always ready to peep out.

Antonia's young betrothed arrived. Tenderly sensing the inmost feelings of her erratic parent, she sang one of Padre Martini's motets which she knew the councillor had made Angela sing for him again and again in the palmy days of their love.

The councillor shed copious tears. He had never heard even Angela sing so. The sound of Antonia's voice was very strange and unusual, resembling now the breath of the Aeolian harp, now the warbling of the nightingale. There seemed to be no room in the human breast for such tones. Antonia, on fire with love and joy, sang and sang and sang all her loveliest melodies; while in the intervals, B— played as only a man intoxicated with delight and enthusiasm can play.

At first, Krespel was ecstatic. Then he grew pensive, still contemplative. Finally, he sprang up, pressed Antonia to his breast and implored her in soft, hollow accents, "Sing no more, if you love me. It breaks my heart. I am afraid ... afraid. Don't sing any more."

"No," said the councillor next day to Doctor R—, "when her color shrank to two dark-red spots on those pale cheeks as she sang, it was not just a silly family likeness. It was what I had feared."

The doctor, whose mien at the start of the conversation had betrayed deep sorrow, replied, "Whether it comes from early overexertion in singing or whether it is the fault of Nature—no matter Antonia suffers from an organic flaw in her chest, the very thing that gives her voice its marvelous power and its strange resonance, which I might almost say goes beyond the limits of human vocal capacity. But an early death will also be the result. If she continues to sing, I give her only six months more, at most."

Krespel felt as if a flowering tree had spread its blossoms into his life for the first time, only to be sawed off at the root so that it could never bud and bloom again.

His mind was made up. He told Antonia all. He offered her the choice of going with her betrothed, yielding to his and the world's persuasion, but going to an early death; or giving to her father in his old age a tranquillity and delight such as he had never known and living a long life herself.

Antonia fell sobbing into her father's arms. Feeling the heart rending nature of the moments to come, he wanted no plainer words.

He talked to B—. But although the young man protested that not a note should pass Antonia's lips, the councillor knew very well that even B— would never be able to resist the temptation to hear Antonia sing, at least his own arias. And as for the world, the musical public, even if informed of Antonia's ailment, it would certainly go on making its demands for, where enjoyment is concerned, audiences are selfish and thoughtless.

The councillor disappeared with Antonia from F—, and went to H—.

B— was in despair when he found they had left. He followed their trail, overtook the councillor, and arrived in H— at the same time with him.

"Let me see him just once, and then die." Antonia implored.

"Die? Die?" cried the councillor, fiercely angry. An icy chill penetrated the depths of his being. His daughter, the one creature in the whole world who had brought new joy to his life, who alone had reconciled him to existence, was snatching herself forcibly from his heart; and he hoped for the disaster to come.

B— was sent to the piano. Antonia sang, and Krespel played the violin merrily until the red spots appeared on Antonia's cheeks. Then he called a halt.

But as B— was taking leave of Antonia, she suddenly collapsed with a loud cry.

"I supposed," Krespel told me, "I supposed she was really dead, as I had expected, and, having once taken my place on this detached summit, I remained quite placid and self-possessed. I took B—, who stood there petrified, looking like a silly sheep, by the shoulders and said," (the councillor dropped into his singsong intonation) "Since you have really succeeded, my valued piano master, in murdering your sweetheart, as was your wish and intention, you need have no further hesitation about departing unless you would care to excuse me for a moment while I run that shiny hunting knife through your heart, so that my daughter (who, as you see, has turned rather pale) may regain some of her color from your esteemed blood. Run along, do. But at that I might toss a bit of a knife after you!' I must have looked rather shocking as I spoke, for he gave a cry of deepest horror, tore himself loose, and ran out of the door and downstairs."

When the councillor started to lift up Antonia, who was lying senseless on the floor, after B— had rushed off she opened her eyes with a deep sigh, but apparently closed them again in death a moment later. At this, Krespel broke out in loud, disconsolate laments.

Summoned by the housekeeper, the doctor declared Antonia's condition an acute but not at all dangerous attack. Indeed, she recovered more quickly than the councillor had dared to hope. She now clung to Krespel with the most fervent and childlike love. She followed out his pet inclinations, his mad whims and notions. She helped take apart old violins, and glue together new ones. "I don't want to sing any more, I want to live for you," she would often say with a gentle smile to her father when someone had asked her to perform and she had declined. The councillor, however, tried to spare her such moments as much as possible. This was why he disliked to take her out in company, and earnestly avoided all music. He realized very well, indeed, how painful it must be for Antonia to give up altogether the art in which she had attained such perfection.

When the councillor bought the marvelous violin that he later buried with Antonia, and was about to take it apart, Antonia looked at him sadly, and objected in gentle entreaty, "This one, too?"

The councillor could not have said himself what unknown power compelled him to leave the violin undissected and to play on it.

He had scarcely bowed the first notes when Antonia cried on joyously, "Why, it's I—I'm singing again!"

Truly, the silvery, bell-like tone of the instrument had a special and marvelous quality of its own. It seemed to come from the human breast. Krespel was deeply stirred. He played perhaps more compellingly than ever before. When he carried some bold passage up and down the scale with full volume and deep expression, Antonia would clasp her hands, and ecstatically cry, "Oh, I did that well; really, I did that well!"

From that time on there was a great tranquillity and serenity in her life. Often she would tell the councillor. "I think I'd like to sing something, father." Then Krespel would take the violin and play Antonia's sweetest melodies, and she would be blissfully happy.

One night, shortly before my arrival, the councillor seemed to hear someone playing his pianoforte in the next room, and soon he could clearly make out a prelude in the habitual manner of B—. He tried to get up, but it was as if he were held in bands of iron.

Now Antonia joined in, her voice as soft as a breath, then rising and rising to a crashing fortissimo. Finally, those marvelous tones swept into the deeply moving song—in the devout style of the old masters—that B— had once composed for Antonia. Krespel said, his state of mind was past understanding, for an awful dread, was coupled with such bliss as he had never known. Suddenly there was a dazzling brightness around him, in which he saw B— and Antonia embracing and regarding each other in ecstasy. The tones of the song and the accompanying piano went on without Antonia's being seen to sing or B—'s touching the piano.

The councillor now fell into a sort of swoon in which the image and the music faded away. When he awoke, the awful horror of his dream still remained. He rushed into Antonia's room.

She lay on the couch with her eyes closed, smiling sweetly, her hands devoutly folded, as if she were asleep and dreaming of heavenly transports. But she was dead.

Don Juan
Or, The Fabulous Adventure which Befell a Commercial Traveler

The sharp clang of a bell and the loud announcement of the imminent rise of the curtain brought me out of my gentle torpor. The orchestra was tuning up amid the throbbing of bass instruments, the boom of kettledrums and the blare of trumpets. An oboe emitted a clear, light A; the violins tuned in, and I rubbed my eyes. Had Satan, who is never idle when it comes to mischief, betwitched me?

A moment's reflection proved to me that I was wrong. I realized where I was; namely, in the hotel room which I had engaged the night before after arriving utterly exhausted. The imposing, bell rope dangled over my nose. I tugged lustily at it, and a servant appeared.

"What on earth is this music?" I asked him. "Is somebody giving a concert here?"

"No, your excellency," he answered. (I had ordered champagne yesterday.)

"I see that your excellency does not know that this hotel is connected with the theater next door. Behind this tapestry is a door which opens on to a small corridor leading directly to Loge Number 23, 'the visitor's box.'"

"What! A theater next door? A visitor's box?"

"Yes, sir. It is a small box for two persons, or three at most. It is for distinguished guests only, a fine box upholstered in green, with a screen in front, and right next to the stage. If it please your excellency, we are giving *Don Juan* tonight, the opera by the celebrated Herr Mozart of Vienna. We can put the ticket on your hotel bill.

The words "Don Juan" propelled me so swiftly into the corridor that the servant had not finished speaking before I was on the threshold of Loge 23. As I sat down, I noted that, for such a modest town, the theater was spacious, tastefully decorated and brilliantly illumined. The loges and orchestra seats were packed. And the opening accords of the overture convinced me that I was about to enjoy Mozart's masterpiece thoroughly, if only the singers matched the orchestra.

With the Andante, I experienced a sensation of terror. Panic, fear, gripped me. The infernal *regno del pianto* filled me with terrifying intimations of horror to come. The jubilation of the seventh measure of the Allegro was no more and no less than crime exultant. Out of the black night I saw the red-hot claws of fiery demons loom menacingly over the lives of happy mortals who danced merrily upon the thin lid that covered the bottomless pit. I was aware of the conflict between human nature and the unknown; and I knew what hideous powers lay about us and how they were even now preparing to corrupt us. Then the storm abated, and the curtain rose.

Leporello strides into the black night. He is cold and vexed. He wraps his mantle tightly about him as he makes for the pavilion. *Notte a giorno faticar*, I heard. What? Italian? Italian in this German city? *Ah, che piacere!* I heard. Was it possible? Was I to hear everything just as the great master had conceived it in his heart and produced it out of his very soul?

Then Don Juan storms out, Donna Elvira clinging to the seducer's cloak. I was rapt at the stage business. To be sure, Donna Elvira might be taller, more slender and statelier of gait. But what a head! Her eyes flash love and scorn, hatred and despair; they are the flame that blazes from a pyramid of light! Her dark hair, in loosened braids, streams over her neck; her white nightdress betrays charms dangerous to gaze upon. Her heart throbbed, grievously betrayed. What a voice!

Non sperar se non m'uccidi. The tones, molten of ethereal metal, flash like lightning through the storm of instruments. How can Don Juan tear himself loose? Indeed, does he wish to tear himself loose? Could he not push her back with a blow of the fist, and flee forever? Is it his crime that made him powerless, or is it the inner conflict of love and hate that robs him of courage and strength?

The old father has paid with his life for his folly. How dared he fall upon his enemy in the dark? Don Juan and Leporello move down stage, conversing. Don Juan sheds his coat, appears splendent in his torn red and silver satin cloak. A noble, powerful figure, with virile features; a thin, distinguished nose; piercing eyes; soft and sensuous lips; and, over his eyes, a play of brows distinctly satanic. He is at once handsome and sinister. The magic of the serpent is his, and never a woman upon whom he has cast his gaze but is driven, by a mysterious spell, to make for her own destruction. Leporello, his shadow, a tall, lean man, clad in red and white, bustles about him; white trousers, a striped red and white waistcoat, a red jacket and a white hat, its red feather acock, constitute his costume. Leporello's features are at once kindly, knavish, lascivious, and ironically impertinent. His black eyebrows stand out in contrast with the gray of his head and beard. Old though he be, he belongs in Don Juan's following. He must inevitably be Don Juan's henchman.

Now they have scaled the wall. Enter Donna Anna and Don Ottavio, accompanied by torchbearers, he a delicate, foppish mannikin, almost twenty-one years old, and, as Anna's bridegroom, probably living in the house. How else, indeed, could he be so swiftly summoned? At the first outcry, had he wished, he could have rushed to the Commander's rescue. But he had first to groom himself make certain that he looked smart. Besides, he was none too anxious to venture out into the night air.

Ma qual mal, s'offre, o dei, spettacolo funesto agli occhi miei! The burden of Don Juan's despair over the crime he has committed animates the heart-rending tones of the recitative and duet. It is not merely Don Juan's action which spells his ruin, brings death to his father-in-law and wrings tears from his heart. There must be an acute inner struggle before his ruin is encompassed. No less tall of stature, Donna Elvira joins the group. She is beautiful, but *passée*.

As she denounces the seducer (*Tu nido d'inganni*), and the compassionate Leporello aptly interjects, "*parla como un libro stampato*," I became aware of someone behind me, or at my side. I realized with a pang that anyone might readily open the door of my loge and slip in. Here I sat, fortunate enough to be alone in my box to welter in enjoyment of Mozart's masterpiece. Here I sat, every fiber of my soul clutching and entwining this marvel of beauty as with polyp arms, drawing it so deeply into myself that the slightest word, superfluous or stupid, would have broken the spell of this poetry and music. Should I allow myself to be distracted? No, I vowed; I would take no notice of my neighbor. Absorbed in the spectacle, I would avoid his glance or word. My chin cupped in my palm, my back turned to the intruder, I looked on at the play.

As the performance unfolded, I was pleased to find that it kept all the promise of its splendid beginning. Little Zerlina, filled with love and longing, does her best to console a doltish but good-natured Masetto. Her ways and tone are delightful. In the wild aria *Fin ch'han dal vino*, Don Juan bares his most secret heart and indulges his contempt for the sorry little people about him. What purpose do they serve? What were they invented for, if not to afford his lust the occasion to encroach upon their feeble thoughts and deeds? He frowns, ever more visibly; the contraction of his brows is more dramatic.

The masks appear, their terzetto a prayer rising to heaven in shafts of pellucid light. The middle curtain rises, disclosing a scene of merrymaking, with glasses clinking as the peasants and other masks dance in a mad whirl at Don Juan's behest. The trio of plotters, sworn to vengeance, appear, and the atmosphere becomes more formal until the opening of the dance. Zerlina is rescued. In the thundering finale, Don Juan draws his sword and faces his foes, every inch a hero. He wrests the bridegroom's dress sword from the latter's feeble hand and, like doughty Roland, hews his way to freedom through the rabble, as it dissolves in confusion, varlet tumbling over varlet before him.

Several times as I was watching, I thought I had felt a soft warm breath against the back of my head, and heard the rustle of a silk dress. The person in my loge was obviously a woman; but, lost as I was in a world of poetry, I paid no need. The curtain fell upon Act I. I shook myself out of my reverie and glanced at my neighbor. To my amazement, I found Donna Anna standing behind me, clad in the very costume I had just seen on the stage. I looked up; she fastened her piercing soulful gaze upon me. Speechless, I stared at her. Her mouth, as I saw it, curled in an ironic suave smile, in the radiance of which I saw my awkwardness reflected. I felt I must address her, but could not, because my tongue cleaved to my palate. Presently, words came to me willy-nilly.

"How in the world are you here?" I asked her. She replied in purest Tuscan that, if I knew no Italian, she would have reluctantly to forego the pleasure of my company. She knew no other language, she said with a shrug of the shoulders. Her words were music. Her deep blue eyes gained in expression as she spoke; with each flash of lightning which they darted I felt a glowing stream coursing through me, making every pulse of my body beat faster, and every fiber of my nerves twitch. There could be no doubt; it was, indeed, Donna Anna who was with me. The possibility of explaining how she could be both in my loge and on the stage, at one and the same time, never entered my mind. Just as a happy dream combines the strangest phenomena, so that a man of faith can understand the supernatural and accept it wholly with the so-called natural apparitions of life, so now, in the presence of this wonderful woman, I sank into a sort of somnambulism in which I recognized the secret connections binding me so intimately to her. This sensation was so vivid that, even when she was on the stage, she could not avoid me.

How happy I would be, my dear Theodore, to relate each word of the fascinating conversation which now took place between the signora and me. She spoke in Tuscan with all that language's light graceful charm, but I must write in German. In translation, therefore, every word she said must necessarily ring dull and flat, every sentence clumsy. As she spoke to me of *Don Juan* and of her part, I seemed for the first time to glimpse the depths of their masterpiece, to plumb their mysteries and clearly to recognize the fantastic apparitions of an eerie world. Music was her entire life, she told me. Often, too, she felt that, while she sang, she could divine within her innermost self many arcane things which no words could express.

"Yes, then, indeed, I can divine it!" she went on joyously, her eyes flashing, her voice gaining in intensity. "But all remains cold and dead around me, and while the audience claps a difficult roulade or a successful movement, icy hands grip my glowing heart! But you understand me, I am sure, I *know* that *you, too,* are aware of the wonderful romantic, kingdom alive with the celestial magic of musical tones."

"What!" I said in amazement. "O you curious, wonderful woman, do you mean that you know me? Did not the enchanted madness of love and its eternal longing, as you portrayed them in your latest opera, proceed from your innermost self? I have understood you; your soul has revealed itself to me in your song!"

"Yes," she replied, and named me by my Christian name. "I have sung you; I am your melodies."

The bell of the theater rang. A slight pallor drained the cold from Donna Anna's face which was innocent of make-up. She clapped her hand on her heart as though she felt a sudden pain and whispered:

"O unhappy Anna, now your most fearsome times are at hand."

Whereupon, she vanished from my loge.

The first act had charmed me; but after this extraordinary adventure, I reacted to the music quite differently and in a very singular manner. It was as though a long promised fulfillment of the loveliest dreams of another world were really coming to life. It was as though the most clandestine thoughts of the soul bewitched were being exorcised in tones and were being forced miraculously to materialize in the raptest perceptions. During Donna Anna's scene felt myself trembling with an intoxication of pleasure. A warm, soft breath passed over me, unconsciously I closed my eyes. Then a fiery kiss seemed to burn upon my lips, but it was like a tone that is held long by the singer, a tone of eternally thirsting desire.

The finale began amid frivolous merrymaking (*Gia la mensae preparate*) as Don Juan sat between two girls whom he caressed, and one cork popped after another, releasing the effervescent spirits that had been hermetically imprisoned and allowing them to exercise their full freedom. The scene represents a small room, with a large Gothic window looking out into the night in the background. As Elvira reminds the traitor of all his vows, one could see lightning flash across the windows and hear the muffled rumbling of the approaching storm. At last comes the mighty knocking at the door; Elvira and the maidens flee, and to the ghastly accompaniment of chords from the infernal world of spirits, enters the marble colossus. Beside the statue of the Commander, Don Juan seemed a veritable pygmy. The ground shook beneath the giant's thundering tread.

Through the storm, through the thunder, through the howling of demons, Don Juan screams "No!" that dread monosyllable which marks that the hour of his downfall is at hand. The statue disappears heavy smoke fills the room, and, from its clouds, hideous larvae take shape. Amid the torments of a wind of Hell, Don Juan weaves his way among the demons, now visible for a moment, now hidden from view. There is an explosion; it is as though a myriad thunderbolts were striking.

Don Juan and the demons have disappeared without anyone knowing how they did it. Leporello lies unconscious in one corner of the room. How salutory it is, now, to see the remaining person ages as they seek in vain a Don Juan who has been snatched, by the infernal powers, from a human vengeance. Then, only, could the spectator feel that he had escaped the awful circle of the spirits of Hell.

Donna Anna looked utterly different: a mortal pallor spread over her face; her eyes were set in a dead stare; her voice quivered unevenly; but, by that token, she achieved a heart-rending effect in the short duo with the pretty little bridegroom. (The latter, now that Heaven has successfully taken over the dangerous office of avenger, wishes to celebrate the wedding at once.) To crown the performance, the entire chorus rounded out the work into a magnificent whole.

I hastened towards my room in a state of high excitement. I do not think I had ever been so exalted emotionally. The waiter, intercepting me, ushered me to the main table. Mechanically I followed him. Because of the town fair, the company was brilliant, and the subject of the conversation was this evening's rendition of *Don Juan*. Praise of the Italians and of the quality of their playing was general; yet a casual observation, ventured waggishly here and there, proved that no speaker entertained the slightest conception of the deeper meaning of this, the opera of all operas. Don Ottavio, according to one auditor, had given an excellent performance, Donna Anna had been too passionate for the taste of another. Shouldn't a decent measure of moderation rule the stage, he carped and shouldn't an excess of passion be avoided? That passion, that aggressive force, which dominates the recital of the attack had alarmed and confused him. Whereupon, he took a pinch of snuff and proffered his neighbor an indescribably sage glance.

The neighbor, taking the floor, declared that the Italian woman was, nevertheless, very pretty, indeed. But, he pursued, she was too careless in the matters of clothing and make-up. Hadn't we noticed? Why, in one scene, a single lock of her hair, falling out of place, wholly obscured her profile!

Another guest hummed *Fin ch'han dal vino* softly, which inspired a lady to remark that she was least satisfied with Don Juan. "He was much too dark," she explained. "He was too sinister and too earnest; that frivolous, sportive character must be interpreted with a light, airy grace!"

But the final explosion came in for a long eulogy. As for myself, having had my fill of such chatter, I hastened to my room.

In Loge Number 23

How cramped, how sultry that musty room seemed to me, my dear Theodore! At midnight, I thought I heard your voice. I remember that you spoke my name clearly. Then there was a rustling behind the tapestry that covered the door connecting my room with the theater.

What is it that restrains me from revisiting the scene of my wonderful adventure? Perhaps I shall see you, and see her, the woman who fills and permeates my entire being? How easy it would be to carry in the small table, two lights and writing materials!

The waiter is coming with the punch I ordered. He finds the tapestried door open. He follows me into the loge and looks at me dubiously. I motion to him; he places my drink on the table. Then he withdraws, with a question on the tip of his tongue and another dubious glance cast at me over his shoulder. I turn my back upon him, and lean over the edge of the loge and look into the deserted house. The architecture of the theater, magically illumined by my lights, emerges, strange, ghostly and fey out of the shadowy darkness. A draught blowing through the theater rustles the curtain. What if it should go up? Suppose Donna Anna, terrified by the hideous larvae should suddenly appear before me? "Donna Anna!" I cry out her name involuntarily. "Donna Anna!"

My cry re-echoes through the deserted room, but the spirits of the instruments come to life. A matchless harmony rises tremulously as though the beloved name animated this music. I cannot quell a secret tremor within me, but it sweeps soothingly, consolingly through my nerves.

I master my mood once again and feel impelled, my dear Theodore, at least to indicate to you how today I believe I at last understand the divine master's glorious work in its profoundest sense. None but a poet can understand a poet; none but a romantic spirit may pass through the portals of romanticism; none but a spirit transported with poetry and consecrated in the Holy of Holies can comprehend what the ordained utters out of his inspiration.

If we consider the poem of *Don Juan* without attaching a deeper significance to it, if we limit ourselves to its historical side, we can not possibly conceive how Mozart ever thought out and composed such music. Boldly put, a *bon vivant*, who loves wine and women immoderately, dares wantonly to invite a man of stone to his merry board, the statue representing the old father whom he killed in self-defense. This outline holds little of the poetical. Let us honestly confess that such a man is scarcely worthy of the distinction conferred upon him by the infernal powers when they consider him as a quite extraordinary adornment of Hell. Nor can he really be said to deserve the honor when the man of stone, possessed by the transfigured soul of the dead Commander, takes the trouble to alight from his horse in order to admonish the sinner to repentance. Nor, finally, is he important enough for Satan to send his stoutest henchmen to effect, in the most terrifying manner imaginable, the translation of Don Juan to the infernal realms.

You may take my word for it, Theodore: Nature endowed Don Juan with all the favors she heaps upon her darlings. He received every gift which, tending toward the divine, raises a man above the humdrum, pedestrian, workaday world and above the uniformly manufactured products, hastily flung out of workshops like ciphers and obliged to be properly numbered before they can hope to possess the slightest value. His was a powerful and magnificent body, a personality radiating that spark which kindles the most sublime feelings in the soul, a profound sensibility, a swift and instinctive understanding.

But such is the terrible consequence of sin that the Fiend retained the power to beguile this man, and to set traps all along the road he traveled, striving for that perfection which most expresses his godlike nature. This conflict between the divine and the demonic powers creates the conception of earthly life, just as the solution of hard-won victory embodies the idea of supernatural life. The demands upon life, exacted by his physical and mental attributes, filled Don Juan with unfailing enthusiasm. Insatiable in his desires, fired by a longing which seethed through the blood in his veins, he was driven to the greedy, restless seizure of all the phenomena of this earthly world, hoping in vain to find satisfaction in them.

Certainly there can be no feeling that we experience here below that so exalts man's innermost nature as love. In its occult and potent workings, it destroys and transfigures the most intimate elements of existence. No wonder, then, that Don Juan hoped to still, in love, the longing which rent his heart. And it was there precisely that the Devil cast the noose about his neck. Through the cunning of man's ageless enemy, Don Juan was led to believe that love and the enjoyment of woman might already fulfill upon earth what exists in our hearts as a heavenly promise only.

He was determined to translate into material reality that infinite longing which weds us to the supernatural. Flitting from one beautiful woman to another still more beautiful; enjoying their several charms progressively from a white-hot ardor to satiety and to a frenzy of destruction; forever believing himself mistaken in his choice; forever hoping to find the ideal of ultimate satisfaction; Don Juan, at the last, inevitably found all mortal life a stale, dull, and unprofitable performance. More, since he despised humanity, anyhow, he rebelled against that apparition which at first spelled the zenith of life for him, only to disappoint him bitterly in the end. And so he reached a point where the enjoyment of woman ceased to afford his senses the slightest satisfaction. In it, instead, he found an occasion to vent his impious scorn of Nature and the Creator.

Don Juan was moved by a profound contempt for the ordinary view of life, since he felt much superior to it. He scoffed bitterly at a humanity which hoped to find, in felicitous love and its subsequent bourgeois union, even the merest fulfillment of the higher desires which a treacherous nature has inimically laid in our hearts. This contempt and mockery reached their limits whenever the possibility of such a union arose. He was particularly rebellious then, and spared no pains to combat that unknown Being who guides our destiny. For to Don Juan, that Being seemed but a monster of malice playing a cruel game with the pitiful creatures of his mocking moods—creatures, incidentally, whose downfall Don Juan was himself eager to encompass. Does he seize every opportunity to seduce a loved bride or to destroy the happiness of a pair of lovers? Does any fierce, powerful blow of his fail to inflict pain enough or to visit the direst blight upon his victims? If so, it is because in such acts he triumphs over the malignant monster, and his triumph exalts him, ever more surely, above our narrow life, above Nature, above the Creator. Ever more fervently, too, he wishes himself out of and beyond this life, yet the upshot of it all is his descent into Hell. The seduction of Anna and all that goes with it marks the summit of his attainment.

With regard to the loftiest endowments which Nature can offer, Donna Anna is the feminine counterpart of Don Juan. Just as, originally, he was a noble and splendid man, so she is a divine woman, against whose chastity of spirit the Devil is powerless. All the arts of Hell concentrated upon her person could ruin her in only an earthly fashion. No sooner has Satan accomplished this ruin, but Hell, in accordance with the dictates of Heaven, must immediately undertake the office of avenger.

Don Juan, with a sneer, invites the statue of the old man he slew to a merry feast. Now, for the first time, the transfigured spirit sees Don Juan as the fallen man or Adam cast out of a Paradise. He is filled with sorrow for the sinner, and does not disdain to appear in terrifying form in order to move him to repentance. But the soul of Don Juan is too vexed and corrupted. The very salvation of Heaven can bring no ray of hope to lighten his darkness or to awaken him to a better life.

Doubtless you are wondering, my dear Theodore, why I should have discussed the seduction of Anna. At this time of night, with thoughts and ideas rising from distant worlds to storm my soul, I shall do my best to explain, briefly, how the interplay and conflict of these two natures (Don Juan's and Donna Anna's) appears to me in the music, regardless of the text.

I have already said that Donna Anna is the counterpart of Don Juan. Suppose Donna Anna had been destined by Heaven to preserve a love which Satan crushed? Suppose, further, that this love had availed to show Don Juan the divine nature that dwelled within him? Suppose she had been able to cure the despair of his vain striving? When he first saw her, it was at the height of his criminal career, and therefore too late for him to feel aught but a fiendish lust to corrupt her. She was swept by the ardors of a superhuman sensuality; a fire from hell burned through her body, and she was not saved! Don Juan and none else could fire her with that lascivious madness she lavished upon him in their embrace. Her sin expressed the overpoweringly destructive fury of the hellish spirits within her. The fell deed done, he sought to flee.

As for her, the realization of her ruin hovered above her like a hideous monster spewing poisonous death, then twined itself about her being in an agony of torture. A host of facts seized and rent her.

There was her father killed by Don Juan. There was her betrothal to the frigid, effeminate, commonplace Don Ottavio, whom she had once thought she loved. Now even the love raging in a destructive flame through the inmost recesses of her flesh, ablaze at the moment of her highest pleasure, but at present aglow with annihilating hatred, racked her being.

Her soul the prey of mortal torment, Donna Anna feels that nothing short of Don Juan's destruction can bring her peace. But this peace spells her own earthly downfall. Incessantly, therefore, she urges her indifferent bridegroom to seek vengeance. She herself pursues the betrayer, and knows pause only after the subterranean powers have dragged Don Juan to the bottomless pit.

But, this done, she will not yield to the bridegroom, as he presses her to wed him. *Lasci, o caro, un anno ancora, allo sfoga del mio cor!* She will not outlive that year; Don Ottavio will never embrace this woman whose devotion saved her from becoming Satan's destined bride.

How keenly and overwhelmingly I feel this in the heart-rending harmony of the first recitative during the narration of the nocturnal assault! Even Donna Anna's scene in the second act (her *Crudele*, regarded superficially, applies to Don Ottavio only) voices, in intimate remembrance and in a wonderfully apt conjunction, that disposition of the soul which consumes all earthly happiness. What else should we find in the words of the remarkable passage added, and uttered perhaps unconsciously by the poet: *"forse un giorno il cielo ancore sentirà pietà di mi"*?

The clock strikes two. A warm electric breath fans my cheek. I am aware of the soft fragrance of delicate Italian perfume which my neighbor exhaled yesterday. A rapt feeling surges within me which I know that I can express only in music. The night air blows so sharply through the house, the keys of the piano rustle. O heaven! it is as though I hear Anna's voice from a far distance, borne upon the pinions of the swelling tones of an aerial orchestra. *Non mi du bell' idol mio!*

"Open out before me, O distant unknown spirit world; open out, O land of genii and jinn; open out, O realm of all splendor, whence a mystic and celestial pain falls on me like a joy ineffable, fulfilling beyond all measure everything that was ever promised to the enraptured soul here below! Let me enter the circle of blessed apparitions! Let the dreams sent to me from this enchanted kingdom now terrify me as I shudder, now calm me as a friendly messenger to earthly men.

And, in the hour when sleep holds my body captive in leaden bonds, let these dreams waft my spirit gently into the ethereal fields!"

Midday Conversation at the Main Table
(Epilogue)

THE SAGE MAN
(*tapping his snuff box sharply*)
It really is most misfortunate that we shall have no more good opera for a long time! That is what comes of this stupid overacting.

MULATTO FACE
Quite so! I've said the same thing often enough, God knows. The role of Donna Anna always affected her deeply. Yesterday she was like one possessed. They say she lay unconscious throughout the second intermission. In her scene in Act II, I hear she had a kind of nervous fit. . . .

INSIGNIFICANT PERSON
Oh, do tell me . . . ?

MULATTO FACE
I repeat, she had nervous seizures. In fact, they couldn't carry her out of the theater.

MYSELF
Good Lord! I hope she isn't seriously ill! We shall hear the signora soon again, eh?

SAGE MAN
(*taking a pinch of snuff from his box*)
That is scarcely likely. You see, the signora died at exactly two o'clock this morning.

The Mines of Falun

On a hot sunny July day all the people of Gothaborg were assembled by the waterside. A rich East Indiaman, safely returned from distant lands, lay at anchor in the rocky harbor, the long pennant, the Swedish flag, waving gaily in the clear, warm air, while hundreds of boats of all kind, filled with jubilant sailors, floated on the mirror-like surface of the Goathaelf, and the cannon on Masthuggetorg sent its resounding greeting far across the open sea. The gentlemen of the East India Company wandered up and down by the harbor and with smiling faces counted up their gains, delighted with the way in which their undertakings improved year by year and dear Gothaborg bloomed ever more fresh and lovely as trade grew more flourishing. And therefore everybody looked with pleasure on these good gentlemen, and rejoiced with them, for with their earnings came strength and energy into the brisk life of the whole town.

The crew of the East Indiaman, about a hundred and fifty strong landed from many boats and started off to keep the Honsung. That is the name of the feast which the sailors celebrate on such occasions, and which often lasts several days. Musicians in marvelously colored garments went ahead, with fiddles, pipes, oboes, and trumpets which they played upon valiantly, while others sang merry songs to their accompaniment. These were followed by the sailors, two by two. Some with coats and hats decorated with gaily colored ribbons were waving flags, others danced and jumped, and all shouted and made merry so that the gay noise could be heard a great distance.

Thus the joyous procession went through the docks, through the suburbs to Haga, there to drink and make merry to their hearts' desire.

The finest beer flowed there in streams, and tankard after tankard was emptied. As is always the case when sailors return from a long voyage, a number of smart young women were soon there to greet them. Dancing began, the festivities got wilder and wilder, the rejoicings louder and more exciting.

One single sailor, a slim good-looking youth, scarcely twenty years of age, had slipped away from the turmoil and seated himself on a bench beside the door of the inn.

A few sailors came out to him, and one of them, laughing loudly, cried out: "Elis Frobom! Elis Frobom! Are you being a miserable fool again and wasting this good time in silly brooding? Listen here, Elis, if you are going to stay away from our Honsung, you had better stay away from the ship as well. At this rate you will never become a decent, hard-working sailor. You have courage and are brave in face of danger, but you can't drink, and you would rather keep your ducats in your pockets than throw them to the landlubbers here! Drink, fellow, or may the sea devils, the whole pack of them, fall upon you!"

Elis Frobom jumped up from the bench, stared at the sailors with glowing eyes, took up a brimming cup of spirits and emptied it at one draught. Then he said, "There, Joens, now you see that I can drink as well as any of you, and the captain can decide what sort of sailor I am. But now hold your tongue and get away from here. I hate your wild merriment. What I am doing out here is no concern of yours."

"Now, now," replied Joens, "I know you have always been a Neriker and they are all gloomy and sad, and don't really enjoy a sailor's life. Wait a bit, Elis, I will send someone out to you who'll soon get you away from that bench to which you seem to have been nailed."

In a very short time a smart young girl came out of the door of the inn and sat beside the gloomy Elis, who was again seated, dumb and brooding, on the bench. The girl's profession was obvious from her clothes and her manner, but she was still young enough to have retained freshness and charm in her yet pleasing features. There was no sign of repellent shamelessness about her, rather an expression of yearning sorrow lay in her dark eyes.

"Elis! aren't you going to take any part in the gaieties of your comrades? Don't you feel any pleasure in having once again escaped the threatening dangers of the treacherous sea, and being back again in your own country?"

Thus spoke the girl in a gentle, quiet voice, putting her arm round the youth's shoulders. Elis Frobom, as though waking from a dream, gazed into the girl's eyes, took her hand and pressed it tightly. It was obvious that her soft whisper had sunk deep into his heart.

"Ah," he said at last, "happiness and pleasure are not for me. At least, I cannot take part in the orgies of my companions. Go in, my dear child, dance and make merry with the others if it gives you pleasure, but leave sad, miserable Elis out here alone; he will only spoil all your pleasure. But wait — I like you, and you must think well of me when I have gone to sea again."

So saying he took two shining ducats from his pocket, drew a fine East Indian shawl from under his coat, and gave both to the girl. Tears came into her eyes. She stood up, laid the money on the bench, and said, "Oh, keep your ducats, they only make me unhappy, but this beautiful shawl, I will keep it to wear in memory of you, and next year when you keep Honsung here you won't find me."

With that, she went, not back into the inn, but, both hands, before her face, away down the road.

Once again Elis Frobom sank back into his gloomy meditations, until, when the merrymaking in the inn had reached its loudest, he called out, "Oh, would that I were lying at the bottom of the deepest sea, for there is nobody left alive with whom I could be happy."

A deep, gruff voice behind him replied, "You must have suffered a very great unhappiness, young man, if already, with life just opening before you, you wish yourself dead."

Elis looked around and saw an old miner leaning with folded arms against the wall of the inn and looking down on him with eager, searching eyes.

Looking up at him, Elis felt like a man who, thinking himself lost in a lonely place, suddenly sees a well-known figure coming towards him, offering a welcoming hand. He pulled himself together and explained that his father had been a skillful pilot but had been lost at sea in a storm from which he himself had been rescued in a marvelous manner. Both his brothers had been soldiers and had fallen in battle. He had been keeping his poor, lonely mother on the splendid earnings of his East Indian voyages. Destined from childhood for a sailor's life, a sailor he had remained, thinking himself very lucky to get into the service of the East India Company.

This voyage had been even more prosperous than usual, and every member of the crew had received a good sum of money apart from his wages, so that with his pockets full of ducats he had gone joyfully off to the cottage where his mother lived. But strange faces had gazed at him from the windows, and the young woman who had finally opened the door to him, and to whom he explained who he was, told him coldly that his mother had died three months before, and that the few rags left over when the funeral expenses were paid were lying at the town hall waiting for him to claim them. His mother's death was breaking his heart; he felt himself forsaken by everyone lonely as one wrecked on a desert island, helpless, miserable. His whole life at sea appeared to him as a useless, purposeless activity. Yes, when he considered that his mother had probably been wretchedly cared for by strangers, it seemed to him even infamous and horrible that he ever went to sea and did not rather stay at home to look after and care for her. His comrades had brought him forcibly to the Honsung, and he had himself thought that perhaps the merriment around him and the strong drink would deaden his sorrow, but instead of that he felt as though his heart must break.

"Yes," said the old miner, "you will soon be at sea again, Elis, and then your sorrow will be forgotten in a short time. Old people die. That is only natural, and you yourself have said that your mother's was but a poor, miserable existence."

"Ah," sighed Elis, "nobody believes in my unhappiness; most people chide me for being silly and foolish, and that is what makes me feel so forsaken. I do not want to go to sea again. I have a horror of the life. And it used to be my greatest joy when the sails were unfurled like stately wings, and the ship glided over the water, and the waves rippled or blustered, making merry music, and the wind whistled through the rigging. Then I shouted gaily with my comrades on the deck, and if I had the watch on a still, dark night, I thought of the happiness of returning home, and how my good old mother would rejoice when Elis returned! Ah, yes! then I could make merry at the Honsung, when I had poured my ducats into my mother's lap, when I had given her the lovely shawls and the other gifts I had brought her from distant lands.

"How her eyes would light up with pleasure when she folded her arms, quite overcome with happiness and excitement, when she tripped busily about, and brought out the finest beer which she had stored up for Elis's return. And when I sat with her in the evenings I used to tell her about all the queer people I met, about their customs and habits, about anything strange I had seen during my long voyages. She loved to hear it, and in return told me about my father's wonderful voyages to the Far North, interspersed with many a terrifying seaman's legend which I had heard hundreds of times but could not hear too often. Ah! who can give that happiness back to me! No, never again will I go to sea! What should I do among my comrades who would only laugh me to scorn, and how should I enjoy work which would seem but a wearisome expense of energy for nothing!"

"I have listened to you gladly, young man," said the old miner as Elis ceased speaking, "just as I have watched you during the last few hours without your noticing it, and felt pleased with your behavior. Everything which you have done or spoken is a sign that yours is a retiring, pious, childlike disposition, and high heaven could not give you a more precious gift. But you have never been suited for a sailor's life. How should so quiet, almost somber a Neriker (for that you are one, your features, your whole bearing, show) fit into the wild, restless life at sea? You are wise to forsake such a life. But you don't want to fold your arms and sit back yet? Take my advice, Elis Frobom, go to Falun and become a miner. You are young, strong, certainly you would soon be a good apprentice, then a hewer, master miner, and always higher up the ladder. You have useful money in your pockets, invest that, add your earnings, and you will soon own a miner's license and a share in the mine. Take my advice, become a miner."

Elis Frobom was startled by the old man's words. "What?" he cried, "what are you advising me to do? I am to leave the beautiful free earth, the bright, sunny heavens which surround me, reviving, refreshing. I am to leave all that and go down into the terrifying depths of the underworld to dig and bore like a mole for minerals and metals just for the sake of vile profit?"

"You are all alike," cried the old man angrily, "you are all scornful of anything you do not understand. Vile profit! As though all the horrible torments which are part of commerce above ground were nobler than the work of a miner, to whose knowledge, to whose unwearying toil Nature opens her most secret treasure hoards. And you talk of vile profit, Elis Frobom! This is a matter of something much higher. If the blind mole bores into the earth following blind instinct, it may well be that in the deepest shafts by the faint light of the lantern the human eye becomes more clear-sighted, yes, that at last, growing stronger and stronger, it may see in the marvelous metals a reflection of that which is hidden above the clouds. You know nothing of mining, Elis Frobom, let me explain it to you."

With these words the old man seated himself on the bench beside Elis and began to describe in great detail the workings of a mine, and took great trouble to paint it in the most living colors to make it real to one who knew nothing of it. He spoke of the mines of Falun, in which, he said, he had worked since his boyhood; he described the great pit head with its dark-brown walls through which one passed; he spoke of the immeasurable richness in lovely metals of the principal shaft. He grew more and more vivacious, his eyes more glowing. He wandered among the shafts as in a magic garden. The minerals came to life, the fossils moved, the wonderful pyrope, the almandine, blazed in the light of the lanterns, the rock crystal caught the light and sparkled.

Elis listened eagerly; he was completely enthralled by the old man's strange manner of speaking of the underground wonders as though he were among them at the moment. Oppression seized him; he felt as though he were already in the pits with the old man, and a powerful magic was keeping him there so that he should never again see the friendly light of day. And yet he felt as though the old man had opened to him a new, unknown world to which he belonged, and the magic of that new world had really been his secret since his childhood.

"I have shown you, Elis Frobom," said the old man at last, "all the glories of a realm for which Nature really designed you. Go and think it over and then do as your feelings dictate."

With that the old man jumped hastily up from the bench and strode away without speaking another word to Elis or turning for another glance. He was soon out of sight.

In the meantime, the noise in the inn had ceased. The strong beer and spirits had exerted their power. Many of the sailors had slipped away with their sweethearts, others lay about in corners and snored. Elis, who had now no home, rented a tiny attic in the inn, in which to sleep.

Hardly had he lain down, tired and weary as he was, than dreams began to weave their spell over him. He thought he was on a beautiful ship under full sail on a sea smooth as glass, under a sky overcast with dark clouds. But when he looked down into the water, he soon realized that what he had imagined to be sea was really a solid, transparent, glittering mass, in which in some strange manner the whole ship melted away, so that he was left standing on a floor of crystal, and could see over him a vault of shining black stone. For what he had thought were clouds was stone. He hurried forward, urged by an unknown power, but at the same moment everything around him began to move, and, like ruffled waves, marvelous flowers and plants of shining metal rose from the floor, the flowers and leaves creeping out of the depths and intertwining in the most charming manner. The floor was so transparent that Elis could see quite clearly the roots of the plants; but searching ever deeper he saw, far down, innumerable beautiful young female figures, their white arms encircling one another; and in their hearts were the roots of those plants which were growing up around him. When the girls laughed a sweet harmony filled the great vault, and the wonderful metal flowers grew taller and more lovely.

An indescribable feeling of mingled pain and pleasure seized the youth, a world of love, longing, and ardent desire flooded his heart. "Down, down to you," he cried, and threw himself with outstretched arms on the crystal floor. But it gave under him and he was left to swim in shimmering ether. "Well, Elis Frobom, how do you like this glorious place?" cried a powerful voice, and Elis found at his side the old miner, but as he looked at him he appeared to turn into a gigantic figure in glowing bronze. The chill of terror began to spread over Elis, but in that instant there was a flash as of lightning in the depths, and the earnest face of a majestic woman appeared. Elis felt the delight in his heart growing and growing until it became almost a crushing dread. The old man had thrown his arm round him, and cried: "Take care, Elis Frobom, that is the Queen, you can still look up."

Involuntarily he turned his head and realized that the stars in the night sky were shining through a crack in the vault. A soft voice called his name as though in inconsolable sorrow. It was the voice of his mother. He thought he saw her figure through the crack over head. But it was a lovely young woman who thrust her hand down through the crack and called his name. "Carry me above," he cried to the old man, "I belong to the upper world with its friendly sky." "Take care," muttered the old man, "Frobom, be true to the Queen to whom you have surrendered."

When the youth looked down again into the calm face of the majestic woman, he felt his whole being melting into the glittering stone. He screamed aloud in nameless terror, and woke from the wonderful dream whose beauty and horror found an echo deep in his soul.

"It had to be, I suppose," said Elis to himself, when he had pulled himself together, "I had to have such a curious dream. The old miner told me so much about the wonders of the underworld that my whole being is full of it, and in all my life I never had such strange feelings as now. Perhaps I am still dreaming. No, no — I must be ill. I will go out into the open, the fresh sea breezes will cure me."

He got up quickly and hurried down to the harbor where the merriment of the Honsung was just beginning again. But he soon noticed that he had no pleasure in anything, that he could not keep his mind on anything, that ideas, wishes, he was unable to put into words, kept going through his head. He thought with deep sorrow about his dead mother; then it seemed to him that his one desire was to meet the girl who had spoken so kindly to him yesterday. Then he feared that if the girl came out of one of the lanes towards him it would prove to be the old miner of whom, in spite of himself, he was in dread. And yet he would gladly have heard from the old man more about the wonders of the mines.

He stood looking down into the water, these thoughts driving backwards and forwards through his head. It seemed as though the silvery waves froze into a glittering glimmer in which the lovely great ships melted away, as though the dark clouds which were just gathering in the bright sky were sinking and turning into a vault of stone. He was back in the midst of his dream again, looking again into the earnest face of the majestic woman, and the disturbing anxiety and longing took hold of him anew.

His comrades shook him out of his dream to follow in their procession. But now he felt that an unknown voice was whispering ceaselessly in his ear: "What, are you still here? — away — away — your home is in the mines of Falun. There you shall see all the glory of which you have dreamed — go, go to Falun!"

For three days Elis Frobom wandered about the streets of Gothaborg, followed the whole time by the marvelous figures of his dream, exhorted all the time by the unknown voice.

On the fourth day Elis stood at the gate leading out of the town on the way of Gefle. A big man went through just ahead of him. Elis thought he recognized the old miner and was impelled to hurry after him, but he could not catch up with him.

Disquieted, he followed him.

Elis knew quite well that he was on the road to Falun, and that pacified him strangely, for he was certain that Fate had spoken to him through the voice of the old miner, and was now leading him to his destiny.

Certainly he noticed often that, when he was not quite sure which road to take, the old man suddenly appeared from behind rocks or bushes and walked ahead of him for a while without looking round, disappearing again quickly when the way became plain.

At last, after days of hard walking, Elis saw in the distance two large lakes, between which arose thick columns of steam. As he climbed higher and higher towards the west, he was able to make out in the smoke a few towers and black roofs. The old man stood gigantic before him, pointed with outstretched arm at this smoke and disappeared again among the rocks.

"This is Falun," cried Elis, "the goal of my journey." He was right, for people who came up with him at that moment confirmed the fact that the town of Falun lay there between the two lakes, Runn and Warpann, and that he was then climbing Guffris Hill on which was the great pit head of the mine.

Elis went cheerfully on, but when he reached the monstrous abyss leading to the underworld, the blood froze in his veins, and he remained rooted to the ground at the sight of the terrible destruction.

As is well known, the great entrance to the mine of Falun is twelve hundred feet long, six hundred feet wide and one hundred and eighty feet deep. The dark-brown walls are vertical at first, then they slope away owing to enormous heaps of rubble and fragments. Both here and in the walls remains of the woodwork of old shafts are visible, strong, closely packed tree trunks grooved together at one end in the same way as the walls of log cabins. No tree, no blade of grass grew among the bare, crumbling, stony chasms and the jagged cliffs which were formed into strange shapes, sometimes like enormous stone beasts, sometimes like human forms of gigantic proportions. At the bottom lay in wild disorder stones, dross, burnt-out ore; and stupefying sulphur fumes rose eternally as though an infernal brew was always being prepared there, whose steam destroyed all the green things in Nature. One could believe that here Dante descended into the Inferno with all its desperate torments, all its horrors.

As Elis Frobom looked down into the chasm he remembered what an old helmsman on his ship had told him long ago. As he lay in a fever, he said, he felt suddenly that the sea had rolled away and left him looking down into a measureless pit in which he could see all the fearful creatures which live on the floor of the ocean writhing horribly among strange shellfish and corals and wonderful stones, until with wide-open jaws they lay motionless in death. Such a sight, declared the old sailor, was a sign of a speedy death in the waves, and shortly afterwards he did fall accidentally from the deck into the sea and was not seen again. It was brought back to Elis's mind by the sight of the pit, which reminded him of the old helmsman's description of the pit into which he looked when the waters rolled back. The black stones and blue and red dross of the metal looked to him like horrible creatures stretching out their ugly polypus arms towards him. Just at that time some of the miners were climbing out of the depths, and in their dark working clothes, with their black faces, they looked like hateful monsters trying laboriously to make themselves a road to the surface.

Elis felt himself shaken with horror, and, what had never happened to him at sea, a feeling of giddiness overcame him; it seemed to him that unseen hands were drawing him down into the abyss.

With closed eyes he stumbled away, and only when he was far from the pit head, descending Guffris Hill, and looked up to the bright, sunny sky, did all his fear leave him. He breathed freely again, and cried from the depths of his soul: "Oh, God, what are all the terrors of the ocean compared to the horror which inhabits that rocky chasm! Let the gale rage, let the black clouds sink to meet the raging waves, the beautiful, kindly sun very soon conquers them, and beneath his friendly rays the storm soon calms down; but those rays never pierce that black pit, and no soft spring breeze ever refreshes the air down there. No, I do not want to join you, you black earthworms, I could never accustom myself to your gloomy life!"

Elis decided to spend the night in Falun, and early the next morning to set out on his return to Gothaborg.

When he reached the market place, the Helsingtorget, he found a great crowd of people assembled.

A long procession of miners in festal attire, led by musicians, had just come to a halt in front of a stately house. A tall, slim, middle-aged man came out and looked round with a friendly smile. One could recognize the true Dalecarlian from his upright carriage, open brown, and dark-blue, beaming eyes. The miners encircled him, to each one he gave a hearty handshake and a friendly word.

Elis made inquiries and found that this man was Pehrson Dahlsjo, engineer and owner of a fine Bergsfralse near Stora-Kopparberg. "Bergsfralse" is the Swedish word for land granted for copper and silver mines. The owners of such Fralsen have shares in the mines for the workings of which they are responsible.

Elis was also told that it was the last day of the sitting of the court, and on that day it was usual for the miners to go in procession to the surveyor, the overseer, and the owners, and at each place to be entertained.

Looking at these fine, stately men with their open, friendly faces, he forgot the earthworms he had seen at the pit head.

The evident happiness of these people, which seemed to break out afresh through the crowd when Pehrson Dahlsjo came out, was evidently something very different from the wild, mad merrymaking of the sailors at the Honsung.

The heart of the quiet youth was deeply touched by the manner in which the miners took their pleasure. He felt indescribably happy, but he could hardly keep back his tears when some of the younger men began to sing an old song, a very simple but deeply moving melody in praise of mining.

When the song ended, Pehrson Dahlsjo threw open the doors of his house and all the miners went in. Involuntarily Elis followed and stood on the threshold so that he could overlook the whole hall in which the miners were taking their places on benches. A large meal was spread out before them.

The door opposite Elis opened, and a lovely girl in festal attire entered the hall. Tall and slim, with dark hair wound in many plaits round her head, her lovely dress fastened with rich clasps, she moved with the charm and grace of blooming youth. All the miners stood up and a quite murmur ran through the rows: "Ulla Dahlsjo — how God's blessing has descended on our excellent manager in that beautiful and good child." The eyes of even the oldest miners sparkled as Ulla shook hands with them one after another and gave them friendly greeting. Then she fetched beautiful silver jugs and poured out such excellent beer as was at that time only to be found in Falun, and handed it to the guests, her face all the time beaming with innocent pleasure.

As Elis Frobom caught sight of the girl, it seemed to him that a flash of lightning went through him and awakened again all the love, the joy, the ardor which he had thought dead. It was Ulla Dahlsjo who in that ominous dream had held out to him a helping hand; he thought now that he could understand the deeper meaning of that dream, and, forgetting the old miner, thanked the fate which had brought him to Falun.

But standing there on the threshold, he felt that he was an unnoticed stranger, miserable, disconsolate and alone, and he wished that he had died before he saw Ulla Dhalsjo, for now he must perish miserably of love and longing. He could not bring himself to take his eyes off the girl, and as she passed quite close to him, he spoke her name in a shaky undertone. Ulla looked round and noticed poor Elis, who stood there with burning cheeks and downcast eyes, motionless, unable to utter a word.

Ulla went up to him and said with a sweet smile, "Ah, you must be a stranger, dear friend! I can tell that by your sailor's clothes. But why are you standing there on the threshold? Come along in and enjoy yourself with us." And she took him by the hand, drew him into the hall and, handing him a tankard of beer, said, "Drink, dear friend, to your welcome."

It seemed to Elis as though he were in the paradise of a glorious dream, from which he must awake to indescribable misery. He emptied the tankard mechanically. At that moment Pehrson Dahlsjo came up to him, shook him by the hand in friendly greeting and inquired whence he came and what had brought him to Falun.

The warmth of the noble liquor spread through Elis's veins. He grew courageous and cheerful as he gazed into the eyes of the gallant Pehrson, and explained how he, the son of a sailor, brought up to the sea from childhood, had just returned from the East Indies to find that his mother, whom he had kept in comfort with his wages, had died during his last voyage, so that he was now alone in the world, how repugnant the wild life of a sailor had become to him, that his greatest longing was to become a miner and that he should try to get taken on as a miner at Falun. This last wish, so contrary to what he had felt but a few moments previously, was drawn from him involuntarily as though he had not been able to help saying it, almost as though he had expressed his deepest desires, desires in which he himself had not previously believed.

Pehrson Dahlsjo looked earnestly at the young man as though he wanted to read his inmost thoughts; then he said: "I do not imagine, Elis Frobom, that sheer frivolity is driving you away from your previous occupation, or that you have not weighed carefully all the hardships and difficulties of a miner's life before making your decision. It is an old belief that the powerful elements in which a miner works destroy him unless he puts forth his whole strength to gain the mastery over them, and puts aside all other thoughts which might weaken the wholehearted devotion he owes to his work in earth and fire. If you have really given careful thought to your desire and really wish to devote yourself to mining, then you have come at the right moment. I am short of workmen. You can, if you like, stay here now, and tomorrow morning go down the mine with the mine inspector who will show you your duties."

The heart of Elis beat high at these words. He thought no more of the fear he had felt looking down into that horrible abyss of hell. He was filled with joy and delight at the thought of seeing the lovely Ulla every day, of living under the same roof with her; the sweetest hopes were his.

Pehrson Dahlsjo informed the assembled miners that a young man had just arrived who wished to apprentice himself to mining, and introduced Elis to them.

They all looked with pleasure on the vigorous youth, and said that he was a born miner with his fine, strong limbs, and that they doubted not that he had his share of diligence and piety.

One of the miners, an elderly man, approached Elis, and shaking him by the hand said that he was the chief inspector of Pehrson Dahlsjo's mine, and that he would make it his care to see that Elis was instructed in everything necessary. Elis had to sit by him, and over a tankard of beer the old man began to explain the work.

Elis suddenly remembered the old miner of Gothaborg, and was able to repeat almost everything the old man had said to him. "Oh," cried the inspector in astonishment, "Elis Frobom, where did you learn all that? Why! there can be no doubt that in a short time you will be the best apprentice in the mine."

The lovely Ulla, moving about among the guests and waiting on them, gave many friendly nods to Elis, and disposed him to be really happy. "Now," she said, "you are no longer a stranger but belong here and not on the treacherous sea. Falun with its rich hills is your home." Heaven itself opened before the young man's eyes at Ulla's words. It was noticed that Ulla liked to be near him, and that even Pehrson Dahlsjo in his quiet, earnest way looked on him with pleasure.

Elis's heart beat fast when he stood once more by the smoking abyss, and, clothed in his miner's outfit, the heavy iron-shod Dalecarlian shoes on his feet, went down for the first time into the mine with the inspector. At first the hot steam nearly suffocated him, then a cutting wind nearly extinguished the lamps they carried. Deeper and deeper they went, at last down a narrow iron ladder, and Elis Frobom discovered that all his dexterity in climbing, learned in the rigging of ships, was of no use to him here.

At last they reached the deepest shaft, and the inspector showed Elis what he was to do.

Elis thought of the lovely Ulla; like a beautiful angel her form floated over him and he forgot all his horror of the depths, and all the difficulties of his work. He was certain that his dearest hopes could only be realized if he worked with all his might, with all the strength of which his body was capable, and so it happened that in a remarkably short time he was as good a worker as any in the mine.

Each day Pehrson Dahlsjo grew fonder of the hard-working quiet youth and often told him that he had found in him not only a good workman but also a well-loved son. Ulla also showed her feelings more and more openly. Often when Elis was going to his work and there was anything dangerous to be done, she begged him with tears in her eyes to guard himself against accident. And when he came back, she ran joyfully to meet him and was always ready with the finest beer or some good things to refresh him.

Elis's heart beat high with joy when one day Pehrson Dahlsjo said to him that, though he had brought no money with him, yet, because of his activity and his economy, he would certainly one day own a share in a mine or even become a mine owner; and then no owner in Falun would refuse his request if he begged for his daughter's hand. He longed to say how deeply he loved Ulla and that all his hopes were fixed on gaining her, but an unconquerable shyness and, even more, a doubt whether Ulla really loved him kept him from speaking.

One day Elis was working in the deepest shaft, the sulphur fumes so thick around him that his lamp gave out only a tiny glimmer and he could hardly distinguish the different strata in the rock. Suddenly he heard, as though from an even deeper shaft, a knocking as though somebody was using a pick. As such work is not possible in the depths, and Elis knew for certain that he was the only person who had come down that day, the inspector having sent the other men to work in another direction, there seemed to him something sinister in the sounds. He put down his tools and listened to the hollow sounds which seemed to come nearer and nearer. Then he noticed a dark shadow, and as a blast of cold air blew aside the sulphur fumes, he saw the old miner of Gothaborg beside him. "Good luck!" cried the old man, "good luck, Elis Frobom, down here in the earth! Well — how do you like the work, comrade?"

Elis wanted to ask him how he got into the shaft; but hitting the rock with his hammer with such force that sparks flew and the echo went through the shaft like thunder, the old man shouted in a terrible voice: "This is a wonderful trap-vein, but to you, you worthless, rascally good-for-nothing, it is only a Trumm, not worth a blade of grass. Down here you are nothing but a blind mole, to whom the prince of metals will always be unfriendly, and up on the surface you dare attempt nothing. So you want to win Pehrson Dahlsjo's daughter as your wife, and for that reason work down here, neither caring for your work nor thinking about it? Take care, false creature, that the prince of metals, whom you scorn, does not take you and throw you against the rocks until all your bones are broken. And Ulla shall never be your wife, I warn you!"

A furious anger rose in Elis at the insolent words of the old man. "What are you doing here in my master's mine, where I work with all my strength, as is my duty? Go away as you came, or we'll see down here which of us will manage to brain the other." With these words Elis took his stand in front of the old man and swung the iron hammer with which he had been working. The old man gave a mocking laugh, and a feeling of terror went through Elis as he watched him climb the narrow ladder like a squirrel and disappear into the darkness.

Elis felt paralyzed, he could not work any longer, and so he followed the other out of the shaft. The old inspector, just then returning from the other shaft, noticed him, and cried: "In heaven's name, what has happened to you, Elis, you are so deathly pale! Have the sulphur fumes, to which you are not yet accustomed, upset you? Drink this, young man, that will help." Elis took a long pull at the brandy bottle which the inspector held out to him, and, thus strengthened, related what had happened to him in the mine, also how he had made the acquaintance of the sinister old man in Gothaborg.

The inspector listened quietly, then he shook his head and said: "Elis Frobom, that was old Torbern, and now I know that the story which is told about him is more than a fairy tale. More than a hundred years ago there was here in Falun a miner named Torbern. He is said to have been one of the first to make a success of mining in Falun, and in his day the output was far richer than it is now. Nobody understood mining as Torbern did, his knowledge was so great that he was head of all the mining in Falun. He seemed to possess greater strength than anybody else, to know exactly where to find the richest veins, added to which he was a gloomy, serious man, without wife or child, even without a home in Falun, rarely coming up from the mine into the light of day, but always working in the depths. And so naturally the story soon began to get about that he was in alliance with the secret power which rules the underworld and makes the metals. In spite of Torbern's stern warnings that misfortune would follow unless the miners went to their work only from a feeling of real love for the wonderful minerals and metals, the mines were enlarged for the sake of gain, until at last on the Feast of St. John, in the year 1687, the terrible disaster occurred which opened the enormous chasm and wrecked the mines so completely that only through great labor and much skill have some of the shafts been made workable again. Torbern was never seen again; it was thought that he was buried under the ruins. Soon afterwards, as the work improved, many of the diggers swore that they had seen old Torbern down the mines and that he had given them much good advice and pointed out to them some rich veins. Others had seen the old man wandering about the pit head, sometimes lamenting, sometimes shouting angrily. Other youths have come here, as you have done, saying that an old miner had advised them to work in the mines and to come to Falun. That always happened when there was a shortage of labor, and was probably old Torbern's way of helping. If it was really old Torbern with whom you quarreled in the mine, and if he spoke of a wonderful trap-vein, then there is certainly a rich vein of iron there, and tomorrow we will search for it. You know that here the iron veins are called trap-veins, and that the 'Trumm' is a vein of that kind that splits into many pieces."

When Elis, deep in thought, entered Pehrson Dahlsjo's house that day, Ulla did not come as usual to meet him. With lowered gaze, and, as Elis thought, eyes red with weeping. Ulla sat there, and by her side a handsome young man who held her hand fast in his was trying to cheer her up by his merry talk of which Ulla did not appear to be taking much notice. Elis stared at the couple, a horrid fear taking hold of him, till Pehrson Dahlsjo drew him aside into another room and said: "Now, Elis Frobom, you will soon be able to show your love to me, and your faithfulness, for I have always looked upon you as a son, and soon you will be that completely. That man is the rich merchant, Eric Olawsen, of Gothaborg. He has my consent to marry my daughter; they will go to Gothaborg and you will then be alone here with me, my only support in my old age. Why, Elis, have you nothing to say? You blench. I hope my plans do not upset you, and that you will not wish to leave me as well! but I hear Eric Olawsen calling me. I must go!"

And Pehrson went back into the other room.

Elis felt as though thousands of sharp knives were being driven into his heart. He could not speak; tears would not come. In wild despair he rushed out of the house—away—away—to the pit head. If the enormous chasm was terrifying by daylight, how much more awful was it now that night had fallen and the moon was just rising to look down upon the rocks, which seemed more than ever like a restless crowd of horrible monsters, ghastly fiends moving about on the smoking floor, their terrible eyes flashing upwards and their gigantic claws stretching ever towards the world of man.

"Torbern—Torbern," called Elis with a dreadful voice which echoed through the desolate chasm, "Torbern—here I am! You were right, I have been a rascally sort of worker, and given myself over to stupid hopes in the world above ground. Down there lies my treasure, my life, my all! Torbern! come down with me, show me the richest trap-veins, there I will work and dig, and never more see the light of day. Torbern! Torbern! come down with me."

Elis took steel and flint out of his pocket, lit his lamp and descended to the shaft where he had been working, but the old man did not appear. But how surprised he was in the deepest shaft to see the trap-vein, clear and distinct, so that he could even distinguish the streaks and faults in it.

As he looked more and more closely at the wonderful vein in the rock, it seemed as though a blinding light lit up the whole shaft and its walls became as transparent as pure crystal. The ominous dream which he had dreamed in Gothaborg came back to him. He looked again into the heavenly regions where grew lovely metal trees and plants whose fruit and flowers were precious stones. He saw the maidens; he gazed again into the noble face of the mighty Queen. She caught hold of him, drew him down, pressed him to her breast, a thrill of wonder went through him and he was conscious only of feeling that he was swimming in a blue, transparent, sparkling mist.

"Elis Frobom, Elis Frobom!" cried a strong voice from above and the light of torches flooded the shaft. Pehrson Dahlsjo himself had come with the inspector who had seen Elis rushing like one possessed towards the pit head.

They found him standing motionless, his face pressed to the cold stone.

"What are you doing here by night, you rash young man?" cried Pehrson. "Pull yourself together, and come up with us; who knows what good news you will hear up there!"

In deep silence Elis followed Pehrson Dahlsjo, who continued to scold him for running into such danger.

It was already broad daylight when they reached the house. With a loud cry Ulla threw herself into Elis's arms, and called him by the sweetest names. But Pehrson spoke to Elis: "You fool! do you suppose that I have not known for a long time that you love Ulla, and that all your work for me was for her sake? Have I not also known for a long time that Ulla loves you from the bottom of her heart? Could I wish for a better son-in-law, a more hard-working, honest miner than you, my brave Elis? But your silence angered me, hurt me."

"But did we know," Ulla interrupted her father, "how much we loved each other?"

"Let that be as it will," went on Pehrson, "it annoyed me that Elis was not open and honest with me about his love for you, and because I wanted to try you also, I invented the fairy tale about Eric Olawsen yesterday, which soon brought you to your senses. You foolish man! Eric Olawsen has long been married, and to you, Elis Frobom, I give my daughter, for, I repeat, I could not wish a better son-in-law."

Tears of joy ray down Elis's cheeks. So much happiness had come so unexpectedly upon him that it seemed to him he was again in the midst of a wonderful dream.

By Pehrson Dahlsjo's orders the miners assembled at midday for a feast. Ulla had put on her finest attire and looked more lovely than ever, so that everybody exclaimed: "Ah, what a lovely bride our brave Elis Frobom has won! Now may heaven bless them both!"

The horror of the previous night was still to be seen on Elis's pale face, and he often stood staring straight before him as though far removed from what was going on around him.

"What is the matter, my Elis?" asked Ulla. Elis held her tight in his arms and said, "Yes, yes! you are really mine, and now everything will be right."

Yet in the midst of his joy it sometimes seemed to Elis as though an ice-cold hand were laid on him and a dark voice said: "Have you everything you desire now that you have won Ulla? Poor fool! Have you not looked on the face of the Queen?"

He was nearly overcome by an unspeakable dread. The thought was ever with him that one of the miners would rise before him, a gigantic figure, and he would recognize Torbern, come to remind him in terrible form of that underground kingdom of stone and metal to which he had made his submission.

And yet he had no idea why the ghostly old man was so hostile to him, or what, indeed, mining had to do with his love for Ulla.

Pehrson noticed Elis's strange behavior and put it down to the pain he had suffered and to the night in the mine. Not so Ulla who, filled with secret dread, pressed her lover to tell her what horrible experience it was that he had suffered, which cut her off so completely. Elis felt that his heart woud break. In vain he tried to tell his loved one of the marvelous sight he had seen in the mine. It was as though an unknown power was forcibly shutting his mouth, as though the terrible face of the Queen was looking at him, and if he spoke her name, then, as at the sight of the head of Medusa, everything around would turn to stone. All that loveliness, which down the mine had filled him with the deepest ecstasy, seemed now to be a hell of desperate misery tricked out for his temptation.

Pehrson Dahlsjo ordered Elis to stay at home for a few days in order to recover from the illness from which he seemed to be suffering. During this time the love which shone forth bright and clear from Ulla's childlike and pure heart overcame any remembrance of that ominous adventure in the mine. Elis revived completely in this atmosphere of love and happiness, and believed firmly that no evil power had any further influence over him.

When next he went down the mine, everything seemed different to him. The most wonderful seams lay opened before his eyes, he worked with redoubled vigor, he forgot everything; when he reached the surface again he had to force himself to remember Pehrson Dahlsjo and even his Ulla; he felt as though he were divided in two, as though his real, his better, self remained down in the depths of the earth, resting in the arms of the Queen, while the rest of him sought his unhappy couch in Falun. If Ulla spoke to him of their love and how happily they would live together, he began to talk about the wonders of the mine, the priceless treasures which lay hidden there, and became so involved in such marvelous and unintelligible descriptions that the poor girl was overcome with fear and anxiety and could not understand how Elis had suddenly changed so completely.

Elis often told the mine inspector of the wonderful seams he had found, and when the miners could find nothing but barren rock, he laughed ironically and said that of course he alone understood the secret signs, the momentous writing which the Queen herself engraved on the stone, and it was really sufficient to understand these signs without making clear what the meaning was.

The old inspector looked sadly at the young man talking, with wild, glittering eyes, of the wonderful paradise buried deep in the earth.

"Oh, sir," he whispered softly into Pehrson Dahlsjo's ear, "the wicked Torbern has bewitched the young man."

"Don't believe such old miner's yarns, old man," answered Pehrson Dahlsjo. "Love has turned his head, that is all. Wait till the wedding is over, then there will be an end of these stories of rich seams and treasures and underground paradises."

The day Pehrson Dahlsjo had appointed for the wedding came round at last. Days beforehand, Elis Frobom was quieter, graver more retiring than ever, but more in love with Ulla. He could not bear to be parted from her for an instant and for that reason he did not go to the mines; he appeared to have forgotten his strange behavior and no word of the underground kingdom crossed his lips. Ulla was full of joy. She had lost her fear that the threatening powers of the underworld, of which she had heard old miners speak, should lure her Elis to destruction. And Pehrson Dahlsjo said laughingly to the old inspector, "There, you see, it was only love for Ulla which turned Elis Frobom's head."

Early on the wedding morning—it was midsummer day—Elis knocked on his bride's door. She opened it and started back in terror when she saw Elis already dressed for the wedding, but deathly pale and with dark flaming eyes. "I only want," he said in a light, unsteady voice, "to tell you, my beloved Ulla, that we are standing on the brink of the greatest happiness which human beings can experience on earth. It has all been revealed to me tonight. Down at the bottom of the mine, buried in chloride and mica, lies the cherry-red, sparkling almandine on which our life lines are engraved. I must fetch that to give you as a wedding present. It is more lovely than the finest blood-red carbuncle; and when, knit together by our great love, we look into its beaming light, we shall be able to see clearly how our inner life is bound up with that wonderful branch which grows out of the heart of the Queen at the center of the world. It is only necessary for me to bring this stone up to the light of day, and that I will do now. Take care of yourself in the meantime, my beloved Ulla! I shall soon be back."

With tears in her eyes, Ulla begged her lover to refrain from this chimerical undertaking, for she had a foreboding of great misfortune; but Elis assured her that without the stone he would never again have peace, and that there could be no question of danger. He embraced her fervently and left her.

The guests had assembled to accompany the bride and bridegroom to the Kopparberg church where the wedding was to take place. A crowd of gaily dressed girls who, according to the custom of the country, were to lead the bride to the church, were laughing and joking round Ulla. The musicians finished turning up and began a gay wedding march. It was nearly midday, and there was still no sign of Elis. Suddenly a crowd of miners rushed in, anxiety and horror in their pale faces, and announced that a terrible landslide had destroyed Dahlsjo's mine completely.

"Elis—my Elis—dead—dead!" Ulla shrieked and fell unconscious. Now, for the first time, Pehrson heard from the inspector that in the early morning Elis had gone to the pit head and descended the mine, where he was quite alone, for all the others had been invited to the wedding. The miners hurried out, but all search was hopeless. No trace of Elis Frobom was found. It was certain that he was buried under the fall: and so misery and sorrow entered the house of Pehrson Dahlsjo in that moment when he had thought to assure himself peace and quiet for his old age.

The brave mine owner Pehrson Dahlsjo had long been dead, his daughter Ulla long vanished, nobody in Falun knew anything of them anymore, for more than fifty years had elapsed since Elis

Frobom's unlucky wedding day. Then it happened one day that miners trying a crosscut between two shafts deep down found the body or young miner in vitriolic water. When they brought it to the surface, it appeared to have been turned to stone.

To the onlookers the youth seemed to be in a deep sleep, the features were so well preserved; there was no sign of decay about the festal attire which he wore, even the flowers in his buttonhole seemed quite fresh. Everybody in the neighborhood gathered at the pit head where the youth had been carried, but nobody recognized his face and none of the miners remembered one of their number having disappeared. They were just about to carry the corpse to Falun when there appeared in the distance an old woman hobbling along on crutches. "Here comes the old midsummer woman!" cried some of the miners. The old crone had received this name from the fact that for many years on midsummer day she had appeared out of nowhere, gazed down the mine shaft, and, wringing her hands, crept sighing and moaning round the pit head before disappearing again.

Hardly had the old woman caught sight of the youth than she let fall both her crutches and, raising her arms to heaven, cried in tones of heart-rending sorrow: "Oh, Elis Frobom—oh, my dear love." And kneeling beside the corpse she seized the stiff hands and pressed them to her breast in which, like a holy flame under a covering of ice, there beat a heart full of passionate love. "Ah," she said at last, "none, none of you remember poor Ulla Dahlsjo who, fifty years ago, was the happy bride of this youth. When in misery and sorrow I left Falun and went to Ornas, old Torbern comforted me and promised me that I should see my Elis, who was buried by a fall of stone on our wedding day, again on this earth, and so, year after year, filled with longing and true love, I have come and gazed down into the pit. And today I have seen him! Oh, my Elis—my beloved!"

And she threw her thin arms round the youth and held him as though she would never let him go, while the people stood, deeply moved, around her.

Fainter and fainter came the old woman's sobs and moans until at last they ceased altogether.

The miners drew near; they wanted to lift her away, but she had breathed her last over the corpse of her bridegroom. Then the onlookers noticed that the corpse that they had thought turned to stone was beginning to turn to dust.

In the Kopparberg church where, fifty years before, the couple should have been married, his dust was laid to rest beside the body of his faithful bride.

Balzac

1799 May 20. Honoré de Balzac born in Tours, France.

1816–19 Works as a law clerk but quits to pursue a writing career.

1819–24 In five years writes six novels under a pseudonym and collaborates with a number of hack writers. Begins an affair with Mme. de Berny in 1822. (When she dies in 1836, he writes *Le lys dans la vallée*, an idealized version of their love.)

1825–30 Enters business as a publisher, but by 1828 is on the verge of bankruptcy and accrues debts that remain for the rest of his life. Publishes *Le dernier chouan* in 1829 under his own name and garners public attention. The first of the *Scenes of Private Life* is published in 1830. Starts to write the stories and novels that will comprise *La comédie humaine*.

1831–33 Becomes interested in the occult and adopts Emanuel Swendenborg's theosophy which informs such works as *La peau de chagrin* (1831) and the trilogy *Le livre mystique* (1832–35). Begins corresponding with Evelina Hanska in 1832. Balzac's letters result in the posthumous *Lettres à l'étrangère*. (Hanska's letters are destroyed.) By 1833, he decides to link disconnected stories by using recurring characters.

1842–48 A new edition of his works appear in 1842 and for the first time carries the name *La comédie humaine*. Begins another expanded edition of *La comédie humaine* in 1845. Finishes the last of his completed stories by 1848, when his health begins to decline.

1850 Marries Evelina Hanska in March. Balzac dies on August 18 in Paris.

Honoré de Balzac

Just as Hugo was the last great champion of the romantic virtues of heroism (although he was a republican and without a sense of humor), Balzac was the first celebrant of the new era of democratic, capitalistic, industrial society. He was its critic and historian also. In the work of Hugo as in the work of the medieval romances, money and the effects of money play an inconspicuous part in the scheme of living; even the poor, upon whom Hugo lavishes so much agreeable sentiment, are never considered in relation to the economic system which makes them poor, but as unfortunates, slighted children of God upon whom the more fortunate are constrained to exercise charity and pity.

The acquisition of money is the central passion of Balzac himself, and it is the mainspring of the characters of nearly all of his fictional creations. He and Stendhal (whose career as a novelist somewhat antedated Balzac's), alone among nineteenth century novelists, did not disdain money (or profess to) or discount its importance in the scheme of life under industrialism. Balzac was not repelled, like so many writers of his time, by the idea that prosperity, pleasant living, pleasant enjoyment of the amenities might be gained by peaceful trade, instead of by pillage; that the individual, whatever his birth, might of his own talents win to the ease and comfort, luxury and freedom of the mind and spirit by supplying the wants and needs of his fellow man, instead of, by force of arms, taking what his fellows produced.

Balzac saw all the evil that this new opportunity could produce: he saw the miser centering all his passion on the accumulation of gold, never spending it, never making use of it and causing misery to all who were dependent upon him or were subject to his lust for gold. He saw the clever *arrivistes*, winning their way to power through money by crushing and killing those less clever;

he saw new artificial classes arising on a new basis of possessions; he saw, in fine, all the disagreeable and sordid factors in the new touchstone of success—money.

But he did not, like the middle class dilettantes of his period who rooted like any swine for cash, make a show of disdaining money. Money was frankly what he was after as a writer. Others wanted fame; Balzac wanted money. That he never quite attained his objective, that he wore himself out paying off old debts and died just when he had finally attained a degree of wealth, is one of the fortunate ironies of life, unfortunate for Balzac but fortunate for the rest of humanity.

For the fact is Balzac reproduced in novels every phase of the society of his time. Future students of his period will go to Balzac, and not to the historians, to learn what life was like in Paris during the greater part of the nineteenth century. He was a meticulous observer; he was a faithful reporter; and he had a sense of drama.

Honoré de Balzac was born in 1799 at Tours, the country of Rabelais. He had many of the qualities celebrated by the creator of *Gargantua and Pantagruel*: he was stout, broad-shouldered, sanguine, inclined to fatness, a prodigious eater and drinker, coarse, clumsy, close to the soil, nearer to the peasant than to the nobility. He had full sensual lips, thick black hair, coarse as the mane of a horse, and deep brown eyes which shone with a steady luster. He was educated at the College Vendôme in Tours and, when the Balzac family moved to Paris, he was entered as a notary's apprentice with the view to his taking up the legal profession.

The law was not to Balzac's taste, however, for he had early conceived the ambition to conquer Paris with his literary gifts. He proposed a plan to his father, which his father finally yielded to: his father was to contribute a small amount for his support until he had tried out his gifts. If he was able to sustain himself as a writer, he would be permitted to go on with a literary career; if he did not, he was to take up law again.

The future creator of a teeming world of fictional types took an attic room near the Père Lachaise, and entered upon the titanic labors which were to produce ninety-six novels, any number of short stories, and literary hackwork of all kinds and finally kill him prematurely. In *Père Goriot* he pictures Rastignac, an ambitious young man, standing on the Butte above Paris in the evening, looking down on the city and vowing to conquer that city by brain and will, no matter what it cost him. In the same way we are sure that Balzac, looking out of the window from his garret over the rooftops of Paris, vowed that he would conquer Paris by the labors of his pen. He had to practice every economy. His room was cold and cheerless, drab and sparsely furnished. He worked through the night, wrapped up in blankets, and with a pot of coffee beside him. To obtain a lower price for his room he agreed to make his bed, sweep the room and keep it tidy. He permitted himself a short walk in the morning as the only form of exercise; his food was scanty — rolls, a paste of sardines and olive oil, coffee and some fruit. Later he would starve himself for days at a time and then eat enough to kill him — six dozen oysters, two whole chickens, slices of roast, salad and cheese — and wash it down with a magnum of wine.

He tried a tragedy and soon found he had no sense of dramatic technique. Time was pressing. He turned to novel writing. He had not had much experience in life, but he had read a great many novels. He turned out five novels in one year, under a pseudonym, all of which were accepted, but none of which had any considerable merit. But he got a thousand francs apiece for them. He had proved to his family that he could earn a living by his pen.

Balzac gave up writing for a time and with his meager savings started a publishing house with the idea of bringing out cheap one-volume editions of the classics; but he failed in this because he had not reckoned on the competition he would have to meet. He had also set up as a bookseller to distribute his own publications, as the result of which other booksellers declined to purchase his wares. Again on a trip to Italy, he had an idea (which later proved correct) that the silver mines of Sardinia were not exhausted and, since silver at the time was at a premium, he set about examining the mines, returned to Paris for capital, got the money needed, and applied for permission to work the mines. Unfortunately he had told others of his idea while in Italy, and one of these beat him to the concession. His ideas, however, had been correct: the mines made a fortune for the man whom he guilelessly told about it.

Balzac's publishing idea had been a grandiose one, for he

meant to edit the classics himself, write prefaces for them, and be his own printer, agent, distributor, and bookseller. He persuaded his father to put money into the scheme. At first things seemed to work out all right, but then the booksellers combined against him; he went bankrupt and was overburdened with debts. He spent some months in a debtor's prison before he was able to make arrangements with his creditors which would allow him to pay off his debts by installments.

To pay off his debts he plunged again into writing. Writing did not come easy to him. He did not have a natural, easy facility; he could not, like his friend Gautier, hastily turn off a newspaper article which would be a marvel of felicitous phrasing while standing at a counter in the newspaper office with the editor waiting for the sheets. Balzac never learned to write easily nor did he ever acquire any charm of style. Like Theodore Dreiser in America after him, he always wrote graceless prose with only occasional lapses into felicity: like Dreiser he was not so much concerned with the way of saying a thing as with what he had to say. His style, therefore, was always somewhat distasteful to the more exacting French critics.

Gautier has given us his reminiscences of Balzac as a worker. All the world has heard about Balzac's habit of working all day and all night, keeping awake by drinking vast quantities of strong coffee. But, as Gautier reveals to us, Balzac got as much sleep as the average person requires. He merely distributed sleep over periods when other people were awake. Gautier tells how Balzac would come to his house in the early morning after working all night and, being ravenously hungry, would make innumerable sandwiches of sardine paste and fall asleep with his clothes on, asking Gautier to wake him in an hour. This Gautier would invariably fail to do, and Balzac would sleep soundly until nightfall, when he would wake up in a high state of excitability and hurl maledictions on his benefactor, crying out that he had thus lost so many thousand francs for the chapters he might have written of his novel. This performance was repeated day in and day out, and Balzac, getting plenty of sleep all the time, entertained the delusion that he did not need sleep and rarely got it, and then only when some one betrayed him into the hands of Morpheus.

Balzac turned out many novels under a pseudonym before he dared to acknowledge the work that came from his pen. Then he wrote *The Physiology of Marriage*, a Rabelaisian analysis of the institution of wedlock, which had an excellent sale but which did not help his literary reputation. He followed this by *La Peau de Chagrin*, a half supernatural, half psychological novel which some critics consider the finest of his novels. It established his reputation; it was translated into German and English. It made an impression on Goethe.

It was not until after Balzac had written his most famous classics, *Eugénie Grandet and Père Goriot*, that he conceived the idea of linking all his past and future novels together, with some of the same central characters reappearing from time to time, of treating every phase of contemporary French society and of calling the whole work, the *Human Comedy*. Dante had called his principal poem the *Inferno* and had peopled it with Florentines of his time. So Balzac would write an *Inferno* of Parisian society, peopling it with go-getters, misers, rakes, peasants, novelists, journalists, frivolous high society persons, bankers, actors, mountebanks. Always in debt, he struggled on with his gigantic task until at last he achieved a degree of security and a certain happiness—only to die.

—*from* Titans of Literature *by Burton Rascoe*

La Grande Bretèche

"Ah! Madame," replied Doctor Horace Bianchon to the lady at whose house he was supping, "it is true that I have many terrible histories in my repertory; but every tale has its due hour in a conversation, according to the clever saying reported by Chamfort and said to the Duc de Fronsac: "There are ten bottles of champagne between your joke and the present moment."

"But it is past midnight; what better hour could you have?" said the mistress of the house.

"Yes, tell us, Monsieur Bianchon," urged the assembled company.

At a gesture from the complying doctor, silence reigned.

"About a hundred yards from Vendôme," he said, "on the banks of the Loir, is an old brown house, covered with very steep roofs, and so completely isolated that there is not so much as an evil-smelling tannery, nor a shabby inn such as you see at the entrance of all little towns, in its neighborhood. In front of this dwelling is a garden overlooking the river, where the box edgings, once carefully clipped, which bordered the paths, now cross them and straggle as they fancy. A few willows with their roots in the Loir have made a rapid growth, like the enclosing hedge, and together they half hide the house. Plants which we call weeds drape the bank towards the river with their beautiful vegetation. Fruit trees, neglected for half a score of years, no longer yield a product, and their shoots and suckers have formed an undergrowth. The espaliers are like a hornbeam hedge. The paths, formerly gravelled, are full of purslain; so that, strictly speaking, there are no paths at all.

"From the crest of the mountain, on which hang the ruins of the old castle of Vendôme (the only spot whence the eye can look down into this enclosure) we say to ourselves that at an earlier period, now difficult to determine, this corner of the earth was the delight of some gentleman devoted to roses and tulips, in a word, to horticulture, but above all possessing a keen taste for good fruits. An arbor is still standing, or rather the remains of one, and beneath it is a table which time has not yet completely demolished.

"From the aspect of this garden, now no more, the negative joys of the peaceful life of the provinces can be inferred, just as we infer the life of some worthy from the epitaph on his tomb. To complete the sad and tender ideas which take possession of the soul, a sundial on the wall bears this inscription, Christian yet bourgeois, 'ULTIMATUM COGITA.' The roofs are dilapidated, the blinds always closed, the balconies are filled with swallows' nests, the gates are locked. Tall herbs and grasses trace in green lines the chinks and crevices of the stone portico; the locks are rusty. Sun and moon, summer and winter and snow have rotted the wood, warped the planks, and worn away the paint. The gloomy silence is unbroken save by the birds, the cats, the martens, the rats, the mice, all free to scamper or fly, and to fight, and to eat themselves up.

"An invisible hand has written the word 'MYSTERY' everywhere. If, impelled by curiosity, you wish to look at this house, on the side towards the road you will see a large gate with an arched top, in which the children of the neighborhood have made large holes. This gate, as I heard later, had been disused for ten years. Through these irregular holes you can observe the perfect harmony which exists between the garden side, and the courtyard side of the premises. The same neglect everywhere. Lines of grass surround the paving stones. Enormous cracks furrow the walls, the blackened eaves of which are festooned with pellitory. The steps of the portico are disjointed, the rope of the bell is rotten, the gutters are dropping apart. What fire from heaven has fallen here? What tribunal has ordained that salt be cast upon this dwelling? Has God been mocked here; or France betrayed? These are the questions we ask as we stand there; the reptiles crawl about but they give no answer.

"This empty and deserted house is a profound enigma, whose solution is known to none. It was formerly a small fief, and is called La Grande Bretèche. During my stay at Vendôme, where Desplein had sent me in charge of a rich patient, the sight of this strange dwelling was one of my keenest pleasures. It was better than a ruin. A ruin possesses memories of positive authenticity; but this habitation, still standing, though slowly demolished by an avenging hand, contained some secret, some mysterious thought, — it betrayed at least a strange caprice.

"More than once of an evening I jumped the hedge, now a tangle, which guarded the enclosure. I braved the scratches; I walked that garden without a master, that property which was neither public nor private; for hours I stayed there contemplating its decay. Not even to obtain the history which underlay (and to which no doubt was due) this strange spectacle would I have asked a single question of any gossiping countryman. Standing there I invented enchanting tales; I gave myself up to debauches of melancholy which fascinated me. Had I known the reason, perhaps a common one, for this strange desertion, I should have lost the unwritten poems with which I intoxicated myself. To me this sanctuary evoked the most varied images of human life darkened by sorrows; sometimes it was a cloister without the nuns; sometimes a graveyard and its peace, without the dead who talk to you in epitaphs; today the house of the leper, tomorrow that of the Atrides; but above all was it the provinces with their composed ideas, their hourglass life.

"Often I wept there, but I never smiled. More than once an involuntary terror seized me, as I heard above my head the muffled whirr of a ringdove's wings hurrying past. The soil is damp; care must be taken against the lizards, the vipers, the frogs, which wander about with the wild liberty of nature; above all, it is well not to fear cold, for there are moments when you feel an icy mantle laid upon your shoulders like the hand of the Commander on the shoulder of Don Juan. One evening I shuddered; the wind had caught and turned a rusty vane. Its creak was like a moan issuing from the house; at a moment, too, when I was ending a gloomy drama in which I explained to myself the monumental dolor of that scene.

"That night I returned to my inn, a prey to gloomy thoughts. After I had supped the landlady entered my room with a mysterious air, and said to me, 'Monsieur, Monsieur Regnault is here.'

"'Who is Monsieur Regnault?'

"'Is it possible that Monsieur doesn't know Monsieur Regnault? Ah, how funny!' she said, leaving the room.

"Suddenly I beheld a long, slim man, clothed in black, holding his hat in his hand, who presented himself, much like a ram about to leap on a rival, and showed me a retreating forehead, a small, pointed head and a livid face, in color somewhat like a glass of dirty water. You would have taken him for the usher of a minister. This unknown personage wore an old coat much worn in the folds, but he had a diamond in the frill of his shirt, and gold earrings in his ears.

"'Monsieur, to whom have I the honor of speaking?' I said.

"He took a chair, sat down before my fire, laid his hat on my table and replied, rubbing his hands: 'Ah! it is very cold. Monsieur, I am Monsieur Regnault.'

"I bowed, saying to myself: '*Il bondo cani!* seek!'

"'I am,' he said, 'the notary of Vendôme.'

"'Delighted, monsieur,' I replied, 'but I am not in the way of making my will,—for reasons, alas, too well-known to me.'

"'One moment!' he resumed, raising his hand as if to impose silence; 'Permit me, monsieur, permit me! I have learned that you sometimes enter the garden of La Grande Bretèche and walk there—'

"'Yes, monsieur.'

"'One moment!' he said, repeating his gesture. 'That action constitutes a misdemeanor. Monsieur, I come in the name and as testamentary executor of the late Comtesse de Merret to beg you to discontinue your visits. One moment! I am not a Turk; I do not wish to impute a crime to you. Besides, it is quite excusable that you, a stranger, should be ignorant of the circumstances which compel me to let the handsomest house in Vendôme go to ruin. Nevertheless, monsieur, as you seem to be a person of education, you no doubt know that the law forbids trespassers on enclosed property. A hedge is the same as a wall. But the state in which that house is left may well excuse your curiosity. I should be only too glad to leave you free to go and come as you liked there, but charged as I am to execute the wishes of the testatrix, I have the honor, monsieur, to request that you do not again enter that garden. I myself, monsieur, have not, since the reading of the will, set foot in that house, which, as I have already had the honor to tell you, I hold under the will of Madame de Merret. We have only taken account of the number of the doors and windows so as to assess the taxes which I pay annually from the funds left by the late countess for that purpose. Ah, monsieur, that will made a great deal of noise in Vendôme!'

"There the worthy man paused to blow his nose. I respected his loquacity, understanding perfectly that the testamentary bequest of Madame de Merret had been the most important event of his life, the head and front of his reputation, his glory, his Restoration. So then, I must bid adieu to my beautiful reveries, my romances! I was not so rebellious as to deprive myself of getting the truth, as it were officially, out of the man of law, so I said, —

"'Monsieur, if it is not indiscreet, may I ask the reason of this singularity?'

"'At these words a look which expressed the pleasure of a man who rides a hobby passed over Monsieur Regnault's face. He pulled up his shirt collar with a certain conceit, took out his snuffbox, opened it, offered it to me, and on my refusal, took a strong pinch himself. He was happy. A man who hasn't a hobby doesn't know how much can be got out of life. A hobby is the exact medium between a passion and a monomania. At that moment I understood Sterne's fine expression to its fullest extent, and I formed a complete idea of the joy with which my Uncle Toby—Trim assisting—bestrode his war-horse.

"'Monsieur,' said Monsieur Regnault, 'I was formerly head clerk to Maitre Roguin in Paris. An excellent lawyer's office of which you have doubtless heard? No! And yet a most unfortunate failure made it, I may say, celebrated. Not having the means to buy a practice in Paris at the price to which they rose in 1816, I came here to Vendôme, where I have relations, — among them a rich aunt, who gave me her daughter in marriage.'

"Here he made a slight pause, and then resumed: —

"'Three months after my appointment was ratified by Monseigneur the Keeper of the Seals, I was sent for one evening just as I was going to bed (I was not then married) by Madame la Comtesse de Merret, then living in her château at Merret. Her lady's maid, an excellent girl who is now serving in this inn, was at the door with the countess's carriage. Ah! one moment! I ought to tell you, monsieur, that Monsieur le Comte de Merret had gone to die in Paris about two months before I came here. He died a miserable death from excesses of all kinds, to which he gave himself up. You understand? Well, the day of his departure Madame la Comtesse left La Grande Bretèche, and dismantled it. They do say that she even burned the furniture, and the carpets, and all appurtenances whatsoever and wheresoever contained on the premises leased to the said — Ah! beg pardon; what am I saying? I thought I was dictating a lease. Well, monsieur, she burned everything, they say, in the meadow at Merret. Were you ever at Merret, monsieur?'

"Not waiting for me to speak, he answered for me: 'No. Ah! it is a fine spot? For three months, or thereabouts,' he continued, nodding his head, 'Monsieur le Comte and Madame la Comtesse had been living at La Grande Bretèche in a very singular way. They admitted no one to the house; madame lived on the ground floor, and monsieur on the first floor. After Madame le Comtesse was left alone she never went to church. Later, in her own château she refused to see the friends who came to visit her. She changed greatly after she left La Grande Bretèche and came to Merret. That dear woman (I say dear, though I never saw her but once, because she gave me this diamond), — that good lady was very ill; no doubt she had given up all hope of recovery, for she died without calling in a doctor; in fact, some of our ladies thought she was not quite right in her mind. Consequently, monsieur, my curiosity was greatly excited when I learned that Madame de Merret needed my services; and I was not the only one deeply interested; that very night, though it was ate, the whole town knew I had gone to Merret.'

"The good man paused a moment to arrange his facts, and then continued: 'The lady's maid answered rather vaguely the questions which I put to her as we drove along; she did, however, tell me that her mistress had received the last sacraments that day from the curate of Merret, and that she was not likely to live through the night. I reached the château about eleven o'clock. I went up the grand staircase. After passing through a number of dark and lofty rooms, horribly cold and damp, I entered the state bedroom where Madame la Comtesse was lying. In consequence of the many stories that were told about this lady (really, monsieur, I should never end if I related all of them) I expected to find her a fascinating coquette. Would you believe it, I could scarcely see her at all in the huge bed in which she lay. It is true that the only light in that vast room, with friezes of the old style powdered with dust enough to make you sneeze on merely looking at them, was one Argand lamp. Ah! but you say you have never been at Merret. Well, monsieur, the bed was one of those old-time beds with a high tester covered with flowered chintz. A little night table stood by the bed, and on it I noticed a copy of the "Imitation of Christ."

"'Allow me a parenthesis,' he said, interrupting himself. 'I bought that book subsequently, also the lamp, and presented them to my wife. In the room was a large sofa for the woman who was taking care of Madame de Merret, and two chairs. That was all. No fire. The whole would not have made ten lines of an inventory. Ah! my dear monsieur, could you have seen her as I saw her then, in that vast room hung with brown tapestry, you would have imagined you were in the pages of a novel. It was glacial, — better than that, funereal,' added the worthy man, raising his arm theatrically and making a pause. Presently he resumed:

"'By dint of peering round and coming close to the bed I at length saw Madame de Merret, thanks to the lamp which happened to shine on the pillows. Her face was as yellow as wax, and looked like two hands joined together. Madame la Comtesse wore a lace cap, which, however, allowed me to see her fine hair, white as snow. She was sitting up in the bed, but apparently did so with difficulty. Her large black eyes, sunken no doubt with fever, and almost lifeless, hardly moved beneath the bones where the eyebrows usually grow. Her forehead was damp. Her fleshless hands were like bones covered with thin skin; the veins and muscles could all be seen. She must once have been very handsome, but now I was seized with — I couldn't tell you what feeling, as I looked at her. Those who buried her said afterwards that no living creature had ever been as wasted as she without dying. Well, it was awful to see. Some mortal disease had eaten up that woman till there was nothing left of her but a phantom. Her lips, of a pale violet, seemed not to move when she spoke. Though my profession had familiarized me with such scenes, in bringing me often to the bedside of the dying, to receive their last wishes, I must say that the tears and the anguish of families and friends which I have witnessed were as nothing compared to this solitary woman in that vast building. I did not hear the slightest noise, I did not see the movement which the breathing of the dying woman would naturally give to the sheet that covered her; I myself remained motionless, looking at her in a sort of stupor. Indeed. I fancy I am there still. At last her large eyes moved; she tried to lift her right hand, which fell back upon the bed; then these words issued from her lips like a breath, for her voice was no longer a voice, —

"'"I have awaited you with impatience."

"'Her cheeks colored. The effort to speak was great. The old woman who was watching her here rose and whispered in my ear: "Don't speak; Madame la Comtesse is past hearing the slightest sound; you would only agitate her." I sat down. A few moments later Madame de Merret collected all her remaining strength to move her right arm and put it, not without great difficulty, under her bolster. She paused an instant; then she made a last effort and withdrew her hand which now held a sealed paper. Great drops of sweat rolled from her forehead.

"'"I give you my will," she said. "Oh, my God! Oh!"

"'That was all. She seized a crucifix which lay on her bed, pressed it to her lips and died. The expression of her fixed eyes still makes me shudder when I think of it. I brought away the will. When it was opened I found that Madame de Merret had appointed me her executor. She bequeathed her whole property to the hospital of Vendôme, save and excepting certain bequests. The following disposition was made of La Grande Bretèche. I was directed to leave it in the state in which it was at the time of her death for a period of fifty years from the date of her decease; I was to forbid all access to it, by any and every one, no matter who; to make no repairs, and to put by from her estate a yearly sum to pay watchers, if they were necessary, to insure the faithful execution of these intentions. At the expiration of that time the estate was, if the testatrix's will had been carried out in all particulars, to belong to my heirs (because, as monsieur is doubtless well aware, notaries are forbidden by law to receive legacies); if otherwise, then La Grande Bretèche was to go to whoever might establish a right to it, but on condition of fulfilling certain orders contained in a codicil annexed to the will and not to be opened until the expiration of the fifty years. The will has never been attacked, consequently—'

"Here the oblong notary, without finishing his sentence, looked at me triumphantly. I made him perfectly happy with a few compliments.

"'Monsieur,' I said, in conclusion, 'you have so deeply impressed that scene upon me that I seem to see the dying woman, whiter than the sheets; those glittering eyes horrify me; I shall dream of her all night. But you must have formed some conjectures as to the motive of that extraordinary will.'

"'Monsieur,' he replied, with comical reserve, 'I never permit myself to judge of the motives of those who honor me with the gift of a diamond.'

"However, I managed to unloose the tongue of the scrupulous notary so far that he told me, not without long digressions, certain opinions on the matter emanating from the wise-heads of both sexes whose judgments made the social law of Vendôme. But these opinions and observations were so contradictory, so diffuse, that I well-nigh went to sleep in spite of the interest I felt in this authentic story. The heavy manner and monotonous accent of the notary, who was no doubt in the habit of listening to himself and making his clients and compatriots listen to him, triumphed over my curiosity. Happily, he did at last go away.

"'Ha, ha! monsieur,' he said to me at the head of the stairs, 'many persons would like to live their forty-five years longer, but, one moment!'—here he laid the forefinger of his right hand on his nose as if he meant to say, Now pay attention to this!—'in order to do that, to do *that*, they ought to skip the sixties.'

"I shut my door, the notary's jest, which he thought very witty, having drawn me from my apathy; then I sat down in my armchair and put both feet on the andirons. I was plunged in a romance *à la* Radcliffe, based on the notarial disclosures of Monsieur Regnault, when my door, softly opened by the hand of a woman, turned noiselessly on its hinges.

"I saw my landlady, a jovial, stout woman, with a fine, good-humored face, who had missed her true surroundings; she was from Flanders, and might have stepped out of a picture by Teniers.

"'Well, monsieur', she said, 'Monsieur Regnault has no doubt recited to you his famous tale of La Grande Bretèche?'

"'Yes, Madame Lepas.'

"'What did he tell you?'

"I repeated in a few words the dark and chilling story of Madame de Merret as imparted to me by the notary. At each sentence my landlady ran out her chin and looked at me with the perspicacity of an inn-keeper, which combines the instinct of a policeman, the astuteness of a spy, and the cunning of a shopkeeper.

"'My dear Madame Lepas,' I added, in conclusion, 'you evidently know more than that. If not, why did you come up here to me?'

"'On the word, now, of an honest woman, just as true as my name is Lepas—'

"'Don't swear, for your eyes are full of the secret. You knew Monsieur de Merret. What sort of man was he?'

"'Goodness! Monsieur de Merret? well, you see, he was a handsome man, so tall you never could see the top of him,—a very worthy gentleman from Picardy, who had, as you may say, a temper of his own; and he knew it. He paid every one in cash so as to have no quarrels. But, I tell you, he could be quick. Our ladies thought him very pleasant.'

"'Because of his temper?' I asked.

"'Perhaps,' she replied. 'You know, monsieur, a man must have something to the fore, as they say, to marry a lady like Madame de Merret, who, without disparaging others, was the handsomest and the richest woman in Vendôme. She had an income of nearly twenty thousand francs. All the town was at the wedding. The bride was so dainty and captivating, a real little jewel of a woman. Ah! they were a fine couple in those days!'

"'Was their home a happy one?'

"'Hum, hum! yes and no, so far as any one can say; for you know well enough that the like of us don't live hand and glove with the like of them. Madame de Merret was a good woman and very charming, who no doubt had to bear a good deal from her husband's temper; we all liked her though she was rather haughty. Bah! that was her bringing up, and she was born so. When people are noble—don't you see?'

"'Yes, but there must have been some terrible catastrophe, for Monsieur and Madame de Merret to separate violently.'

"'I never said there was a catastrophe, monsieur; I know nothing about it.'

"'Very good; now I am certain that you know all.'

"'Well, monsieur, I'll tell you all I do know. When I saw Monsieur Regnault coming after you I knew he would tell you about Madame de Merret and La Grande Bretèche; and that gave me the idea of consulting monsieur, who seems to be a gentleman of good sense, incapable of betraying a poor woman like me, who has never done harm to any one, but who is, somehow, troubled in her conscience. I have never dared to say a word to the people about here, for they are all gossips, with tongues like steel blades. And there's never been a traveller who has stayed as long as you have, monsieur, to whom I could tell all about the fifteen thousand francs—'

"'My dear Madame Lepas,' I replied, trying to stop the flow of words, 'if your confidence is of a nature to compromise me, I wouldn't hear it for worlds.'

"'Oh, don't be afraid,' she said, interrupting me. 'You'll see—'

"This haste to tell made me quite certain I was not the first to whom my good landlady had communicated the secret of which I was to be the sole repositary, so I listened.

"'Monsieur,' she said, 'when the Emperor sent the Spanish and other prisoners of war to Vendôme I lodged one of them (at the cost of the government),—a young Spaniard on parole. But in spite of his parole he had to report every day to the sub-prefect. He was a grandee of Spain, with a name that ended in *os* and in *dia*, like all Spaniards—Bagos de Férédia. I wrote his name on the register, and you can see it if you like. Oh, he was a handsome young fellow for a Spaniard, who, they tell me, are all ugly. He wasn't more than five feet two or three inches, but he was well made. He had pretty little hands which he took care of—ah, you should just have seen him! He had as many brushes for those hands as a woman has for her head. He had fine black hair, a fiery eye, a rather copper-colored skin, but it was pleasant to look at all the same. He wore the finest linen I ever saw on any one, and I have lodged princesses, and, among others, General Bertrand, the Duc and Duchesse d'Abrantès, Monsieur Decazes and the King of Spain. He didn't eat much; but he had such polite manners and was always so amiable that I couldn't find fault with him. Oh! I did really love him, though he never said four words a day to me; if any one spoke to him, he never answered,— that's an oddity those grandees have, a sort of mania, so I'm told. He read his breviary like a priest, and he went to mass and to all the services regularly. Where do you think he sat? close to the chapel of Madame de Merret. But as he took that place the first time he went to church nobody attached any importance to the fact, though it was remembered later. Besides, he never took his eyes off his prayer book, poor young man!'

"My jovial landlady paused a moment, overcome with her recollections; then she continued her tale:

"'From that time on, monsieur, he used to walk up the mountain every evening to the ruins of the castle. It was his only amusement, poor man! and I dare say it recalled his own country; they say Spain is all mountains. From the first he was always late at night in coming in. I used to be uneasy at never seeing him before the stroke of midnight; but we got accustomed to his ways and gave him a key to the door, so that we didn't have to sit up. It so happened that one of our grooms told us that one evening when he went to bathe his horses he thought he saw the grandee in the distance, swimming in the river like a fish. When he came in I told him he had better take care not to get entangled in the sedges; he seemed annoyed that any one had seen him in the water. Well, monsieur, one day, or rather, one morning, we did not find him in his room; he had not come in. He never returned. I looked about and into everything, and at last I found a writing in a table drawer where he had put away fifty of those Spanish gold coins called "portugaise," which bring a hundred francs apiece; there were also diamonds worth ten thousand francs sealed up in a little box. The paper said that in case he should not return some day, he bequeathed to us the money and the diamonds, with a request to found masses of thanksgiving to God for his escape and safety. In those days my husband was living, and he did everything he could to find the young man. But, it was the queerest thing! he found only the Spaniard's clothes under a big stone in a sort of shed on the banks of the river, on the castle side, just opposite to La Grande Bretèche. My husband went so early in the morning that no one saw him. He burned the clothes after we had read the letter, and gave out, as Comte Férédia requested, that he had fled. The subprefect sent the whole gendarmerie on his traces, but bless your heart! they never caught him. Lepas thought the Spaniard had drowned himself. But, monsieur, I never thought so. I think he was somehow mixed up in Madame de Merret's trouble; and I'll tell you why. Rosalie has told me that her mistress had a crucifix she valued so much that she was buried with it, and it was made of ebony and silver; now when Monsieur de Férédia first came to lodge with us he had just such a crucifix, but I soon missed it. Now, monsieur, what do you say? isn't it true that I need have no remorse about those fifteen thousand francs? are not they rightfully mine?'

"'Of course they are. But how is it you have never questioned Rosalie?' I said.

"'Oh, I have, monsieur; but I can get nothing out of her. That girl is a stone wall. She knows something, but there is no making her talk.'

"After a few more remarks, my landlady left me, a prey to a romantic curiosity, to vague and darkling thoughts, to a religious terror that was something like the awe which comes upon us when we enter by night a gloomy church and see in the distance beneath the arches a feeble light; a formless figure glides before us, the sweep of a robe—of priest or woman—is heard; we shudder. La Grande Bretèche, with its tall grasses, its shuttered windows, its rusty railings, its barred gates, its deserted rooms, rose fantastically and suddenly before me. I tried to penetrate that mysterious dwelling and seek the knot of this most solemn history, this drama which had killed three persons.

"Rosalie became to my eyes the most interesting person in Vendôme. Examining her, I discovered the traces of an ever-present inward thought. In spite of the health which bloomed upon her dimpled face, there was in her some element of remorse, or of hope; her attitude bespoke a secret, like that of devotees who pray with ardor, or that of a girl who has killed her child and forever after hears its cry. And yet her postures were naïve, and even vulgar; her silly smile was surely not criminal; you would have judged her innocent if only by the large neckerchief of blue and red squares which covered her vigorous bust, clothed, confined, and set off by a gown of purple and white stripes. 'No,' thought I; 'I will not leave Vendôme without knowing the history of La Grande Bretèche. I'll even make love to Rosalie, if it is absolutely necessary.'

"'Rosalie!' I said to her one day.

"'What is it, monsieur?'

"'You are not married, are you?'

She trembled slightly.

"'Oh! when the fancy takes me to be unhappy there'll be no lack of men,' she said, laughing.

"She recovered instantly from her emotion, whatever it was; for all women, from the great lady to the chambermaid of an inn, have a self-possession of their own.

"'You are fresh enough and taking enough to please a lover,' I said, watching her. 'But tell me, Rosalie, why did you take a place at an inn after you left Madame de Merret? Didn't she leave you an annuity?'

"'Oh, yes, she did. But, monsieur, my place is the best in all Vendôme.'

"This answer was evidently what judges and lawyers call 'dilatory.'

Rosalie's position in this romantic history was like that of a square on a checkerboard; she was at the very center, as it were, of its truth and its interest; she seemed to me to be tied into the knot of it. The last chapter of the tale was in her, and, from the moment that I realized this, Rosalie became to me an object of attraction. By dint of studying the girl I came to find in her, as we do in every woman whom we make a principal object of our attention, that she had a host of good qualities. She was clean, and careful of herself, and therefore handsome. Some two or three weeks after the notary's visit I said to her, suddenly: 'Tell me all you know about Madame de Merret.'

"'Oh, no!' she replied, in a tone of terror, 'don't ask me that, monsieur.'

"'I persisted in urging her. Her pretty face darkened, her bright color faded, her eyes lost their innocent, liquid light.

"'Well!' she said, after a pause, 'if you will have it so, I will tell you; but keep the secret.'

"'I'll keep it with the faithfulness of a thief, which is the most loyal to be found anywhere.'

"'If it is the same to you, monsieur, I'd rather you kept it with your own.'

"Thereupon, she adjusted her neckerchief and posed herself to tell the tale; for it is very certain that an attitude of confidence and security is desirable in order to make a narration. The best tales are told at special hours, — like that in which we are now at table. No one ever told a story well, standing or fasting.

"If I were to reproduce faithfully poor Rosalie's diffuse eloquence, a whole volume would scarce suffice. But as the event of which she now gave me a hazy knowledge falls into place between the facts revealed by the garrulity of the notary, and that of Madame Lepas, as precisely as the mean terms of an arithmetical proposition lie between its two extremes, all I have to do is to tell it to you in few words. I therefore give a summary of what I heard from Rosalie.

"The chamber which Madame de Merret occupied at La Grande Bretèche was on the ground floor. A small closet about four feet in depth was made in the wall, and served as a wardrobe. Three months before the evening when the facts I am about to relate to you happened, Madame de Merret had been so seriously unwell that her husband left her alone in her room and slept himself in a chamber on the first floor. By one of those mere chances which it is impossible to foresee, he returned, on the evening in question, two hours later than usual from the club where he went habitually to read the papers and talk politics with the inhabitants of the town. His wife thought him at home and in bed and asleep. But the invasion of France had been the subject of a lively discussion; the game of billiards was a heated one; he had lost forty francs, an enormous sum for Vendôme, where everybody hoards his money, and where manners and customs are restrained within modest limits worthy of all praise,—which may, perhaps, be the source of a certàin true happiness which no Parisian cares anything at all about.

"For some time past Monsieur de Merret had been in the habit of asking Rosalie, when he came in, if his wife were in bed. Being told, invariably, that she was, he at once went to his own room with the contentment that comes of confidence and custom. This evening, on returning home, he took it into his head to go to Madame de Merret's room and tell her his ill-luck, perhaps to be consoled for it. During dinner he had noticed that his wife was coquettishly dressed; and as he came from the club the thought crossed his mind that she was no longer ill, that her convalescence had made her lovelier than ever,—a fact he perceived, as husbands are wont to perceive things, too late.

"Instead of calling Rosalie, who at that moment was in the kitchen watching a complicated game of 'brisque,' at which the cook and the coachman were playing, Monsieur de Merret went straight to his wife's room by the light of his lantern, which he had placed on the first step of the stairway. His step, which was easily recognized, resounded under the arches of the corridor. Just as he turned the handle of his wife's door he fancied he heard the door of the closet, which I mentioned to you, shut; but when he entered, Madame de Merret was alone, standing before the fireplace. The husband thought to himself that Rosalie must be in the closet; and yet a suspicion, which sounded in his ears like the ringing of bells, made him distrustful. He looked at his wife, and fancied he saw something wild and troubled in her eyes.

"'You are late in coming home,' she said. That voice, usually so pure and gracious, seemed to him slightly changed.

"Monsieur de Merret made no answer, for at that moment Rosalie entered the room. Her appearance was a thunderbolt to him. He walked up and down the room with his arms crossed, going from one window to another with a uniform movement.

"'Have you heard anything to trouble you?' asked his wife, timidly, while Rosalie was undressing her. He made no answer.

"'You can leave the room,' said Madame de Merret to the maid. 'I will arrange my hair myself.'

"She guessed some misfortune at the mere sight of her husband's face, and wished to be alone with him.

"When Rosalie was gone, or supposed to be gone, for she went no further than the corridor, Monsieur de Merret came to his wife and stood before her. Then he said, coldly:

"'Madame, there is some one in your closet.'

"She looked at her husband with a calm air, and answered, 'No, monsieur.'

"That 'no' agonized Monsieur de Merret, for he did not believe it. And yet his wife had never seemed purer nor more saintly than she did at that moment. He rose and went towards the closet to open the door; Madame de Merret took him by the hand and stopped him; she looked at him with a sad air and said, in a voice that was strangely shaken: 'If you find no one, remember that all is over between us.'

"The infinite dignity of his wife's demeanor restored her husband's respect for her, and suddenly inspired him with one of those resolutions which need some wider field to become immortal.

"'No, Josephine,' he said, 'I will not look there. In either case we should be separated forever. Listen to me: I know the purity of your soul, I know that you lead a saintly life; you would not commit a mortal sin to save yourself from death.'

"At these words, Madame de Merret looked at her husband with a haggard eye.

"'Here is your crucifix,' he went on. 'Swear to me before God that there is no one in that closet and I will believe you; I will not open that door.'

"Madame de Merret took the crucifix and said 'I swear it.'

"'Louder!' said her husband; 'repeat after me, — I swear before God that there is no person in that closet.'

"She repeated the words composedly.

"'That is well,' said Monsieur de Merret, coldly. After a moment's silence he added, examining the ebony crucifix inlaid with silver, 'That is a beautiful thing; I did not know you possessed it; it is very artistically wrought.'

"'I found it at Duvivier's,' she replied; 'he bought it of a Spanish monk when those prisoners-of-war passed through Vendôme last year.'

"'Ah!' said Monsieur de Merret, replacing the crucifix on the wall.

He rang the bell. Rosalie was not long in answering it. Monsieur de Merret went quickly up to her, took her into the recess of a window on the garden side, and said to her in a low voice:—

"'I am told that Gorenflot wants to marry you, and that poverty alone prevents it, for you have told him you will not be his wife until he is a master-mason. Is that so?'

"'Yes, monsieur.'

"'Well, go and find him; tell him to come here at once and bring his trowel and other tools. Take care not to wake any one at his house but himself; he will soon have enough money to satisfy you. No talking to any one when you leave this room, mind, or—'

"He frowned. Rosalie left the room. He called her back; 'Here, take my passkey,' he said.

"Monsieur de Merret, who had kept his wife in view while giving these orders, now sat down beside her before the fire and began to tell her of his game of billiards, and the political discussions at the club. When Rosalie returned she found Monsieur and Madame de Merret talking amicably.

"The master had lately had the ceilings of all the reception rooms on the lower floor restored. Plaster is very scarce at Vendôme, and the carriage of it makes it expensive. Monsieur de Merret had therefore ordered an ample quantity for his own wants, knowing that he could readily find buyers for what was left. This circumstance inspired the idea that now possessed him.

"'Monsieur, Gorenflot has come,' said Rosalie.

"'Bring him in,' said her master.

"Madame de Merret turned slightly pale when she saw the mason.

"'Gorenflot,' said her husband, 'fetch some bricks from the coach-house,—enough to wall up that door; use the plaster that was left over, to cover the wall.'

"Then he called Rosalie and the mason to the end of the room, and, speaking in a low voice, added, 'Listen to me, Gorenflot; after you have done this work you will sleep in the house; and tomorrow morning I will give you a passport into a foreign country, and six thousand francs for the journey. Go through Paris where I will meet you. There, I will secure to you legally another six thousand francs, to be paid to you at the end of ten years if you still remain out of France. For this sum, I demand absolute silence on what you see and do this night. As for you, Rosalie, I give you a dowry of ten thousand francs, on condition that you marry Gorenflot, and keep silence, if not—'

"'Rosalie,' said Madame de Merret, 'come and brush my hair.'

"The husband walked up and down the room, watching the door, the mason, and his wife, but without allowing the least distrust or misgiving to appear in his manner. Gorenflot's work made some noise; under cover of it Madame de Merret said hastily to Rosalie, while her husband was at the farther end of the room. 'A thousand francs annuity if you tell Gorenflot to leave a crevice at the bottom;' then aloud she added, composedly, 'Go and help the mason.'

"Monsieur and Madame de Merret remained silent during the whole time it took Gorenflot to wall up the door. The silence was intentional on the part of the husband to deprive his wife of all chance of saying words with a double meaning which might be heard within the closet; with Madame de Merret it was either prudence or pride.

"When the wall was more than half up, the mason's tool broke one of the panes of glass in the closet door; Monsieur de Merret's back was at that moment turned away. The action proved to Madame de Merret that Rosalie had spoken to the mason. In that one instant she saw the dark face of a man with black hair and fiery eyes. Before her husband turned the poor creature had time to make a sign with her head which meant 'Hope.'

"By four o'clock, just at dawn, for it was in the month of September, the work was done. Monsieur de Merret remained that night in his wife's room. The next morning, on rising, he said, carelessly: 'Ah! I forgot, I must go to the mayor's office about that passport.'

"He put on his hat, made three steps to the door, then checked himself, turned back, and took the crucifix.

"His wife trembled with joy; 'He will go to Duvivier's,' she thought.

"The moment her husband had left the house she rang for Rosalie. 'The pick-axe!' she cried, 'the pick-axe! I watched how Gorenflot did it; we shall have time to make a hole and close it again.'

"In an instant Rosalie had brought a sort of cleaver, and her mistress, with a fury no words can describe, began to demolish the wall. She had knocked away a few bricks, and was drawing back to strike a still more vigorous blow with all her strength, when she saw her husband behind her. She fainted.

"'Put madame on her bed,' said her husband, coldly.

"Foreseeing what would happen, he had laid this trap for his wife; he had written to the mayor, and sent for Duvivier. The jeweller arrived just as the room had been again put in order.

"'Duvivier,' said Monsieur de Merret, 'I think you bought some crucifixes of those Spaniards who were here last year?'

"'No, monsieur, I did not.'

"'Very good; thank you,' he said, with a tigerish glance at his wife. 'Jean,' he added to the footman, 'serve my meals in Madame de Merret's bedroom; she is very ill, and I shall not leave her till she recovers.'

"For twenty days that man remained beside his wife. During the first hours, when sounds were heard behind the walled door, and Josephine tried to implore mercy for the dying stranger, he answered, without allowing her to utter a word:—

"'You swore upon the cross that no one was there.'"

As the tale ended the women rose from table, and the spell under which Bianchon had held them was broken. Nevertheless, several of them were conscious of a cold chill as they recalled the last words.

A Passion in the Desert

"The sight was fearful!" she exclaimed, as we left the menagerie of Monsieur Martin.

She had been watching that daring speculator as he went through his wonderful performance in the den of the hyena.

"How is it possible," she continued, "to tame those animals so as to be certain that he can trust them?"

"You think it a problem," I answered, interrupting her, "and yet it is a natural fact."

"Oh!" she cried, an incredulous smile flickering on her lip.

"Do you think that beasts are devoid of passions?" I asked. "Let me assure you that we teach them all the vices and virtues of our own state of civilization."

She looked at me in amazement.

"The first time I saw Monsieur Martin," I added, "I exclaimed, as you do, with surprise. I happened to be sitting beside an old soldier whose right leg was amputated, and whose appearance had attracted my notice as I entered the building. His face, stamped with the scars of battle, wore the undaunted look of a veteran of the wars of Napoleon. Moreover, the old hero had a frank and joyous manner which attracts me wherever I meet it. He was, doubtless, one of those old campaigners whom nothing can surprise, who find something to laugh at in the last contortions of a comrade, and will bury a friend or rifle his body gayly; challenging bullets with indifference; making short shrift for themselves or others; and fraternizing, as a usual thing, with the devil. After looking very attentively at the proprietor of the menagerie as he entered the den, my companion curled his lip with that expression of satirical contempt which well-informed men sometimes put on to mark the difference between themselves and dupes. As I uttered my exclamation of surprise at the coolness and courage of Monsieur Martin, the old soldier smiled, shook his head, and said with a knowing glance, 'An old story!'

" 'How do you mean, an old story?' I asked. 'If you could explain the secret of this mysterious power, I should be greatly obliged to you.'

"After a while, during which we became better acquainted, we went to dine at the first restaurant we could find after leaving the menagerie. A bottle of champagne with our dessert brightened the recollections of the old man and made them singularly vivid. He related to me a circumstance in his early history which proved that he had ample cause to pronounce Monsieur Martin's performance 'an old story.' "

When we reached her house, she was so persuasive and captivating, and made me so many pretty promises, that I consented to write down for her benefit the story told me by the old hero. On the following day I sent her this episode of an historical epic, which might be entitled, "The French in Egypt."

At the time of General Desaix's expedition to Upper Egypt a Provençal soldier, who had fallen into the hands of the Maugrabins, was marched by those tireless Arabs across the desert which lies beyond the cataracts of the Nile. To put sufficient distance between themselves and the French army and thus insure their safety, the Maugrabins made a forced march, and did not halt until after nightfall. They then camped about a well shaded with palm trees, near which they had previously buried a stock of provisions. Not dreaming that the thought of escape could enter their captive's mind, they merely bound his wrists, and lay down to sleep themselves, after eating a few dates and giving their horses a feed of barley. When the bold Provençal saw his enemies too soundly asleep to watch him, he used his teeth to pick up a scimitar, with which, steadying the blade by means of his knees, he contrived to cut through the cord which bound his hands, and thus recovered his liberty. He at once seized a carbine and a poniard, took the precaution to lay in a supply of dates, a small bag of barley, some powder and ball, buckled on the scimitar, mounted one of the horses, and spurred him in the direction where he supposed the French army to be. Impatient to meet the outposts, he pressed the horse, which was already wearied, so severely that the poor animal fell dead with his flanks torn, leaving the Frenchman alone in the midst of the desert.

After marching for a long time through the sand with the dogged courage of an escaping galley slave, the soldier was forced to halt as the darkness drew on; for his utter weariness compelled him to rest, though the exquisite sky of an Eastern night might well have tempted him to continue the journey. Happily he had reached a slight elevation, at the top of which a few palm trees shot upward, whose leafage, seen from a long distance against the sky, had helped to sustain his hopes. His fatigue was so great that he threw himself down on a block of granite, cut by Nature into the shape of a camp-bed, and slept heavily, without taking the least precaution to protect himself while asleep. He accepted the loss of his life as inevitable, and his last waking thought was one of regret for having left the Maugrabins, whose nomad life began to charm him now that he was far away from them and from every other hope of succor.

He was wakened by the sun, whose pitiless beams falling vertically upon the granite rock produced an intolerable heat. The Provençal had ignorantly flung himself down in a contrary direction to the shadows thrown by the verdant and majestic fronds of the palm trees. He gazed at these solitary monarchs and shuddered. They recalled to his mind the graceful shafts crowned with long weaving leaves which distinguish the Saracenic columns of the cathedral of Arles. The thought overcame him, and when, after counting the trees, he threw his eyes upon the scene around him, an agony of despair convulsed his soul. He saw a limitless ocean. The sombre sands of the desert stretched out till lost to sight in all directions; they glittered with dark lustre like a steel blade shining in the sun. He could not tell if it were an ocean or a chain of lakes that lay mirrored before him. A hot vapor swept in waves above the surface of this heaving continent. The sky had the Oriental glow of translucent purity which disappoints because it leaves nothing for the imagination to desire. The heavens and the earth were both on fire.

Silence added its awful and desolate majesty. Infinitude, immensity pressed down upon the soul on every side; not a cloud in the sky, not a breath in the air, not a rift on the breast of the sand, which was ruffled only with little ridges scarcely rising above its surface. Far as the eye could reach the horizon fell away into space, marked by a slender line, slim as the edge of a sabre, — like as in summer seas a thread of light parts this earth from the heaven it meets.

The Provençal clasped the trunk of a palm tree as if it were the body of a friend. Sheltered from the sun by its straight and slender shadow, he wept; and presently sitting down he remained motionless, contemplating with awful dread the implacable nature stretched out before him. He cried aloud, as if to tempt the solitude to answer him. His voice, lost in the hollows of the hillock, sounded afar with a thin resonance that returned no echo; the echo came from the soldier's heart. He was twenty-two years old, and he loaded his carbine.

"Time enough!" he muttered, as he put the liberating weapon on the sand beneath him.

Gazing by turns at the burnished blackness of the sand and the blue expanse of the sky, the soldier dreamed of France. He smelt in fancy the gutters of Paris; he remembered the towns through which he had passed, the faces of his comrades, and the most trifling incidents of his life. His southern imagination saw the pebbles of his own Provence in the undulating play of the heated air, as it seemed to roughen the far-reaching surface of the desert. Dreading the dangers of this cruel mirage, he went down the little hill on the side opposite to that by which he had gone up the night before. His joy was great when he discovered a natural grotto, formed by the immense blocks of granite which made a foundation for the rising ground. The remnants of a mat showed that the place had once been inhabited, and close to the entrance were a few palm trees loaded with fruit. The instinct which binds men to life woke in his heart. He now hoped to live until some Maugrabin should pass that way; possibly he might even hear the roar of cannon, for Bonaparte was at that time over-running Egypt. Encouraged by these thoughts, the Frenchman shook down a cluster of the ripe fruit under the weight of which the palms were bending; and as he tasted this unhoped for manna, he thanked the former inhabitant of the grotto for the cultivation of the trees, which the rich and luscious flesh of the fruit amply attested. Like a true Provençal, he passed from the gloom of despair to a joy that was half insane. He ran back to the top of the hill, and busied himself for the rest of the day in cutting down one of the sterile trees which had been his shelter the night before.

Some vague recollection made him think of the wild beasts of the desert, and foreseeing that they would come to drink at a spring which bubbled through the sand at the foot of the rock, he resolved to protect his hermitage by felling a tree across the entrance. Notwithstanding his eagerness, and the strength which the fear of being attacked while asleep gave to his muscles, he was unable to cut the palm tree in pieces during the day; but he succeeded in bringing it down. Towards evening the king of the desert fell; and the noise of his fall, echoing far, was like a moan from the breast of Solitude. The soldier shuddered, as though he had heard a voice predicting evil. But, like an heir who does not long mourn a parent, he stripped from the beautiful tree the arching green fronds—its poetical adornment—and made a bed of them in his refuge. Then, tired with his work and by the heat of the day, he fell asleep beneath the red vault of the grotto.

In the middle of the night his sleep was broken by a strange noise. He sat up; the deep silence that reigned everywhere enabled him to hear the alternating rhythm of a respiration whose savage vigor could not belong to a human being. A terrible fear, increased by the darkness, by the silence, by the rush of his waking fancies, numbed his heart. He felt the contraction of his hair, which rose on end as his eyes, dilating to their full strength, beheld through the darkness two faint amber lights. At first he thought them an optical delusion; but by degrees the clearness of the night enabled him to distinguish objects in the grotto, and he saw, within two feet of him, an enormous animal lying at rest.

Was it a lion? Was it a tiger? Was it a crocodile? The Provençal had not enough education to know in what subspecies he ought to class the intruder; but his terror was all the greater because his ignorance made it vague. He endured the cruel trial of listening, of striving to catch the peculiarities of this breathing without losing one of its inflections, and without daring to make the slightest movement. A strong odor, like that exhaled by foxes, only far more pungent and penetrating, filled the grotto. When the soldier had tasted it, so to speak, by the nose, his fear became terror; he could no longer doubt the nature of the terrible companion whose royal lair he had taken for a bivouac. Before long, the reflection of the moon, as it sank to the horizon, lighted up the den and gleamed upon the shining, spotted skin of a panther.

The lion of Egypt lay asleep, curled up like a dog, the peaceable possessor of a kennel at the gate of a mansion; its eyes, which had opened for a moment, were now closed; its head was turned towards the Frenchman. A hundred conflicting thoughts rushed through the mind of the panther's prisoner. Should he kill it with a shot from his musket? But ere the thought was formed, he saw there was no room to take aim; the muzzle would have gone beyond the animal. Suppose he were to wake it? The fear kept him motionless. As he heard the beating of his heart through the dead silence, he cursed the strong pulsations of his vigorous blood, lest they should disturb the sleep which gave him time to think and plan for safety. Twice he put his hand on his scimitar, with the idea of striking off the head of his enemy; but the difficulty of cutting through the close-haired skin made him renounce the bold attempt. Suppose he missed his aim? It would, he knew, be certain death. He preferred the chances of a struggle, and resolved to await the dawn. It was not long in coming. As daylight broke, the Frenchman was able to examine the animal. Its muzzle was stained with blood. "It has eaten a good meal," thought he, not caring whether the feast were human flesh or not; "it will not be hungry when it wakes."

It was a female. The fur on the belly and on the thighs was of sparkling whiteness. Several little spots like velvet made pretty bracelets round her paws. The muscular tail was also white, but it terminated with black rings. The fur of the back, yellow as dead gold and very soft and glossy, bore the characteristic spots, shaded like a full-blown rose, which distinguish the panther from all other species of *felis*. This terrible hostess lay tranquilly snoring, in an attitude as easy and graceful as that of a cat on the cushions of an ottoman. Her bloody paws, sinewy and well-armed, were stretched beyond her head, which lay upon them; and from her muzzle projected a few straight hairs called whiskers, which shimmered in the early light like silver wires. If he had seen her lying thus imprisoned in a cage, the Provençal would have admired the creature's grace, and the strong contrasts of vivid color which gave to her robe an imperial splendor; but as it was, his sight was jaundiced by sinister forebodings. The presence of the panther, though she was still asleep, had the same effect upon his mind as the magnetic eyes of a snake produce, we are told, upon the nightingale. The soldier's courage oozed away in presence of this silent peril, though he was a man who gathered nerve before the mouths of cannon belching grapeshot. And yet, ere long, a bold thought entered his mind, and checked the cold sweat which was rolling from his brow. Roused to action, as some men are when, driven face to face with death, they defy it and offer themselves to their doom, he saw a tragedy before him, and he resolved to play his part with honor to the last.

"Yesterday," he said, "the Arabs might have killed me."

Regarding himself as dead, he waited bravely, but with anxious curiosity, for the waking of his enemy. When the sun rose, the panther suddenly opened her eyes; then she stretched her paws violently, as if to unlimber them from the cramp of their position. Presently she yawned and showed the frightful armament of her teeth, and her cloven tongue, rough as a grater.

"She is like a dainty woman," thought the Frenchman, watching her as she rolled and turned on her side with an easy and coquettish movement. She licked the blood from her paws, and rubbed her head with a reiterated movement full of grace.

"Well done! dress yourself prettily, my little woman," said the Frenchman, who recovered his gayety as soon as he had recovered his courage. "We are going to bid each other good morning;" and he felt for the short poniard which he had taken from the Maugrabins.

At this instant the panther turned her head towards the Frenchman and looked at him fixedly, without moving. The rigidity of her metallic eyes and their insupportable clearness made the Provençal shudder. The beast moved towards him; he looked at her caressingly, with a soothing glance by which he hoped to magnetize her. He let her come quite close to him before he stirred; then, with a touch as gentle and loving as he might have used to a pretty woman, he slid his hand along her spine from the head to the flanks, scratching with his nails the flexible vertebrae which divide the yellow back of a panther. The creature drew up her tail voluptuously, her eyes softened, and when for the third time the Frenchman bestowed this self-interested caress, she gave vent to a purr like that with which a cat expresses pleasure; but it issued from a throat so deep and powerful that the sound echoed through the grotto like the last chords of an organ rolling along the roof of a church. The Provençal, perceiving the value of his caresses, redoubled them, until they had completely soothed and lulled the imperious courtesan.

When he felt that he had subdued the ferocity of his capricious companion, whose hunger had so fortunately been appeased the night before, he rose to leave the grotto. The panther let him go; but as soon as he reached the top of the little hill she bounded after him with the lightness of a bird hopping from branch to branch, and rubbed against his legs, arching her back with the gesture of a domestic cat. Then looking at her guest with an eye that was growing less inflexible, she uttered the savage cry which naturalists liken to the noise of a saw.

"My lady is exacting," cried the Frenchman, smiling. He began to play with her ears and stroke her belly, and at last he scratched her head firmly with his nails. Encouraged by success, he tickled her skull with the point of his dagger, looking for the right spot where to stab her; but the hardness of the bone made him pause, dreading failure.

The sultana of the desert acknowledged the talents of her slave by lifting her head and swaying her neck to his caresses, betraying satisfaction by the tranquillity of her relaxed attitude. The Frenchman suddenly perceived that he could assassinate the fierce princess at a blow, if he struck her in the throat; and he had raised the weapon, when the panther, surfeited perhaps with his caresses, threw herself gracefully at his feet, glancing up at him with a look in which, despite her natural ferocity, a flicker of kindness could be seen. The poor Provençal, frustrated for the moment, ate his dates as he leaned against a palm tree, casting from time to time an interrogating eye across the desert in the hope of discerning rescue from afar, and then lowering it upon his terrible companion, to watch the chances of her uncertain clemency. Each time that he threw away a date-stone the panther eyed the spot where it fell with an expression of keen distrust; and she examined the Frenchman with what might be called commercial prudence. The examination, however, seemed favorable, for when the man had finished his meagre meal she licked his shoes and wiped off the dust, which was caked into the folds of the leather, with her rough and powerful tongue.

"How will it be when she is hungry?" thought the Provençal. In spite of the shudder which this reflection cost him, his attention was attracted by the symmetrical proportions of the animal, and he began to measure them with his eye. She was three feet in height to the shoulder, and four feet long, not including the tail. That powerful weapon, which was round as a club, measured three feet. The head, as large as that of a lioness, was remarkable for an expression of crafty intelligence; the cold cruelty of a tiger was its ruling trait, and yet it bore a vague resemblance to the face of an artful woman. As the soldier watched her, the countenance of this solitary queen shone with savage gayety like that of Nero in his cups: she had slaked her thirst for blood, and now wished for play. The Frenchman tried to come and go, and accustom her to his movements. The panther left him free, as if contented to follow him with her eyes, seeming, however, less like a faithful dog watching his master's movements with affection, than a huge Angora cat uneasy and suspicious of them. A few steps brought him to the spring, where he saw the carcass of his horse, which the panther had evidently carried there. Only two thirds was eaten. The sight reassured the Frenchman; for it explained the absence of his terrible companion and the forbearance which she had shown to him while asleep.

This first good luck encouraged the reckless soldier as he thought of the future. The wild idea of making a home with the panther until some chance of escape occurred entered his mind, and he resolved to try every means of taming her and of turning her good will to account. With these thoughts he returned to her side, and noticed joyfully that she moved her tail with an almost imperceptible motion. He sat down beside her fearlessly, and they began to play with each other. He held her paws and her muzzle, twisted her ears, threw her over on her back, and stroked her soft, warm flanks. She allowed him to do so; and when he began to smooth the fur of her paws, she carefully drew in her murderous claws, which were sharp and curved like a Damascus blade. The Frenchman kept one hand on his dagger, again watching his opportunity to plunge it into the belly of the too-confiding beast; but the fear that she might strangle him in her last convulsions once more stayed his hand. Moreover, he felt in his heart a foreboding of remorse which warned him not to destroy a hitherto inoffensive creature. He even fancied that he had found a friend in the limitless desert. His mind turned back, involuntarily, to his first mistress, whom he had named in derision "Mignonne," because her jealousy was so furious that throughout the whole period of their intercourse he lived in dread of the knife with which she threatened him. This recollection of his youth suggested the idea of teaching the young panther, whose soft agility and grace he now admired with less terror, to answer to the caressing name. Towards evening he had grown so familiar with his perilous position that he was half in love with its dangers, and his companion was so far tamed that she had caught the habit of turning to him when he called, in falsetto tones, "Mignonne!"

As the sun went down Mignonne uttered at intervals a prolonged, deep, melancholy cry.

"She is well brought up," thought the gay soldier. "She says her prayers." But the jest only came into his mind as he watched the peaceful attitude of his comrade.

"Come, my pretty blonde, I will let you go to bed first," he said, relying on the activity of his legs to get away as soon as she fell asleep, and trusting to find some other resting place for the night. He waited anxiously for the right moment, and when it came he started vigorously in the direction of the Nile. But he had scarcely marched for half an hour through the sand before he heard the panther bounding after him, giving at intervals the saw-like cry which was more terrible to hear than the thud of her bounds.

"Well, well!" he cried, "she must have fallen in love with me! Perhaps she has never met any one else. It is flattering to be her first love."

So thinking, he fell into one of the treacherous quick-sands which deceive the inexperienced traveller in the desert, and from which there is seldom any escape. He felt he was sinking, and he uttered a cry of despair. The panther seized him by the collar with her teeth, and sprang vigorously backward, drawing him, like magic, from the sucking sand.

"Ah, Mignonne!" cried the soldier, kissing her with enthusiasm, "we belong to each other now, — for life, for death! But play me no tricks," he added, as he turned back the way he came.

From that moment the desert was, as it were, peopled for him. It held a being to whom he could talk, and whose ferocity was now lulled into gentleness, although he could scarcely explain to himself the reasons for this extraordinary friendship. His anxiety to keep awake and on his guard succumbed to excessive weariness both of body and mind, and throwing himself down on the floor of the grotto he slept soundly. At his waking Mignonne was gone. He mounted the little hill to scan the horizon, and perceived her in the far distance returning with the long bounds peculiar to these animals, who are prevented from running by the extreme flexibility of their spinal column.

Mignonne came home with bloody jaws, and received the tribute of caresses which her slave hastened to pay, all the while manifesting her pleasure by reiterated purring.

Her eyes, now soft and gentle, rested kindly on the Provençal, who spoke to her lovingly as he would to a domestic animal.

"Ah! Mademoiselle, — for you are an honest girl, are you not? You like to be petted, don't you? Are you not ashamed of yourself? You have been eating a Maugrabin. Well, well! they are animals like the rest of you. But you are not to craunch up a Frenchman; remember that! If you do, I will not love you."

She played like a young dog with her master, and let him roll her over and pat and stroke her, and sometimes she would coax him to play by laying a paw upon his knee with a pretty soliciting gesture.

Several days passed rapidly. This strange companionship revealed to the Provençal the sublime beauties of the desert. The alternations of hope and fear, the sufficiency of food, the presence of a creature who occupied his thoughts,—all this kept his mind alert, yet free: it was a life full of strange contrasts. Solitude revealed to him her secrets, and wrapped him with her charm. In the rising and the setting of the sun he saw splendors unknown to the world of men. He quivered as he listened to the soft whirring of the wings of a bird,—rare visitant!—or watched the blending of the fleeting clouds,—those changeful and many-tinted voyagers. In the waking hours of the night he studied the play of the moon upon the sandy ocean, where the strong simoom had rippled the surface into waves and ever-varying undulations. He lived in the Eastern day; he worshipped its marvellous glory. He rejoiced in the grandeur of the storms when they rolled across the vast plain, and tossed the sand upward till it looked like a dry red fog or a solid death-dealing vapor; and as the night came on he welcomed it with ecstasy, grateful for the blessed coolness of the light of the stars. His ears listened to the music of the skies. Solitude taught him the treasures of meditation. He spent hours in recalling trifles, and in comparing his past life with the weird present.

He grew fondly attached to his panther; for he was a man who needed an affection. Whether it were that his own will, magnetically strong, had modified the nature of his savage princess, or that the wars then raging in the desert had provided her with an ample supply of food, it is certain that she showed no sign of attacking him, and became so tame that he soon felt no fear of her. He spent much of his time in sleeping; though with his mind awake, like a spider in its web, lest he should miss some deliverance that might chance to cross the sandy sphere marked out by the horizon. He had made his shirt into a banner and tied it to the top of a palm tree which he had stripped of its leafage. Taking counsel of necessity, he kept the flag extended by fastening the corners with twigs and wedges; for the fitful wind might have failed to wave it at the moment when the longed-for succor came in sight.

Nevertheless, there were long hours of gloom when hope forsook him; and then he played with his panther. He learned to know the different inflections of her voice and the meanings of her expressive glance; he studied the variegation of the spots which shaded the dead gold of her robe. Mignonne no longer growled when he caught the tuft of her dangerous tail and counted the black and white rings which glittered in the sunlight like a cluster of precious stones. He delighted in the soft lines of her lithe body, the whiteness of her belly, the grace of her charming head: but above all he loved to watch her as she gambolled at play. The agility and youthfulness of her movements were a constantly fresh surprise to him. He admired the suppleness of the flexible body as she bounded, crept, and glided, or clung to the trunk of palm trees, or rolled over and over, crouching sometimes to the ground, and gathering herself together as she made ready for her vigorous spring. Yet, however vigorous the bound, however slippery the granite block on which she landed, she would stop short, motionless, at the one word "Mignonne."

One day, under a dazzling sun, a large bird hovered in the sky. The Provençal left his panther to watch the new guest. After a moment's pause the neglected sultana uttered a low growl.

"The devil take me! I believe she is jealous!" exclaimed the soldier, observing the rigid look which once more appeared in her metallic eyes. "The soul of Sophronie has got into her body!"

The eagle disappeared in ether, and the Frenchman, recalled by the panther's displeasure, admired afresh her rounded flanks and the perfect grace of her attitude. She was as pretty as a woman. The blonde brightness of her robe shaded, with delicate gradations, to the dead-white tones of her furry thighs; the vivid sunshine brought out the brilliancy of this living gold and its variegated brown spots with indescribable lustre. The panther and the Provençal gazed at each other with human comprehension. She trembled with delight — the coquettish creature! — as she felt the nails of her friend scratching the strong bones of her skull. Her eyes glittered like flashes of lightning, and then she closed them tightly.

"She has a soul!" cried the soldier, watching the tranquil repose of this sovereign of the desert, golden as the sands, white as their pulsing light, solitary and burning as they.

"Well," she said, "I have read your defense of the beasts. But tell me what was the end of this friendship between two beings so formed to understand each other."

"Ah, exactly," I replied. "It ended as all great passions end, — by a misunderstanding. Both sides imagine treachery, pride prevents an explanation, and the rupture comes about through obstinacy."

"Yes," she said, "and sometimes a word, a look, an exclamation suffices. But tell me the end of the story."

"That is difficult," I answered. "But I will give it to you in the words of the old veteran, as he finished the bottle of champagne and exclaimed: 'I don't know how I could have hurt her, but she suddenly turned upon me as if in fury, and seized my thigh with her sharp teeth; and yet (as I afterwards remembered) not cruelly. I thought she meant to devour me, and I plunged my dagger into her throat. She rolled over with a cry that froze my soul; she looked at me in her death-struggle, but without anger. I would have given all the world—my cross, which I had not then gained, all, everything—to have brought her back to life. It was as if I had murdered a friend, a human being. When the soldiers who saw my flag came to my rescue they found me weeping. Monsieur,' he resumed after a moment's silence, 'I went through the wars in Germany, Spain, Russia, France; I have marched my carcass wellnigh over all the world; but I have seen nothing comparable to the desert. Ah, it is grand! glorious!'

"'What were your feelings there?' I asked.

"'They cannot be told, young man. Besides, I do not always regret my panther and my palm tree oasis: I must be very sad for that. But I will tell you this: in the desert there is all—and yet nothing.'

"'Stay!— explain that.'

"'Well, then,' he said, with a gesture of impatience, 'God is there, and man is not.'"

The Hidden Masterpiece

I

On a cold morning in December, towards the close of the year 1612, a young man, whose clothing betrayed his poverty, was standing before the door of a house in the Rue des Grands-Augustins, in Paris. After walking to and fro for some time with the hesitation of a lover who fears to approach his mistress, however complying she may be, he ended by crossing the threshold and asking if Maitre François Porbus were within. At the affirmative answer of an old woman who was sweeping out one of the lower rooms the young man slowly mounted the stairway, stopping from time to time and hesitating, like a newly fledged courtier doubtful as to what sort of reception the king might grant him.

When he reached the upper landing of the spiral ascent, he paused a moment before laying hold of a grotesque knocker which ornamented the door of the *atelier* where the famous painter of Henry IV—neglected by Marie de Medicis for Rubens—was probably at work. The young man felt the strong sensation which vibrates in the soul of great artists when, in the flush of youth and of their ardor for art, they approach a man of genius or a masterpiece. In all human sentiments there are, as it were, primeval flowers bred of noble enthusiasms, which droop and fade from year to year, till joy is but a memory and glory a lie. Amid such fleeting emotions nothing so resembles love as the young passion of an artist who tastes the first delicious anguish of his destined fame and woe,—a passion daring yet timid, full of vague confidence and sure discouragement. Is there a man, slender in fortune, rich in his springtime of genius, whose heart has not beaten loudly as he approached a master of his art? If there be, that man will forever lack some heartstring, some touch, I know not what, of his brush, some fibre in his creations; some sentiment in his poetry. When braggarts, self-satisfied and in love with themselves, step early into the fame which belongs rightly to their future achievements, they are men of genius only in the eyes of fools. If talent is to be measured by youthful shyness, by that indefinable modesty which men born to glory lose in the practice of their art, as a pretty woman loses hers among the artifices of coquetry, then this unknown young man might claim to be possessed of genuine merit. The habit of success lessens doubt; and modesty, perhaps, is doubt.

Worn down with poverty and discouragement, and dismayed at this moment by his own presumption, the young neophyte might not have dared to enter the presence of the master to whom we owe our admirable portrait of Henry IV, if chance had not thrown an unexpected assistance in his way. An old man mounted the spiral stairway. The oddity of his dress, the magnificence of his lace ruffles, the solid assurance of his deliberate step, led the youth to assume that this remarkable personage must be the patron, or at least the intimate friend, of the painter. He drew back into a corner of the landing and made room for the newcomer; looking at him attentively and hoping to find either the frank good nature of the artistic temperament, or the serviceable disposition of those who promote the arts. But on the contrary he fancied he saw something diabolical in the expression of the old man's face,—something, I know not what, which has the quality of alluring the artistic mind.

Imagine a bald head, the brow full and prominent and falling with deep projection over a little flattened nose turned up at the end like the noses of Rabelais and Socrates; a laughing, wrinkled mouth; a short chin boldly chiselled and garnished with a gray beard cut into a point; sea-green eyes, faded perhaps by age, but whose pupils, contrasting with the pearl-white balls on which they floated, cast at times magnetic glances of anger or enthusiasm. The face in other respects was singularly withered and worn by the weariness of old age, and still more, it would seem, by the action of thoughts which had undermined both soul and body. The eyes had lost their lashes, and the eyebrows were scarcely traced along the projecting arches where they belonged. Imagine such a head upon a lean and feeble body, surround it with lace of dazzling whiteness worked in meshes like a fish slice, festoon the black velvet doublet of the old man with a heavy gold chain, and you will have a faint idea of the exterior of this strange individual, to whose appearance the dusky light of the landing lent fantastic coloring. You might have thought that a canvas of Rembrandt without its frame had walked silently up the stairway, bringing with it the dark atmosphere which was the sign manual of the great master. The old man cast a look upon the youth which was full of sagacity; then he rapped three times upon the door, and said, when it was opened by a man in feeble health, apparently about forty years of age, "Good morning, maître."

Porbus bowed respectfully, and made way for his guest, allowing the youth to pass in at the same time, under the impression that he came with the old man, and taking no further notice of him; all the less perhaps because the neophyte stood still beneath the spell which holds a heaven-born painter as he sees for the first time an *atelier* filled with the materials and instruments of his art. Daylight came from a casement in the roof and fell, focussed as it were, upon a canvas which rested on an easel in the middle of the room, and which bore, as yet, only three or four chalk lines. The light thus concentrated did not reach the dark angles of the vast *atelier*; but a few wandering reflections gleamed through the russet shadows on the silvered breastplate of a horseman's cuirass of the fourteenth century as it hung from the wall, or sent sharp lines of light upon the carved and polished cornice of a dresser which held specimens of rare pottery and porcelains, or touched with sparkling points the rough-grained texture of ancient gold-brocaded curtains, flung in broad folds about the room to serve the painter as models for his drapery. Anatomical casts in plaster, fragments and torsos of antique goddesses amorously polished by the kisses of centuries, jostled each other upon shelves and brackets. Innumerable sketches, studies in the three crayons, in ink, and in red chalk covered the walls from floor to ceiling; color-boxes, bottles of oil and turpentine, easels and stools upset or standing at right angles, left but a narrow pathway to the circle of light thrown from the window in the roof, which fell full on the pale face of Porbus and on the ivory skull of his singular visitor.

The attention of the young man was taken exclusively by a picture destined to become famous after those days of tumult and revolution, and which even then was precious in the sight of certain opinionated individuals to whom we owe the preservation of the divine afflatus through the dark days when the life of art was in jeopardy. This noble picture represents the Mary of Egypt as she prepares to pay for her passage by the ship. It is a masterpiece, painted for Marie de Medicis, and afterwards sold by her in the days of her distress.

"I like your saint," said the old man to Porbus, "and I will give you ten golden crowns over and above the queen's offer; but as to entering into competition with her—the devil!"

"You do like her, then?"

"As for that," said the old man, "yes, and no. The good woman is well set-up, but— she is not living. You young men think you have done all when you have drawn the form correctly, and put everything in place according to the laws of anatomy. You color the features with flesh tones,—mixed beforehand on your palette,—taking very good care to shade one side of the face darker than the other; and because you draw now and then from a nude woman standing on a table, you think you can copy nature; you fancy yourselves painters, and imagine that you have got at the secret of God's creations! Pr-r-r-r!—To be a great poet it is not enough to know the rules of syntax and write faultless grammar. Look at your saint, Porbus. At first sight she is admirable; but at the very next glance we perceive that she is glued to the canvas, and that we cannot walk round her. She is a silhouette with only one side, a semblance cut in outline, an image that can't turn round nor change her position. I feel no air between this arm and the background of the picture; space and depth are wanting. All is in good perspective; the atmospheric gradations are carefully observed, and yet in spite of your conscientious labor I cannot believe that this beautiful body has the warm breath of life. If I put my hand on that firm, round throat I shall find it cold as marble. No, no, my friend, blood does not run beneath that ivory skin; the purple tide of life does not swell those veins, nor stir those fibers which interlace like network below the translucent amber of the brow and breast. This part palpitates with life, but that other part is not living; life and death jostle each other in every detail. Here, you have a woman; there, a statue; here again, a dead body. Your creation is incomplete. You have breathed only a part of your soul into the well-beloved work. The torch of Prometheus went out in your hands over and over again; there are several parts of your painting on which the celestial flame never shone."

"But why is it so, my dear master?" said Porbus humbly, while the young man could hardly restrain a strong desire to strike the critic.

"Ah! that is the question," said the little old man. "You are floating between two systems, — between drawing and color, between the patient phlegm and honest stiffness of the old Dutch masters and the dazzling warmth and abounding joy of the Italians. You have tried to follow, at one and the same time, Hans Holbein and Titian, Albrecht Dürer and Paul Veronese. Well, well! it was a glorious ambition, but what is the result? You have neither the stern attraction of severity nor the deceptive magic of the chiaroscuro. See! at this place the rich, clear color of Titian has forced out the skeleton outline of Albrecht Dürer, as molten bronze might burst and overflow a slender mould. Here and there the outline has resisted the flood, and holds back the magnificent torrent of Venetian color. Your figure is neither perfectly well painted nor perfectly well drawn; it bears throughout the signs of this unfortunate indecision. If you did not feel that the fire of your genius was hot enough to weld into one the rival methods, you ought to have chosen honestly the one or the other, and thus attained the unity which conveys one aspect, at least, of life. As it is, you are true only on your middle plane. Your outlines are false; they do not round upon themselves; they suggest nothing behind them. There is truth here," said the old man, pointing to the bosom of the saint; "and here," showing the spot where the shoulder ended against the background; "but there," he added, returning to the throat, "it is all false. Do not inquire into the why and wherefore. I should fill you with despair."

The old man sat down on a stool and held his head in his hands for some minutes in silence.

"Master," said Porbus at length, "I studied that throat from the nude; but, to our sorrow, there are effects in nature which become false or impossible when placed on canvas."

"The mission of art is not to copy nature, but to represent it. You are not an abject copyist, but a poet," cried the old man, hastily interrupting Porbus with a despotic gesture. "If it were not so, a sculptor could reach the height of his art by merely molding a woman. Try to mold the hand of your mistress, and see what you will get, — ghastly articulations, without the slightest resemblance to her living hand; you must have recourse to the chisel of a man who, without servilely copying that hand, can give it movement and life. It is our mission to seize the mind, soul, countenance of things and beings. Effects! effects! what are they? the mere accidents of the life, and not the life itself. A hand, — since I have taken that as an example, — a hand is not merely a part of the body, it is far more; it expresses and carries on a thought which we must seize and render. Neither the painter nor the poet nor the sculptor should separate the effect from the cause, for they are indissolubly one. The true struggle of art lies there. Many a painter has triumphed through instinct without knowing this theory of art as a theory.

"Yes," continued the old man vehemently, "you draw a woman, but you do not *see* her. That is not the way to force an entrance into the arcana of Nature. Your hand reproduces, without an action of your mind, the model you copied under a master. You do not search out the secrets of form, nor follow its windings and evolutions with enough love and perseverance. Beauty is solemn and severe, and cannot be attained in that way: we must wait and watch its times and seasons, and clasp and hold it firmly ere it yields to us. Form is a Proteus less easily captured, more skilful to double and escape, than the Proteus of fable; it is only at the cost of struggle that we compel it to come forth in its true aspects. You young men are content with the first glimpse you get of it; or, at any rate, with the second or the third. This is not the spirit of the great warriors of art, — invincible powers, not misled by will-o'-the-wisps, but advancing always until they force Nature to lie bare in her divine integrity. That was Raphael's method," said the old man, lifting his velvet cap in homage to the sovereign of art; "his superiority came from the inward essence which seems to break from the inner to the outer of his figures. Form with him was what it is with us, — a medium by which to communicate ideas, sensations, feelings; in short, the infinite poesy of being. Every figure is a world; a portrait, whose original stands forth like a sublime vision, colored with the rainbow tints of light, drawn by the monitions of an inward voice, laid bare by a divine finger which points to the past of its whole existence as the source of its given expression. You clothe your women with delicate skins and glorious draperies of hair, but where is the blood which begets the passion or the peace of their souls, and is the cause of what you call 'effects'? Your saint is a dark woman; but this, my poor Porbus, belongs to a fair one. Your figures are pale, colored phantoms, which you present to our eyes; and you call that painting! art! Because you make something which looks more like a woman than a house, you think you have touched the goal; proud of not being obliged to write *currus venustus* or *pulcher homo* on the frame of your picture, you think yourselves majestic artists like our great forefathers. Ha, ha! you have not got there yet, my little men; you will use up many a crayon and spoil many a canvas before you reach that height. Undoubtedly a woman carries her head this way and her petticoats that way; her eyes soften and droop with just that look of resigned gentleness; the throbbing shadow of the eyelashes falls exactly thus upon her cheek. That is it, and—that is *not it*. What lacks? A mere nothing; but that mere nothing is ALL. You have given the shadow of life, but you have not given its fulness, its being, its— I know not what—soul, perhaps, which floats vaporously about the tabernacle of flesh; in short, that flower of life which Raphael and Titian culled. Start from the point you have now attained, and perhaps you may yet paint a worthy picture: you grew weary too soon. Mediocrity will extol your work; but the true artist smiles. O Mabuse! O my master!" added this singular person, "you were a thief; you have robbed us of your life, your knowledge, your art! But at least," he resumed after a pause, "this picture is better than the paintings of that rascally Rubens, with his mountains of Flemish, flesh daubed with vermilion, his cascades of red hair, and his hurly-burly of color. At any rate, you have got the elements of color, drawing, and sentiment,—the three essential parts of art."

"But the saint is sublime, good sir!" cried the young man in a loud voice, waking from a deep revery. "These figures, the saint and the boatman, have a subtle meaning which the Italian painters cannot give. I do not know one of them who could have invented that hesitation of the boatman."

"Does the young fellow belong to you?" asked Porbus of the old man.

"Alas, maître, forgive my boldness," said the neophyte, blushing.

"I am all unknown; only a dauber by instinct. I have just come to Paris, that fountain of art and science."

"Let us see what you can do," said Porbus, giving him a red crayon and a piece of paper.

The unknown copied the saint with an easy turn of his hand.

"Oh! oh!" exclaimed the old man, "what is your name?"

The youth signed the drawing: Nicolas Poussin.

"Not bad for a beginner," said the strange being who had discoursed so wildly. "I see that it is worth while to talk art before you. I don't blame you for admiring Porbus's saint. It is a masterpiece for the world at large; only those who are behind the veil of the holy of holies can perceive its errors. But you are worthy of a lesson, and capable of understanding it. I will show you how little is needed to turn that picture into a true masterpiece. Give all your eyes and all your attention; such a chance of instruction may never fall in your way again. Your palette, Porbus."

Porbus fetched his palette and brushes. The little old man turned up his cuffs with convulsive haste, slipped his thumb through the palette charged with prismatic colors, and snatched, rather than took, the handful of brushes which Porbus held out to him. As he did so his beard, cut to a point, seemed to quiver with the eagerness of an incontinent fancy; and while he filled his brush he muttered between his teeth:—

"Colors fit to fling out of the window with the man who ground them,—crude, false, revolting! who can paint with them?"

Then he dipped the point of his brush with feverish haste into the various tints, running through the whole scale with more rapidity than the organist of a cathedral runs up the gamut of the *O Filii* at Easter.

Porbus and Poussin stood motionless on either side of the easel, plunged in passionate contemplation.

"See, young man," said the old man without turning round, "see how with three or four touches and a faint bluish glaze you can make the air circulate round the head of the poor saint, who was suffocating in that thick atmosphere. Look how the drapery now floats, and you see that the breeze lifts it; just now it looked like heavy linen held out by pins. Observe that the satiny luster I am putting on the bosom gives it the plump suppleness of the flesh of a young girl. See how this tone of mingled reddish-brown and ochre warms up the cold grayness of that large shadow where the blood seemed to stagnate rather than flow. Young man, young man! what I am showing you now no other master in the world can teach you. Mabuse alone knew

The Hidden Masterpiece 103

the secret of giving life to form. Mabuse had but one pupil, and I am he. I never took a pupil, and I am an old man now. You are intelligent enough to guess at what should follow from the little that I shall show you today."

"While he was speaking, the extraordinary old man was giving touches here and there to all parts of the picture. Here two strokes of the brush, there one, but each so telling that together they brought out a new painting, — a painting steeped, as it were, in light. He worked with such passionate ardor that the sweat rolled in great drops from his bald brow; and his motions seemed to be jerked out of him with such rapidity and impatience that the young Poussin fancied a demon, incased within the body of this singular being, was working his hands fantastically like those of a puppet without, or even against, the will of their owner. The unnatural brightness of his eyes, the convulsive movements which seemed the result of some mental resistance, gave to this fancy of the youth a semblance of truth which reacted upon his lively imagination. The old man worked on, muttering half to himself, half to his neophyte: —

"Paf! paf! paf! that is how we butter it on, young man. Ah! my little pats, you are right; warm up that icy tone. Come, come! — pon, pon, pon, — " he continued, touching up the spots where he had complained of a lack of life, hiding under layers of color the conflicting methods, and regaining the unity of tone essential to an ardent Egyptian.

"Now see, my little friend, it is only the last touches of the brush that count for anything. Porbus put on a hundred; I have only put on one or two. Nobody will thank us for what is underneath, remember that!"

At last the demon paused; the old man turned to Porbus and Poussin, who stood mute with admiration, and said to them, —

"It is not yet equal to my Beautiful Nut-girl; still, one can put one's name to such a work. Yes, I will sign it," he added, rising to fetch a mirror in which to look at what he had done. "Now let us go and breakfast. Come, both of you, to my house. I have some smoked ham and good wine. Hey! hey! in spite of the degenerate times we will talk painting; we are strong ourselves. Here is a little man," he continued, striking Nicolas Poussin on the shoulder, "who has the faculty."

Observing the shabby cap of the youth, he pulled from his belt a leathern purse from which he took two gold pieces and offered them to him, saying, —

"I buy your drawing."

"Take them," said Porbus to Poussin, seeing that the latter trembled and blushed with shame, for the young scholar had the pride of poverty; "take them, he has the ransom of two kings in his pouch."

The three left the *atelier* and proceeded, talking all the way of art, to a handsome wooden house standing near the Pont Saint-Michel, whose window-casings and arabesque decoration amazed Poussin. The embryo painter soon found himself in one of the rooms on the ground floor seated, beside a good fire, at a table covered with appetizing dishes, and, by unexpected good fortune, in company with two great artists who treated him with kindly attention.

"Young man," said Porbus, observing that he was speechless, with his eyes fixed on a picture, "do not look at that too long, or you will fall into despair."

It was the Adam of Mabuse, painted by that wayward genius to enable him to get out of the prison where his creditors had kept him so long. The figure presented such fulness and force of reality that Nicolas Poussin began to comprehend the meaning of the bewildering talk of the old man. The latter looked at the picture with a satisfied but not enthusiastic manner, which seemed to say, "I have done better myself."

"There is life in the form," he remarked. "My poor master surpassed himself there; but observe the want of truth in the background. The man is living, certainly; he rises and is coming towards us; but the atmosphere, the sky, the air that we breathe, see, feel,—where are they? Besides, that is only a man; and the being who came first from the hand of God must needs have had something divine about him which is lacking here. Mabuse said so himself with vexation in his sober moments."

Poussin looked alternately at the old man and at Porbus with uneasy curiosity. He turned to the latter as if to ask the name of their host, but the painter laid a finger on his lips with an air of mystery, and the young man, keenly interested, kept silence, hoping that sooner or later some word of the conversation might enable him to guess the name of the old man, whose wealth and genius were sufficiently attested by the respect which Porbus showed him, and by the marvels of art heaped together in the picturesque apartment.

Poussin, observing against the dark panelling of the wall a magnificent portrait of a woman, exclaimed aloud, "What a beautiful Giorgione!"

"No," remarked the old man, "that is only one of my early daubs."

"Zounds!" cried Poussin naïvely; "are you the king of painters?"

The old man smiled, as if long accustomed to such homage. "Maître Frenhofer," said Porbus, "could you order up a little of your good Rhine wine for me?"

"Two casks," answered the host; "one to pay for the pleasure of looking at your pretty sinner this morning, and the other as a mark of friendship."

"Ah! if I were not so feeble," resumed Porbus, "and if you would consent to let me see your Beautiful Nut-girl, I too could paint some lofty picture, grand and yet profound, where the forms should have the living life."

"Show my work!" exclaimed the old man, with deep emotion. "No, no! I have still to bring it to perfection. Yesterday, towards evening, I thought it was finished. Her eyes were liquid, her flesh trembled, her tresses waved—she breathed! And yet, though I have grasped the secret of rendering on a flat canvas the relief and roundness of nature, this morning at dawn I saw many errors. Ah! to attain that glorious result, I have studied to their depths the masters of color. I have analyzed and lifted, layer by layer, the colors of Titian, king of light. Like him, great sovereign of art, I have sketched my figure in light clear tones of supple yet solid color; for shadow is but an accident,—remember that, young man. Then I worked backward, as it were; and by means of half-tints, and glazings whose transparency I kept diminishing little by little, I was able to cast strong shadows deepening almost to blackness. The shadows of ordinary painters are not of the same texture as their tones of light. They are wood, brass, iron, anything you please except flesh in shadow. We feel that if the figures changed position the shady places could not be wiped off, and would remain dark spots which never could be made luminous. I have avoided that blunder, though many of our most illustrious painters have fallen into it. In my work you will see whiteness beneath the opacity of the broadest shadow. Unlike the crowd of ignoramuses, who fancy they draw correctly because they can paint one good vanishing line, I have not dryly outlined my figures, nor brought out superstitiously minute anatomical details; for, let me tell you, the human body does not end off with a line. In that respect sculptors get nearer to the truth of nature than we do. Nature is all curves, each wrapping or overlapping another. To speak rigorously, there is no such thing as drawing. Do not laugh, young man; no matter how strange that saying seems to you, you will understand the reasons for it one of these days. A line is a means by which man explains to himself the effect of light upon a given object;

but there is no such thing as a line in nature, where all things are rounded and full. It is only in modelling that we really draw,—in other words, that we detach things from their surroundings and put them in their due relief. The proper distribution of light can alone reveal the whole body. For this reason I do not sharply define lineaments; I diffuse about their outline a haze of warm, light half-tints, so that I defy any one to place a finger on the exact spot where the parts join the groundwork of the picture. If seen near by this sort of work has a woolly effect, and is wanting in nicety and precision; but go a few steps off and the parts fall into place; they take their proper form and detach themselves,—the body turns, the limbs stand out, we feel the air circulating around them.

"Nevertheless," he continued, sadly, "I am not satisfied; there are moments when I have my doubts. Perhaps it would be better not to sketch a single line. I ask myself if I ought not to grasp the figure first by its highest lights, and then work down to the darker portions. Is not that the method of the sun, divine painter of the universe? O Nature, Nature! who has ever caught thee in thy flights? Alas! the heights of knowledge, like the depths of ignorance, lead to unbelief. I doubt my work."

The old man paused, then resumed. "For ten years I have worked, young man; but what are ten short years in the long struggle with Nature? We do not know the time it cost Pygmalion to make the only statue that ever walked—"

He fell into a revery and remained, with fixed eyes, oblivious of all about him, playing mechanically with his knife.

"See, he is talking to his own soul," said Porbus in a low voice.

The words acted like a spell on Nicolas Poussin, filling him with the inexplicable curiosity of a true artist. The strange old man, with his white eyes fixed in stupor, became to the wondering youth something more than a man; he seemed a fantastic spirit inhabiting an unknown sphere, and waking by its touch confused ideas within the soul. We can no more define the moral phenomena of this species of fascination than we can render in words the emotions excited in the heart of an exile by a song which recalls his fatherland. The contempt which the old man affected to pour upon the noblest efforts of art, his wealth, his manners, the respectful deference shown to him by Porbus, his work guarded so secretly,—a work of patient toil, a work no doubt of genius, judging by the head of the Virgin which Poussin had so naively admired, and which, beautiful beside even the Adam of Mabuse, betrayed the imperial touch of a great artist, — in short, everything about the strange old man seemed beyond the limits of human nature. The rich imagination of the youth fastened upon the one perceptible and clear clew to the mystery of this supernatural being, — the presence of the artistic nature, that wild impassioned nature to which such mighty powers have been confided, which too often abuses those powers, and drags cold reason and common souls, and even lovers of art, over stony and arid places, where for such there is neither pleasure nor instruction; while to the artistic soul itself, — that white-winged angel of sportive fancy, — epics, works of art, and visions rise along the way. It is a nature, an essence, mocking yet kind, fruitful though destitute. Thus, for the enthusiastic Poussin, the old man became by sudden transfiguration Art itself, — art with all its secrets, its transports, and its dreams.

"Yes, my dear Porbus," said Frenhofer, speaking half in revery, "I have never yet beheld a perfect woman; a body whose outlines were faultless and whose flesh-tints — Ah! where lives she?" he cried, interrupting his own words; "where lives the lost Venus of the ancients, so long sought for, whose scattered beauty we snatch by glimpses? Oh! to see for a moment, a single moment, the divine completed nature, — the ideal, — I would give my all of fortune. Yes; I would search thee out, celestial Beauty! in thy farthest sphere. Like Orpheus, I would go down to hell to win back the life of art — " "Let us go," said Porbus to Poussin; "he neither sees nor hears us any longer."

"Let us go to his *atelier*," said the wonder-struck young man.

"Oh! the old dragon has guarded the entrance. His treasure is out of reach. I have not waited for your wish or urging to attempt an assault on the mystery."

"Mystery! then there is a mystery?"

"Yes," answered Porbus. "Frenhofer was the only pupil Mabuse was willing to teach. He became the friend, savior, father of that unhappy man, and he sacrificed the greater part of his wealth to satisfy the mad passions of his master. In return, Mabuse bequeathed to him the secret of relief, the power of giving life to form, — that flower of nature, our perpetual despair, which Mabuse had seized so well that once, having sold and drunk the value of a flowered damask which he should have worn at the entrance of Charles V, he made his appearance in a paper garment painted to resemble damask. The splendor of the stuff attracted the attention of the emperor, who, wishing to compliment the old drunkard, laid a hand upon his shoulder and discovered the deception. Frenhofer is a man carried away by the passion of his art; he sees above and beyond what other painters see. He has meditated deeply on color and the absolute truth of lines; but by dint of much research, much thought, much study, he has come to doubt the object for which he is searching. In his hours of despair he fancies that drawing does not exist, and that lines can render nothing but geometric figures. That, of course, is not true; because with a black line which has no color we can represent the human form. This proves that our art is made up, like nature, of an infinite number of elements. Drawing gives the skeleton, and color gives the life; but life without the skeleton is a far more incomplete thing than the skeleton without the life. But there is a higher truth still,—namely, that practice and observation are the essentials of a painter; and that if reason and poesy persist in wrangling with the tools, the brushes, we shall be brought to doubt, like Frenhofer, who is as much excited in brain as he is exalted in art. A sublime painter, indeed; but he had the misfortune to be born rich, and that enables him to stray into theory and conjecture. Do not imitate him. Work! work! painters should theorize with their brushes in their hands."

"We will contrive to get in," cried Poussin, not listening to Porbus, and thinking only of the hidden masterpiece.

Porbus smiled at the youth's enthusiasm, and bade him farewell with a kindly invitation to come and visit him.

Nicolas Poussin returned slowly towards the Rue de la Harpe and passed, without observing that he did so, the modest hostelry where he was lodging. Returning presently upon his steps, he ran up the miserable stairway with anxious rapidity until he reached an upper chamber nestling between the joists of a roof *en colombage*,—the plain, slight covering of the houses of old Paris. Near the single and gloomy window of the room sat a young girl, who rose quickly as the door opened, with a gesture of love; she had recognized the young man's touch upon the latch.

"What is the matter?" she asked.

"It is—it is," he cried, choking with joy, "that I feel myself a painter! I have doubted it till now; but today I believe in myself. I can be a great man. Ah, Gillette, we shall be rich, happy! There is gold in these brushes!"

The Hidden Masterpiece 109

Suddenly he became silent. His grave and earnest face lost its expression of joy; he was comparing the immensity of his hopes with the mediocrity of his means. The walls of the garret were covered with bits of paper on which were crayon sketches; he possessed only four clean canvases. Colors were at that time costly, and the poor gentleman gazed at a palette that was well-nigh bare. In the midst of this poverty he felt within himself an indescribable wealth of heart and the superabundant force of consuming genius. Brought to Paris by a gentleman of his acquaintance, and perhaps by the monition of his own talent, he had suddenly found a mistress,—one of those generous and noble souls who are ready to suffer by the side of a great man; espousing his poverty, studying to comprehend his caprices, strong to bear deprivation and bestow love, as others are daring in the display of luxury and in parading the insensibility of their hearts. The smile which flickered on her lips brightened as with gold the darkness of the garret and rivalled the effulgence of the skies; for the sun did not always shine in the heavens, but she was always here,—calm and collected in her passion, living in his happiness, his griefs; sustaining the genius which overflowed in love ere it found in art its destined expression.

"Listen, Gillette; come!"

The obedient, happy girl sprang lightly on the painter's knee. She was all grace and beauty, pretty as the springtime, decked with the wealth of feminine charm, and lighting all with the fire of a noble soul.

"O God!" he exclaimed, "I can never tell her!"

"A secret!" she cried; "then I must know it."

Poussin was lost in thought.

"Tell me."

"Gillette, poor, beloved heart!"

"Ah! do you want something of me?"

"Yes."

"If you want me to pose as I did the other day," she said, with a little pouting air, "I will not do it. Your eyes say nothing to me, then. You look at me, but you do not think of me."

"Would you like me to copy another woman?"

"Perhaps," she answered, "if she were very ugly."

"Well," continued Poussin, in a grave tone, "if to make a great painter it were necessary to pose to some one else—"

"You are testing me," she interrupted; "you know well that I would not do it."

Poussin bent his head upon his breast like a man succumbing to joy or grief too great for his spirit to bear.

"Listen," she said, pulling him by the sleeve of his worn doublet, "I told you, Nick, that I would give my life for you; but I never said—never!—that I, a living woman, would renounce my love."

"Renounce it?" cried Poussin. "If I showed myself thus to another you would love me no longer; and I myself, I should feel unworthy of your love. To obey your caprices, ah, that is simple and natural! in spite of myself, I am proud and happy in doing thy dear will; but to another, fy!"

"Forgive me, my own Gillette," said the painter, throwing himself at her feet. "I would rather be loved than famous. To me thou art more precious than fortune and honors. Yes, away with these brushes burn those sketches! I have been mistaken. My vocation is to love thee,—thee alone! I am not a painter, I am thy lover. Perish art and all its secrets!"

She looked at him admiringly, happy and captivated by his passion. She reigned; she felt instinctively that the arts were forgotten for her sake, and flung at her feet like grains of incense.

"Yet he is only an old man," resumed Poussin. "In you he would see only a woman. You are the perfect woman whom he seeks."

"Love should grant all things!" she exclaimed, ready to sacrifice love's scruples to reward the lover who thus seemed to sacrifice his art to her. "And yet," she added, "it would be my ruin. Ah, to suffer for thy good! Yes, it is glorious! But thou wilt forget me. How came this cruel thought into thy mind?"

"It came there, and yet I love thee," he said, with a sort of contrition. "Am I, then, a wretch?"

"Let us consult Père Hardouin."

"No, no! it must be a secret between us."

"Well, I will go; but thou must not be present," she said. "Stay at the door, armed with thy dagger. If I cry out, enter and kill the man."

Forgetting all but his art, Poussin clasped her in his arms.

"He loves me no longer!" thought Gillette, when she was once more alone.

She regretted her promise. But before long she fell a prey to an anguish far more cruel than her regret; and she struggled vainly to drive forth a terrible fear which forced its way into her mind. She felt that she loved him less as the suspicion rose in her heart that he was less worthy than she had thought him.

II

Three months after the first meeting of Porbus and Poussin, the former went to see Maître Frenhofer. He found the old man a prey to one of those deep, self-developed discouragements, whose cause, if we are to believe the mathematicians of health, lies in a bad digestion, in the wind, in the weather, in some swelling of the intestines, or else, according to casuists, in the imperfections of our moral nature; the fact being that the good man was simply worn out by the effort to complete his mysterious picture. He was seated languidly in a large oaken chair of vast dimensions covered with black leather; and without changing his melancholy attitude he cast on Porbus the distant glance of a man sunk in absolute dejection.

"Well, maître," said Porbus, "was the ultramarine, for which you journeyed to Brussels, worthless? Are you unable to grind our new white? Is the oil bad, or the brushes restive?"

"Alas!" cried the old man, "I thought for one moment that my work was accomplished; but I must have deceived myself in some of the details. I shall have no peace until I clear up my doubts. I am about to travel; I go to Turkey, Asia, Greece, in search of models. I must compare my picture with various types of Nature. It may be that I have up *there*," he added, letting a smile of satisfaction flicker on his lip, "Nature herself. At times I am half afraid that a breath may wake this woman, and that she will disappear from sight."

He rose suddenly, as if to depart at once. "Wait," exclaimed Porbus. "I have come in time to spare you the costs and fatigues of such a journey."

"How so?" asked Frenhofer, surprised.

"Young Poussin is beloved by a woman whose incomparable beauty is without imperfection. But, my dear master, if he consents to lend her to you, at least you must let us see your picture."

The old man remained standing, motionless, in a state bordering on stupefaction. "What!" he at last exclaimed, mournfully. "Show my creature, my spouse? — tear off the veil with which I have chastely hidden my joy? It would be prostitution! For ten years I have lived with this woman; she is mine, mine alone! she loves me! Has she not smiled upon me as, touch by touch, I painted her? She has a soul, — the soul with which I endowed her. She would blush if other eyes than mine beheld her. Let her be seen? — where is the husband, the lover, so debased as to lend his wife to dishonor? When you paint a picture for the court you do not put your whole soul into it; you sell to courtiers your tricked-out lay figures. My painting is not a picture; it is a sentiment, a passion! Born in my *atelier*, she must remain a virgin there. She shall not leave it unclothed. Poesy and women give themselves bare, like truth, to lovers only. Have we the model of Raphael, the Angelica of Ariosto, the Beatrice of Dante? No, we see but their semblance. Well, the work which I keep hidden behind bolts and bars is an exception to all other art. It is not a canvas; it is a woman, — a woman with whom I weep and laugh and think and talk. Would you have me resign the joy of ten years, as I might throw away a worn-out doublet? Shall I, in a moment, cease to be father, lover, creator? — this woman is not a creature; she is my creation. Bring your young man; I will give him my treasures, — paintings of Correggio, Michelangelo, Titian; I will kiss the print of his feet in the dust, — but make him my rival? Shame upon me! Ha! I am more a lover than I am a painter. I shall have the strength to burn my Nut-girl ere I render my last sigh; but suffer her to endure the glance of a man, a young man, a painter? — No, no! I would kill on the morrow the man who polluted her with a look! I would kill you, — you, my friend, — if you did not worship her on your knees; and think you I would submit my idol to the cold eyes and stupid criticisms of fools? Ah, love is a mystery! its life is in the depths of the soul; it dies when a man says, even to his friend, Here is she whom I love."

The old man seemed to renew his youth; his eyes had the brilliancy and fire of life, his pale cheeks blushed a vivid red, his hands trembled. Porbus, amazed by the passionate violence with which he uttered these words, knew not how to answer a feeling so novel and yet so profound. Was the old man under the thraldom of an artist's fancy? Or did these ideas flow from the unspeakable fanaticism produced at times in every mind by the long gestation of a noble work? Was it possible to bargain with this strange and whimsical being?

Filled with such thoughts, Porbus said to the old man, "Is it not woman for woman? Poussin lends his mistress to your eyes."

"What sort of mistress is that?" cried Frenhofer. "She will betray him sooner or later. Mine will be to me forever faithful."

"Well," returned Porbus, "then let us say no more. But before you find, even in Asia, a woman as beautiful, as perfect, as the one I speak of you, may be dead, and your picture forever unfinished."

"Oh, it is finished!" said Frenhofer. "Whoever sees it will find a woman lying on a velvet bed, beneath curtains; perfumes are exhaling from a golden tripod by her side: he will be tempted to take the tassels of the cord that holds back the curtain; he will think he sees the bosom of Catherine Lescaut, — a model called the Beautiful Nut-girl; he will see it rise and fall with the movement of her breathing. Yet — I wish I could be sure — "

"Go to Asia, then," said Porbus hastily, fancying he saw some hesitation in the old man's eye.

Porbus made a few steps towards the door of the room. At this moment Gillette and Nicolas Poussin reached the entrance of the house. As the young girl was about to enter, she dropped the arm of her lover and shrank back as if overcome by a presentiment. "What am I doing here?" she said to Poussin, in a deep voice, looking at him fixedly.

"Gillette, I leave you mistress of your actions; I will obey your will. You are my conscience, my glory. Come home; I shall be happy, perhaps, if you, yourself — "

"Have I a self when you speak thus to me? Oh, no! I am but a child. Come," she continued, seeming to make a violent effort. "If our love perishes, if I put into my heart a long regret, thy fame shall be the guerdon of my obedience to thy will. Let us enter. I may yet live again, — a memory on thy palette."

Opening the door of the house the two lovers met Porbus coming out. Astonished at the beauty of the young girl, whose eyes were still wet with tears, he caught her all trembling by the hand and led her to the old master.

"There!" he cried; "is she not worth all the masterpieces in the world?"

Frenhofer quivered. Gillette stood before him in the ingenuous, simple attitude of a young Georgian, innocent and timid, captured by brigands and offered to a slave-merchant. A modest blush suffused her cheeks, her eyes were lowered, her hands hung at her sides, strength seemed to abandon her, and her tears protested against the violence done to her purity. Poussin cursed himself, and repented of his folly in bringing this treasure from their peaceful garret. Once more he became a lover rather than an artist; scruples convulsed his heart as he saw the eye of the old painter regain its youth and, with the artist's habit, disrobe as it were the beauteous form of the young girl. He was seized with the jealous frenzy of a true lover.

"Gillette!" he cried; "let us go."

At this cry, with its accent of love, his mistress raised her eyes joyfully and looked at him; then she ran into his arms.

"Ah! you love me still?" she whispered, bursting into tears.

Though she had had strength to hide her suffering, she had none to hide her joy.

"Let me have her for one moment," exclaimed the old master, "and you shall compare her with my Catherine. Yes, yes; I consent!" There was love in the cry of Frenhofer as in that of Poussin, mingled with jealous coquetry on behalf of his semblance of a woman; he seemed to revel in the triumph which the beauty of his virgin was about to win over the beauty of the living woman.

"Do not let him retract," cried Porbus, striking Poussin on the shoulder. "The fruits of love wither in a day; those of art are immortal."

"Can it be," said Gillette, looking steadily at Poussin and at Porbus, "that I am nothing more than a woman to him?"

She raised her head proudly; and as she glanced at Frenhofer with flashing eyes she saw her lover gazing once more at the picture he had formerly taken for a Giorgione.

"Ah!" she cried, "let us go in; he never looked at me like that !"

"Old man!" said Poussin, roused from his meditation by Gillette's voice, "see this sword. I will plunge it into your heart at the first cry of that young girl. I will set fire to your house, and no one shall escape from it. Do you understand me?"

His look was gloomy and the tones of his voice were terrible. His attitude, and above all the gesture with which he laid his hand upon the weapon, comforted the poor girl, who half forgave him for thus sacrificing her to his art and to his hopes of a glorious future.

Porbus and Poussin remained outside the closed door of the *atelier*, looking at one another in silence. At first the painter of the Egyptian Mary uttered a few exclamations: "Ah, she unclothes herself!" — "He tells her to stand in the light!" — "He compares them!" but he grew silent as he watched the mournful face of the young man; for though old painters have none of such petty scruples in presence of their art, yet they admire them in others, when they are fresh and pleasing. The young man held his hand on his sword, and his ear seemed glued to the panel of the door. Both men, standing darkly in the shadow, looked like conspirators waiting the hour to strike a tyrant.

"Come in! come in!" cried the old man, beaming with happiness. "My work is perfect; I can show it now with pride. Never shall painter, brushes, colors, canvas, light, produce the rival of Catherine Lescaut, the Beautiful Nut-girl."

Porbus and Poussin, seized with wild curiosity, rushed into the middle of a vast *atelier* filled with dust, where everything lay in disorder, and where they saw a few paintings hanging here and there upon the walls. They stopped before the figure of a woman, life-sized and half nude, which filled them with eager admiration.

"Do not look at that," said Frenhofer, "it is only a daub which I made to study a pose; it is worth nothing. Those are my errors," he added, waving his hand towards the enchanting compositions on the walls around them.

At these words Porbus and Poussin, amazed at the disdain which the master showed for such marvels of art, looked about them for the secret treasure, but could see it nowhere.

"There it is!" said the old man, whose hair fell in disorder about his face, which was scarlet with supernatural excitement. His eyes sparkled, and his breast heaved like that of a young man beside himself with love.

"Ah!" he cried, "you did not expect such perfection? You stand before a woman, and you are looking for a picture! There are such depths on that canvas, the air within it is so true, that you are unable to distinguish it from the air you breathe. Where is art? Departed, vanished! Here is the form itself of a young girl. Have I not caught the color, the very life of the line which seems to terminate the body? The same phenomenon which seems to terminate the body? The same phenomenon which we notice around fishes in the water is also about objects which float in air. See how these outlines spring forth from the background. Do you not feel that you could pass your hand behind those shoulders? For seven years have I studied these effects of light coupled with form. That hair,—is it not bathed in light? Why, she breathes! That bosom,—see! Ah! who would not worship it on bended knee? The flesh palpitates! Wait, she is about to rise; wait!"

"Can you see anything?" whispered Poussin to Porbus.

"Nothing. Can you?"

"No."

The two painters drew back, leaving the old man absorbed in ecstasy, and tried to see if the light, falling plumb upon the canvas at which he pointed, had neutralized all effects. They examined the picture, moving from right to left, standing directly before it, bending, swaying, rising by turns.

"Yes, yes; it is really a canvas," cried Frenhofer, mistaking the purpose of their examination. "See, here is the frame, the easel; these are my colors, my brushes." And he caught up a brush which he held out to them with a naïve motion.

"The old rogue is making game of us," said Poussin, coming close to the pretended picture. "I can see nothing here but a mass of confused color, crossed by a multitude of eccentric lines, making a sort of painted wall."

"We are mistaken. See!" returned Porbus. Coming nearer, they perceived in a corner of the canvas the point of a naked foot, which came forth from the chaos of colors, tones, shadows hazy and undefined, misty and without form, — an enchanting foot, a living foot. They stood lost in admiration before this glorious fragment breaking forth from the incredible, slow, progressive destruction around it. The foot seemed to them like the torso of some Grecian Venus, brought to light amid the ruins of a burned city.

"There is a woman beneath it all!" cried Porbus, calling Poussin's attention to the layers of color which the old painter had successively laid on, believing that he thus brought his work to perfection. The two men turned towards him with one accord, beginning to comprehend, though vaguely, the ecstasy in which he lived.

"He means it in good faith," said Porbus.

"Yes, my friend," answered the old man, rousing from his abstraction, "we need faith; faith in art. We must live with our work for years before we can produce a creation like that. Some of these shadows have cost me endless toil. See, there on her cheek, below the eyes, a faint half-shadow; if you observed it in Nature you might think it could hardly be rendered. Well, believe me, I took unheard of pains to reproduce that effect. My dear Porbus, look attentively at my work, and you will comprehend what I have told you about the manner of treating form and outline. Look at the light on the bosom, and see how by a series of touches and higher lights firmly laid on I have managed to grasp light itself, and combine it with the dazzling whiteness of the clearer tones; and then see how, by an opposite method, — smoothing off the sharp contrasts and the texture of the color, — I have been able, by caressing the outline of my figure and veiling it with cloudy half-tints, to do away with the very idea of drawing and all other artificial means, and give to the form the aspect and roundness of Nature itself. Come nearer, and you will see the work more distinctly; if too far off it disappears. See! there, at that point, it is, I think, most remarkable." And with the end of his brush he pointed to a spot of clear light color.

Porbus struck the old man on the shoulder, turning to Poussin as he did so, and said, "Do you know that he is one of our greatest painters?"

"He is a poet even more than he is a painter," answered Poussin gravely.

"There," returned Porbus, touching the canvas, "is the ultimate end of our art on earth."

"And from thence," added Poussin, "it rises, to enter heaven."

"How much happiness is there! — upon that canvas," said Porbus.

The absorbed old man gave no heed to their words, he was smiling at his visionary woman.

"But sooner or later, he will perceive that there is nothing there," cried Poussin.

"Nothing there! — upon my canvas?" said Frenhofer, looking first at the two painters, and then at his imaginary picture.

"What have you done?" cried Porbus, addressing Poussin.

The old man seized the arm of the young man violently, and said to him, "You see nothing? — clown, infidel, scoundrel, dolt! Why did you come here? My good Porbus," he added, turning to his friend, "is it possible that you, too, are jesting with me? Answer; I am your friend. Tell me, can it be that I have spoiled my picture?"

Porbus hesitated, and feared to speak; but the anxiety painted on the white face of the old man was so cruel that he was constrained to point to the canvas and utter the word, "See!"

Frenhofer looked at his picture for the space of a moment, and staggered.

"Nothing! nothing! after toiling ten years!"

He sat down and wept.

"Am I then a fool, an idiot? Have I neither talent nor capacity? Am I no better than a rich man who walks, and can only walk? Have I indeed produced nothing?"

He gazed at the canvas through tears. Suddenly he raised himself proudly and flung a lightning glance upon the two painters.

"By the blood, by the body, by the head of Christ, you are envious men who seek to make me think she is spoiled, that you may steal her from me. I — I see her!" he cried. "She is wondrously beautiful!"

At this moment Poussin heard the weeping of Gillette as she stood, forgotten, in a corner.

"What troubles thee, my darling?" asked the painter, becoming once more a lover.

"Kill me!" she answered. "I should be infamous if I still loved thee, for I despise thee. I admire thee; but thou hast filled me with horror. I love, and yet already I hate thee."

While Poussin listened to Gillette, Frenhofer drew a green curtain before his Catherine, with the grave composure of a jeweller locking his drawers when he thinks that thieves are near him. He cast at the two painters a look which was profoundly dissimulating, full of contempt and suspicion; then, with convulsive haste, he silently pushed them through the door of his *atelier*. When they reached the threshold of his house he said to them, "Adieu, my little friends."

The tone of this farewell chilled the two painters with fear.

On the morrow Porbus, alarmed, went again to visit Frenhofer, and found that he had died during the night, after having burned his paintings.

Mérimée

1803	September 28. Prosper Mérimée born in Paris, France.
1819–23	Studies law at the University of Paris for four years but never practices. Instead, devotes himself to learning foreign languages. In 1822 writes his first play, *Cromwell*, with the encouragement of his friend, Stendhal.
1825–29	Produces two literary hoaxes, which influence the early development of Romanticism: *Le Théâtre de Clara Gazul* (1825), allegedly translated from Spanish, and *La Guzla*, allegedly translated from Illyrian (1827). In 1829, he publishes his highly regarded historical novel, *La Chronique du temps de Charles IX*. His first short story appears in *La Revue de Paris*, and other stories follow that same year.
1831–34	Meets Jenny Dacquin with whom he corresponds for the rest of his life. The letters are published posthumously in *Lettres à une inconnue* (Letters to an Unknown Girl). Has an affair with George Sands in 1833. Is named inspector general of historical monuments and travels throughout Europe and the Orient. Produces books on travel, as well as on architecture and archeology.
1841–53	Publishes *Colomba*, a collection of stories, in 1841 and is elected to the French Academy in 1843. *Nouvelles*, another collection, appears in 1852. It contains "Carmen," the story on which Bizet later bases his opera. Through the acquaintance of Empress Eugenie, he is made a senator in 1853.
1870	Sept 23. Mérimée dies in Cannes, France.

Prosper Mérimée

Prosper Mérimée came of a family of artists. His father, a man of varied culture, was a good painter, who wrote a book on the technique of his art; his mother was also a painter, well-known for her portraits of children; she had a talent for storytelling, and was accustomed to keep her little sitters quiet while she was painting them by telling them interesting tales. The portrait which she painted of her only son in his fifth year gives an equally favorable impression of her talent and of her child's looks. The face possesses a style of beauty very uncommon in such a young boy; for there is something of the pride and intellectual superiority of the distinguished man in this infantine countenance framed in fair, soft curls. The eyes are innocent and frank, but there is mischief in the curve of the sagacious, firmly closed lips. The bearing is that of a little prince. One can quite well understand how this child one day, seeing his parents, who had pretended to be angry with him, laugh behind his back at his tears of repentance, determined "never to ask forgiveness," a determination which he adhered to as a man. His mother, with whom he lived until her death in 1852, was a woman of remarkable strength of character, in whose mind the philosophy of the eighteenth century had engendered such an aversion for every form of religious belief that she would not even allow her son to be baptized—a circumstance which he, in later life, used to mention with a certain satirical satisfaction. To a pious and amiable lady who was using all her eloquence to induce him to undergo the ceremony, he replied: "I will, upon one condition, and that is, that you stand godmother, and carry me, dressed in a long white frock, in your arms."

The outward events of Mérimée's life may be simply and shortly narrated. At the age of twenty-two, after completing the legal studies which form part of the education of most well-to-do young Frenchmen, he made a brilliant *début* as an author. During the following six years he led an independent life in the social circles belonging to the Liberal Opposition, dividing his time between literature and the pursuit of pleasure. In 1831, when his political friends came into power, he was appointed Inspector of Historical Monuments, as successor to Vitet, in whose footsteps he had already followed as an author. He fulfilled the duties of his office zealously and capably. Repeated tours in Spain and England, one in the East, and two in Greece, completed his peculiar training and enriched him with stores of impressions of foreign characters and customs. His extraordinary proficiency as a linguist enabled him to reap every advantage from his travels; he moved about in foreign countries like a native. It is especially unusual for a Frenchman to know as many languages as Mérimée did. He spoke English, Spanish (in all its dialects, including the gipsy language), Italian, modern Greek, and Russian, and had thoroughly studied the literatures of these languages, besides mastering those of ancient Greece and Rome. In his official capacity he published accounts of his travels in France, full of erudite detail; these and some studies on episodes in Roman history procured his election to the Académie des Inscriptions in 1841. In 1844 he was made a member of the Académie Française. Under the Second Empire, as an old friend of the Countess Montijo, he was on intimate terms with the Imperial family; and he and Octave Feuillet were long the only literary ornaments of the new court. In 1853 he was made a Senator. The appointment was beneath his dignity, and his acceptance of it injured his reputation, in spite of the fact that he almost never took part in the deliberations of the Chamber. During his last illness Mérimée heard of the fall of the Empire. He died at Cannes on the 23rd of September 1870.

The inner life of this man, as revealed by his books, is by no means so simple. The character of the youth who went out into the world at eighteen was composed of many conflicting elements. He was exceedingly proud; bold and bashful at the same time. He had an audacious intellect and a shy, reserved disposition. To conceal the shyness, which wounded his pride, he assumed either a stiff, cold manner, or an appearance of frivolity tinged with cynicism. This cynicism became a kind of mannerism with him in conversation with men. As a youth he was certainly not so suspicious and reserved as he afterwards became, but it is a mistake to attribute his general scepticism to any one particular disappointment. He met, like the rest of us, with many disappointments, and was often roughly disillusioned; he was deceived by friends, sacrificed by the woman he loved; he learned to know the world, learned that life is warfare, and that a man has not only to protect himself against false and untrustworthy friends, secret and open enemies, but also against those who, as he himself puts it, "do evil for evil's sake." But if the germs of suspicion had not been in him from the first, a dozen consecutive bitter experiences would not have cured him of faith in his fellow men; for the man of a trustful nature has always had at least an equal number of contrary experiences which outweigh the others. But Mérimée's nature was as critical as it was productive, and men of his character are apt to make the rule by which we judge the professional critic — that he only deserves trust in proportion as he shows distrust — the rule of their lives. We can imagine the suffering which his own poetic impressionability entailed on a man with Mérimée's highly developed critical sense.

The critical temperament is above everything truthful; and Mérimée was remarkably so. His natural audacity, moreover, impelled him to say exactly what he thought, regardless of conventionalities. One sees from his letters how frank he was by nature, how inclined to speak the undisguised truth, and how impatient of conventional falsehoods and even of alleviating or embellishing circumlocutions. This is especially noticeable in the first volume of *Lettres à une inconnue*. Even in these love letters Mérimée is almost rude when it seems to him that the object of his affections has expressed some merely conventional opinion. Though his fear of ridicule and his ever-increasing scepticism did not dispose him to knight-errantry or lead him to court martyrdom, he nevertheless, in his fiftieth year, committed a chivalrous folly of which most men of the world would only be capable in their extreme youth. When his friend, the notorious Libri, was found guilty of having abused his position as public librarian to the extent of appropriating and selling a number of valuable books belonging to the nation, Mérimée, unable to believe Libri capable of such an action, undertook his rehabilitation with an ardor worthy of a better cause, and attacked the committee of investigation and the judges in an article in the *Revue des deux Mondes* (April 15, 1852), the sparkling wit of which recalls Paul Louis Courier's pamphlets. A professed Don Quixote could not have acted more foolishly; nor is the case much altered if what the initiated maintain is true, namely, that his ardor was inspired rather by Madame Libri than by her husband.

Under the Empire, and even as a courtier, Mérimée preserved his freedom of speech. I am not referring to the fact that he, as a rule, spoke disparagingly of Napoleon III, which is not particularly to his credit, seeing that he accepted office under that prince's government; but even in conversation with members of the Imperial family he combined frankness with courtesy. Writing in July 1859, he tells that the Empress had asked him in Spanish what he thought of the speech made by the Emperor on his return from Italy. "In order," he writes, "to be both straightforward and courtier-like, I answered, '*Muy necesario!*' (Very necessary)."

Mérimée's natural tendency to outspokenness was, however, held in check by his pride and shyness. He early learned that the man who makes a naïve public display of his feelings not only lays himself open to ridicule, but invites the sympathy and familiarity of the vulgar crowd; and, as a youth, he resolved that he would never wear his heart upon his sleeve. Nor did it need all his mistrust to discover that the great majority of these around him who made a frank and childlike display of their feelings knew very well what they were about. The men who published their noblemindedness, their earnestness, their love of morality and religion, their patriotism, etc., in the great marketplace of publicity, always seemed to him either to be angling for applause or to be actuated by some business motive. He could not fail to see how well it pays, as a rule, to give expression to noble sentiments and warm feeling, and he found it difficult to suppose others ignorant of the fact. In any case, he could not bring himself to do as they did; he was one of those who cannot bear to proclaim the fact that they love virtue and hate vice, and to be always singing the praises of "the Good, the True, and the Beautiful."

To avoid all comradeship with the calculating "men of feeling," and to protect his emotional life from the gaze of the profane, Mérimée had recourse to the expedient of concealing his quivering sensibility under steely irony, as under a coat of mail. He determined rather to appear worse than he was, than to run the risk of being taken for one of these models of all the virtues. With this aim in view he dealt so hardly with himself that he lost his first fresh, simple naturalness, and acquired instead a manner which, though still natural and simple, was, nevertheless, distinctly a cultivated manner. In *The Etruscan Vase*, the one of his tales which gives most insight into his own intellectual and emotional life, we read of the hero, Saint-Clair: "He was born with a tender and loving heart; but, at an age when one is liable to receive impressions which last for the rest of one's life, too frank a display of his tenderheartedness drew down upon him the ridicule of his companions. He was proud and ambitious, and valued the good opinion of others, as all children do. Thenceforward he made it his study to conceal all the outward manifestations of what he regarded as a dishonorable weakness. He attained his aim, but his victory cost him dear. He succeeded in hiding the emotions of his feeling heart from others, but, by shutting them up in his own breast, he made them a thousand times more painful. In society he acquired the lamentable reputation of being unfeeling and careless, and in solitude his restless imagination created torments for him which were the more unbearable because he would confide them to no one." It is impossible to ignore the direct self-portraiture in this character sketch, though the coloring is too somber.

—*from* Main Currents in Nineteenth Century Literature, Vol. 5, *by George Morris Cohen Brandes*

Mateo Falcone

Coming out of Porto-Vecchio, and turning northwest toward the center of the island, the ground is seen to rise very rapidly, and, after three hours' walk by tortuous paths, blocked by large boulders of rocks, and sometimes cut by ravines, the traveller finds himself on the edge of a very broad *mâquis*, or open plateau. These plateaus are the home of the Corsican shepherds, and the resort of those who have come in conflict with the law. The Corsican peasant sets fire to a certain stretch of forest to spare himself the trouble of manuring his lands: so much the worse if the flames spread further than is needed. Whatever happens, he is sure to have a good harvest by sowing upon this ground, fertilized by the ashes of the trees which grew on it. When the corn is gathered, they leave the straw because it is too much trouble to gather. The roots, which remain in the earth without being consumed, sprout, in the following spring, into very thick shoots, which, in a few years, reach to a height of seven or eight feet. It is this kind of underwood which is called *mâquis*. It is composed of different kinds of trees and shrubs mixed up and entangled as in a wild state of nature. It is only with hatchet in hand that man can open a way through, and there are *mâquis* so dense and so thick that not even the wild sheep can penetrate them.

If you have killed a man, go into the *mâquis* of Porto-Vecchio, with a good gun and powder and shot, and you will live there in safety. Do not forget to take a brown cloak, furnished with a hood, which will serve as a coverlet and mattress. The shepherds will give you milk, cheese, chestnuts, and you will have nothing to fear from the hand of the law, nor from the relatives of the dead, except when you go down into the town to renew your stock of ammunition.

When I was in Corsica in 18— Mateo Falcone's house was half a league from this *mâquis*. He was a comparatively rich man for that country, living handsomely, that is to say, without doing anything, from the produce of his herds, which the shepherds, a sort of nomadic people, led to pasture here and there over the mountains. When I saw him, two years after the event that I am about to tell, he seemed about fifty years of age at the most. Imagine a small, but robust man, with jet-black, curly hair, an aquiline nose, thin lips, large and piercing eyes, and a deeply tanned complexion. His skill in shooting passed for extraordinary, even in his country, where there are so many crack shots. For example, Mateo would never fire on a sheep with swanshot, but, at one hundred and twenty paces, he would strike it with a bullet in its head or shoulders as he chose. He could use his gun at night as easily as by day, and I was told the following example of his adroitness, which will seem almost incredible to those who have not travelled in Corsica. A lighted candle was placed behind a transparent piece of paper, as large as a plate, at eighty paces off. He put himself into position, then the candle was extinguished, and in a minute's time, in complete darkness, he shot and pierced the paper three times out of four.

With this conspicuous talent Mateo Falcone had earned a great reputation. He was said to be a loyal friend, but a dangerous enemy; in other respects he was obliging and gave alms, and he lived at peace with everybody in the district of Porto-Vecchio. But it is told of him that when at Corte, where he had found his wife, he had very quickly freed himself of a rival reputed to be equally formidable in love as in war; at any rate, people attributed to Mateo a certain gunshot which surprised his rival while in the act of shaving before a small mirror hung in his window. After the affair had been hushed up, Mateo married. His wife Giuseppa at first presented him with three daughters, which enraged him, but finally a son came whom he named Fortunato; he was the hope of the family, the inheritor of its name. The girls were well married; their father could reckon in case of need upon the poniards and rifles of his sons-in-law. The son was only ten years old, but he had already shown signs of a promising disposition.

One autumn day Mateo and his wife set out early to visit one of their flocks in a clearing of the *mâquis*. Little Fortunato wanted to go with them, but the clearing was too far off; besides, it was necessary that someone should stay and mind the house; so his father refused. We shall soon see that he had occasion to repent of this.

He had been gone several hours and little Fortunato was quietly lying out in the sunshine, looking at the blue mountains, and thinking that on the following Sunday he would be going to town to have dinner at his uncle's the corporal, when his meditations were suddenly interrupted by the firing of a gun. He got up and turned toward that side of the plain from which the sound had proceeded. Other shots followed, fired at irregular intervals, and each time they came nearer and nearer until he saw a man on the path which led from the plain to Mateo's house. He wore a pointed cap like a mountaineer, he was bearded, and clothed in rags, and he dragged himself along with difficulty, leaning on his gun. He had just received a gunshot in the thigh.

This man was a *bandit* (Corsican for one who is proscribed) who, having set out at night to get some powder from the town, had fallen on the way into an ambush of Corsican soldiers. After a vigorous defense he had succeeded in escaping, but they gave chase hotly, firing at him from rock to rock. He was only a little in advance of the soldiers, and his wound made it out of the question for him to reach the *mâquis* before being overtaken.

He came up to Fortunato and said —

"Are you the son of Mateo Falcone?"

"Yes."

"I am Gianetto Sanpiero. I am pursued by the yellow-collars. Hide me, for I can not go any further."

"But what will my father say if I hide you without his permission?"

"He will say that you did right."

"How do you know?"

"Hide me quickly; they are coming."

"Wait till my father returns."

"Good Lord! how can I wait? They will be here in five minutes. Come, hide me, or I will kill you."

Fortunato replied with the utmost coolness —

"Your gun is unloaded, and there are no more cartridges in your *carchera*."

"I have my stiletto."

"But could you run as fast as I can?"

With a bound he put himself out of reach.

"You are no son of Mateo Falcone! Will you let me be taken in front of his house?"

The child seemed moved.

"What will you give me if I hide you?" he said, drawing nearer.

The bandit felt in the leather pocket that hung from his side and took out a five-franc piece, which he had put aside, no doubt, for powder. Fortunato smiled at the sight of the piece of silver, and, seizing hold of it, he said to Gianetto —

"Don't be afraid."

He quickly made a large hole in a haystack which stood close by the house. Gianetto crouched down in it, and the child covered him up so as to leave a little breathing space, and yet in such a way as to make it impossible for anyone to suspect that the hay concealed a man. He acted, further, with the ingenious cunning of the savage. He fetched a cat and her kittens and put them on the top of the haystack to make believe that it had not been touched for a long time. Then he carefully covered over with dust the blood stains which he had noticed on the path near the house, and, this done, he lay down again in the sun with the utmost sangfroid.

Some minutes later six men with brown uniform with yellow collars, commanded by an adjutant, stood before Mateo's door. This adjutant, was a distant relative of the Falcones. (It is said that further degrees of relationship are recognized in Corsica than anywhere else.) His name was Tiodoro Gamba; he was an energetic man, greatly feared by the banditti, and had already hunted out many of them.

"Good day, youngster," he said, coming up to Fortunato. "How you have grown! Did you see a man pass just now?"

"Oh, I am not yet so tall as you, cousin," the child replied, with a foolish look.

"You soon will be. But, tell me, have you not seen a man pass by?"

"Have I seen a man pass by?"

"Yes, a man with a pointed black velvet cap and a waistcoat embroidered in red and yellow."

"A man with a pointed cap and a waistcoat embroidered in scarlet and yellow?"

"Yes; answer sharply and don't repeat my questions."

"The priest passed our door this morning on his horse Piero. He asked me how papa was, and I replied—"

"You are making game of me, you rascal. Tell me at once which way Gianetto went, for it is he we are after; I am certain he took this path."

"How do you know that?"

"How do I know that? I know you have seen him."

"How can one see passers-by when one is asleep?"

"You were not asleep, you little demon; the gunshots would wake you."

"You think, then, cousin, that your guns make noise enough? My father's rifle makes much more noise."

"May the devil take you, you young scamp. I am absolutely certain you have seen Gianetto. Perhaps you have even hidden him. Here, you fellows, go into the house, and see if our man is not there. He could only walk on one foot, and he has too much common sense, the villain, to have tried to reach the *mâquis* limping. Besides, the traces of blood stop here."

"Whatever will papa say?" Fortunato asked, with a chuckle. "What will he say when he finds out that his house has been searched during his absence?"

"Do you know that I can make you change your tune, you scamp?" cried the adjutant Gamba, seizing him by the ear. "Perhaps you will speak when you have had a thrashing with the flat of a sword."

Fortunato kept on laughing derisively.

"My father is Mateo Falcone," he said significantly.

"Do you know, you young scamp, that I can take you away to Corte or to Bastia? I shall put you in a dungeon, on a bed of straw, with your feet in irons, and I shall guillotine you if you do not tell me where Gianetto Sanpiero is."

The child burst out laughing at this ridiculous menace.

"My father is Mateo Falcone," he repeated.

"Adjutant, do not let us embroil ourselves with Mateo," one of the soldiers whispered.

Gamba was evidently embarrassed. He talked in a low voice with his soldiers, who had already been all over the house. It was not a lengthy operation, for a Corsican hut only consists of a single square room. The furniture comprises a table, benches, boxes and utensils for cooking and hunting. All this time little Fortunato caressed his cat, and seemed, maliciously, to enjoy the confusion of his cousin and the soldiers.

One soldier came up to the haycock. He looked at the cat and carelessly stirred the hay with his bayonet, shrugging his shoulders as though he thought the precaution ridiculous. Nothing moved, and the face of the child did not betray the least agitation.

The adjutant and his band were in despair; they looked solemnly out over the plain, half inclined to return the way they had come; but their chief, convinced that threats would produce no effect upon the son of Falcone, thought he would make one last effort by trying the effect of favors and presents.

"My boy," he said, "you are a wide-awake young dog, I can see. You will get on. But you play a dangerous game with me; and, if I did not want to give pain to my cousin Mateo, devil take it! I would carry you off with me."

"Bah!"

"But, when my cousin returns I shall tell him all about it, and he will give you the whip till he draws blood for having told me lies."

"How do you know that?"

"You will see. But, look here, be a good lad and I will give you something."

"You had better go and look for Gianetto in the *mâquis*, cousin, for if you stay any longer it will take a cleverer fellow than you to catch him."

The adjutant drew a watch out of his pocket, a silver watch worth quite ten crowns. He watched how little Fortunato's eyes sparkled as he looked at it, and he held out the watch at the end of its steel chain.

"You rogue," he said, "you would like to have such a watch as this hung round your neck, and to go and walk up and down the streets of Porto-Vecchio as proud as a peacock; people would ask you the time, and you would reply, 'Look at my watch!'"

"When I am grown up, my uncle the corporal will give me a watch."

"Yes; but your uncle's son has one already—not such a fine one as this, however—for he is younger than you."

The boy sighed.

"Well, would you like this watch, kiddy?"

Fortunato ogled the watch out of the corner of his eyes, just as a cat does when a whole chicken is given to it. It dares not pounce upon the prey, because it is afraid a joke is being played on it, but it turns its eyes away now and then, to avoid succumbing to the temptation, licking its lips all the time as though to say to its master, "What a cruel joke you are playing on me!"

The adjutant Gamba, however, seemed really willing to give the watch. Fortunato did not hold out his hand; but he said to him with a bitter smile—

"Why do you make fun of me?"

"I swear I am not joking. Only tell me where Gianetto is, and this watch is yours."

Fortunato smiled incredulously, and fixed his black eyes on those of the adjutant. He tried to find in them the faith he would fain have in his words.

"May I lose my epaulettes," cried the adjutant, "if I do not give you the watch upon that condition! I call my men to witness, and then I can not retract."

As he spoke, he held the watch nearer and nearer until it almost touched the child's pale cheeks. His face plainly expressed the conflict going on in his mind between covetousness and the claims of hospitality. His bare breast heaved violently almost to suffocation. All the time the watch dangled and twisted and even hit the tip of his nose. By degrees he raised his right hand toward the watch, his finger ends touched it; and its whole weight rested on his palm although the adjutant still held the end of the chain loosely . . . . The watch face was blue . . . . The case was newly polished . . . . It seemed blazing in the sun like fire . . . . The temptation was too strong.

Fortunato raised his left hand at the same time, and pointed with his thumb over his shoulder to the haycock against which he was leaning. The adjutant understood him immediately, and let go the end of the chain. Fortunato felt himself sole possessor of the watch. He jumped up with the agility of a deer, and stood ten paces distant from the haycock, which the soldiers at once began to upset.

It was not long before they saw the hay move, and a bleeding man came out, poniard in hand; when, however, he tried to rise to his feet his stiffening wound prevented him from standing. He fell down. The adjutant threw himself upon him and snatched away his dagger. He was speedily and strongly bound, in spite of his resistance.

Gianetto was bound and laid on the ground like a bundle of fagots. He turned his head toward Fortunato, who had come up to him.

"Son of—," he said to him more in contempt than in anger.

The boy threw to him the silver piece that he had received from him, feeling conscious that he no longer deserved it; but the outlaw took no notice of the action. He merely said in a cool voice to the adjutant—

"My dear Gamba, I can not walk; you will be obliged to carry me to the town."

"You could run as fast as a kid just now," his captor retorted brutally. "But don't be anxious, I am glad enough to have caught you: I would carry you for a league on my own back and not feel tired. All the same, my friend, we will make a litter for you out of the branches and your cloak. The farm at Crespoli will provide us with horses."

"All right," said the prisoner, "I hope you will put a little straw on your litter to make it easier for me."

While the soldiers were busy, some making a rough stretcher out of chestnut boughs and others dressing Gianetto's wound, Mateo Falcone and his wife suddenly appeared in a turning of the path from the *mâquis*. The wife came in bending laboriously under the weight of a huge sack of chestnuts, while her husband jaunted up carrying his gun in one hand, and a second gun slung in his shoulder belt. It is considered undignified for a man to carry any other burden but his weapons.

When he saw the soldiers, Mateo's first thought was that they had come to arrest him. But he had no ground for this fear, he had never quarrelled with the law. On the contrary, he bore a good reputation. He was, as the saying is, particularly well thought of. But he was a Corsican, and mountain bred, and there are but few Corsican mountaineers who, if they search their memories sufficiently, can not recall some little peccadillo, some gunshot, or dagger thrust, or such-like bagatelle. Mateo's conscience was clearer than most, for it was fully ten years since he had pointed his gun at any man; yet at the same time he was cautious, and he prepared to make a brave defense if needs be.

"Wife, put down your sack," he said, "and keep yourself in readiness."

She obeyed immediately. He gave her the gun which was slung over his shoulder, as it was likely to be the one that would inconvenience him the most. He held the other gun in readiness, and proceeded leisurely toward the house by the side of the trees which bordered the path, ready to throw himself behind the largest trunk for cover, and to fire at the least sign of hostility. His wife walked close behind him holding her reloaded gun and her cartridges. It was the duty of a good housewife, in case of a conflict, to reload her husband's arms.

On his side, the adjutant was very uneasy at the sight of Mateo advancing thus upon them with measured steps, his gun pointed and finger on trigger.

"If it happens that Gianetto is related to Mateo," thought he, "or he is his friend, and he means to protect him, two of his bullets will be put into two of us as sure as a letter goes to the post, and he will aim at me in spite of our kinship! ..."

In this perplexity, he put on a bold face and went forward alone toward Mateo to tell him what had happened, greeting him like an old acquaintance. But the brief interval which separated him from Mateo seemed to him of terribly long duration.

"Hullo! Ah! my old comrade," he called out. "How are you, old fellow? I am your cousin Gamba."

Mateo did not say a word, but stood still; and while the other was speaking, he softly raised the muzzle of his rifle in such a manner that by the time the adjutant came up to him it was pointing skyward.

"Good day, brother," said the adjutant, holding out his hand. "It is a very long time since I saw you."

"Good day, brother."

"I just called in when passing to say 'good day' to you and cousin Pepa. We have done a long tramp today; but we must not complain of fatigue, for we have taken a fine catch. We have got hold of Gianetto Sanpiero."

"Thank Heaven!" exclaimed Giuseppa. "He stole one of our milch goats last week."

Gamba rejoiced at these words.

"Poor devil!" said Mateo, "he was hungry."

"The fellow fought like lion," continued the adjutant, slightly nettled. "He killed one of the men, and, not content to stop there he broke Corporal Chardon's arm; but that is not of much consequence, for he is only a Frenchman . . . Then he hid himself so cleverly that the devil could not have found him. If it had not been for my little cousin Fortunato, I should never have discovered him."

"Fortunato?" cried Mateo.

"Fortunato?" repeated Giuseppa.

"Yes; Gianetto was concealed in your haycock there, but my little cousin showed me his trick. I will speak of him to his uncle the corporal, who will send him a nice present as a reward. And both his name and yours will be in the report which I shall send to the superintendent."

"Curse you!" cried Mateo under his breath.

By this time they had rejoined the company. Gianetto was already laid on his litter, and they were ready to set out. When he saw Mateo in Gamba's company he smiled a strange smile; then, turning toward the door of the house, he spat on the threshold.

"It is the house of a traitor!" he exclaimed.

No man but one willing to die would have dared to utter the word "traitor" in connection with Falcone. A quick stroke from a dagger, without need for a second, would have immediately wiped out the insult. But Mateo made no other movement beyond putting his hand to his head like a dazed man.

Fortunato went into the house when he saw his father come up. He reappeared shortly carrying a jug of milk, which he offered with downcast eyes to Gianetto.

"Keep off me!" roared the outlaw.

Then, turning to one of the soldiers, he said —

"Comrade, give me a drink of water."

The soldier placed the flask in his hands, and the bandit drank the water given him by a man with whom he had but now exchanged gunshots. He then asked that his hands might be tied crossed over his breast instead of behind his back.

"I prefer," he said, "to lie down comfortably."

They granted him his request. Then, at a sign from the adjutant, they set out, first bidding adieu to Mateo, who answered never a word, and descended at a quick pace toward the plain.

Well-nigh ten minutes elapsed before Mateo opened his mouth. The child looked uneasily first at his mother, then at his father, who leant on his gun, looking at him with an expression of concentrated anger.

"Well, you have made a pretty beginning," said Mateo at last in a voice calm, but terrifying, to those who knew the man.

"Father," the boy cried out, with tears in his eyes, just ready to fall at his knees.

"Out of my sight!" shouted Mateo.

The child stopped motionless a few steps off his father, and began to sob.

Giuseppa came near him. She had just seen the end of the watch chain hanging from out his shirt.

"Who gave you that watch?" she asked severely.

"My cousin the adjutant."

Falcone seized the watch, and threw it against a stone with such force that it broke into a thousand pieces.

"Woman," he said, "is this my child?"

Giuseppa's brown cheeks flamed brick red.

"What are you saying, Mateo? Do you know to whom you are speaking?"

"Yes, very well. This child is the first traitor of his race."

Fortunato's sobs and hiccoughs redoubled, and Falcone kept his lynx eyes steadily fixed on him. At length he struck the ground with the butt end of his gun; then he flung it across his shoulder, retook the way to the *mâquis*, and ordered Fortunato to follow him. The child obeyed.

Giuseppa ran after Mateo, and seized him by the arm.

"He is your son," she said in a trembling voice, fixing her black eyes on those of her husband, as though to read all that was passing in his mind.

"Leave go," replied Mateo; "I am his father."

Giuseppa kissed her son, and went back crying into the hut. She threw herself on her knees before an image of the Virgin, and prayed fervently. When Falcone had walked about two hundred yards along the path he stopped at a little ravine and went down into it. He sounded the ground with the butt end of his gun, and found it soft and easy to dig. The spot seemed suitable to his purpose.

"Fortunato go near to that large rock."
The boy did as he was told, then knelt down.
"Father, father, do not kill me!"
"Say your prayers!" repeated Mateo in a terrible voice.
The child repeated the Lord's Prayer and the Creed, stammering and sobbing. The father said "Amen!" in a firm voice at the close of each prayer.
"Are those all the prayers you know?"
"I know also the Ave Maria and Litany, that my aunt taught me, father."
"It is long, but never mind."
The child finished the Litany in a faint voice.
"Have you finished?"
"Oh, father, forgive me! forgive me! I will never do it again. I will beg my cousin the corporal with all my might to pardon Gianetto!"
He went on imploring. Mateo loaded his rifle and took aim.
"May God forgive you!" he said.
The boy made a frantic effort to get up and clasp his father's knees, but he had no time. Mateo fired, and Fortunato fell stone dead.

Without throwing a single glance at the body, Mateo went back to his house to fetch a spade with which to bury his son. He had only returned a little way along the path when he met Giuseppa, who had run out alarmed by the sound of firing.

"What have you done?" she cried.
"Justice!"
"Where is he?"
"In the ravine; I am going to bury him. He died a Christian. I shall have a mass sung for him. Let someone tell my son-in-law Tiodoro Bianchi to come and live with us."

The Pearl of Toledo

Who can tell me when the sun is most beautiful, at rising, or at setting? Who can tell me whether of the Olive or the Almond is the most beautiful of trees? Who can tell me whether Andalusia or Valencia sends forth the bravest knight? What man can tell me who is the fairest of women? I will tell you who is the fairest of women. She is Aurora de Vargas, the Pearl of Toledo.

The Pearl of Toledo

Swarthy Tuzani has called for his lance, he has called for his buckler; his lance he grasps in his strong right hand; his buckler hangs from his neck. He goes down to his stable, and considers well his forty good steeds; in due order he considers them all, and he says:

"Berja is the fleetest and trustiest of all. On her strong back will I carry away the Pearl of Toledo, as mine will I bear her away, or by Allah, Cordova shall see me no more."

So he sets forth and he rides on his way, till at length he reaches Toledo, and he meets an old man hard by Zucatin.

"Old man, with the snowy beard, carry this letter to Don Guttiera, to Don Guttiera de Saldaña. If he is a man he will come and meet me in single combat, near to the fountain of Almami. The Pearl of Toledo must belong to one of us two."

The old man has taken the letter, he has taken and carried it to the Count de Saldaña, as he sat playing chess with the Pearl of Toledo. The Count has read the letter, he has read the parchment, and with his closed fist does he smite the table so mightily that all the chessmen have fallen to the ground. Then he rises and calls for his lance and his good steed, and all trembling does the Pearl of Toledo arise, for she has perceived and understood that he is going forth to combat.

"My Lord Guttiera de Saldaña, go not hence I pray, go not hence, but play still this game with me."

"No longer will I play at chess; I will play at the game of lances by the fountain of Almami."

And the tears of Aurora availed not to stay him; for naught stays a knight who goes forth to combat. Then the Pearl of Toledo took her mantle, and mounting upon her mule she went her way to the fountain of Almami.

All about the fountain is the grass crimson, crimson too the waters of the fountain; but it is not the blood of a Christian that stains the green sward, that stains the waters of the fountain. The swarthy Tuzani lies there with his face to the sky. The lance of Don Guttiera is splintered in his breast: all his life blood spends itself drop by drop. His faithful steed, Berja, looks down upon him weeping, for she can not heal the wound of her master.

The Pearl of Toledo alights from her mule. "Take heart, good sir, for you will live yet to wed some fair Moorish maiden; my hand has cunning to heal the wound made by my knight."

"O Pearl so white, O Pearl so fair, draw forth from my breast the splinter of lance which rends it. The cold of the steel chills me and freezes my heart."

In all confidence she approached him, but he, with a last effort, gathered together his failing strength, and with his saber's sharp blade, gashed the face so fair, so tender.

The Game of Backgammon

The sails hung motionless, clinging to the masts; the sea was as smooth as glass; the heat was stifling and the calm discouraging.

During a sea voyage the resources of amusement open to passengers on board ship are soon exhausted. Anyone who has spent four months together in a wooden house of one hundred and twenty feet in length knows this fact, alas! only too well. When you see the first lieutenant coming toward you you know that he will first begin talking about Rio de Janeiro, from whence he came; then of the famous Essling Bridge, which he saw made by the Marine Guards to which he belonged. After the fifteenth day you know exactly the expressions he is fond of, even the punctuation of his sentences and the different intonations of his voice. When did he ever miss dwelling sadly on the word "emperor" when he pronounced it for the first time in his recital? ... He invariably added, "If you had only seen him then!!!" (three exclamation marks to denote his admiration). And the incident of the trumpeter's horse, and the ball that rebounded and carried away a cartridge box which contained seven thousand five hundred francs in money and jewelry, etc., etc.! The second lieutenant is a great politician; he makes critical remarks every day on the last number of the *Constitutionnel* which he brought from Brest, or, if he leaves the sublime heights of politics to descend to literature, he sets you to rights on the last vaudeville he saw played. Good Lord! The Commissioner of the Navy has a very interesting story to relate. How he enchanted us the first time he told us his escape from the pontoon at Cadiz, but, by the twentieth repetition, upon my word, it is barely endurable! ...

And the ensigns and the midshipmen! ... The recollection of their conversation makes my hair stand on end. Generally speaking, the captain is the least tedious person on board. In his position of despotic commander he is in a state of secret hostility against the whole staff; he annoys and oppresses at times, but there is a certain amount of pleasure to be gained by inveighing against him. If he is furiously angry with some of his subordinates, his superior tone is a pleasure to listen to, which is some slight consolation.

On board the vessel on which I was sailing the officers were the best fellows going, all good company, liking each other as brothers, but bored of each other all the same. The captain was the gentlest of men, and, what is very rare, was nothing of a busybody. He was always unwilling to exercise his authoritative power. But, in spite of all, the voyage seemed terribly long, especially when the calm set in which overtook us a few days only before we made land! . . .

One day, after dinner, which want of employment had made us spin out as long as it was humanly possible, we were all assembled on the bridge, watching the monotonous but ever majestic spectacle of a sunset over the sea. Some were smoking, others were re-reading for the twentieth time one of the thirty volumes which comprised our wretched library; all were yawning till the tears ran down their cheeks. One ensign, who was sitting by me, was amusing himself, with the gravity worthy of a serious occupation, by letting the poniard, worn ordinarily by naval officers in undress, fall, point downward, on the planks of the deck. It was as amusing as anything else on board, and required skill to throw the point so that it should stick in the wood quite perpendicularly. I wanted to follow the ensign's example, and, not having a poniard with me, I tried to borrow the captain's, but he refused it me. He was singularly attached to that weapon, and it would have vexed him to see it put to such a futile use. It had formerly belonged to a brave officer who had been mortally wounded in the last war. I guessed a story would be forthcoming, nor was I mistaken. The captain began before he was asked for it, but the officers, who stood round us, and who knew the misfortunes of Lieutenant Roger by heart, soon beat a circumspect retreat. Here is the captain's story almost in his own words:

Roger was three years older than I when I first knew him; he was a lieutenant and I was an ensign. He was quite one of the best officers on our staff; he was, moreover, goodnatured, talented, quick and well educated; in a word, he was a fascinating young fellow. But unfortunately he was rather proud and sensitive; this arose, I think, from the fact of his being an illegitimate child, and his fear that his birth might make people look down upon him; but, to tell the truth, the greatest of all his faults was a passionate and ever-present desire to take the lead wherever he was. His father, whom he had never seen, made him an allowance which would have been more than enough for his needs, had he not been the soul of generosity. All that he had was at the service of his friends. When he drew his quarter's pay, and met a friend with a sad and anxious face, he would say—

"Why, mate, what's the matter? You look as though you had difficulty in making your pockets jingle when you slap them; come, here is my purse, take what you want, and have dinner with me."

A very pretty young actress came to Brest named Gabrielle, and she quickly made conquest among the naval and army officers. She was not a perfect beauty, but she had a good figure, fine eyes, a small foot and a pleasant, saucy manner; these things are all very delightful when one is voyaging between the latitudes of twenty and twenty-five years of age. She was, in addition, the most capricious of her sex, and her style of playing did not belie this reputation. Sometimes she played enchantingly, and one would have called her a *comédienne* of the highest order; on the following day she would be cold and lifeless in the very same piece: she would deliver her part as a child recites its catechism. But more than all else it was the story told of her which I am about to relate that interested our young men. It seems she had been kept in sumptuous style by a Parisian senator, who, it was said, committed all sorts of follies for her sake. One day this man put his hat on in her house; she begged him to take it off, and even complained that he showed a want of respect toward her. The senator burst out laughing, shrugged his shoulders and said, as he elaborately settled himself in his chair, "The least I can do is to make myself at home in the house of a girl whom I keep." Gabrielle's white hand smacked his face as soundly as though she had a navy's hand, and she also paid him back for his words by throwing his hat to the other end of the room. From that moment there was a complete rupture between them. Bankers and generals made considerable offers to the lady, but she refused them all and became an actress, so that she could, as she expressed it, live independently.

When Roger saw her and learnt her history, he decided that she was—must be his, and with the somewhat uncouth freedom with which we sailors are credited, he took the following methods to show her how much he was affected by her charms. He bought the rarest and loveliest flowers to be found in Brest, had them made into a bouquet which he tied with a beautiful rose-colored ribbon, and in the knot he carefully placed a roll of twenty-five napoleons, all he possessed for the time being. I remember accompanying him behind the scenes during an interval between the acts. He paid Gabrielle a brief compliment upon the grace with which she wore her costume, offered her the bouquet and asked leave to call upon her. He managed to get through all this in about three words.

Whilst Gabrielle only saw the flowers and the handsome youth who offered them to her, she smiled upon him, accompanying her smile with a most gracious bow; but when she held the bouquet between her hands and felt the weight of the gold, her face changed more rapidly than the surface of the sea when roused by a tropical hurricane; and certainly it could scarcely have looked more evil, for she hurled the bouquet and the napoleons with all her strength at my poor friend's head, so that he carried the marks of it on his face for more than a week after. The manager's bell rang and Gabrielle went on and played wildly.

Covered with confusion, Roger picked up his bouquet and packet of gold, went to a café, offered the bouquet (but not the money) to the girl at the desk, and tried to forget his cruel mistress in a glass of punch. But he did not succeed, and, in spite of his vexation at not being able to show himself without a black eye, he fell madly in love with the enraged Gabrielle. He wrote her twenty letters a day, and such letters!—abject, tender, full of obsequious phrases that might have been addressed to a princess. The first were returned to him unopened, and the rest received no answer. Roger, however, kept up hope, until he discovered that the theater orange-seller wrapped up his oranges in Roger's love-letters, which Gabrielle, with the very refinement of maliciousness, had given him. This was a terrible blow to our friend's pride; but his passion did not die out. He talked of asking the actress to marry him, and threatened to blow his brains out when we told him that the Minister for Marine Affairs would never give his consent.

While all this was going on the officers of a regiment of the line in the garrison at Brest wished to make Gabrielle repeat a vaudeville couplet, and she refused the encore out of pure caprice. The officers and the actress both remained so obstinate that it came to the former hooting until the curtain had to be dropped and the latter left the stage. You know what the pit of a garrison town is like. The officers plotted together to hiss her without intermission the next day and for a few days after, and not allow her to play a single part unless she made humble amends for her bad behavior. Roger had taken no part in these proceedings; but he heard of the scandal which put the whole theater in an uproar that very night, and also the plans for revenge which were being hatched for the morrow. He immediately made up his mind what he would do.

When Gabrielle made her appearance the next night an ear-splitting noise of hooting and catcalls rose from the officers' seats. Roger, who had purposely placed himself near the roisterers, got up and harangued the noisiest in such scathing language that the whole of their fury was soon turned on himself. He then drew his notebook from his pocket, and, with the utmost *sangfroid*, wrote down the names cried out to him from all sides; he would have arranged to fight with the whole regiment if a great many naval officers had not come up, out of loyalty to their order, and taken part against his adversaries. The hubbub was something frightful.

The whole garrison was confined for several days, but when we regained liberty, there was a terrible score to settle. There were threescore of us at the rendezvous. Roger, alone, fought three officers in succession; he killed one, and badly wounded the other two without receiving a scratch. I, as luck would have it, came off less fortunately; a cursed lieutenant, who had been a fencing master, gave me a neat thrust through the chest which nearly finished me. The duel, or rather battle, was a fine sight, I can tell you. The naval officers had gained the victory, and the regiment was obliged to leave Brest.

You may guess that our superior officers did not overlook the author of the quarrel. They placed a guard outside his door for a fortnight.

When his term of arrest was over I came out of hospital and went to see him. Judge my surprise when I entered his room and found him sitting at breakfast *tête-à-tête* with Gabrielle. They seemed to have been on friendly terms for some time, and already called each other thee and thou, and drank out of the same glass. Roger introduced me to his mistress as his dearest friend, and told her I had been wounded in the slight skirmish on her behalf. This charming young girl then condescended to kiss me, for all her sympathies were with fighters.

They spent three months together in perfect happiness, and never left each other for a moment. Gabrielle seemed to love him to distraction, and Roger declared that he had never known love before he met Gabrielle.

One day a Dutch frigate came into harbour. The officers gave us a dinner, and we drank deeply of all sorts of wines; but when the cloth was removed, we did not know what to do, for these gentlemen spoke very bad French. We began to play. The Dutchmen seemed to have plenty of money; and their first lieutenant especially offered to play such high stakes that none of us cared to take a hand with him. But Roger, who did not play as a rule, felt it incumbent upon him to uphold the honor of his country in the matter. So he played for the stakes that the Dutch lieutenant fixed. At first he gained, then he lost, and after several ups and downs of gaining and losing they stopped without anything having been done on either side. We returned this dinner, and invited the Dutch officers. Again we played, and Roger and the lieutenant set to work afresh. In short, they played for several days, meeting either in cafés or on board ship; they tried all kinds of games, backgammon more than any, always increasing their wagers until they came to the point of playing for twenty-five napoleons each game. It was an enormous sum for poverty-stricken officers like us—more than two months' pay! At the week's end Roger had lost every penny he possessed, and more than three or four thousand francs which he had borrowed on all sides.

You will gather that Roger and Gabrielle had ended by sharing household and purse in common, that is to say that Roger, who had just received a large payment on account of his allowance, contributed ten or twenty times more than the actress. He always considered that this sum, large as was his share in it, belonged chiefly to his mistress, and he had only kept back for his own expenses about fifty napoleons. He was, however, obliged to draw from this reserve to go on playing, and Gabrielle did not make the slightest objection.

The housekeeping money went the same way as his pocket money. Very soon Roger was reduced to playing his last twenty-five napoleons. The game was long and hotly contested, and it was horrible to see the intense efforts Roger made to gain it. The moment came when Roger, who held the dice-box, had only one more chance left to win; I think he wanted to get six, four. The night was far advanced, and an officer who had been looking at their play had fallen asleep in an armchair. The Dutchman was tired out and drowsy; moreover, he had drunk too much punch. Roger alone was wide awake and a prey to the depths of despair. He trembled as he threw the dice. He threw them so roughly upon the board that the shock knocked a candle over on to the floor. The Dutchman turned his head first toward the candle, which had covered his new trousers with wax, then he looked at the dice. They showed six and four. Roger, who was as pale as death, received his twenty-five napoleons, and they went on playing. Chance again favored my unlucky friend, who, however, made blunder upon blunder, and secured points as though he wanted to lose. The Dutch lieutenant lost his head, and doubled and quadrupled his stakes; he lost every time. I can see him now—a tall, fair man of a phlegmatic nature, whose face seemed made of wax. At last he got up, after he lost forty thousand francs, and paid it without his features betraying the least trace of emotion.

"We will not take into account what we have played for tonight," said Roger. "You were more than half asleep. I do not want your money."

"You are joking," replied the phlegmatic Dutchman; "I played well, but the dice were against me. I am quite capable of winning off you always. Good evening!"

And he went out.

We learnt next day that, made desperate by his losses, he had blown out his brains in his room, after drinking a bowl of punch.

The forty thousand francs that Roger had won from him were spread out on the table, and Gabrielle gazed at them with a smile of satisfaction.

"See how rich we are!" she said. "What shall we do with all this money?"

Roger did not answer her; he seemed stunned since the Dutchman's death.

"We can do a thousand delicious things," she went on. "Money gained so easily ought to be spent as lightly. Let us set up a carriage, and snap our fingers at the Maritime Prefect and his wife. I want some diamonds and some Cashmere shawls. Ask for a holiday, and let us go to Paris; we could never spend so much money here!"

She stopped to look at Roger, whose eyes were fixed on the ceiling; his head was leant on his hand, and he had not heard a word; he seemed to be a prey to the most miserable thoughts.

"What on earth's wrong with you, Roger?" she cried, leaning her hand on his shoulder. "You will make me pull faces at you presently. I can not get a word out of you."

"I am very unhappy," he said at length, with a smothered sigh.

"Unhappy! Why, I do believe you regret having pinked that big *mynheer*."

He raised his head and looked at her with haggard eyes.

"What does it matter?" she went on. "Why mind if he did take the thing tragically and blew out his few brains? I don't pity losing players; and his money is better in our hands than in his. He would have wasted it in drinking and smoking, whilst we will do a thousand lovely things with it, each one nicer than the last."

Roger walked about the room with his head bent on his breast, his eyes half closed and filled with tears. "You would have been sorry for him if you had seen him."

"Don't you know," said Gabrielle to him, "that people who do not know how romantically sensitive you are might imagine you had been cheating?"

"And if it were the truth?" he cried in hollow tones, stopping before her.

"Bah!" she answered, smiling; "you are not clever enough to cheat at play."

"Yes, I cheated, Gabrielle; I cheated—wretch that I am!"

She understood from his agitation of mind that he spoke but too truly. She sat down on a couch and remained speechless for some time.

"I would much rather you had killed ten men than cheated at play," she said at length in a very troubled voice.

There was a deathlike silence for half an hour. They both sat on the same sofa, and never looked at each other once. Roger got up first and wished her good night in a calm voice.

"Good night," she replied in cold and hard tones.

Roger has since told me that he would have killed himself that very day if he had not been afraid that his comrades would have guessed the reason for his suicide. He did not wish his memory to be disgraced.

Gabrielle was as gay as usual next day. She seemed, already, to have forgotten the confidences of the previous evening. But Roger became gloomy, capricious and morose. He avoided his friends, and scarcely left his rooms, often passing a whole day without saying a word to his mistress. I attributed his melancholy to an honorable, but excessive sensitiveness, and tried several times to console him; but he put me at a distance by affecting a supreme indifference toward his unhappy partner. One day he even inveighed against the Dutch nation in violent terms, and tried to make me believe that there was not a single honorable man in Holland. All the same, he tried secretly to find out the Dutch lieutenant's relatives; but no one could give him any information about them.

Six weeks after that unlucky game of backgammon Roger found a note in Gabrielle's rooms, written by an admirer who thanked her for the kind feeling she had shown him. Gabrielle was the very personification of untidiness, and the note in question had been left by her on her mantelpiece. I do not know whether she was unfaithful to Roger or not, but he believed her to be so, and his anger was frightful. His love and a remnant of pride were the only feelings which still attached him to life, and the strongest of these sentiments was thus suddenly destroyed. He overwhelmed the proud actress with insults; and was so violent that I do not know how he refrained from striking her.

"No doubt," he said to her, "this puppy gave you lots of money. It is the only thing you love. You would give yourself to the dirtiest of our sailors if he had anything to pay you with."

"Why not?" retorted the actress icily. "Yes, I would take payment from a sailor; but *I should not have stolen it!*"

Roger uttered a cry of rage. He tremblingly drew his sword, and for one second looked at Gabrielle with the eyes of a madman; then he collected himself with a tremendous effort, threw the weapon at her feet, and rushed from the room to prevent himself yielding to the temptation which beset him.

That same evening I passed his lodging at a late hour, and, seeing his light burning, I went in to borrow a book. I found him busy, writing. He did not disturb himself, and scarcely seemed to notice my presence in his room. I sat down by his desk and studied his features; they were so much altered that anyone else but I would hardly have recognized him. All at once I noticed a letter already sealed on his desk, addressed to myself. I immediately opened it. In it Roger announced to me his intention to put an end to himself, and gave me various instructions to carry out. While I read this, he went on writing the whole time without noticing me. He was bidding farewell to Gabrielle. You can judge of my astonishment, and of what I felt bound to say to him. I was thunderstruck by his decision.

"What! you want to kill yourself when you are so happy?"

"My friend," he said, as he hid his letter, "you know nothing about it; you do not know me; I am a rascal; I am so guilty that a prostitute has power to insult me; and I am so aware of my baseness that I have no power to strike her."

He then related the story of the game of backgammon, and all that you already know. As I listened I was as moved as he was. I did not know what to say to him; with tears in my eyes I pressed his hands, but I could not speak. Then the idea came to me to try and show him that he need not reproach himself with having intentionally caused the ruin of the Dutchman, and that, after all, he had only made him lose, by his ... cheating ... twenty-five napoleons.

"Then," he cried, with bitter irony, "I am a petty thief and not a great one. I, who was so ambitious, to be nothing but a scurvy little scoundrel!"

He shrieked with laughter.

I burst into tears.

Suddenly the door opened and Gabrielle rushed into his arms.

"Forgive me!" she cried, strangling him almost in her passion; "forgive me! I know it now; I love only you; and I love you better now than if you had not done what you blame yourself for. If you like, I will steal; I have stolen before now . . . . Yes, I have stolen; I took a gold watch . . . . What worse could one do?"

Roger shook his head incredulously, but his face seemed to brighten.

"No, my poor child," he said, gently repulsing her. "I must kill myself; there is no other course for me. I suffer so greatly that I can not bear my grief."

"Very well, then, if you intend to die, Roger, I shall die with you. What is life to me without you? I have plenty of courage; I have fired pistols; I shall kill myself like anyone else. Besides, I have played at tragedy and am used to it." At first there were tears in her eyes, but this last idea amused her, and even Roger could not help smiling with her. "You are laughing, my soldier-boy," she cried, clapping her hands and hugging him; "you will not kill yourself."

All the time she embraced him she was first crying, then laughing, then swearing like a sailor; for she was not, like many women, afraid of a coarse word.

In the meantime I possessed myself of Roger's pistols and poniard; then I turned to him and said—

"My dear Roger, you have a mistress and a friend who love you. Believe me, there can still be happiness for you in this life." I embraced him and went out, leaving him alone with Gabrielle.

I do not believe we should have succeeded in doing more than delaying his fatal design if he had not received an order from the Admiralty to set out as first lieutenant on board a frigate bound for a cruise in the Indian seas—if it could first cross the lines of the English fleet, which blockaded the port. It was a dangerous venture. I put it to him that it would be much better to die nobly by an English bullet than to put an inglorious end to his life himself, without rendering any service to his country. So he promised to live. He distributed half the forty thousand francs to maimed sailors or the widows and orphans of seamen; the rest he gave to Gabrielle, who at first vowed to him only to use the money for charitable purposes. She fully meant to keep her word, poor girl! but enthusiasm with her was short-lived. I have heard since that she gave some thousands of francs to the poor, but she spent the remainder on finery.

Roger and I boarded the fine frigate *La Galatée*; our men were brave, experienced, and well-drilled, but our commander was an idiot, who thought himself a Jean Bart because he could swear better than an army captain, because he murdered French, and because he had never studied the theory of his profession, the practice of which he understood only very indifferently. However, fate favored us at the outset. We got well out of the roadstead—thanks to a gust of wind which compelled the blockading fleet to give us a wide berth— and we began our cruise by burning an English sloop and an East Indiaman off the coast of Portugal.

We were slowly sailing toward the Indian seas, hampered by contrary winds and our captain's bad handling of the ship, whose stupidity increased the danger of our cruise. Sometimes we were chased by superior forces, sometimes pursued by merchant vessels; we did not pass a single day without some fresh adventure. But neither the risky life he led nor the labors caused him by the irksome ship-duties devolving upon him could distract Roger from the sad thoughts which unceasingly haunted him. He who was once considered the most brilliant and active officer in our port now found it almost a burden to fulfil simply his duty. As soon as he was off duty he would shut himself in his cabin without either books or papers, and the unhappy man passed whole hours lying in his cot, for he could not sleep.

One day, noticing his depression, I ventured to say to him—

"Good gracious, my boy, you grieve over nothing! Granted you filched twenty-five napoleons from a big Dutchman, you show as much remorse as though you had taken more than a million. Now, tell me, when you loved the wife of the Prefect of . . . did you mind at all? Nevertheless, she was worth more than twenty-five napoleons."

He turned over on his mattress without a word.

"After all," I continued, "your crime, since you persist in calling it so, had an honorable motive and arose from a lofty mind."

He turned his head and looked at me furiously.

"Yes, for if you had lost what would have become of Gabrielle? She—poor girl!—would have sold her last garment for you . . . . If you had lost she would have been reduced to misery . . . . It was for her, out of love for her, you cheated. There are people who die for love ... will kill themselves for it .... You, my dear Roger, did more. For a man of our order it takes more courage to ... steal, to put it baldly, than to commit suicide."

("Now, perhaps," the captain interrupted his story to say, "I appear ridiculous to you. I assure you that my friendship for Roger endowed me with a timely eloquence that I am not equal to nowadays; and, devil take it, in saying what I did I spoke in good earnest, and I believed all I said. Ah, I was young then!")

Roger did not make any answer for a long time; then he held out his hand to me.

"My friend," he said, making a great effort over himself. "you think too well of me. I am a cowardly wretch. When I cheated the Dutchman my only thought was to win the twenty-five napoleons, that was all. I never thought of Gabrielle, and that is why I despise myself .... I, to hold my honor in less esteem than twenty-five napoleons! ... What baseness! Yes, I could be happy if I could tell myself I stole to keep Gabrielle from wretchedness .... No! ... no! I did not think of her .... I was not in love at that moment. ... I was a player .... I was a thief .... I stole money to possess it myself, ... and the deed has so degraded me, and debased me, that I now have no more courage left nor love .... I can see it; I do not think any longer of Gabrielle .... I am a broken-down man."

He was so wretched, that if he had asked me to hand him his pistols to kill himself I believe I should have given them to him.

One Friday, that day of ill omen, we discovered that a big English frigate, the *Alcestis*, was chasing us. She carried fifty-eight guns, and we but thirty-eight. We put on all sail to escape from her, but her pace was faster than ours, and she gained on us every minute. It was very evident that before night we should be obliged to engage in an unequal battle. Our captain called Roger to his cabin, where they consulted together for more than a quarter of an hour. Roger came up on the deck again, took me by the arm, and drew me aside.

"In two hours' time," he said, "we shall be engaged. That rash man who struts the quarter-deck has lost his wits. He has two courses to choose from: the first, and the most honorable, would be to let the enemy come up to us, then to board the ship determinedly with a hundred or so of our best men; the other course, which is not bad, but rather cowardly, is to lighten ourselves by throwing some of our guns overboard. Then we could make for the near coast of Africa, which we shall soon find to larboard. The English captain would soon be obliged to give up the chase, for fear of grounding;

but our . . . captain is neither coward nor hero. He will let himself be destroyed by gunshots a good distance off, and after some hours' fight he will honorably lower his flag. So much the worse for you. The Portsmouth pontoons will be your fate. I have no desire to see them."

"Possibly," I said, "our first shots will damage the enemy sufficiently to compel her to abandon the chase."

"Listen, I do not mean to be taken prisoner; I shall kill myself. It is time I ended it all. If by ill luck I am only wounded, give me your word of honor that you will throw me overboard. It is the proper deathbed for a good sailor."

"What nonsense!" I exclaimed. "What a charge to make me undertake!"

"You will be fulfilling the duty of a true friend. You know I shall have to die. I have only consented not to take my own life in the hope of being killed; you must remember that. Come, promise me this; if you refuse, I shall go and ask this service from the boatswain's mate, who will not refuse me."

After reflecting for some time, I said to him—

"I give you my word to do what you wish, provided that you are mortally wounded, with no hope of recovery. In that case I consent to spare you further suffering."

"I shall be mortally wounded or I shall be killed outright."

He held out his hand to me, and I shook it firmly. After that he was calmer, and even a kind of martial cheerfulness shone in his face. Toward three o'clock in the afternoon the enemy's guns began to play in our rigging. We then clewed up some of our sails, crossed the bows of the *Alcestis*, and started a rattling fire, which the English returned vigorously. After about an hour's fight out captain, who did nothing methodically, wanted to try to board the enemy; but we had already many dead and wounded, and the remainder of our crew had lost heart. Our rigging, besides, had suffered severely, and our masts were badly damaged. Just as we were taking in sail, to approach the English vessel, our large mast, which had nothing to stay it, fell with a horrible noise. The *Alcestis* took advantage of the confusion into which this accident threw us. She came broadside up to our stern and opened fire upon us within half a pistol range of us; she riddled shot through our unfortunate frigate fore and aft, and we were only in a position to point two small guns at her. At that moment I was standing near Roger, who was busy trying to cut the shrouds which still held the fallen mast. I felt my arm pressed forcibly; I turned round and saw him laid flat on the deck covered with blood. He had received a charge of grapeshot in the stomach.

"What can we do, lieutenant?" cried the captain, running up.

"Nail our flag to this piece of mast and sink the ship."

The captain left him at that, for he did not in the least relish the advice.

"Come," said Roger, "remember your promise."

"It is nothing," I said; "you will get over it."

"Throw me overboard!" he cried, and he swore fearfully and seized me by my coattails; "you see well enough that I can not recover. Throw me into the sea; I do not want to see our flag taken."

Two sailors came up to carry him below.

"To your guns, you knaves!" he cried with all his strength: "use grapeshot, and aim on the deck. And as for you, if you fail to keep your word I will curse you and think of you as the most cowardly and vile of men!"

His wound was certainly mortal. I saw the captain call a midshipman and give him the order to lower the flag.

"Give me a shake of the hand," I said to Roger. And at that moment our flag was lowered . . . .

"Captain, there is a whale to larboard!" interrupted an ensign, running to us.

"A whale?" cried the captain joyfully and leaving his story unfinished. "Quick! launch the longboat and the yawl, too! All longboats into the water! Bring the harpoons and ropes!" . . .

I never knew how poor Lieutenant Roger died.

The Etruscan Vase

Auguste Saint-Clair was not at all a favorite in Society, the chief reason being that he only cared to please those who took his own fancy. He avoided the former and sought after the latter. In other respects he was absentminded and indolent. One evening, on coming out of the Italian Opera, the Marquise A— asked him his opinion on the singing of Mlle. Sontag. "Yes, Madam," Saint-Clair replied, smiling pleasantly, and thinking of something totally different. This ridiculous reply could not be set down to shyness, for he talked with great lords and noted men and women and even with Society women with as much ease as though he were their equal. The Marquise put down Saint-Clair as a stupid, impertinent boor.

One Monday he had an invitation to dine with Madam B—. She paid him a good deal of attention, and on leaving her house, he remarked that he had never met a more agreeable woman. Madam B— spent a month collecting witticisms at other people's houses, which she dispensed in one evening at her own. Saint-Clair called upon her again on the Thursday of the same week. This time he grew a little tired of her. Another visit decided him never to enter her salon again. Madam B— gave out that Saint-Clair was an ill-bred young man, and not good form.

He was naturally tenderhearted and affectionate, but at an age when lasting impressions are taken too easily. His too demonstrative nature had drawn upon him the sarcasm of his comrades. He was proud and ambitious, and stuck to his opinion like an obstinate child. Henceforth he made a point of hiding any outward sign of what might seem discreditable weakness. He attained his end, but the victory cost him dear. He learnt to hide his softer feelings from others, but the repression only increased their force a hundredfold. In Society he bore the sorry reputation of being heartless and indifferent; and, when alone, his restless imagination conjured up hideous torments—all the worse because unshared.

How difficult it is to find a friend! Difficult! Is it possible to find two men anywhere who have not a secret from each other? That Saint-Clair had little faith in friendship was easily seen. With young Society people his manner was cold and reserved. He asked no questions about their secrets; and most of his actions and all his thoughts were mysteries to them. A Frenchman loves to talk of himself; therefore Saint-Clair was the unwilling recipient of many confidences. His friends—that is to say, those whom he saw about twice a week—complained of his indifference to their confidences. They felt that indiscretion should be reciprocal; for, indeed, he who confides his secret to us unasked generally takes offense at not learning ours in return.

"He keeps his thoughts to himself," grumbled Alphonse de Thémines one day.

"I could never place the least confidence in that deuced Saint-Clair," added the smart colonel.

"I think he is half a Jesuit," replied Jules Lambert. "Someone swore to me that he had met him twice coming out of St. Sulpice.

Nobody knows what he thinks about. I must say I never feel at ease with him."

They separated. Alphonse encountered Saint-Clair in the Boulevard Italien. He was walking with his eyes on the ground, not noticing anyone. Alphonse stopped him, took his arm, and, before they had reached the Rue de la Paix, he had related to him the whole history of his love affairs with Madam —, whose husband was so jealous and so violent.

The same evening Jules Lambert lost his money at cards. After that he thought he had better go and dance. While dancing, he accidentally knocked against a man, who had also lost his money and was in a very bad temper. Sharp words followed, and a challenge was given and taken. Jules begged Saint-Clair to act as his second, and, at the same time, borrowed money from him, which he was never likely to return.

After all, Saint-Clair was easy enough to live with. He was no one's enemy but his own; he was obliging, often genial, rarely tiresome; he had travelled much and read much, but never obtruded his knowledge or his experiences unasked. In personal appearance he was tall and well made; he had a dignified and refined expression—almost always too grave, but his smile was pleasing and very attractive.

I am forgetting one important point. Saint-Clair paid attention to all women, and sought their society more than that of men. It was difficult to say whether he was in love; but if this reserved being felt love, the beautiful Countess Mathilde de Coursy was the woman of his choice. She was a young widow, at whose house he was often seen. To prove their friendship there was the evidence first of the almost exaggerated politeness of Saint-Clair toward the Countess, and *vice versâ*; then his habit of never pronouncing her name in public, or if obliged to speak of her, never with the slightest praise; also, before Saint-Clair was introduced to her, he had been passionately fond of music, and the Countess equally so of painting. Since they had become acquainted their tastes had changed. Lastly, when the Countess visited a health resort the previous year, Saint-Clair followed her in less than a week.

My duty as novelist obliges me to reveal that early one morning in the month of July, a few moments before sunrise, the garden gate of a country house opened, and a man crept out with the stealthiness of a burglar fearing discovery. This country house belonged to Madam de Coursy, and the man was Saint-Clair. A woman muffled in a cape, came to the gate with him, stood with her head out and watched him as long as she could, until he was far along the path which led by the park wall. Saint-Clair stopped, looked round cautiously, and signed with his hand for the woman to go in. The clearness of a summer dawn enabled him to distinguish her pale face. She stood motionless where he had left her. He went back to her, and took her tenderly in his arms. He meant to compel her to go in; but he had still a hundred things to say to her. Their conversation lasted ten minutes, till at last they heard the voice of a peasant going to his work in the fields. One more kiss passed between them, the gate was shut, and Saint-Clair with a bound reached the end of the footpath. He followed a track evidently well-known to him, and ran along, striking the bushes with his stick and almost jumping for joy. Sometimes he stopped, or sauntered slowly, looking at the sky, which was flushed in the east with purple. In fact, anyone meeting him would have taken him for an escaped lunatic. After half an hour's walk he reached the door of a lonely little house which he had rented for the season. He let himself in with a key, and then, throwing himself on the couch, he fell into a daydream, with vacant eyes and a happy smile playing on his lips. His mind was filled with bright reflections. "How happy I am!" he kept repeating. "At last I have met a heart that understands mine .... Yes, I have found my ideal. ... I have gained at the same time a friend and a lover. ... What depth of soul! ... What character! ... No, she has never loved anyone before me." How soon vanity creeps into human affairs! "She is the loveliest woman in Paris," he thought, and his imagination conjured up all her charms. "She has chosen me before all the others. She had the flower of Society at her feet. That colonel of hussars, gallant, goodlooking and not too stout; that young author, who paints in water-colors so well, and who is such a capital actor; that Russian Lovelace, who has been in the Balkan campaign and served under Diébitch; above all, Camille T—, who is brilliantly clever, has good manners and a fine saber cut across his forehead .... She has dismissed them all for me! ..." Then came the refrain —"Oh, how happy I am! how happy I am!" and he got up and opened the window, for he could scarcely breathe. First he walked about; then he tossed on his couch.

A happy lover is almost as tedious as an unhappy one. One of my friends, who is generally in one or other of these conditions, found that the only way of getting any attention was to give me an excellent breakfast, over which he could unburden himself on the subject of his amors. When the coffee was finished he was obliged to choose a totally different topic of conversation.

As I can not give breakfast to all my readers, I make them a present of Saint-Clair's ecstasies. Besides, it is impossible always to live in cloudland. Saint-Clair was tired; he yawned, stretched his arms, saw that it was broad day and at last slept. When he awoke he saw by his watch that he had hardly time to dress and rush off to Paris, to attend a luncheon party of several of his young friends.

They had just uncorked another bottle of champagne. I leave my readers to guess how many had preceded it. It is sufficient to know that they had reached that stage which comes quickly enough at a young men's dinner party, when everybody speaks at once, and when the steady heads get anxious for those who can not carry so much.

"I wish," said Alphonse de Thémines, who had never missed a chance of talking about England—"I wish that it was the custom in Paris, as it is in London, for each one to propose a toast to his mistress. If it were we should find out for whom our friend Saint-Clair sighs." And, while uttering these words, he filled up his own glass and those of his neighbors.

Saint-Clair felt slightly embarrassed, but was about to reply when Jules Lambert prevented him.

"I heartily approve this custom," he said, raising his glass; "and I adopt it. To all the milliners of Paris, with the exception of those past thirty, the one-eyed and the lame."

"Hurrah! hurrah!" shouted the anglomaniacs. Saint-Clair rose, glass in hand.

"Gentlemen," said he, "I have not such a large heart as has our friend Jules, but it is more constant—a constancy all the more faithful since I have been long separated from the lady of my thoughts. Nevertheless I am sure that you will approve of my choice, even if you are not already my rivals. To Judith Pasta, gentlemen! May we soon welcome back the first *tragédienne* of Europe."

Thémines was about to criticise the toast, but was interrupted by acclamation. Saint-Clair having parried this thrust, believed himself safe for the rest of the day.

The conversation turned first on theaters. From the criticism of the drama they wandered to political topics. From the Duke of Wellington they passed to English horses. From English horses to women, by a natural connection of ideas; for, to young men, a good horse first, and then a beautiful mistress, are the two most desirable objects.

Then they discussed the means of acquiring these coveted treasures. Horses are bought, women also are bought; only we do not so talk of them. Saint-Clair, after modestly pleading inexperience in this delicate subject, gave as his opinion that the chief way to please a woman is to be singular, to be different from others. But he did not think it possible to give a general prescription for singularity.

"According to your view," said Jules, "a lame or humpbacked man would have a better chance of pleasing than one of ordinary make."

"You push things too far," retorted Saint-Clair, "but I am willing to accept all the consequences of my proposition. For example, if I were humpbacked, instead of blowing out my brains I would make conquests. In the first place, I would try my wiles on those who are generally tenderhearted; then on those women — and there are many of them — who set up for being original — eccentric, as they say in England. To begin with, I should describe my pitiful condition, and point out that I was the victim of Nature's cruelty. I should try to move them to sympathy with my lot, I should let them suspect that I was capable of a passionate love. I should kill one of my rivals in a duel, and I should pretend to poison myself with a feeble dose of laudanum. After a few months they would not notice my deformity, and then I should be on the watch for the first signs of affection. With women who aspire to originality conquest is easy. Only persuade them that it is a hard-and-fast rule that a deformed person can never have a love affair, they will immediately then wish to prove the opposite."

"What a Don Juan!" cried Jules.

"As we have not had the misfortune of being born deformed," said Colonel Beaujeu, "we had better get our legs broken, gentlemen."

"I fully agree with Saint-Clair," said Hector Roquantin, who was only three and a half feet high. "We constantly see beautiful and fashionable women giving themselves to men whom you fine fellows would never dream of."

"Hector, just ring the bell for another bottle, will you?" said Thémines casually.

The Etruscan Vase 157

The dwarf got up and everyone smiled, recalling the fable of the fox without a tail.

"As for me," said Thémines, renewing the conversation, "the longer I live, the more clearly I see that the chief singularity which attracts even the most obdurate, is passable features"—and he threw a complaisant glance in a mirror opposite—"passable features and good taste in dress," and he filliped a crumb of bread off his coat.

"Bah!" cried the dwarf, "with good looks and a coat by Staub, there are plenty of women to be had for a week at a time, but we should be tired of them at the second meeting. More than that is needed to win what is called love. ... You must ..."

"Stop!" interrupted Thémines. "Do you want an apt illustration? You all know what kind of man Massigny was. Manners like an English groom, and no more conversation than his horse. ... But he was as handsome as Adonis, and could tie his cravat like Brummel. Altogether he was the greatest bore I have ever met."

"He almost killed me with weariness," said Colonel Beaujeu. "Only think, I once had to travel two hundred leagues with him!"

"Did you know," asked Saint-Clair, "that he caused the death of poor Richard Thornton, whom you all knew?"

"But," objected Jules, "I thought he was assassinated by brigands near Fondi?"

"Granted; but Massigny was at all events an accomplice in the crime. A party of travellers, Thornton among them, had arranged to go to Naples together to avoid attacks from brigands. Massigny asked to be allowed to join them. As soon as Thornton heard this, he set out before the others, apparently to avoid being long with Massigny. He started alone, and you know the rest."

"Thornton took the only course," said Thémines; "he chose the easiest of two deaths. We should all have done the same in his place." Then, after a pause, "You grant me," he went on, "that Massigny was the greatest bore on earth?"

"Certainly," they all cried with one accord.

"Don't let us despair," said Jules; "let us make an exception in favor of ... especially when he divulges his political intrigues."

"You will next grant me," continued Thémines, "that Madam de Coursy is as clever a woman as can be found anywhere."

A moment's silence followed. Saint-Clair looked down and fancied that all eyes were fixed on himself.

"Who disputes it?" he said at length, still bending over his plate apparently to examine more closely the flowers painted in the china.

"I maintain," said Jules, raising his voice—"I maintain that she is one of the three most fascinating women in Paris."

"I knew her husband," said the Colonel, "he often showed me her charming letters."

"Auguste," interrupted Hector Roquantin, "do introduce me to the Countess. They say you can do anything with her."

"When she returns to Paris at the end of autumn, . . ." murmured Saint-Clair, "I—I believe she does not entertain visitors in the country."

"Will you listen to me?" exclaimed Thémines.

Silence was restored. Saint-Clair fidgeted upon his chair like a prisoner before his judges.

"You did not know the Countess three years ago because you were then in Germany, Saint-Clair," went on Alphonse de Thémines, with aggravating coolness. "You can not form any idea, therefore, of her as she was then; lovely, with the freshness of a rose, and as lighthearted and gay as a butterfly. Perhaps you do not know that among all her many admirers Massigny was the one she honored with her favors? The most stupid and ridiculous of men turned the head of the most fascinating amongst women. Do you suppose that a deformed person could have done as much? Nonsense; believe me, with a good figure and a first-rate tailor, only boldness in addition is needed."

Saint-Clair was in a most awkward position. He longed to fling back the lie direct in the speaker's face, but was restrained from fear of compromising the Countess. He would have liked to have said something to defend her, but he was tongue-tied. His lips trembled with rage, and he tried to find some indirect means of forcing a quarrel, but could not.

"What," exclaimed Jules, with astonishment, "Madam de Coursy gave herself to Massigny? Frailty, thy name is woman!"

"The reputation of a woman being of such small moment, it is, of course, allowable to pull it to pieces for the sake of a little sport," observed Saint-Clair in a dry and scornful tone, "and—"

But as he spoke he remembered with dismay a certain Etruscan vase that he had noticed a hundred times upon the mantelpiece in the Countess's house in Paris. He knew that it was a gift from Massigny, who had brought it back with him from Italy; and—overwhelming coincidence!—it had been taken by the Countess from Paris to her country house. Every evening when Mathilde took the flowers out of her dress she put them in this Etruscan vase.

Speech died upon his lips. He could neither see nor think of anything but of that Etruscan vase.

"How absurd," cries a critic, "to suspect his mistress from such a trifle!"

"Have you ever been in love, my dear critic?"

Thémines was in too good a humor to take offense at the tone Saint-Clair had used when speaking to him, and replied lightly and with great good nature—

"I can only repeat what I heard in Society. It passed as a true story while you were in Germany. However, I scarcely know Madam de Coursy. It is eighteen months since I was at her house. Very likely I am wrong, and the story was a fabrication of Massigny's. But let us return to our discussion, for whether my illustration be false or not does not affect my point. You all know that the cleverest woman in France, whose works—"

The door opened, and Théodore Néville came in. He had just returned from Egypt.

"Theodore, you have soon come back!" He was overwhelmed with questions.

"Have you brought back a real Turkish costume?" asked Thémines. "Have you got an Arabian horse and an Egyptian groom?"

"What sort of man is the Pasha?" said Jules. "When will he make himself independent? Have you seen a head cut off with a single stroke of the saber?"

"And the *almées*," said Roquantin. "Are the Cairo women beautiful?"

"Did you meet General L—?" asked Colonel Beaujeu. "Has he organized the army of the Pasha? Did Colonel C— give you a sword for me?"

"And the Pyramids? The cataracts of the Nile? And the statue of Memnon? Ibrahim Pasha?" etc. They all talked at once; Saint-Clair only brooded on the Etruscan vase.

Théodore sat crosslegged. He had learnt that habit in Egypt, and did not wish to lose it in France. He waited till his questioners were tired, and then spoke as fast as he could to save himself from being easily interrupted.

"The Pyramids! upon my word they are a regular humbug. They are not so high as I expected. Strasburg Cathedral is only four yards lower. I passed by the antiquities. Do not talk to me about them. The very sight of hieroglyphics makes me faint. There are plenty of travellers who worry themselves over these things! My object was to study the nature and manners of all the strange people that jostle against each other in the streets of Alexandria and of Cairo. Turks, Bedouins, Copts, Fellahs, Môghrebins. I drew up a few hasty notes when I was in the quarantine hospital. What infamous places they are! I hope none of you fellows are nervous about infection! I smoked my pipe calmly in the midst of three hundred plague-stricken people. Ah! Colonel, you would admire the well-mounted cavalry out there. I must show you some superb weapons that I have brought back. I have a *djerid* which belonged to a famous Mourad Bey. I have a *yataghan* for you, Colonel, and a *khandjar* for Auguste. You must see my *metchlâ* and *bournous* and *hhaick*. Do you know I could have brought back any number of women with me? Ibrahim Pasha has such numbers imported from Greece that they can be had for nothing. ... But I had to think of my mother's feelings. ... I talked much with the Pasha. He is a thoroughly intelligent and unprejudiced man. You would hardly credit it, but he knows everything about our affairs. Upon my honor, he knows the smallest secrets of our Cabinet. I gleaned much valuable information from him on the state of parties in France. ... Just now he is taken up with statistics. He subscribes to all our papers. Would you believe it?—he is a pronounced Bonapartist, and talks of nothing but Napoleon. 'Ah! what a great man *Bounabardo* was!' he said to me; 'Bounabardo,' that is how he pronounces Bonaparte."

"Giourdina, meaning Jourdain," murmured Thémines.

"At first," continued Théodore, "Mohamed Ali was extremely reserved with me. All the Turks are very suspicious, you know, and he took me for a spy, or a Jesuit, the devil he did! He had a perfect horror of Jesuits. But, after several visits, he recognized that I was an unprejudiced traveller, anxious to inform myself at first hand of Eastern manners, customs and politics. Then he unbosomed himself and spoke freely to me. At the third and last audience he granted me I ventured to ask His Excellency why he did not make himself independent of the Porte. 'By Allah!' he replied, 'I wish it indeed, but I fear the Liberal papers which govern your country would not support me if I proclaimed the independence of Egypt.' He is a fine old man, with a long white beard. He never smiles. He gave us some first-rate confections; but the gift that pleased him most of all I offered him was a collection of costumes of the Imperial Guard by Charlet."

"Is the Pasha of a romantic turn of mind?" asked Thémines.

"He does not trouble himself much about literature; but you

know, of course, that Arabian literature is entirely romantic. They have a poet called Melek Ayatalnefous-Ebn-Esraf, who has recently published a book of Meditations, compared with which Lamartine's read like classic prose. I took lessons in Arabic directly I got to Cairo, in order to read the Koran. I did not need to have many lessons before I was able to judge of the supreme beauty of the prophet's style, and of the baldness of all our translations. Look here, would you like to see Arabian handwriting? This word in gold letters is *Allah*, which means God."

As he spoke he showed them a very dirty letter, which he took out of a scented silk purse.

"How long were you in Egypt?" asked Thémines.

"Six weeks."

And the traveller proceeded to hold forth on everything from beginning to end. Saint-Clair left soon after his arrival, and went in the direction of his country house. The impetuous gallop of his horse prevented him from thinking consecutively, but he felt vaguely that his happiness in life had gone forever, and that it had been shattered by a dead man and an Etruscan vase.

After reaching home he threw himself on the same couch upon which he had dreamed for so long and so deliciously, and analyzed his happiness the evening before. His most cherished dream had been that his mistress was different from other women, that she had not loved nor ever would love anyone but himself. Now this exquisite dream must perish in the light of a sad and cruel reality. "I have had a beautiful mistress, but nothing more. She is clever; she is therefore all the more to be blamed for loving Massigny! . . . I know she does love me now . . . with her whole soul . . . as she can love. But to be loved in the same fashion as Massigny has been loved! . . . She has yielded herself up to my attentions, my importunities, my whims. But I have been deceived. There has been no sympathy between us. Whether her lover were Massigny, or myself, was equally the same to her. He is handsome, and she loves him for his good looks. She amuses herself with me for a time. 'I may as well love Saint-Clair,' she says to herself, 'since the other is dead! And if Saint-Clair dies, or I tire of him, who knows?'

"I firmly believe the devil listens invisible behind a tortured wretch like myself. The enemy of mankind is tickled by the spectacle, and as soon as the victim's wounds begin to heal, the devil is waiting to reopen them."

Saint-Clair thought he heard a voice murmur in his ears—

> The peculiar honor
> Of being the successor ...

He sat up on the couch and threw a savage glance round him. How glad he would have been to find someone in his room! He would have torn him limb from limb without any hesitation.

The clock struck eight. At eight-thirty the Countess expected him. Should he disappoint her? Why, indeed, should he ever see Massigny's mistress again? He lay down again on the couch and shut his eyes. "I will try to sleep," he said. He lay still for half a minute, then he leapt to his feet and ran to the clock to see how the time was going. "How I wish it were half-past eight!" he thought. "It would be too late then for me to start." If only he were taken ill. He had not the courage to stop at home unless he had an excuse. He walked up and down his room, then he sat down and took a book, but he could not read a syllable. He sat down in front of his piano, but had not enough energy to open it. He whistled; then he looked out of his window at the clouds, and tried to count the poplars. At length he looked at the clock again, and saw that he had not succeeded in whiling away more than three minutes. "I can not help loving her." he burst out, grinding his teeth and stamping his feet; "she rules me, and I am her slave, just as Massigny was before me. Well, since you have not sufficient courage to break the hated chain, poor wretch, you must obey."

He picked up his hat and rushed out.

When we are carried away by a great passion it is some consolation to our self-love to look down from the height of pride upon our weakness. "I certainly am weak," he said to himself; "but what if I wish to be so?"

As he walked slowly up the footpath which led to the garden gate, he could see in the distance a white face standing out against the dark background of trees. She beckoned to him with her handkerchief. His heart beat violently, and his knees trembled under him; he could not speak, and he had become so nervous that he feared lest the Countess should read his ill-humor.

He took the hand she held out to him, and kissed her brow, because she threw herself into his arms. He followed her into her sitting room in silence, though scarce able to suppress his bursting sighs.

A single candle lighted the Countess's room. They sat down, and Saint-Clair noticed his friend's coiffure; a single rose was in her hair. He had given her, the previous evening, a beautiful English engraving of Leslie's "Duchess of Portland" (whose hair was dressed in the same fashion), and Saint-Clair had merely remarked to the Countess, "I like that single rose better than all your elaborate coiffures," He did not like jewels, and inclined to the opinion of a noble lord who once remarked coarsely, "The devil has nothing left to teach women who overdress themselves and coil their hair fantastically." The night before, while playing with the Countess's pearl necklace (he always would have something between his hands when talking), Saint-Clair had said, "You are too pretty, Mathilde, to wear jewels; they are only meant to hide defects." Tonight the Countess had stripped herself of rings, necklaces, earrings and bracelets, for she stored up his most trivial remarks. He noticed, above everything else in a woman's toilet, the shoes she wore; and, like many other men, he was quite mad on this point. A heavy shower had fallen at sunset, and the grass was still very wet; in spite of this the Countess walked on the damp lawn in silk stockings and black satin slippers. . . . Suppose she were to take cold?

"She loves me," said Saint-Clair to himself.

He sighed at his folly, but smiled at Mathilde in spite of himself, tossed between his sorry mood and the gratification of seeing a pretty woman, who had sought, by those trifles which have such priceless value in the eyes of lovers, to please him.

The Countess was radiant with love, playfully mischievous and bewitchingly charming. She took something from a Japanese lacquerred box and held it out to him in her little firmly closed hand.

"I broke your watch the other night," she said; "here it is, mended,"

She handed the watch to him and looked at him tenderly, and yet mischievously, biting her lower lip as though to prevent herself from laughing. Oh, what beautiful white teeth she had! and how they gleamed against the ruby red of her lips! (A man looks exceedingly foolish when he is being teased by a pretty women, and replies coldly.) Saint-Clair thanked her, took the watch and was about to put it in his pocket.

"Look at it and open it," she continued. "See if it is mended all right. You, who are so learned, you, who have been to the Polytechnic School, ought to be able to tell that."

"Oh, I didn't learn much there," said Saint-Clair.

He opened the case in an absentminded way, and what was his

surprise to find a miniature portrait of Madam de Coursy painted on the interior of the case? How could he sulk any longer? His brow cleared; he thought no longer of Massigny; he only remembered that he was by the side of a beautiful woman, and that this woman loved him.

"The lark, that harbinger of dawn," began to sing, and long bands of pale light stretched across the eastern clouds. At such an hour did Romeo say farewell to Juliet, and it is the classic hour when all lovers should part.

Saint-Clair stood before a mantelpiece, the key of the garden gate in his hand, his eyes intently fixed on the Etruscan vase, of which we have already spoken. In the depths of his soul he still bore it a grudge, although he was in a much better humor. The simple explanation occurred to his mind that Thémines might have lied about it. While the Countess was wrapping a shawl round her head in order to go to the garden gate with him he began to tap the detested vase with the key, at first gently, then gradually increasing the force of his blows until it seemed as though he would soon smash it to atoms.

"Oh, do be careful!" Mathilde exclaimed. "You will break my beautiful Etruscan vase!"

She snatched the key out of his hands.

Saint-Clair was very angry, but he resigned himself and turned his back on the chimneypiece to avoid temptation. Opening his watch, he began to examine the portrait that had just been given him.

"Who painted it?" he asked.

"Monsieur R—, and it was Massigny who introduced him to my notice. (After Massigny had been in Rome he discovered that he had exquisite taste in art, and constituted himself the Macænas of all young painters.) I really think the portrait is like me, though it is a little too flattering."

Saint-Clair had a burning desire to fling the watch against the wall, to break it beyond all hope of mending. He controlled himself, however, and put the watch in his pocket. Then he noticed that it was daylight, and, entreating Mathilde not to come out with him, he left the house and crossed the garden with rapid strides, and was soon alone in the country.

"Massigny! Massigny!" he burst forth with concentrated rage. "Can I never escape him? . . . No doubt the artist who painted this portrait painted another for Massigny. . . . What a fool I am to imagine for a moment that I am loved with a love equal to my own! . . . just because she put aside her jewels and wore a rose in her hair! . . . Jewels! why, she has a chest full. . . . Massigny, who thought of little else save a woman's toilet, was a lover of jewelry! . . . Yes, she had a gracious nature, it must be granted; she knows how to gratify the tastes of her lovers. Damn it! I would rather a hundred times that she were a courtesan and gave herself for money. Just because she was my mistress and unpaid I thought she loved me indeed."

Soon another still more unhappy idea presented itself. In a few weeks' time the Countess would be out of mourning, and Saint-Clair had promised to marry her as soon as her year of widowhood was over. He had promised. Promised? No. He had never spoken of it, but such had been his intention and the Countess had understood it so. But for him this was as good as an oath. Last night he would have given a throne to hasten the time for acknowledging his love publicly; now the very thought of marrying the former mistress of Massigny filled him with loathing.

"Nevertheless, I owe it to her to marry her," he said to himself, "and it shall be done. No doubt she thinks, poor woman, I heard all about her former *liaison*; it seems to have been generally known. Besides, she did not then know me. . . . She can not understand me; she thinks that I am only such another lover as Massigny."

Then he said to himself, and not without a certain pride—

"For three months she has made me the happiest man living; such happiness is worth the sacrifice of my life."

He did not go to bed, but rode about among the woods the whole of the morning. In one of the pathways of the woods of Verrières he saw a man mounted on a fine English horse, who called him immediately by his name while he was still far off. It was Alphonse de Thémines. To a man in Saint-Clair's state of mind solitude is particularly desirable, and this encounter with Thémines changed his bad humour into a furious temper. Thémines did not notice his mood, or perhaps took a wicked pleasure in thwarting it. He talked and laughed and joked without noticing that he did not receive any response. Saint-Clair soon tried to turn his horse aside into a narrow track, hoping the bore would not follow him; but it was of no use, bores do not leave their prey so easily. Thémines pulled the bridle in the same direction, increased his horse's pace to keep by Saint-Clair's side and complacently continued the conversation.

I have said that the path was a narrow one. The two horses could hardly walk abreast. It was not, therefore, to be wondered at that even so good a horseman as Thémines should graze against Saint-Clair's foot as he walked along with him. This put the finishing touch to his anger, and he could not contain himself any longer. He rose in his stirrups and struck Thémines' horse sharply across the nose with his whip.

"What the devil is the matter with you, Auguste?" cried Thémines.
"Why do you strike my horse?"
"Why do you pursue me?" roared Saint-Clair.
"Have you lost your senses, Saint-Clair? You forget to whom you are talking."
"I know quite well that I am talking to a puppy."
"Saint-Clair! . . . you must be mad, I think. . . . Listen to me. Tomorrow you will either apologize to me, or you will account for your insolent conduct."
"Tomorrow, then, sir—"
Thémines stopped his horse; Saint-Clair pushed his on, and very soon disappeared among the trees.

He was calmer now. He was silly enough to believe in presentiments. He felt sure he would be killed on the morrow, and that would be a suitable ending to his condition. Only one more day of anxieties and torments to endure. He went home and sent a note by his servant to Colonel Beaujeu. He wrote several letters, after which he dined with a good appetite, and was promptly at the little garden gate by 8.30.

                    *   *   *

"What is the matter with you today, Auguste?" said the Countess. "You are unusually lively, and yet your gaiety does not move me to laugh. Last night you were just a trifle dull, and I was the gay one! We have changed parts today. I have a racking headache."

"Dear one, I admit it. Yes, I was very tedious yesterday, but today I have been out, I took exercise, and I feel quite excited."

"On the other hand, I overslept myself this morning, and rose late. I had bad dreams."

"Ah! dreams? Do you believe in dreams?"
"What nonsense!"
"I believe in them. I am sure that you had a dream which foretold some tragic event."

"Good heavens! I never remember my dreams. Once I recollect

... that I saw Massigny in my dreams; so, you see, it was not very entertaining."

"Massigny! But I should have thought you would have been pleased at seeing him again!"

"Poor Massigny!"

"Why 'poor Massigny'?"

"Please tell me, Auguste, what is wrong with you tonight. Your smile is perfectly diabolic, and you seem to be making game of yourself."

"Ah! now you are treating me as badly as your old dowager friends treat me."

"Yes, Auguste, you wear the same expression today that you put on before people whom you do not like."

"That is unpardonable in me. Come, give me your hand."

He kissed her hand with ironical gallantry, and they gazed at each other studiously for a minute. Saint-Clair was the first to drop his eyes.

"How difficult it is," he exclaimed, "to live in this world without being thought ill of! One ought really never to talk of anything but the weather and hunting, or eagerly to discuss with your old friends the reports of their benevolent societies."

He picked up a paper from the table near him.

"Come, here is your lace-cleaner's bill. Let us discuss that, sweetheart; then you can not say I am ill tempered."

"Really, Auguste, you amaze me. ..."

"This handwriting puts me in mind of a letter I found this morning. I must explain that I have fits of untidiness occasionally, and I was arranging my papers. Well, then, I found a love letter from a dressmaker with whom I fell in love at sixteen. She had a trick of writing each word most fantastically, and her style was equal to her writing. Well, I was foolish enough then to be vexed that my mistress could not write as well as Madame de Sévigné, and I left her abruptly. In reading over this letter today I see that this dressmaker really did love me."

"Really! a woman whom you kept?"

"In fine style on fifty francs a month. But I could not afford more, as my guardian only allowed me a little money at a time, for he said that youths who had money ruined themselves and others."

"What became of this woman?"

"How should I know? ... Probably she died in a hospital."

"Auguste, ... if that were true you would not speak so flippantly."

"Well, then, to tell you the truth, she is married to a respectable man, and when I came of age I gave her a small dowry."

"How good of you! ... But why do you try to make yourself out so evil?"

"Oh, I am good enough. ... The more I think of it the more I persuade myself that this woman really did care for me. ... But on the other hand, it is difficult to discern true feeling under such a ridiculous expression of it."

"You ought to have shown me your letter. I should not have been jealous . . . . We women have finer tact than you, and we can tell at a glance, from the style of a letter, whether the writer is sincere, or feigning a passion he does not really feel."

"But what a number of times you have allowed yourself to be taken in by fools and rogues!"

As he spoke he looked at the Etruscan vase with a threatening glance, to which his voice responded, but Mathilde went on without noticing anything.

"Come, now, all you men wish to pose as Don Juans. You fancy you are making dupes when often you have encountered only Doña Juana, who is much more cunning than yourselves."

"I perceive that with your superior wit you ladies scent out rakes in every place. I doubt not also that our friend Massigny, who was both a stupid and a coxcomb, became, when dead, spotless and a martyr."

"Massigny? He was not a fool; then too there are silly women to be found. I must tell you a story about Massigny. But surely have I not told it you already?"

"Never," replied Saint-Clair tremblingly.

"Massigny fell in love with me after his return from Italy. My husband knew him and introduced him to me as a man of taste and culture. Those two were just made for each other. Massigny was most attentive to me from the first; he gave me some water-color sketches which he had bought from Schroth, as his own paintings, and talked of music and art in the most divertingly superior manner. One day he sent me an incredibly ridiculous letter. He said, among other things, that I was the best woman in Paris; therefore he wished to be my lover. I showed the letter to my cousin Julie. We were then both very silly, and we resolved to play him a trick. One evening we had several visitors, among them being Massigny. My cousin said to me, 'I am going to read you a declaration of love which I received this morning.' She took the letter and read it amidst peals of laughter. ... Poor Massigny! ..."

Saint-Clair fell on his knees uttering a cry of joy. He seized the Countess's hand and covered it with tears and kisses. Mathilde was surprised beyond measure, and thought at first he had gone mad. Saint-Clair could only murmur, "Forgive me! forgive me!" When he rose to his feet he was radiant; he was happier than on the day when Mathilde had said to him for the first time, "I love you."

"I am the guiltiest and most stupid of men," he cried; "for two days I have misjudged you . . . and never given you a chance to clear yourself. . . ."

"You suspected me? . . . And of what?"

"Oh! idiot that I was! . . . they told me you had loved Massigny, and—"

"Massigny!" and she began to laugh; then soon quickly growing more earnest, "Auguste," she said, "how could you be so foolish as to harbor such suspicions, and so hypocritical as to hide them from me?"

Her eyes filled with tears.

"I implore you to forgive me."

"Of course I forgive you, beloved . . . but let me first swear. . . ."

"Oh! I believe you, I believe you; do not say any more about it."

"But in Heaven's name what put such an improbable notion in your head?"

"Nothing, nothing in the world except my accursed temper . . . and . . . would you believe it? that Etruscan vase which I knew Massigny had given you."

The Countess clasped her hands together in amazement, and then she burst into shouts of laughter.

"My Etruscan vase! my Etruscan vase!"

Saint-Clair was obliged to join in the laughter himself, although great tears rolled down his cheeks. He seized Mathilde in his arms. "I will not let you go," he said, "until you pardon me."

"Yes, I forgive you, though you are so foolish," she replied, kissing him tenderly. "You make me very happy today; it is the first time I have seen you shed tears, and I thought that you could not weep."

Then she struggled from his embrace, and, snatching the Etruscan vase, broke it into a thousand pieces on the floor. It was a valuable and unique work, painted in three colors, and represented the fight between a Lapithe and a Centaur.

For several hours Saint-Clair was the happiest and the most ashamed of men.

"Well," said Roquantin to Colonel Beaujeu, when he met him in the evening at Tortoni's, "is this news true?"

"Too true, my friend," answered the Colonel sadly.

"Tell me, how did it come about?"

"Oh! just as it should. Saint-Clair began by telling me he was in the wrong, but that he wished to draw Thémines' fire before begging his pardon. I could do no other than accede. Thémines wished to draw lots who should fire first. Saint-Clair insisted that Thémines should. Thémines fired; and I saw Saint-Clair turn round once and then fell stone dead. I have often remarked, in the case of soldiers when they have been shot, this strange turning round which precedes death."

"How very extraordinary!" said Roquantin. "But Thémines, what did he do?"

"Oh, what is usual on these occasions: he threw his pistol on the ground remorsefully, with such force that he broke the hammer. It was an English pistol of Manton's. I don't believe there is a gunmaker in Paris who could make such another."

The Countess shut herself up in her country house for three whole years without seeing anyone; winter and summer, there she lived, hardly going out of her room. She was waited upon by a mulatto woman who knew of the attachment between Saint-Clair and herself. She scarcely spoke a word to her day after day. At the end of three years her cousin Julie returned from a long voyage. She forced her way into the house and found poor Mathilde thin and pale, the very ghost of the beautiful and fascinating woman she had left behind. By degrees she persuaded her to come out of her solitude, and took her to Hyères. The Countess languished there for three or four months, and then died of consumption brought on by her grief—so said Dr. M—, who attended her.

Hawthorne

1630	William Hathorne arrives from England and settles near Boston. Town annals record Judge Hathorne ordering Quakers to be publicly whipped.
1692	Judge John Hathorne sits on preliminary hearings of the Salem witchcraft trials.
1804	July 4. Nathaniel Hawthorne born in Salem, Massachusetts.
1808	Father dies and family moves in with maternal grandparents.
1825–37	Graduates from Bowdoin College. Classmates include Franklin Pierce and Henry Wadsworth Longfellow. Spends time reading, writing, and traveling throughout New England.
1837	*Twice-Told Tales* is published. Meets Sophia Peabody, his future wife, and her sister, Elizabeth, who publishes his children's books. Through them becomes acquainted with Emerson, Thoreau, Ellery Channing, Margaret Fuller, and other literary figures.
1839–42	Works as a measurer in the Boston Custom House. Develops a friendship with Longfellow and meets James Russell Lowell. In 1841 joins the commune Brook Farm. An expanded second edition of *Twice-Told Tales* appears in 1842, and he marries Sophia. Writes short stories at the Old Manse, his new home.
1846–51	Works as a surveyor of the port of Boston. In 1846 *Mosses from an Old Manse* appears. From 1850–51 *The Scarlet Letter, The House of Seven Gables*, and *The Snow-Image and Other Twice-Told Tales* appear. Develops a friendship with Herman Melville.
1852–58	Writes a campaign biography, *The Life of Franklin Pierce*, in 1852. Appointed to the consulship of Liverpool by Pierce the following year.
1858–60	The Hawthornes live in Italy for two years.
1864	May 19. Hawthorne dies in Plymouth, New Hampshire.

Nathaniel Hawthorne

Our first great psychological novelist, Hawthorne was simultaneously Poe's only serious competitor in the short story. After the juvenile attempt at a novel, Hawthorne devoted himself exclusively for many years to the production of tales and sketches, until he had nearly a hundred of them to show; and in many of them the same qualities which were later to be welded in his long works had been foreshadowed, tested and explored. Taking for his province the conscience of Puritanism, and the decay of old families, he began to fashion out of legends and his own fancy the sort of half-dreamlike, half-real fantasies that had earlier occupied Irving. Instead of the legends of New York, he unearthed those of New England. But after he had found his materials, he looked far more deeply beneath the surface than ever Irving had been able to do. There was little of the sunny inconsequentiality of the New Yorker in this sober descendant of John Hathorne, Puritan scourge and witch-hunter of old Salem. The reading of life in his stories was to be far more serious, and his judgments far more severe. His art, too, much less spontaneous, was to be by long odds the more subtle and refined. His vision encompassed the shadowy depths of existence, and out of that shade he wrought the greatest books of any American up to his time. That there was much of life he left out of account in them cannot be denied, his contemporary and erstwhile friend, Melville, was to probe even deeper into the shadows; but in Hawthorne's books, on the whole, we find the largest body of considerable art produced up to his day in America. The sporadic bursts of power and insight, as in Melville's *Moby-Dick*, did not outweigh the impressive totality of Hawthorne's output.

Nevertheless Hawthorne's early attempts were inauspicious and they were patently modeled upon Irving's familiar essays in the

Sketch Book, Bracebridge Hall, etc. This was recognized by contemporary critics, and Park Benjamin, writing in the *New England Magazine* for October, 1835, remarked that the young author was "the most pleasing writer of fanciful prose, except Irving, in the country." Such youthful pieces as "The Old Apple Dealer," painting a faithful and humble picture of a rustic character, or the innocuous "A Rill from the Town Pump" and "A Village Uncle," setting forth the homely virtues of simple lives and provincial scenes, are quite specifically in the Irving vein. When, however, Hawthorne produced a sketch like "Sights from a Steeple," he was beginning to discover his own voice, although its mannerisms and accents were still those of Irving. Geoffrey Crayon never worked with more Dutch faithfulness of detail than Hawthorne showed in "Main Street," "Snowflakes," and the numerous other slight pieces. Strangely enough, there was never any great advance in artistry or any increase in depth and significance, though Hawthorne continued to write such sketches up almost to the time of *The Scarlet Letter*, or, in other words, as long as he continued to write short pieces at all. It was as if Hawthorne's powers, while expanding in scope, remained essentially what they had been after his first period of journeyman work.

However, it cannot be doubted that the tales which Hawthorne began to publish in Christmas books and magazines spoke definitively of a new voice in our literature; the sketches seemed to be of Irving, but the stories were new-minted. A technical debt to Scott, and an occasional flavor of Brockden Brown, are all that can be detected in the way of extraneous influence in them. The legends of the Dutch, as exploited by Irving, had become the legends of the Puritans, in the hands of Hawthorne. "Sleepy Hollow" had been exchanged for the Essex Woods where Young Goodman Brown witnessed the witches' Sabbath; "Rip Van Winkle" had been expanded and metamorphosed into "Wakefield." Just as Hawthorne concerned himself with the inexplicable evidences of the supernatural, and sometimes with what was weird and evil, Henry James later found in *The Turn of the Screw* a method of developing the Hawthorne interests even further. In fact, James saw much in Hawthorne that must have given him guidance and aid throughout his career, and it was symptomatic that he proclaimed "the fine thing in Hawthorne is that he cared for the deeper psychology, and that, in his way, he tried to become familiar with it." Moreover, Hawthorne's insistence upon the reality of spirit and the unreality of matter, equally impressed James; in Hawthorne's stories there were to be observed "glimpses of a great field, of the whole deep mystery of man's soul and conscience. They are moral, and their interest is moral; they deal with something more than the mere accidents and conventionalities, the surface occurrences of life."

It is this more serious concern with man's inner life that so sets Hawthorne apart from all the American writers of fiction who preceded him. Neither Cooper, Irving, Brown nor Poe entertained this concern for the psychological and moral issues which were to be the great focus of fiction until the realists arrived on the scene. The romancers were content to depict those surface occurrences which James reprehended; the apocalyptics were concerned, it is true, with madness, horror and various agonies of the psyche, but it was a largely external concern, an interest held for the sensational, pictorial and melodramatic effects that could be gained by it. Moral issues seldom invaded the domain of Brown and Poe; and it was not until the advent of Melville that a real seriousness of intention found expression through the apocalyptic vision. Hawthorne's great distinction was in taking seriously what had been neglected or overlooked by all his predecessors, and making great art of the inner drama of conscience which his own Puritan New England inheritance dictated. This is the justification for the use of allegory which, in some cases, became a juggernaut and destroyed the framework of the story it was intended to vivify. Through allegory Hawthorne was able to retain the "surface occurrences of life" and yet invest them with a meaning transcending their mundane aspects. When he succeeded, it was greatly; when he failed, the results were lamentable. A "Young Goodman Brown" or an "Ethan Brand" explored regions hitherto untouched; while a "Celestial Railroad" or a "Bosom Serpent" seemed only to stand like stiff caricatures of John Bunyan.

The great stories of Hawthorne are not so numerous as might be supposed; they stand out clearly from the highly competent ones, and most of them have been well anthologized: "Young Goodman Brown," "The Birthmark," "Ethan Brand," "Rappacini's Daughter" and "The Artist of the Beautiful." In these, as in many others of his tales, there is a curious thing to note: they all deal, in one way and another, with the theme of solitude — of removal from society, or of isolation. The novel which was to have crowned all Hawthorne's efforts, *The Ancestral Footstep*, also deals with this theme, and one recognizes again the absolute primacy of this factor in Hawthorne's genius. Secrecy of the heart, stories locked within the bosoms of men, unrecognized impulses which spring from the inner life, these are the themes of the short stories; their characters are solitary men and women, and they are put into action against a backdrop of solitude.

—*from* The Shapers of American Fiction, 1798–1947, *by George Snell*

The Ambitious Guest

One September night a family had gathered round their hearth and piled it high with the drift-wood of mountain streams, the dry cones of the pine, and the splintered ruins of great trees that had come crashing down the precipice. Up the chimney roared the fire, and brightened the room with its broad blaze. The faces of the father and mother had a sober gladness; the children laughed; the eldest daughter was the image of Happiness at seventeen; and the aged grandmother, who sat knitting in the warmest place, was the image of Happiness grown old. They had found the "herb, heart's-ease," in the bleakest spot of all New England. This family was situated in the Notch of the White Hills, where the wind was sharp throughout the year, and pitilessly cold in the winter — giving their cottage all its fresh inclemency, before it descended on the valley of the Saco. They dwelt in a cold spot and a dangerous one; for a mountain towered above their heads, so steep, that the stones would often rumble down its sides, and startle them at midnight.

The daughter had just uttered some simple jest, that filled them all with mirth, when the wind came through the Notch, and seemed to pause before their cottage — rattling the door, with a sound of wailing and lamentation, before it passed into the valley. For a moment it saddened them, though there was nothing unusual in the tones. But the family were glad again, when they perceived that the latch was lifted by some traveller, whose footsteps had been unheard amid the dreary blast which heralded his approach, and wailed as he was entering, and went moaning away from the door.

Though they dwelt in such a solitude, these people held daily converse with the world. The romantic pass of the Notch is a great artery, through which the lifeblood of internal commerce is continually throbbing, between Maine on one side, and the Green Mountains and the shores of the St. Lawrence on the other. The stagecoach always drew up before the door of the cottage. The wayfarer, with no companion but his staff, paused here to exchange a word, that the sense of loneliness might not utterly overcome him, ere he could pass through the cleft of the mountain, or reach the first house in the valley. And here the teamster, on his way to Portland market, would put up for the night; and, if a bachelor, might sit an hour beyond the usual bedtime, and steal a kiss from the mountain maid at parting. It was one of those primitive taverns where the traveller pays only for food and lodging, but meets with a homely kindness, beyond all price. When the footsteps were heard, therefore, between the outer door and the inner one, the whole family rose up, grandmother, children, and all, as if about to welcome some one who belonged to them, and whose fate was linked with theirs.

The door was opened by a young man. His face at first wore the melancholy expression, almost despondency, of one who travels a wild and bleak road at nightfall and alone, but soon brightened up when he saw the kindly warmth of his reception. He felt his heart spring forward to meet them all, from the old woman, who wiped a chair with her apron, to the little child that held out its arms to him. One glance and smile placed the stranger on a footing of innocent familiarity with the eldest daughter.

"Ah, this fire is the right thing!" cried he; "especially when there is such a pleasant circle round it. I am quite benumbed; for the Notch is just like the pipe of a great pair of bellows; it has blown a terrible blast in my face, all the way from Bartlett."

"Then you are going towards Vermont?" said the master of the house, as he helped to take a light knapsack off the young man's shoulder.

"Yes; to Burlington, and far enough beyond," replied he. "I meant to have been at Ethan Crawford's tonight; but a pedestrian lingers along such a road as this. It is no matter; for, when I saw this good fire, and all your cheerful faces, I felt as if you had kindled it on purpose for me, and were waiting my arrival. So I shall sit down among you, and make myself at home."

The frankhearted stranger had just drawn his chair to the fire, when something like a heavy footstep was heard without, rushing down the steep side of the mountain, as with long and rapid strides, and taking such a leap, in passing the cottage, as to strike the opposite precipice. The family held their breath, because they knew the sound, and their guest held his by instinct.

"The old mountain has thrown a stone at us, for fear we should forget him," said the landlord, recovering himself. "He sometimes nods his head, and threatens to come down; but we are old neighbours, and agree together pretty well, upon the whole. Besides, we have a sure place of refuge hard by, if he should be coming in good earnest."

Let us now suppose the stranger to have finished his supper of bear's meat; and, by his natural felicity of manner, to have placed himself on a footing of kindness with the whole family, so that they talked as freely together as if he belonged to their mountain brood. He was of a proud, yet gentle spirit—haughty and reserved among the rich and great; but ever ready to stoop his head to the lowly cottage door, and be like a brother or a son at the poor man's fireside. In the household of the Notch he found warmth and simplicity of feeling, the pervading intelligence of New England, and a poetry of native growth, which they had gathered, when they little thought of it, from the mountain peaks and chasms, and at the very threshold of their romantic and dangerous abode. He had travelled far and alone; his whole life, indeed, had been a solitary path; for, with the lofty caution of his nature, he had kept himself apart from those who might otherwise have been his companions. The family, too, though so kind and hospitable, had that consciousness of unity among themselves, and separation from the world at large, which, in every domestic circle, should still keep a holy place where no stranger may intrude. But, this evening, a prophetic sympathy impelled the refined and educated youth to pour out his heart before the simple mountaineers, and constrained them to answer him with the same free confidence. And thus it should have been. Is not the kindred of a common fate a closer tie than that of birth?

The secret of the young man's character was a high and abstracted ambition. He could have borne to live an undistinguished life, but not to be forgotten in the grave. Yearning desire had been transformed to hope; and hope, long cherished, had become like certainty, that, obscurely as he journeyed now, a glory was to beam on all his pathway—though not, perhaps, while he was treading it. But, when posterity should gaze back into the gloom of what was now the present, they would trace the brightness of his footsteps, brightening as meaner glories faded, and confess that a gifted one had passed from his cradle to his tomb, with none to recognize him.

"As yet," cried the stranger, his cheek glowing and his eye flashing with enthusiasm, "as yet, I have done nothing. Were I to vanish from the earth tomorrow, none would know so much of me as you; that a nameless youth came up, at nightfall, from the valley of the Saco, and opened his heart to you in the evening, and passed through 11the Notch, by sunrise, and was seen no more. Not a soul would ask—'Who was he?—Whither did the wanderer go?' But I cannot die till I have achieved my destiny. Then let Death come! I shall have built my monument!"

There was a continual flow of natural emotion, gushing forth amid abstracted reverie, which enabled the family to understand this young man's sentiments, though so foreign from their own. With quick sensibility of the ludicrous, he blushed at the ardor into which he had been betrayed.

"You laugh at me," said he, taking the eldest daughter's hand, and laughing himself. "You think my ambition as nonsensical as if I were to freeze myself to death on the top of Mount Washington, only that people might spy at me from the country round about. And truly, that would be a noble pedestal for a man's statue!"

"It is better to sit here by this fire," answered the girl, blushing, "and be comfortable and contented, though nobody thinks about us."

"I suppose," said her father, after a fit of musing, "there is something natural in what the young man says; and if my mind had been turned that way, I might have felt just the same. It is strange, wife, how this talk has set my head running on things that are pretty certain never to come to pass."

"Perhaps they may," observed the wife. "Is the man thinking what he will do when he is a widower?"

"No, no!" cried he, repelling the idea with reproachful kindness. "When I think of your death, Esther, I think of mine too. But I was wishing we had a good farm, in Bartlett, or Bethlehem, or Littleton, or some other township round the White Mountains; but not where they could tumble on our heads. I should want to stand well with my neighbors, and be called 'Squire, and sent to General Court for a term or two; for a plain, honest man may do as much good there as a lawyer. And when I should be grown quite an old man, and you an old woman, so as not to be long apart, I might die happy enough in my bed, and leave you all crying around me. A slate gravestone would suit me as well as a marble one — with just my name and age, and a verse of a hymn, and something to let people know that I lived an honest man and died a Christian."

"There now!" exclaimed the stranger; "it is our nature to desire a monument, be it slate, or marble, or a pillar of granite, or a glorious memory in the universal heart of man."

"We're in a strange way tonight," said the wife, with tears in her eyes. "They say it's a sign of something when folks' minds go a-wandering so. Hark to the children!"

They listened accordingly. The younger children had been put to bed in another room, but with an open door between, so that they could be heard talking busily among themselves. One and all seemed to have caught the infection from the fireside circle, and were outvying each other in wild wishes and childish projects of what they would do, when they came to be men and women. At length a little boy, instead of addressing his brothers and sisters, called out to his mother.

"I'll tell you what I wish, mother," cried he, "I want you and father and grandma'm, and all of us, and the stranger too, to start right away, and go and take a drink out of the basin of the Flume!"

Nobody could help laughing at the child's notion of leaving a warm bed, and dragging them from a cheerful fire, to visit the basin of the Flume — a brook, which tumbles over the precipice, deep within the Notch. The boy had hardly spoken, when a wagon rattled along the road, and stopped a moment before the door. It appeared to contain two or three men, who were cheering their hearts with the rough chorus of a song, which resounded in broken notes, between the cliffs, while the singers hesitated whether to continue their journey, or put up here for the night.

"Father," said the girl, "they are calling you by name."

But the good man doubted whether they had really called him, and was unwilling to show himself too solicitous of gain, by inviting people to patronize his house. He therefore did not hurry to the door; and the lash being soon applied, the travellers plunged into the Notch, still singing and laughing, though their music and mirth came back drearily from the heart of the mountain.

"There, mother!" cried the boy, again. "They'd have given us a ride to the Flume."

Again they laughed at the child's pertinacious fancy for a night ramble. But it happened that a light cloud passed over the daughter's spirit; she looked gravely into the fire, and drew a breath that was almost a sigh. It forced its way, in spite of a little struggle to repress it. Then starting and blushing, she looked quickly round the circle, as if they had caught a glimpse into her bosom. The stranger asked what she had been thinking of.

"Nothing," answered she, with a downcast smile. "Only I felt lonesome just then."

"Oh, I have always had a gift of feeling what is in other people's hearts," said he, half seriously. "Shall I tell the secrets of yours? For I know what to think when a young girl shivers by a warm hearth, and complains of lonesomeness at her mother's side. Shall I put these feelings into words?"

"They would not be a girl's feelings any longer, if they could be put into words," replied the mountain nymph, laughing, but avoiding his eye.

All this was said apart. Perhaps a germ of love was springing in their hearts, so pure that it might blossom in paradise, since it could not be matured on earth; for women worship such gentle dignity as his; and the proud, contemplative, yet kindly soul is oftenest captivated by simplicity like hers. But, while they spoke softly, and he was watching the happy sadness, the light-some shadows, the shy yearnings of a maiden's nature, the wind, through the Notch, took a deeper and drearier sound. It seemed, as the fanciful stranger said, like the choral strain of the spirits of the blast, who, in old Indian times, had their dwelling among these mountains, and made their heights and recesses a sacred region. There was a wail along the road, as if a funeral were passing. To chase away the gloom, the family threw pine-branches on their fire, till the dry leaves crackled, and the flame arose, discovering once again a scene of peace and humble happiness. The light hovered about them fondly, and caressed them all. There were the little faces of the children peeping from their bed apart, and here the father's frame of strength, the mother's subdued and careful mien, the highbrowed youth, the budding girl, and the good old grandam, still knitting in the warmest place. The aged woman looked up from her task, and, with the fingers ever busy, was the next to speak.

"Old folks have their notions," said she, "as well as young ones. You've been wishing and planning, and letting your heads run on one thing and another, till you've set my mind a-wandering too. Now what should an old woman wish for when she can go but a step or two before she comes to her grave? Children, it will haunt me night and day till I tell you."

"What is it, mother?" cried the husband and wife at once.

Then the old woman, with an air of mystery, which drew the circle closer round the fire, informed them that she had provided her grave clothes some years before—a nice linen shroud, a cap with a muslin ruff, and everything of a finer sort than she had worn since her wedding day. But this evening an old superstition had strangely recurred to her. It used to be said, in her younger days, that if anything were amiss with a corpse, if only the ruff were not smooth, or the cap did not set right, the corpse, in the coffin and beneath the clods, would strive to put up its cold hands and arrange it. The bare thought made her nervous,

"Don't talk so, grandmother!" said the girl, shuddering.

"Now," continued the old woman, with singular earnestness, yet smiling strangely at her own folly, "I want one of you, my children—when your mother is dressed, and in the coffin—I want one of you to hold a looking glass over my face. Who knows but I may take a glimpse at myself, and see whether all's right?"

"Old and young, we dream of graves and monuments," murmured the stranger youth. "I wonder how mariners feel when the ship is sinking, and they, unknown and undistinguished, are to be buried together in the ocean—that wide and nameless sepulcher!"

For a moment the old woman's ghastly conception so engrossed the minds of her hearers, that a sound, abroad in the night, rising like the roar of a blast, had grown broad, deep, and terrible before the fated group were conscious of it. The house, and all within it, trembled; the foundations of the earth seemed to be shaken, as if this awful sound were the peal of the last trump. Young and old exchanged one wild glance, and remained an instant, pale, affrighted, without utterance, or power to move. Then the same shriek burst simultaneously from all their lips.

"The Slide! the Slide!"

The simplest words must intimate, but not portray, the unutterable horror of the catastrophe. The victims rushed from their cottage and sought refuge in what they deemed a safer spot—where, in contemplation of such an emergency, a sort of barrier had been reared. Alas! they had quitted their security, and fled right into the pathway of destruction. Down came the whole side of the mountain in a cataract of ruin. Just before it reached the house the stream broke into two branches, shivering not a window there, but overwhelming the whole vicinity, blocked up the road, and annihilated everything in its dreadful course. Long ere the thunder of that great Slide had ceased to roar among the mountains, the mortal agony had been endured, and the victims were at peace. Their bodies were never found.

The next morning the light smoke was seen stealing from the cottage chimney up the mountainside. Within, the fire was yet smoldering on the hearth, and the chairs in a circle round it, as if the inhabitants had but gone forth to view the devastation of the Slide, and would shorty return to thank Heaven for their miraculous escape. All had left separate tokens, by which those who had known the family were made to shed a tear for each. Who has not heard their name? The story had been told far and wide, and will for ever be a legend of these mountains. Poets have sung their fate.

There were circumstances which led some to suppose that a stranger had been received into the cottage on this awful night, and had shared the catastrophe of all its inmates. Others denied that there were sufficient grounds for such a conjecture. Woe for the high-souled youth, with his dream of Earthly Immortality! His name and person utterly unknown; his history, his way of life, his plans—a mystery never to be solved; his death and his existence equally a doubt! Whose was the agony of that death moment?

Night Sketches

BENEATH AN UMBRELLA

Pleasant is a rainy winter's day, within doors! The best study for such a day, or the best amusement,—call it which you will,—is a book of travels, describing scenes the most unlike that somber one which is mistily presented through the windows. I have experienced that fancy is then most successful in imparting distinct shapes and vivid colors to the objects which the author has spread upon his page, and that his words become magic spells to summon up a thousand varied pictures. Strange landscapes glimmer through the familiar walls of the room, and outlandish figures thrust themselves almost within the sacred precincts of the hearth. Small as my chamber is, it has space enough to contain the ocean-like circumference of an Arabian desert, its parched sands tracked by the long line of a caravan, with the camels patiently journeying through the heavy sunshine. Though my ceiling be not lofty, yet I can pile up the mountains of Central Asia beneath it, till their summits shine far above the clouds of the middle atmosphere. And, with my humble means, a wealth that is not taxable, I can transport hither the magnificent merchandise of an Oriental bazaar, and call a crowd of purchasers from distant countries to pay a fair profit for the precious articles which are displayed on all sides. True it is, however, that amid the bustle of traffic, or whatever else may seem to be going on around me, the raindrops will occasionally be heard to patter against my window panes, which look forth upon one of the quietest streets in a New England town. After a time, too, the visions vanish, and will not appear again at my bidding. Then, it being nightfall, a gloomy sense of unreality depresses my spirits, and impels me to venture out before the clock shall strike bedtime, to satisfy myself that the world is not entirely made up of such shadowy materials as have busied me throughout the day. A dreamer may dwell so long among fantasies that the things without him will seem as unreal as those within.

When eve has fairly set in, therefore, I sally forth tightly buttoning my shaggy overcoat, and hoisting my umbrella, the silken dome of which immediately resounds with the heavy drumming of the invisible raindrops. Pausing on the lowest doorstep, I contrast the warmth and cheerfulness of my deserted fireside, with the drear obscurity and chill discomfort into which I am about to plunge. Now come fearful auguries, innumerable as the drops of rain. Did not my manhood cry shame upon me, I should turn back within doors, resume my elbow chair, my slippers, and my book, pass such an evening of sluggish enjoyment as the day has been, and go to bed inglorious. The same shivering reluctance, no doubt, has quelled, for a moment, the adventurous spirit of many a traveller, when his feet, which were destined to measure the earth around, were leaving their last tracks in the home paths.

In my own case, poor human nature may be allowed a few misgivings. I look upward, and discern no sky, not even an unfathomable void, but only a black, impenetrable nothingness, as though heaven and all its lights were blotted from the system of the universe. It is as if nature were dead, and the world had put on black, and the clouds were weeping for her. With their tears upon my cheek, I turn my eyes earthward, but find little consolation here below. A lamp is burning dimly at the distant corner, and throws just enough of light along the street to show, and exaggerate by so faintly showing, the perils and difficulties which beset my path. Yonder dingily white remnant of a huge snowbank,—which will yet cumber the sidewalk till the latter days of March,—over or through that wintry waste must I stride onward. Beyond, lies a certain Slough of Despond, a concoction of mud and liquid filth, ankle-deep, leg-deep, neck-deep,— in a word, of unknown bottom—on which the lamplight does not even glimmer, but which I have occasionally watched, in the gradual growth of its horrors, from morn till nightfall. Should I flounder into it depths, farewell to upper earth! And hark! how roughly sounds the roaring of a stream, the turbulent career of which is partially reddened by the gleam of the lamp, but elsewhere brawls noisily through the densest gloom. Oh, should I be swept away in fording that impetuous and unclean torrent, the coroner will have a job with an unfortunate gentleman, who would fain end his troubles anywhere but in a mudpuddle!

Pshaw! I will linger not another instant at arm's length from these dim terrors, which grow more obscurely formidable, the longer I delay to grapple with them. Now for the onset! And lo! with little damage, save a dash of rain in the face and breast, a splash of mud high up the pantaloons, and the left boot full of ice-cold water, behold me at the corner of the street. The lamp throws down a circle of red light around me; and twinkling onward from corner to corner, I discern other beacons marshalling my way to a brighter scene. But this is a lonesome and dreary spot. The tall edifices bid gloomy defiance to the storm, with their blinds all closed, even as a man winks when he faces a spattering gust. How loudly tinkles the collected rain down the tin spouts! The puffs of wind are boisterous, and seem to assail me from various quarters at once. I have often observed that this corner is a haunt and loitering place for those winds which have no work to do upon the deep, dashing ships against our iron-bound shores; nor in the forest, tearing up the sylvan giants with half a rood of soil at their vast roots. Here they amuse themselves with lesser freaks of mischief. See, at this moment, how they assail yonder poor woman, who is passing just within the verge of the lamplight! One blast struggles for her umbrella, and turns it wrong side outward; another whisks the cape of her cloak across her eyes; while a third takes most unwarrantable liberties with the lower part of her attire. Happily, the good dame is no gossamer, but a figure of rotundity and fleshy substance; else would these aerial tormentors whirl her aloft, like a witch upon a broomstick, and set her down, doubtless, in the filthiest kennel hereabout.

From hence I tread upon firm pavements into the center of the town. Here there is almost as brilliant an illumination as when some great victory has been won, either on the battlefield or at the polls. Two rows of shops, with windows down nearly to the ground, cast a glow from side to side, while the black night hangs overhead like a canopy, and thus keeps the splendor from diffusing itself away. The wet sidewalks gleam with a broad sheet of red light. The raindrops glitter, as if the sky were pouring down rubies. The spouts gush with fire. Methinks the scene is an emblem of the deceptive glare which mortals throw around their footsteps in the moral world; thus bedazzling themselves, till they forget the impenetrable obscurity that hems them in, and that can be dispelled only by radiance from above. And after all, it is a cheerless scene, and cheerless are the wanderers in it. Here comes one who has so long been familiar with tempestuous weather that he takes the bluster of the storm for a friendly greeting, as if it should say, "How fare ye, brother?" He is a retired sea captain, wrapped in some nameless garments of the peajacket order, and is now laying his course towards the Marine Insurance Office, there to spin yarns of gale and shipwreck with a crew of old seadogs like himself. The blast will put in its word among their hoarse voices, and be understood by all of them. Next I meet an unhappy slipshod gentleman, with a cloak flung hastily over his shoulders, running a race with boisterous winds, and striving to glide between the drops of rain. Some domestic emergency or other has blown this miserable man from his warm fireside, in quest of a doctor! See that little vagabond—how carelessly he has taken his stand right underneath a spout, while staring at some object of curiosity in a shop window! Surely the rain is his native element; he must have fallen with it from the clouds, as frogs are supposed to do.

Here is a picture, and a pretty one. A young man and a girl, both enveloped in cloaks, and huddled beneath the scanty protection of a cotton umbrella. She wears rubber overshoes; but he is in his dancing pumps; and they are on their way, no doubt, to some cotillon party, or subscription ball at a dollar a head, refreshments included. Thus they struggle against the gloomy tempest, lured onward by a vision of festal splendor. But ah! a most lamentable disaster. Bewildered by the red, blue, and yellow meteors in an apothecary's window, they have stepped upon a slippery remnant of ice, and are precipitated into a confluence of swollen floods at the corner of two streets. Luckless lovers! Were it my nature to be other than a looker-on in life, I would attempt your rescue. Since that may not be, I vow, should you be drowned, to weave such a pathetic story of your fate as shall call forth tears enough to drown you both anew. Do ye touch bottom, my young friends? Yes; they emerge like a water nymph and a river deity, and paddle hand in hand out of the depth of the dark pool. They hurry homeward, dripping, disconsolate, abashed, but with love too warm to be chilled by the cold water. They have stood a test which proves too strong for many. Faithful, though over head and ears in trouble!

Onward I go, deriving a sympathetic joy or sorrow from the varied aspect of mortal affairs, even as my figure catches a gleam from the lighted windows, or is blackened by an interval of darkness. Not that mine is altogether a chameleon spirit, with no hue of its own. Now I pass into a more retired street, where the dwellings of wealth and poverty are intermingled, presenting a range of strongly contrasted pictures. Here, too, may be found the golden mean. Through yonder casement I discern a family circle—the grandmother, the parents, and the children—all flickering, shadowlike, in the glow of a woodfire. Bluster, fierce blast, and beat, thou wintry rain, against the windowpanes! Ye cannot damp the enjoyment of that fireside. Surely my fate is hard, that I should be wandering homeless here, taking to my bosom night, and storm, and solitude, instead of wife and children. Peace, murmurer! Doubt not that darker guests are sitting round the hearth, though the warm blaze hides all but blissful images. Well; here is still a brighter scene. A stately mansion, illuminated for a ball, with cut glass chandeliers and alabaster lamps in every room, and sunny landscapes hanging round the walls. See! a coach has stopped, whence emerges a slender beauty, who, canopied by two umbrellas, glides within the portal, and vanishes amid lightsome thrills of music. Will she ever feel the night wind and the rain? Perhaps—perhaps! And will Death and Sorrow ever enter that proud mansion? As surely as the dancers will be gay within its halls tonight. Such thoughts sadden, yet satisfy my heart; for they teach me that the poor man, in this mean, weatherbeaten hovel, without a fire to cheer him, may call the rich his brother—brethren by Sorrow, who must be an inmate of both their households—brethren by Death, who will lead them both to other homes.

Onward, still onward, I plunged into the night. Now have I reached the utmost limits of the town, where the last lamp struggles feebly with the darkness, like the farthest star that stands sentinel on the borders of uncreated space. It is strange what sensations of sublimity may spring from a very humble source. Such are suggested by this hollow roar of a subterranean cataract, where the mighty stream of a kennel precipitates itself beneath an iron grate, and is seen no more on earth. Listen awhile to its voice of mystery; and fancy will magnify it, till you start, and smile at the illusion. And now another sound—the rumbling of wheels—as the mailcoach, outward-bound, rolls heavily off the pavements, and splashes through the mud and water of the road. All night long the poor passengers will be tossed to and fro between drowsy watch and troubled sleep, and will dream of their own quiet beds, and awake to find themselves still jolting onward. Happier my lot, who will straightway hie me to my familiar room, and toast myself comfortably before the fire, musing, and fitfully dozing, and fancying a strangeness in such sights as all may see. But first let me gaze at this solitary figure, who comes hitherward with a tin lantern which throws the circular pattern of its punched holes on the ground about him. He passes fearlessly into the unknown gloom, whither I will not follow him.

This figure shall supply me with a moral, wherewith, for lack of a more appropriate one, I may wind up my sketch. He fears not to tread the dreary path before him, because his lantern, which was kindled at the fireside of his home, will light him back to that same fireside again. And thus we, night wanderers through a stormy and dismal world, if we bear the lamp of Faith, enkindled at a celestial fire, it will surely lead us home to that heaven whence its radiance was borrowed.

The Prophetic Pictures

"But this painter!" cried Walter Ludlow, with animation. "He not only excels in his peculiar art, but possesses vast acquirements in all other learning and science. He talks Hebrew with Doctor Mather, and gives lectures in anatomy to Doctor Boylston. In a word, he will meet the best instructed man among us on his own ground. Moreover, he is a polished gentleman—a citizen of the world—yes, a true cosmopolite; for he will speak like a native of each clime and country on the globe, except our own forests, whither he is now going. Nor is this all what I most admire in him."

"Indeed!" said Elinor, who had listened, with a woman's interest to the description of such a man. "Yet this is admirable enough."

"Surely it is," replied her lover, "but far less so than his natural gift of adapting himself to every variety of character, insomuch that all men — and all women too, Elinor — shall find a mirror of themselves in this wonderful painter. But the greatest wonder is yet to be told."

"Nay, if he have more wonderful attributes than these," said Elinor, laughing, "Boston is a perilous abode for the poor gentleman. Are you telling me of a painter, or a wizard?"

"In truth," answered he, "that question might be asked much more seriously than you suppose. They say that he paints not merely a man's features, but his mind and heart. He catches the secret sentiments and passions, and throws them upon the canvas, like sunshine — or perhaps, in the portraits of dark-souled men, like a gleam of infernal fire. It is an awful gift," added Walter, lowering his voice from its tone of enthusiasm. "I shall be almost afraid to sit to him."

"Walter, are you in earnest?" exclaimed Elinor.

"For Heaven's sake, dearest Elinor, do not let him paint the look which you now wear," said her lover, smiling, though rather perplexed. "There: it is passing away now, but when you spoke, you seemed frightened to death, and very sad besides. What were you thinking of?"

"Nothing, nothing," answered Elinor, hastily. "You paint my face with your own fantasies. Well, come for me tomorrow, and we will visit this wonderful artist."

But when the young man had departed, it cannot be denied that a remarkable expression was again visible on the fair and youthful face of his mistress. It was a sad and anxious look, little in accordance with what should have been the feelings of a maiden on the eve of wedlock. Yet Walter Ludlow was the chosen of her heart.

"A look!" said Elinor to herself. "No wonder that it startled him, if it expressed what I sometimes feel. I know, by my own experience, how frightful a look may be. But it was all fancy. I thought nothing of it at the time — I have seen nothing of it since — I did but dream it."

And she busied herself about the embroidery of a ruff, in which she meant that her portrait should be taken.

The painter, of whom they had been speaking, was not one of those native artists who, at a later period than this, borrowed their colors from the Indians, and manufactured their pencils of the furs of wild beasts. Perhaps, if he could have revoked his life and prearranged his destiny, he might have chosen to belong to that school without a master, in the hope of being at least original, since there were no works of art to imitate, nor rules to follow. But he had been born and educated in Europe. People said that he had studied the grandeur or beauty of conception, and every touch of the masterhand, in all the most famous pictures, in cabinets and galleries, and on the walls of churches, till there was nothing more for his powerful mind to learn. Art could add nothing to its lessons, but Nature might. He had therefore visited a world wither none of his professional brethren had preceded him, to feast his eyes on visible images that were noble and picturesque, yet had never been transferred to canvas. America was too poor to afford other temptations to an artist of eminence, though many of the colonial gentry, on the painter's arrival, had expressed a wish to transmit their lineaments to posterity, by means of his skill. Whenever such proposals were made, he fixed his piercing eyes on the applicant, and seemed to look him through and through. If he beheld only a sleek and comfortable visage, though there were a goldlaced coat to adorn the picture, and golden guineas to pay for it, he civilly rejected the task and the reward. But if the face were the index of anything uncommon, in thought, sentiment, or experience; or if he met a beggar in the street, with a white beard and furrowed brow; or if sometimes a child happened to look up and smile; he would exhaust all the art on them that he denied to wealth.

Pictorial skill being so rare in the colonies, the painter became an object of general curiosity. If few or none could appreciate the technical merit of his productions, yet there were points, in regard to which the opinion of the crowd was as valuable as the refined judgment of the amateur. He watched the effect that each picture produced on such untutored beholders, and derived profit from their remarks, while they would as soon have thought of instructing Nature herself, as him who seemed to rival her. Their admiration, it must be owned, was tinctured with the prejudices of the age and country. Some deemed it an offense against the Mosaic law, and even a presumptuous mockery of the Creator, to bring into existence such lively images of his creatures. Others, frightened at the art which could raise phantoms at will, and keep the form of the dead among the living, were inclined to consider the painter as a magician, or perhaps the famous Black Man, of old witch times, plotting mischief in a new guise. These foolish fancies were more than half believed among the mob. Even in superior circles his character was invested with a vague awe, partly rising like smokewreaths from the popular superstitions, but chiefly caused by the varied knowledge and talents which he made subservient to his profession.

Being on the eve of marriage, Walter Ludlow and Elinor were

eager to obtain their portraits, as the first of what, they doubtless hoped, would be a long series of family pictures. The day after the conversation above recorded, they visited the painter's rooms. A servant ushered them into an apartment, where, though the artist himself was not visible, there were personages whom they could hardly forbear greeting with reverence. They knew, indeed, that the whole assembly were but pictures, yet felt it impossible to separate the idea of life and intellect from such striking counterfeits. Several of the portraits were known to them, either as distinguished characters of the day or their private acquaintances. There was Governor Burnett, looking as if he had just received an undutiful communication from the House of Representatives, and were inditing a most sharp response. Mr. Cooke hung beside the ruler whom he opposed, sturdy, and somewhat puritanical, as befitted a popular leader. The ancient lady of Sir William Phipps eyed them from the wall, in ruff and farthingale, an imperious old dame, not unsuspected of witchcraft. John Winslow, then a very young man, wore the expression of warlike enterprise which long afterwards made him a distinguished general. Their personal friends were recognized at a glance. In most of the pictures, the whole mind and character were brought out on the countenance, and concentrated into a single look; so that, to speak paradoxically, the origins hardly resembled themselves so strikingly as the portraits did.

Among these modern worthies there were two old bearded saints, who had almost vanished into the darkening canvas. There was also a pale but unfaded Madonna, who had perhaps been worshipped in Rome, and now regarded the lovers with such a mild and holy look that they longed to worship too.

"How singular a thought," observed Walter Ludlow, "that this beautiful face has been beautiful for above two hundred years! Oh, if all beauty would endure so well! Do you not envy her, Elinor?"

"If earth were heaven, I might," she replied. "But where all things fade, how miscrable to be the one that could not fade!"

"The dark old St. Peter has a fierce and ugly scowl, saint though he be," continued Walter. "He troubles me. But the Virgin looks kindly at us."

"Yes; but very sorrowfully, methinks" said Elinor.

The easel stood beneath these three old pictures, sustaining one that had been recently commenced. After a little inspection they began to recognise the features of their own minister, the Rev. Dr. Colman, growing into shape and life, as it were, out of a cloud.

"Kind old man!" exclaimed Elinor. "He gazes at me as if he were about to utter a word of paternal advice."

"And at me," said Walter, "as if he were about to shake his head and rebuke me for some suspected iniquity. But so does the original. I shall never feel quite comfortable under his eye till we stand before him to be married."

They now heard a footstep on the floor, and, turning, beheld the painter, who had been some moments in the room, and had listened to a few of their remarks. He was a middle-aged man, with a countenance well worthy of his own pencil. Indeed, by the picturesque, though careless arrangement of his rich dress, and, perhaps, because his soul dwelt always among painted shapes, he looked somewhat like a portrait himself. His visitors were sensible of a kindred between the artist and his work, and felt as if one of the pictures had stept from the canvas to salute them.

Walter Ludlow, who was slightly known to the painter, explained the object of their visit. While he spoke, a sunbeam was falling athwart his figure and Elinor's, with so happy an effect that they also seemed living pictures of youth and beauty, gladdened by bright fortune. The artist was evidently struck.

"My easel is occupied for several ensuing days, and my stay in Boston must be brief," said he, thoughtfully; then, after an observant glance, he added: "but your wishes shall be gratified, though I disappoint the Chief Justice and Madame Oliver. I must not lose this opportunity for the sake of painting a few ells of broadcloth and brocade."

The painter expressed a desire to introduce both their portraits into one picture, and represent them engaged in some appropriate action. This plan would have delighted the lovers, but was necessarily rejected, because so large a space of canvas would have been unfit for the room which it was intended to decorate. Two half-length portraits were therefore fixed upon. After they had taken leave, Walter Ludlow asked Elinor, with a smile, whether she knew what an influence over their fates the painter was about to acquire.

"The old women of Boston affirm," continued he, "that after he has once got possession of a person's face and figure, he may paint him in any act or situation whatever—and the picture will be prophetic. Do you believe it?"

"Not quite," said Elinor, smiling, "Yet if he has such magic, there is something so gentle in his manner that I am sure he will use it well."

It was the painter's choice to proceed with both portraits at the same time, assigning as a reason, in the mystical language which he sometimes used, that the faces threw light upon each other. Accordingly, he gave now a touch to Walter, and now to Elinor, and the features of one and the other began to start forth so vividly that it appeared as if his triumphant art would actually disengage them from the canvas. Amid the rich light and deep shade, they beheld their phantom selves. But, though the likeness promised to be perfect, they were not quite satisfied with the expression; it seemed more vague than most of the painter's works. He, however, was satisfied with the prospect of success, and being much interested in the lovers, employed his leisure moments unknown to them, in making a crayon sketch of their two figures. During their sittings, he engaged them in conversation, and kindled up their faces with characteristic traits, which, though continually varying, it was his purpose to combine and fix. At length he announced that at their next visit both the portraits would be ready for delivery.

"If my pencil will but be true to my conception, in the few last touches which I meditate," observed he, "these two pictures will be my very best performances. Seldom, indeed, has an artist such subjects."

While speaking, he still bent his penetrative eye upon them, nor withdrew it till they had reached the bottom of the stairs.

Nothing in the whole circle of human vanities takes stronger hold of the imagination than this affair of having a portrait painted. Yet why should it be so? The looking-glass, the polished globes of the andirons, the mirrorlike water, and all other reflecting surfaces, continually present us with portraits, or rather ghosts, of ourselves, which we glance at and straightway forget them. But we forget them only because they vanish. It is the idea of duration—of earthly immortality—that gives such a mysterious interest to our own portraits. Walter and Elinor were not insensible to this feeling, and hastened to the painter's room, punctually at the appointed hour, to meet those pictured shapes which were to be their representatives with posterity. The sunshine flashed after them into the apartment, but left it somewhat gloomy as they closed the door.

Their eyes were immediately attracted to their portraits, which rested against the farthest wall of the room. At the first glance, through the dim light and the distance, seeing themselves in precisely their natural attitudes, and with all the air that they recognized so well, they uttered a simultaneous exclamation of delight.

"There we stand," cried Walter, enthusiastically, "fixed in sunshine for ever! No dark passions can gather on our faces!"

"No," said Elinor, more calmly; "no dreary change can sadden us."

This was said while they were approaching, and had yet gained only an imperfect view of the pictures. The painter, after saluting them, busied himself at a table in completing a crayon sketch, leaving his visitors to form their own judgment as to his perfected labors. At intervals he sent a glance from beneath his deep eyebrows, watching their countenances in profile, with his pencil suspended over the sketch. They had now stood some moments, each in front of the other's picture, contemplating it with entranced attention, but without uttering a word. At length Walter stepped forward—then back—viewing Elinor's portrait in various lights, and finally spoke.

"Is there not a change?" said he, in a doubtful and meditative tone. "Yes; the perception of its grows more vivid the longer I look. It is certainly the same picture that I saw yesterday; the dress—the features—all are the same, and yet something is altered."

"Is then the picture less like than it was yesterday?" inquired the painter, now drawing near, with irrepressible interest.

"The features are perfect Elinor," answered Walter; "and at the first glance the expression seemed also hers. But I could fancy that the portrait has changed countenance while I have been looking at it. The eyes are fixed on mine with a strangely sad and anxious expression. Nay, it is grief and terror! Is this like Elinor?"

"Compare the living face with the pictured one," said the painter.

Walter glanced sidelong at his mistress and started. Motionless and absorbed—fascinated, as it were—in contemplation of Walter's portrait, Elinor's face had assumed precisely the expression of which he had just been complaining. Had she practiced for whole hours before a mirror, she could not have caught the look so successfully. Had the picture itself been a mirror, it could not have thrown back her present aspect with stronger and more melancholy truth. She appeared quite unconscious of the dialogue between the artist and her lover.

"Elinor," exclaimed Walter, in amazement, "what change has come over you?"

She did not hear him, nor desist from her fixed gaze, till he seized her hand, and thus attracted her notice; then, with a sudden tremor, she looked from the picture to the face of the original.

"Do you see no change in your portrait?" asked she.

"In mine? — None!" replied Walter, examining it. "But let me see! Yes; there is a slight change — an improvement, I think, in the picture, though none in the likeness. It has a livelier expression than yesterday, as if some bright thought were flashing from the eyes, and about to be uttered from the lips. Now that I have caught the look, it becomes very decided."

While he was intent on these observations Elinor turned to the painter. She regarded him with grief and awe, and felt that he repaid her with sympathy and commiseration, though wherefore she could but vaguely guess.

"That look!" whispered she, and shuddered. "How came it there?"

"Madam," said the painter, sadly, taking her hand and leading her apart — "in both these pictures I have painted what I saw. The artist — the true artist — must look beneath the exterior. It is his gift — his proudest, but often a melancholy one — to see the inmost soul, and, by a power indefinable even to himself, to make it glow or darken upon the canvas, in glances that express the thought and sentiment of years. Would that I might convince myself of error in the present instance!"

They had now approached the table, on which were heads in chalk, hands almost as expressive as ordinary faces, ivied church towers, thatched cottages, old thunder-stricken trees, oriental and antique costume, and all such picturesque vagaries of an artist's idle moments. Turning them over with seeming carelessness, a crayon sketch of two figures was disclosed.

"If I have failed," continued he — "if your heart does not see itself reflected in your own portrait — if you have no secret cause to trust my delineation of the other — it is not yet too late to alter them. I might change the action of these figures too. But would it influence the event?"

He directed her notice to the sketch. A thrill ran through Elinor's frame; a shriek was upon her lips; but she stifled it, with the self-command that becomes habitual to all who hide thoughts of fear and anguish within their bosoms. Turning from the table, she perceived that Walter had advanced near enough to have seen the sketch, though she could not determine whether it had caught his eye.

"We will not have the pictures altered," said she, hastily.

"If mine is sad, I shall but look the gayer for the contrast."

"Be it so," answered the painter, bowing. "May your griefs be such fanciful ones that only your picture may mourn for them! For your joys—may they be true and deep, and paint themselves upon this lovely face, till it quite belie my art!"

After the marriage of Walter and Elinor, the pictures formed the two most splendid ornaments of their abode. They hung side by side, separated by a narrow panel, appearing to eye each other constantly, yet always returning the gaze of the spectator. Travelled gentlemen, who professed a knowledge of such subjects, reckoned these among the most admirable specimens of modern portraiture; while common observers compared them with the originals, feature by feature, and were rapturous in praise of the likeness. But it was on a third class,—neither travelled connoisseurs nor common observers, but people of natural sensibility—that the pictures wrought their strongest effect. Such persons might gaze carelessly at first, but, becoming interested, would return day after day and study these painted faces like the pages of a mystic volume. Walter Ludlow's portrait attracted their earliest notice. In the absence of himself and his bride, they sometimes disputed as to the expression which the painter had intended to throw upon the features; all agreeing that there was a look of earnest import, though no two explained it alike. There was less diversity of opinion in regard to Elinor's picture. They differed, indeed, in their attempts to estimate the nature and depth of the gloom that dwelt upon her face, but agreed that it was gloom, and alien from the natural temperament of their youthful friend. A certain fanciful person announced, as the result of much scrutiny, that both these pictures were parts of one design, and that the melancholy strength of feeling in Elinor's countenance bore reference to the more vivid emotion, or, as he termed it, the wild passion, in that of Walter. Though unskilled in the art, he even began a sketch, in which the action of the two figures was to correspond with their mutual expression.

It was whispered among friends, that, day by day, Elinor's face was assuming a deeper shade of pensiveness, which threatened soon to render her too true a counterpart of her melancholy picture. Walter, on the other hand, instead of acquiring the vivid look which the painter had given him on the canvas, became reserved and downcast, with no outward flashes of emotion, however it might be smouldering within. In course of time Elinor hung a gorgeous curtain of purple silk, wrought with flowers, and fringed with heavy golden tassels, before the pictures, under pretence that the dust would tarnish their hues, or the light dim them. It was enough. Her visitors felt that the massive folds of the silk must never be withdrawn, nor the portraits mentioned in her presence.

Time wore on; and the painter came again. He had been far enough to the north to see the silver cascade of the Crystal Hills, and to look over the vast round of cloud and forest from the summit of New England's loftiest mountain. But he did not profane that scene by the mockery of his art. He had also lain in a canoe on the bosom of Lake George, making his soul the mirror of its loveliness and grandeur, till not a picture in the Vatican was more vivid than his recollection. He had gone with the Indian hunters to Niagara, and there again had flung his hopeless pencil down the precipice, feeling that he could as soon paint the roar as aught else that goes to make up the wondrous cataract. In truth, it was seldom his impulse to copy natural scenery, except as a framework for the delineations of the human form and face, instinct with thought, passion, or suffering. With store of such, his adventurous ramble had enriched him: the stern dignity of Indian chiefs; the dusky loveliness of Indian girls; the domestic life of wigwams; the stealthy march; the battle beneath gloomy pinetrees; the frontier fortress with its garrison; the anomaly of the old French partisan, bred in courts, but grown grey in shaggy deserts; such were the scenes and portraits that he had sketched. The glow of perilous moments; flashes of wild feeling; struggles of fierce power — love, hate, grief, frenzy — in a word, all the worn-out heart of the old earth, had been revealed to him under a new form. His portfolio was filled with graphic illustrations of the volume of his memory, which genius would transmute into its own substance, and imbue with immortality. He felt that the deep wisdom in his art, which he had sought so far, was found.

But, amid stern or lovely nature, in the perils of the forest, or its overwhelming peacefulness, still there had been two phantoms, the companions of his way. Like all other men around whom an engrossing purpose wreathes itself, he was insulated from the mass of human kind. He had no aim — no pleasure — no sympathies — but what were ultimately connected with his art. Though gentle in manner, and upright in intent and action, he did not possess kindly feelings; his heart was cold; no living creature could be brought near enough to keep him warm. For these two beings, however, he had felt, in its greatest intensity, the sort of interest which always allied him to the subjects of his pencil. He had pried into their souls with his keenest insight, and pictured the result upon their features with his utmost skill, so as barely to fall short of that standard which no genius ever reached, his own severe conception. He had caught from the duskiness of the future—at least, so he fancied—a fearful secret, and had obscurely revealed it on the portraits. So much of himself—of his imagination and all other powers—had been lavished on the study of Walter and Elinor that he almost regarded them as creations of his own, like the thousands with which he had peopled the realms of Picture. Therefore did they flit through the twilight of the woods, hover on the mist of waterfalls, look forth from the mirror of the lake, nor melt away in the noontide sun. They haunted his pictorial fancy, not as mockeries of life, nor pale goblins of the dead, but in the guise of portraits, each with the unalterable expression which his magic had evoked from the caverns of the soul. He could not recross the Atlantic till he had again beheld the originals of those airy pictures.

"Oh, glorious Art!" thus mused the enthusiastic painter, as he trod the street. "Thou art the image of the Creator's own. The innumerable forms that wander in nothingness start into being at thy beck. The dead live again. Thou recallest them to their old scenes, and givest their grey shadows the luster of a better life, at once earthly and immortal. Thou snatchest back the fleeting moments of History. With thee there is no Past; for, at thy touch, all that is great becomes for ever present; and illustrious men live through long ages, in the visible performance of the very deeds which made them what they are. Oh, potent Art! as thou bringest the faintly-revealed Past to stand in the narrow strip of sunlight which we call Now, canst thou summon the shrouded Future to meet her there? Have I not achieved it? Am I not thy Prophet?"

Thus, with a proud, yet melancholy fervor, did he almost cry aloud as he passed through the toilsome street, among people that knew not of his reveries, nor could understand nor care for them. It is not good for man to cherish a solitary ambition. Unless there be those around him by whose example he may regulate himself, his thoughts, desires, and hopes will become extravagant, and he the semblance, perhaps the reality, of a madman. Reading other bosoms with an acuteness almost preternatural, the painter failed to see the disorder of his own.

"And this should be the house," said he, looking up and down the front before he knocked. "Heaven help my brains! That picture! Methinks it will never vanish. Whether I look at the windows or the door, there it is framed within them, painted strongly, and glowing in the richest tints—the faces of the portraits—the figures and action of the sketch!"

He knocked.

"The portraits! Are they within?" inquired he of the domestic: then recollecting himself—"Your master and mistress? are they at home?"

"They are, sir," said the servant, adding, as he noticed that picturesque aspect of which the painter could never divest himself—"and the portraits too!"

The guest was admitted into a parlor, communicating by a central door with an interior room of the same size. As the first apartment was empty he passed to the entrance of the second, within which his eyes were greeted by those living personages, as well as their pictured representatives, who had long been the objects of so singular an interest. He involuntarily paused on the threshold.

They had not perceived his approach. Walter and Elinor were standing before the portraits, whence the former had just flung back the rich and voluminous folds of the silken curtain, holding its golden tassel with one hand, while the other grasped that of his bride. The pictures, concealed for months, gleamed forth again in undiminished splendor, appearing to throw a somber light across the room, rather than to be disclosed by a borrowed radiance. That of Elinor had been almost prophetic. A pensiveness, and next a gentle sorrow, had successively dwelt upon her countenance, deepening with the lapse of time into a quiet anguish. A mixture of affright would now have made it the very expression of the portrait. Walter's face was moody and dull, or animated only by fitful flashes which left a heavier darkness for their momentary illumination. He looked from Elinor to her portrait and thence to his own, in the contemplation of which he finally stood absorbed.

The painter seemed to hear the step of Destiny approaching behind him on its progress towards its victims. A strange thought darted into his mind. Was not his own the form in which that Destiny had embodied itself, and he a chief agent of the coming evil which he had foreshadowed?

Still Walter remained silent before the picture, communing with it as with his own heart, and abandoning himself to the spell of evil influence that the painter had cast upon the features. Gradually his eyes kindled, while as Elinor watched the increasing wildness of his face her own assumed a look of terror; and when, at last, he turned upon her, the resemblance of both to their portraits was complete.

"Our fate is upon us!" howled Walter. "Die!"

Drawing a knife, he sustained her as she was sinking to the ground, and aimed it at her bosom. In the action and in the look and attitude of each, the painter beheld the figures of his sketch. The picture, with all its tremendous coloring, was finished.

"Hold, madman!" cried he, sternly.

He had advanced from the door, and interposed himself between the wretched beings with the same sense of power to regulate their destiny as to alter a scene upon the canvas. He stood like a magician controlling the phantoms which he had evoked.

"What!" muttered Walter Ludlow, as he relapsed from fierce excitement into sudden gloom. "Does fate impede its own decree?"

"Wretched lady!" said the painter. "Did I not warn you?"

"You did," replied Elinor, calmly, as her terror gave place to the quiet grief which it had disturbed. "But—I loved him!"

Is there not a deep moral in the tale? Could the result of one or of all our deeds be shadowed forth and set before us—some would call it Fate and hurry onward, others be swept along by their passionate desires, and none be turned aside by the PROPHETIC PICTURES.

Young Goodman Brown

Young goodman Brown came forth, at sunset, into the street of Salem village, but put his head back, after crossing the threshold, to exchange a parting kiss with his young wife. And Faith, as the wife was aptly named, thrust her own pretty head into the street, letting the wind play with the pink ribbons of her cap, while she called to goodman Brown.

"Dearest heart," whispered she, softly and rather sadly, when her lips were close to his ear, "pr'y thee, put off your journey until sunrise, and sleep in your own bed tonight. A lone woman is troubled with such dreams and such thoughts, that she's afeard of herself, sometimes. Pray, tarry with me this night, dear husband, of all nights in the year!"

"My love and my Faith," replied young goodman Brown, "of all nights in the year, this one night must I tarry away from thee. My journey, as thou callest it, forth and back again, must needs be done 'twixt now and sunrise. What, my sweet, pretty wife, dost thou doubt me already, and we but three months married!"

"Then, God bless you!" said Faith, with the pink ribbons, "and may you find all well, when you come back."

"Amen!" cried goodman Brown. "Say thy prayers, dear Faith, and go to bed at dusk, and no harm will come to thee."

So they parted; and the young man pursued his way, until being about to turn the corner by the meetinghouse, he looked back, and saw the head of Faith still peeping after him, with a melancholy air, in spite of her pink ribbons.

"Poor little Faith!" thought he, for his heart smote him. "What a wretch am I, to leave her on such an errand! She talks of dreams, too. Methought, as she spoke, there was trouble in her face, as if a dream had warned her what work is to be done tonight. But, no, no! 't would kill her to think it. Well; she's a blessed angel on earth; and after this one night, I'll cling to her skirts and follow her to Heaven."

With this excellent resolve for the future, goodman Brown felt himself justified in making more haste on his present evil purpose. He had taken a dreary road, darkened by all the gloomiest trees of the forest, which barely stood aside to let the narrow path creep through, and closed immediately behind. It was all as lonely as could be; and there is this peculiarity in such a solitude, that the traveler knows not who may be concealed by the innumerable trunks and the thick boughs overhead; so that, with lonely footsteps, he may yet be passing through an unseen multitude.

"There may be a devilish Indian behind every tree," said goodman Brown, to himself; and he glanced fearfully behind him, as he added, "What if the devil himself should be at my very elbow!"

His head being turned back, he passed a crook of the road, and looking forward again, beheld the figure of a man, in grave and decent attire, seated at the foot of an old tree. He arose, at goodman Brown's approach, and walked onward, side by side with him.

"You are late, goodman Brown," said he, "The clock of the Old South was striking as I came through Boston; and that is full fifteen minutes agone."

"Faith kept me back awhile," replied the young man, with a tremor in his voice, caused by the sudden appearance of his companion, though not wholly unexpected.

It was now deep dusk in the forest, and deepest in that part of it where these two were journeying. As nearly as could be discerned, the second traveler was about fifty years old, apparently in the same rank of life as goodman Brown, and bearing a considerable resemblance to him, though perhaps more in expression than features. Still, they might have been taken for father and son. And yet, though the elder person was as simply clad as the younger, and as simple in manner too, he had an indescribable air of one who knew the world, and would not have felt abashed at the governor's dinner table, or in king William's court, were it possible that his affairs should call him thither. But the only thing about him, that could be fixed upon as remarkable, was his staff, which bore the likeness of a great black snake, so curiously wrought, that it might almost be seen to twist and wriggle itself, like a living serpent. This, of course, must have been an ocular deception, assisted by the uncertain light.

"Come, goodman Brown!" cried his fellow traveler, "this is a dull pace for the beginning of a journey. Take my staff, if you are so soon weary."

"Friend," said the other, exchanging his slow pace for a full stop, "having kept covenant by meeting thee here, it is my purpose now to return whence I came. I have scruples, touching the matter thou wot'st of."

"Sayest thou so?" replied he of the serpent, smiling apart. "Let us walk on, nevertheless, reasoning as we go, and if I convince thee not, thou shalt turn back. We are but a little way in the forest yet."

"Too far, too far!" exclaimed the goodman, unconsciously resuming his walk. "My father never went into the woods on such an errand, nor his father before him. We have been a race of honest men and good Christians, since the days of the martyrs. And shall I be the first of the name of Brown, that ever took this path, and kept"—

"Such company, thou wouldst say," observed the elder person, interpreting his pause. "Good, goodman Brown! I have been as well acquainted with your family as with ever a one among the Puritans; and that's no trifle to say. I helped your grandfather, the constable, when he lashed the Quaker woman so smartly through the streets of Salem. And it was I that brought your father a pitch-pine knot, kindled at my own hearth, to set fire to an Indian village, in King Philip's war. They were my good friends, both; and many a pleasant walk have we had along this path, and returned merrily after midnight. I would fain be friends with you, for their sake."

"If it be as thou sayest," replied goodman Brown, "I marvel they never spoke of these matters. Or, verily, I marvel not, seeing that the least rumor of the sort would have driven them from New England. We are a people of prayer, and good works to boot, and abide no such wickedness."

"Wickedness or not," said the traveler with the twisted staff, "I have a very general acquaintance, here in New England. The deacons of many a church have drunk the communion wine with me; the selectmen, of divers towns, make me their chairman; and a majority of the Great and General Court are firm supporters of my interest. The governor and I, too—but these are state secrets."

"Can this be so!" cried goodman Brown, with a stare of amazement at his undisturbed companion. "Howbeit, I have nothing to do with the governor and council; they have their own ways, and are no rule for a simple husbandman, like me. But, were I to go on with thee, how should I meet the eye of that good old man, our minister, at Salem village? Oh, his voice would make me tremble, both Sabbath day and lecture day!"

Thus far the elder traveler had listened with due gravity, but now burst into a fit of irrepressible mirth, shaking himself so violently, that his snakelike staff actually seemed to wriggle in sympathy.

"Ha! ha! ha!" shouted he, again and again; then composing himself, "Well, go on; goodman Brown, go on, but, pr'y thee, don't kill me with laughing!"

"Well, then, to end the matter at once," said goodman Brown, considerably nettled, "there is my wife, Faith. It would break her dear little heart, and I'd rather break my own!"

"Nay, if that be the case," answered the other, "e'en go thy ways, goodman Brown. I would not, for twenty old women like the one hobbling before us, that Faith should come to any harm."

As he spoke, he pointed his staff at a female figure on the path, in whom goodman Brown recognized a very pious and exemplary dame, who had taught him his catechism, in youth, and was still his moral and spiritual adviser, jointly with the minister and deacon Gookin.

"A marvel, truly, that goody Cloyse should be so far in the wilderness, at nightfall!" said he. "But, with your leave, friend, I shall take a cut through the woods, until we have left this Christian woman behind. Being a stranger to you, she might ask whom I was consorting with, and whither I was going."

"Be it so," said his fellow traveler. "Betake you to the woods, and let me keep the path."

Accordingly, the young man turned aside, but took care to watch his companion, who advanced softly along the road, until he had come within a staff's length of the old dame. She, meanwhile, was making the best of her way, with singular speed for so aged a woman, and mumbling some indistinct words, a prayer, doubtless, as she went. The traveler put forth his staff, and touched her withered neck with what seemed the serpent's tail.

"The devil!" screamed the pious old lady.

"Then goody Cloyse knows her old friend?" observed the traveler, confronting her, and leaning on his writhing stick.

"Ah, forsooth, and is it your worship, indeed?" cried the good dame. "Yea, truly is it, and in the very image of my old gossip, goodman Brown, the grandfather of the silly fellow that now is. But, would your worship believe it? my broomstick hath strangely disappeared, stolen, as I suspect, by that unhanged witch, goody Cory and that, too, when I was all anointed with the juice of smallage and cinquefoil and wolfsbane"—

"Mingled with fine wheat and the fat of a newborn babe," said the shape of old goodman Brown.

"Ah, your worship knows the receipt," cried the old lady, cackling aloud. "So, as I was saying, being all ready for the meeting, and no horse to ride on, I made up my mind to foot it; for they tell me, there is a nice young man to be taken into communion tonight. But now your good worship will lend me your arm, and we shall be there in a twinkling."

"That can hardly be," answered her friend. "I may not spare you my arm, goody Cloyse, but here is my staff, if you will."

So saying, he threw it down at her feet, where, perhaps, it assumed life, being one of the rods which its owner had formerly lent to the Egyptian Magi. Of this fact, however, goodman Brown could not take cognizance. He had cast up his eyes in astonishment, and looking down again, beheld neither goody Cloyse nor the serpentine staff, but his fellow traveler alone, who waited for him as calmly as if nothing had happened.

"That old woman taught me my catechism!" said the young man; and there was a world of meaning in this simple comment.

They continued to walk onward, while the elder traveler exhorted his companion to make good speed and persevere in the path, discoursing so aptly, that his arguments seemed rather to spring up in the bosom of his auditor, than to be suggested by himself. As they went, he plucked a branch of maple, to serve for a walking stick, and began to strip it of the twigs and little boughs, which were wet with evening dew. The moment his fingers touched them, they became strangely withered and dried up, as with a week's sunshine. Thus the pair proceeded, at a good free pace, until suddenly, in a gloomy hollow of the road, goodman Brown sat himself down on the stump of a tree, and refused to go any farther.

"Friend," said he, stubbornly, "my mind is made up. Not another step will I budge on this errand. What if a wretched old woman do choose to go to the devil, when I thought she was going to Heaven! Is that any reason why I should quit my dear Faith, and go after her?"

"You will think better of this, by-and-by," said his acquaintance, composedly. "Sit here and rest yourself awhile; and when you feel like moving again, there is my staff to help you along."

Without more words, he threw his companion the maple stick, and was as speedily out of sight, as if he had vanished into the deepening gloom. The young man sat a few moments, by the roadside, applauding himself greatly, and thinking with how clear a conscience he should meet the minister, in his morning walk, nor shrink from the eye of good old deacon Gookin. And what calm sleep would be his, that very night, which was to have been spent so wickedly, but purely and sweetly now, in the arms of Faith! Amidst these pleasant and praiseworthy meditations, goodman Brown heard the tramp of horses along the road, and deemed it advisable to conceal himself within the verge of the forest, conscious of the guilty purpose that had brought him thither, though now so happily turned from it.

On came the hoof tramps and the voices of the riders, two grave old voices, conversing soberly as they drew near. These mingled sounds appeared to pass along the road, within a few yards of the young man's hiding place; but owing, doubtless, to the depth of the gloom, at that particular spot, neither the travelers nor their steeds were visible. Though their figures brushed the small boughs by the wayside, it could not be seen that they intercepted, even for a moment, the faint gleam from the strip of bright sky, athwart which they must have passed. Goodman Brown alternately crouched and stood on tiptoe, pulling aside the branches, and thrusting forth his head as far as he durst, without discerning so much as a shadow. It vexed him the more, because he could have sworn, were such a thing possible, that he recognized the voices of the minister and deacon Gookin, jogging along quietly, as they were wont to do, when bound to some ordination or ecclesiastical council. While yet within hearing, one of the riders stopped to pluck a switch.

"Of the two, reverend Sir," said the voice like the deacon's, "I had rather miss an ordination dinner than tonight's meeting. They tell me that some of our community are to be here from Falmouth and beyond, and others from Connecticut and Rhode Island; besides several of the Indian powows, who, after their fashion, know almost as much deviltry as the best of us. Moreover, there is a goodly young woman to be taken into communion."

"Mighty well, deacon Gookin!" replied the solemn old tones of the minister. "Spur up, or we shall be late. Nothing can be done, you know, until I get on the ground."

The hoofs clattered again, and the voices, talking so strangely in the empty air, passed on through the forest, where no church had ever been gathered, nor solitary Christian prayed. Whither, then, could these holy men be journeying, so deep into the heathen wilderness? Young goodman Brown caught hold of a tree, for support, being ready to sink down on the ground, faint and overburthened with the heavy sickness of his heart. He looked up to the sky, doubting whether there really was a Heaven above him. Yet, there was the blue arch, and the stars brightening in it.

"With Heaven above, and Faith below, I will yet stand firm against the devil!" cried goodman Brown.

While he still gazed upward, into the deep arch of the firmament, and had lifted his hands to pray, a cloud, though no wind was stirring, hurried across the zenith, and hid the brightening stars. The blue sky was still visible, except directly overhead, where this black mass of cloud was sweeping swiftly northward. Aloft in the air, as if from the depths of the cloud, came a confused and doubtful sound of voices. Once, the listener fancied that he could distinguish the accents of townspeople of his own, men and women, both pious and ungodly, many of whom he had met at the communion table, and had seen others rioting at the tavern. The next moment, so indistinct were the sounds, he doubted whether he had heard aught but the murmur of the old forest, whispering without a wind. Then came a stronger swell of those familiar tones, heard daily in the sunshine, at Salem village, but never, until now, from a cloud of night. There was one voice, of a young woman, uttering lamentations, yet with an uncertain sorrow, and entreating for some favor, which, perhaps, it would grieve her to obtain. And all the unseen multitude, both saints and sinners, seemed to encourage her onward.

"Faith!" shouted goodman Brown, in a voice of agony and desperation; and the echoes of the forest mocked him, crying—"Faith! Faith!" as if bewildered wretches were seeking her, all through the wilderness.

The cry of grief, rage, and terror, was yet piercing the night, when the unhappy husband held his breath for a response. There was a scream, drowned immediately in a louder murmur of voices, fading into far-off laughter, as the dark cloud swept away, leaving the clear and silent sky above goodman Brown. But something fluttered lightly down through the air, and caught on the branch of a tree. The young man seized it, and beheld a pink ribbon.

"My Faith is gone!" cried he, after one stupefied moment. "There is no good on earth; and sin is but a name. Come, devil! for to thee is this world given."

And maddened with despair, so that he laughed loud and long, did goodman Brown grasp his staff and set forth again, at such a rate, that he seemed to fly along the forest-path, rather than to walk or run. The road grew wilder and drearier, and more faintly traced, and vanished at length, leaving him in the heart of the dark wilderness, still rushing onward, with the instinct that guides mortal man to evil. The whole forest was peopled with frightful sounds; the creaking of the trees, the howling of wild beasts, and the yell of Indians; while, sometimes, the wind tolled like a distant church bell, and sometimes gave a broad roar around the traveler, as if all Nature were laughing him to scorn. But he was himself the chief horror of the scene, and shrank not from its other horrors.

"Ha! ha! ha!" roared goodman Brown, when the wind laughed at him. "Let us hear which will laugh loudest! Think not to frighten me with your deviltry! Come witch, come wizard, come Indian powow, come devil himself! and here comes goodman Brown. You may as well fear him as he fear you!"

In truth, all through the haunted forest, there could be nothing more frightful than the figure of goodman Brown. On he flew, among the black pines, brandishing his staff with frenzied gestures, now giving vent to an inspiration of horrid blasphemy, and now shouting forth such laughter, as set all the echoes of the forest laughing like demons around him. The fiend in his own shape is less hideous, than when he rages in the breast of man. Thus sped the demoniac on his course, until, quivering among the trees, he saw a red light before him, as when the felled trunks and branches of a clearing have been set on fire, and throw up their lurid blaze against the sky, at the hour of midnight. He paused, in a lull of the tempest that had driven him onward, and heard the swell of what seemed a hymn, rolling solemnly from a distance, with the weight of many voices. He knew the tune; it was a familiar one in the choir of the village meetinghouse. The verse died heavily away, and was lengthened by a chorus, not of human voices, but of all the sounds of the benighted wilderness, pealing in awful harmony together. Goodman Brown cried out; and his cry was lost to his own ear, by its unison with the cry of the desert.

In the interval of silence, he stole forward, until the light glared full upon his eyes. At one extremity of an open space, hemmed in by the dark wall of the forest, arose a rock, bearing some rude, natural resemblance either to an altar or a pulpit, and surrounded by four blazing pines, their tops aflame, their stems untouched, like candles at an evening meeting. The mass of foliage, that had overgrown the summit of the rock, was all on fire, blazing high into the night, and fitfully illuminating the whole field. Each pendent twig and leafy festoon was in a blaze. As the red light arose and fell, a numerous congregation alternately shone forth, then disappeared in shadow, and again grew, as it were, out of the darkness, peopling the heart of the solitary woods at once.

"A grave and dark-clad company!" quoth goodman Brown.

In truth, they were such. Among them, quivering to-and-fro, between gloom and splendor, appeared faces that would be seen, next day, at the council board of the province, and others which, Sabbath after Sabbath, looked devoutly heavenward, and benignantly over the crowded pews, from the holiest pulpits in the land. Some affirm, that the lady of the governor was there. At least, there were high dames well known to her, and wives of honored husbands, and widows, a great multitude, and ancient maidens, all of excellent repute, and fair young girls, who trembled, lest their mothers should espy them. Either the sudden gleams of light, flashing over the obscure field, bedazzled goodman Brown, or he recognized a score of the church members of Salem village, famous for their especial sanctity. Good old deacon Gookin had arrived, and waited at the skirts of that venerable saint, his revered pastor. But, irreverently consorting with these grave, reputable, and pious people, these elders of the church, these chaste dames and dewy virgins, there were men of dissolute lives and women of spotted fame, wretches given over to all mean and filthy vice, and suspected even of horrid crimes. It was strange to see, that the good shrank not from the wicked, nor were the sinners abashed by the saints. Scattered, also, among their pale faced enemies, were the Indian priests, or powows, who had often scared their native forest with more hideous incantations than any known to English witchcraft.

"But, where is Faith?" thought goodman Brown; and, as hope came into his heart, he trembled.

Another verse of the hymn arose, a slow and solemn strain, such as the pious love, but joined to words which expressed all that our nature can conceive of sin, and darkly hinted at far more. Unfathomable to mere mortals is the lore of fiends. Verse after verse was sung, and still the chorus of the desert swelled between, like the deepest tone of a mighty organ. And, with the final peal of that dreadful anthem, there came a sound, as if the roaring wind, the rushing streams, the howling beasts, and every other voice of the unconverted wilderness, were mingling and according with the voice of guilty man, in homage to the prince of all. The four blazing pines threw up a loftier flame, and obscurely discovered shapes and visages of horror on the smoke wreaths, above the impious assembly. At the same moment, the fire on the rock shot redly forth, and formed a glowing arch above its base, where now appeared a figure. With reverence be it spoken, the apparition bore no slight similitude, both in garb and manner, to some grave divine of the New England churches.

"Bring forth the converts!" cried a voice, that echoed through the field and rolled into the forest.

At the word, goodman Brown stept forth from the shadow of the trees, and approached the congregation, with whom he felt a loathful brotherhood, by the sympathy of all that was wicked in his heart. He could have well-nigh sworn, that the shape of his own dead father beckoned him to advance, looking downward from a smoke wreath, while a woman, with dim features of despair, threw out her hand to warn him back. Was it his mother? But he had no power to retreat one step, nor to resist, even in thought, when the minister and good old deacon Gookin, seized his arms, and led him to the blazing rock. Thither came also the slender form of a veiled female, led between goody Cloyse, that pious teacher of the catechism, and Martha Carrier, who had received the devil's promise to be queen of hell. A rampant hag was she! And there stood the proselytes, beneath the canopy of fire.

"Welcome, my children," said the dark figure, "to the communion of your grave! Ye have found, thus young, your nature and your destiny. My children, look behind you!"

They turned; and flashing forth, as it were, in a sheet of flame, the fiend worshippers were seen; the smile of welcome gleamed darkly on every visage.

"There," resumed the sable form, "are all whom ye have reverenced from youth. Ye deemed them holier than yourselves, and shrank from your own sin, contrasting it with their lives of righteousness, and prayerful aspirations heavenward. Yet, here are they all, in my worshipping assembly! This night it shall be granted you to know their secret deeds; how hoary bearded elders of the church have whispered wanton words to the young maids of their households; how many a woman, eager for widow's weeds, has given her husband a drink at bed time, and let him sleep his last sleep in her bosom; how beardless youths have made haste to inherit their farthers' wealth; and how fair damsels—blush not, sweet ones!—have dug little graves in the garden, and bidden me, the sole guest, to an infant's funeral. By the sympathy of your human hearts for sin, ye shall scent out all the places—whether in church, bed chamber, street, field, or forest—where crime has been committed, and shall exult to behold the whole earth one stain of guilt, one mighty blood spot. Far more than this! It shall be yours to penetrate, in every bosom, the deep mystery of sin, the fountain of all wicked arts, and which, inexhaustibly supplies more evil impulses than human power —than my power, at its utmost!—can make manifest in deeds. And now, my children, look upon each other."

They did so; and, by the blaze of the hell-kindled torches, the wretched man beheld his Faith, and the wife her husband, trembling before that unhallowed altar.

"Lo! there ye stand, my children," said the figure, in a deep and solemn tone, almost sad, with its despairing awfulness, as if his once angelic nature could yet mourn for our miserable race. "Depending upon one another's hearts, ye had still hoped, that virtue were not all a dream. Now are ye undeceived! Evil is the nature of mankind. Evil must be your only happiness. Welcome, again, my children, to the communion of your race!"

"Welcome!" repeated the fiend worshippers, in one cry of despair and triumph.

And there they stood, the only pair, as it seemed, who were yet hesitating on the verge of wickedness, in this dark world. A basin was hollowed, naturally, in the rock. Did it contain water, reddened by the lurid light? or was it blood? or, perchance, a liquid flame? Herein did the Shape of Evil dip his hand, and prepare to lay the mark of baptism upon their foreheads, that they might be partakers of the mystery of sin, more conscious of the secret guilt of others, both in deed and thought, than they could now be of their own. The husband cast one look at his pale wife, and Faith at him. What polluted wretches would the next glance shew them to each other, shuddering alike at what they disclosed and what they saw!

"Faith! Faith!" cried the husband. "Look up to Heaven, and resist the Wicked One!"

Whether Faith obeyed, he knew not. Hardly had he spoken, when he found himself amid calm night and solitude, listening to a roar of the wind, which died heavily away through the forest. He staggered against the rock and felt it chill and damp, while a hanging twig, that had been all on fire, besprinkled his cheek with the coldest dew.

The next morning, young goodman Brown came slowly into the street of Salem village, staring around him like a bewildered man. The good old minister was taking a walk along the graveyard, to get an appetite for breakfast and meditate his sermon, and bestowed a blessing, as he passed, on goodman Brown. He shrank from the venerable saint, as if to avoid an anathema. Old deacon Gookin was at domestic worship, and the holy words of his prayer were heard through the open window. "What God doth the wizard pray to?" quoth goodman Brown. Goody Cloyse, that excellent old Christian, stood in the early sunshine, at her own lattice, catechising a little girl, who had brought her a pint of morning's milk. Goodman Brown snatched away the child, as from the grasp of the fiend himself. Turning the corner by the meetinghouse, he spied the head of Faith, with the pink ribbons, gazing anxiously forth, and bursting into such joy at sight of him, that she skipt along the street, and almost kissed her husband before the whole village. But, goodman Brown looked sternly and sadly into her face and passed on without a greeting.

Had goodman Brown fallen asleep in the forest, and only dreamed a wild dream of a witch meeting?

Be it so, if you will. But, alas! it was a dream of evil omen for young goodman Brown. A stern, a sad, a darkly meditative, a distrustful, if not a desperate man, did he become, from the night of that fearful dream. On the Sabbath day, when the congregation were singing a holy psalm, he could not listen, because an anthem of sin rushed loudly upon his ear, and drowned all the blessed strain. When the minister spoke from the pulpit, with power and fervid eloquence, and, with his hand on the open bible, of the sacred truths of our religion, and of saintlike lives and triumphant deaths, and of future bliss or misery unutterable, then did goodman Brown turn pale, dreading, lest the roof should thunder down upon the gray blasphemer and his hearers. Often, awaking suddenly at midnight, he shrank from the bosom of Faith, and at morning or eventide, when the family knelt down at prayer, he scowled, and muttered to himself, and gazed sternly at his wife, and turned away. And when he had lived long, and was borne to his grave, a hoary corpse, followed by Faith, an aged woman, and children and grandchildren, a goodly procession, besides neighbors, not a few, they carved no hopeful verse upon his tombstone; for his dying hour was gloom.

The Birthmark

In the latter part of the last century there lived a man of science, an eminent proficient in every branch of natural philosophy, who not long before our story opens had made experience of a spiritual affinity more attractive than any chemical one. He had left his laboratory to the care of an assistant, cleared his fine countenance from the furnace smoke, washed the stain of acids from his fingers, and persuaded a beautiful woman to become his wife. In those days when the comparatively recent discovery of electricity and other kindred mysteries of Nature seemed to open paths into the region of miracle, it was not unusual for the love of science to rival the love of woman in its depth and absorbing energy. The higher intellect, the imaginations the spirit, and even the heart might all find their congenital aliment in pursuits which, as some of their ardent votaries believed, would ascend from one step of powerful intelligence to another, until the philosopher should lay his hand on the secret of creative force and perhaps make new worlds for himself. We know not whether Aylmer possessed this degree of faith in man's ultimate control over Nature. He had devoted himself, however, too unreservedly to scientific studies ever to be weaned from them by any second passion. His love for his young wife might prove the stronger of the two; but it could only be by intertwining itself with his love of science, and uniting the strength of the latter to his own.

Such a union accordingly took place, and was attended with truly remarkable consequences and a deeply impressive moral. One day, very soon after their marriage, Aylmer sat gazing at his wife with a trouble in his countenance that grew stronger until he spoke.

"Georgiana," said he, "has it never occurred to you that the mark upon your cheek might be removed?"

"No, indeed," said she, smiling; but perceiving the seriousness of his manner, she blushed deeply. "To tell you the truth it has been so often called a charm that I was simple enough to imagine it might be so."

"Ah, upon another face perhaps it might," replied her husband; "but never on yours. No, dearest Georgiana, you came so nearly perfect from the hand of Nature that this slightest possible defect, which we hesitate whether to term a defect or a beauty, shocks me, as being the visible mark of earthly imperfection."

"Shocks you, my husband!" cried Georgiana, deeply hurt; at first-reddening with momentary anger, but then bursting into tears. "Then why did you take me from my mother's side? You cannot love what shocks you!"

To explain this conversation it must be mentioned that in the centre of Georgiana's left cheek there was a singular mark, deeply interwoven, as it were, with the texture and substance of her face. In the usual state of her complexion — a healthy though delicate bloom — the mark wore a tint of deeper crimson, which imperfectly defined its shape amid the surrounding rosiness. When she blushed it gradually became more indistinct, and finally vanished amid the triumphant rush of blood that bathed the whole cheek with its brilliant glow. But if any shifting motion caused her to turn pale, there was the mark again, a crimson stain upon the snow, in what Aylmer sometimes deemed an almost fearful distinctness. Its shape bore not a little similarity to the human hand, though of the smallest pygmy size. Georgiana's lovers were wont to say that some fairy at her birth hour had laid her tiny hand upon the infant's cheek, and left this impress there in token of the magic endowments that were to give her such sway over all hearts. Many a desperate swain would have risked life for the privilege of pressing his lips to the mysterious hand. It must not be concealed, however, that the impression wrought by this fairy sign manual varied exceedingly, according to the difference of temperament in the beholders. Some fastidious persons — but they were exclusively of her own sex — affirmed that the bloody hand, as they chose to call it, quite destroyed the effect of Georgiana's beauty, and rendered her countenance even hideous. But it would be as reasonable to say that one of those small blue stains which sometimes occur in the purest statuary marble would convert the Eve of Powers to a monster. Masculine observers, if the birthmark did not heighten their admiration, contented themselves with wishing it away, that the world might possess one living specimen of ideal loveliness without the semblance of a flaw. After his marriage,—for he thought little or nothing of the matter before,—Aylmer discovered that this was the case with himself.

Had she been less beautiful,—if Envy's self could have found aught else to sneer at,—he might have felt his affection heightened by the prettiness of this mimic hand, now vaguely portrayed, now lost, now stealing forth again and glimmering to and fro with every pulse of emotion that throbbed within her heart; but seeing her otherwise so perfect, he found this one defect grow more and more intolerable with every moment of their united lives. It was the fatal flaw of humanity which Nature, in one shape or another, stamps ineffaceably on all her productions, either to imply that they are temporary and finite, or that their perfection must be wrought by toil and pain. The crimson hand expressed the ineludible gripe in which mortality clutches the highest and purest of earthly mold, degrading them into kindred with the lowest, and even with the very brutes, like whom their visible frames return to dust. In this manner, selecting it as the symbol of his wife's liability to sin, sorrow, decay, and death, Aylmer's somber imagination was not long in rendering the birthmark a frightful object, causing him more trouble and horror than ever Georgiana's beauty, whether of soul or sense, had given him delight.

At all the seasons which should have been their happiest, he invariably and without intending it, nay, in spite of a purpose to the contrary, reverted to this one disastrous topic. Trifling as it at first appeared, it so connected itself with innumerable trains of thought and modes of feeling that it became the central point of all. With the morning twilight Aylmer opened his eyes upon his wife's face and recognized the symbol of imperfection; and when they sat together at the evening hearth his eyes wandered stealthily to her cheek, and beheld, flickering with the blaze of the wood fire, the spectral hand that wrote mortality where he would fain have worshipped. Georgiana soon learned to shudder at his gaze. It needed but a glance with the peculiar expression that his face often wore to change the roses of her cheek into a deathlike paleness, amid which the crimson hand was brought strongly out, like a bas-relief of ruby on the whitest marble.

Late one night when the lights were growing dim, so as hardly to betray the stain on the poor wife's cheek, she herself, for the first time, voluntarily took up the subject.

"Do you remember, my dear Aylmer," said she, with a feeble

attempt at a smile, "have you any recollection of a dream last night about this odious hand?"

"None! none whatever!" replied Aylmer, starting; but then he added, in a dry, cold tone, affected for the sake of concealing the real depth of his emotion, "I might well dream of it; for before I fell asleep it had taken a pretty firm hold of my fancy."

"And you did dream of it?" continued Georgiana hastily, for she dreaded lest a gush of tears should interrupt what she had to say. "A terrible dream! I wonder that you can forget it. Is it possible to forget this one expression? — 'It is in her heart now; we must have it out!' Reflect, my husband; for by all means I would have you recall that dream."

The mind is in a sad state when Sleep, the all-involving, cannot confine her spectres within the dim region of her sway, but suffers them to break forth, affrighting this actual life with secrets that perchance belong to a deeper one. Aylmer now remembered his dream. He had fancied himself with his servant Aminadab, attempting an operation for the removal of the birthmark; but the deeper went the knife, the deeper sank the hand, until at length its tiny grasp appeared to have caught hold of Georgiana's heart; whence, however, her husband was inexorably resolved to cut or wrench it away.

When the dream had shaped itself perfectly in his memory, Aylmer sat in his wife's presence with a guilty feeling. Truth often finds its way to the mind close muffled in robes of sleep, and then speaks with uncompassing directness of matters in regard to which we practise an unconscious self-deception during our waking moments. Until now he had not been aware of the tyrannizing influence acquired by one idea over his mind, and of the lengths which he might find in his heart to go for the sake of giving himself peace.

"Aylmer," resumed Georgiana solemnly, "I know not what may be the cost to both of us to rid me of this fatal birthmark. Perhaps its removal may cause cureless deformity; or it may be the stain goes as deep as life itself. Again: do we know that there is a possibility, on any terms, of unclasping the firm gripe of this little hand which was laid upon me before I came into the world?"

"Dearest Georgiana, I have spent much thought upon the subject," hastily interrupted Aylmer. "I am convinced of the perfect practicability of its removal."

"If there be the remotest possibility of it," continued Georgiana, "let the attempt be made at whatever risk. Danger is nothing to me; for life, while this hateful mark makes me the object of your horror and disgust,—life is a burden which I would fling down with joy. Either remove this dreadful hand, or take my wretched life! You have deep science. All the world bears witness of it. You have achieved great wonders. Cannot you remove this little, little mark, which I cover with the tips of two small fingers? Is this beyond your power, for the sake of your own peace, and to save your poor wife from madness?"

"Noblest, dearest, tenderest wife," cried Aylmer rapturously, "doubt not my power. I have already given this matter the deepest thought—thought which might almost have enlightened me to create a being less perfect than yourself. Georgiana, you have led me deeper than ever into the heart of science. I feel myself fully competent to render this dear cheek as faultless as its fellow; and then, most beloved, what will be my triumph when I shall have corrected what Nature left imperfect in her fairest work! Even Pygmalion, when his sculptured woman assumed life, felt not greater ecstasy than mine will be."

"It is resolved, then," said Georgiana, faintly smiling. "And, Aylmer, spare me not, though you should find the birthmark take refuge in my heart at last."

Her husband tenderly kissed her cheek—her right cheek—not that which bore the impress of the crimson hand.

The next day Aylmer apprised his wife of a plan that he had formed whereby he might have opportunity for the intense thought and constant watchfulness which the proposed operation would require; while Georgiana, likewise, would enjoy the perfect repose essential to its success. They were to seclude themselves in the extensive apartments occupied by Aylmer as a laboratory, and where, during his toilsome youth, he had made discoveries in the elemental powers of Nature that had roused the admiration of all the learned societies in Europe. Seated calmly in this laboratory, the pale philosopher had investigated the secrets of the highest cloud region and of the profoundest mines; he had satisfied himself of the causes that kindled and kept alive the fires of the volcano; and had explained the mystery of fountains, and how it is that they gush forth, some so bright and pure, and others with such rich medicinal virtues, from the dark bosom of the earth. Here, too, at an earlier period, he had studied the wonders of the human frame, and attempted to fathom the very process by which Nature assimilates all her precious influences from earth and air, and from the spiritual world, to create and foster man, her masterpiece. The latter pursuit, however, Aylmer had long laid aside in unwilling recognition of the truth—against which all seekers sooner or later stumble—that our great creative Mother, while she amuses us with apparently working in the broadest sunshine, is yet severely careful to keep her own secrets, and, in spite of her pretended openness, shows us nothing but results. She permits us, indeed, to mar, but seldom to mend, and, like a jealous patentee, on no account to make. Now, however, Aylmer resumed these half-forgotten investigations,—not, of course, with such hopes or wishes as first suggested them, but because they involved much physiological truth and lay in the path of his proposed scheme for the treatment of Georgiana.

As he led her over the threshold of the laboratory, Georgiana was cold and tremulous. Aylmer looked cheerfully into her face, with intent to reassure her, but was so started with the intense glow of the birthmark upon the whiteness of her cheek that he could not restrain a strong convulsive shudder. His wife fainted.

"Aminadab! Aminadab!" shouted Aylmer, stamping violently on the floor.

Forthwith there issued from an inner apartment a man of low stature, but bulky frame, with shaggy hair hanging about his visage, which was grimed with the vapors of the furnace. This personage had been Aylmer's underworker during his whole scientific career, and was admirably fitted for that office by his great mechanical readiness, and the skill with which, while incapable of comprehending a single principle, he executed all the details of his master's experiments. With his vast strength, his shaggy hair, his smoky aspect, and the indescribable earthiness that incrusted him, he seemed to represent man's physical nature; while Aylmer's slender figure, and pale, intellectual face, were no less apt a type of the spiritual element.

"Throw open the door of the boudoir, Aminadab," said Aylmer, "and burn a pastil."

"Yes, master," answered Aminadab, looking intently at the lifeless form of Georgiana; and then he muttered to himself, "If she were my wife, I'd never part with that birthmark."

When Georgiana recovered consciousness she found herself breathing an atmosphere of penetrating fragrance, the gentle potency of which had recalled her from her deathlike faintness. The scene around her looked like enchantment. Aylmer had converted those smoky, dingy, somber rooms, where he had spent his brightest years in recondite pursuits, into a series of beautiful apartments not unfit to be the secluded abode of a lovely woman. The walls were hung with gorgeous curtains, which imparted the combination of grandeur and grace that no other species of adornment can achieve; and as they fell from the ceiling to the floor, their rich and ponderous folds, concealing all angles and straight lines, appeared to shut in the scene from infinite space. For aught Georgiana knew, it might be a pavilion among the clouds. And Aylmer, excluding the sunshine, which would have interfered with his chemical processes, had supplied its place with perfumed lamps, emitting flames of various hue, but all uniting in a soft, impurpled radiance. He now knelt by his wife's side, watching her earnestly, but without alarm; for he was confident in his science, and felt that he could draw a magic circle round her within which no evil might intrude.

"Where am I? Ah, I remember," said Georgiana faintly; and she placed her hand over her cheek to hide the terrible mark from her husband's eyes.

"Fear not, dearest!" exclaimed he. "Do not shrink from me! Believe me, Georgiana, I even rejoice in this single imperfection, since it will be such a rapture to remove it."

"Oh, spare me!" sadly replied his wife. "Pray do not look at it again. I never can forget that convulsive shudder."

In order to soothe Georgiana, and, as it were, to release her mind from the burden of actual things, Aylmer now put in practice some of the light and playful secrets which science had taught him among its profounder lore. Airy figures, absolutely bodiless ideas, and forms of unsubstantial beauty came and danced before her, imprinting their momentary footsteps on beams of light. Though she had some indistinct idea of the method of these optical phenomena, still the illusion was almost perfect enough to warrant the belief that her husband possessed sway over the spiritual world. Then again, when she felt a wish to look forth from her seclusion, immediately, as if her thoughts were answered, the procession of external existence flitted across a screen. The scenery and the figures of actual life were perfectly represented, but with that bewitching, yet indescribable difference which always makes a picture, an image, or a shadow so much more attractive than the original. When wearied of this, Aylmer bade her cast her eyes upon a vessel containing a quantity of earth. She did so, with little interest at first; but was soon started to perceive the germ of a plant shooting upward from the soil. Then came the slender stalk; the leaves gradually unfolded themselves; and amid them was a perfect and lovely flower.

"It is magical!" cried Georgiana. "I dare not touch it."

"Nay, pluck it," answered Aylmer: "pluck it, and inhale its brief perfume while you may. The flower will wither in a few moments and leave nothing save its brown seed vessels; but thence may be perpetuated a race as ephemeral as itself."

But Georgiana had no sooner touched the flower than the whole plant suffered a blight, its leaves turning coal-black as if by the agency of fire.

"There was too powerful a stimulus," said Aylmer thoughtfully.

To make up for this abortive experiment, he proposed to take her portrait by a scientific process of his own invention. It was to be effected by rays of light striking upon a polished plate of metal. Georgiana assented; but, on looking at the result, was affrighted to find the features of the portrait blurred and indefinable; while the minute figure of a hand appeared where the cheek should have been. Aylmer snatched the metallic plate and threw it into a jar of corrosive acid.

Soon, however, he forgot these mortifying failures. In the intervals of study and chemical experiment he came to her flushed and exhausted, but seemed invigorated by her presence, and spoke in glowing language of the resources of his art. He gave a history of the long dynasty of the alchemists, who spent so many ages in quest of the universal solvent by which the golden principle might be elicited from all things vile and base. Aylmer appeared to believe that, by the plainest scientific logic, it was altogether within the limits of possibility to discover this long-sought medium; "but," he added, "a philosopher who should go deep enough to acquire the power would attain too lofty a wisdom to stoop to the exercise of it." Not less singular were his opinions in regard to the elixir vitae. He more than intimated that it was at his option to concoct a liquid that should prolong life for years, perhaps interminably; but that it would produce a discord in Nature which all the world, and chiefly the quaffer of the immortal nostrum, would find cause to curse.

"Aylmer, are you in earnest?" asked Georgiana, looking at him with amazement and fear. "It is terrible to possess such power, or even to dream of possessing it."

"Oh, do not tremble, my love," said her husband. "I would not wrong either you or myself by working such inharmonious effects upon our lives; but I would have you consider how trifling, in comparison, is the skill requisite to remove this little hand."

At the mention of the birthmark, Georgiana, as usual, shrank as if a red-hot iron had touched her cheek.

Again Aylmer applied himself to his labors. She could hear his voice in the distant furnace-room giving directions to Aminadab, whose harsh, uncouth, misshapen tones were audible in response, more like the grunt or growl of a brute than human speech. After hours of absence, Aylmer reappeared and proposed that she should now examine his cabinet of chemical products and natural treasures of the earth. Among the former he showed her a small vial, in which, he remarked, was contained a gentle yet most powerful fragrance, capable of impregnating all the breezes that blow across a kingdom. They were of inestimable value, the contents of that little vial; and, as he said so, he threw some of the perfume into the air and filled the room with piercing and invigorating delight.

"And what is this?" asked Georgiana, pointing to a small crystal globe containing a gold-colored liquid. "It is so beautiful to the eye that I could imagine it the elixir of life."

"In one sense it is," replied Aylmer, "or rather, the elixir of immortality. It is the most precious poison that ever was concocted in this world. By its aid I could apportion the lifetime of any mortal at whom you might point your finger. The strength of the dose would determine whether he were to linger out years, or drop dead in the midst of a breath. No king on his guarded throne could keep his life if I, in my private station, should deem that the welfare of millions justified me in depriving him of it."

"Why do you keep such a terrific drug?" inquired Georgiana in horror.

"Do not mistrust me, dearest," said her husband, smiling; "its virtuous potency is yet greater than its harmful one. But see! here is a powerful cosmetic. With a few drops of this in a vase of water, freckles may be washed away as easily as the hands are cleansed. A stronger infusion would take the blood out of the cheek, and leave the rosiest beauty a pale ghost."

"Is it with this lotion that you intend to bathe my cheek?" asked Georgiana, anxiously.

"Oh, no," hastily replied her husband; "this is merely superficial. Your case demands a remedy that shall go deeper."

In his interviews with Georgiana, Aylmer generally made minute inquiries as to her sensations and whether the confinement of the rooms and the temperature of the atmosphere agreed with her. These questions had such a particular drift that Georgiana began to conjecture that she was already subjected to certain physical influences, either breathed in with the fragrant air or taken with her food. She fancied likewise, but it might be altogether fancy, that there was a stirring up of her system—a strange, indefinite sensation creeping through her veins, and tingling, half painfully, half pleasurably, at her heart. Still, whenever she dared to look into the mirror, there she beheld herself pale as white rose and with the crimson birthmark stamped upon her cheek. Not even Aylmer now hated it so much as she.

To dispel the tedium of the hours which her husband found it necessary to devote to the processes of combination and analysis, Georgiana turned over the volumes of his scientific library. In many dark old tomes she met with chapters full of romance and poetry. They were the works of the philosophers of the middle ages, such as Albertus Magnus, Cornelius Agrippa, Paracelsus, and the famous friar who created the prophetic Brazen Head. All these antique naturalists stood in advance of their centuries, yet were imbued with some of their credulity, and therefore were believed, and perhaps imagined themselves to have acquired from the investigation of Nature a power above Nature, and from physics a sway over the spiritual world. Hardly less curious and imaginative were the early volumes of the Transactions of the Royal Society, in which the members, knowing little of the limits of natural possibility, were continually recording wonders or proposing methods whereby wonders might be wrought.

But to Georgiana the most engrossing volume was a large folio from her husband's own hand, in which he had recorded every experiment of his scientific career, its original aim, the methods adopted for its development, and its final success or failure, with the circumstances to which either event was attributable. The book, in truth, was both the history and emblem of his ardent, ambitious, imaginative, yet practical and laborious life. He handled physical details as if there were nothing beyond them; yet spiritualized them all, and redeemed himself from materialism by his strong and eager aspiration towards the infinite. In his grasp the veriest clod of earth assumed a soul. Georgiana, as she read, reverenced Aylmer and loved him more profoundly than ever, but with a less entire dependence on his judgment than heretofore. Much as he had accomplished, she could not but observe that his most splendid successes were almost invariably failures, if compared with the ideal at which he aimed. His brightest diamonds were the merest pebbles, and felt to be so by himself, in comparison with the inestimable gems which lay hidden beyond his reach. The volume, rich with achievements that had won renown for its author, was yet as melancholy a record as ever mortal hand had penned. It was the sad confession and continual exemplification of the shortcomings of the composite man, the spirit burdened with clay and working in matter, and of the despair that assails the higher nature at finding itself so miserably thwarted by the earthly part. Perhaps every man of genius in whatever sphere might recognize the image of his own experience in Aylmer's journal.

So deeply did these reflections affect Georgiana that she laid her face upon the open volume and burst into tears. In this situation she was found by her husband.

"It is dangerous to read in a sorcerer's books," said he with a smile, though his countenance was uneasy and displeased. "Georgiana, there are pages in that volume which I can scarcely glance over and keep my senses. Take heed less it prove as detrimental to you."

"It has made me worship you more than ever," said she.

"Ah, wait for this one success," rejoined he, "then worship me if you will. I shall deem myself hardly unworthy of it. But come, I have sought you for the luxury of your voice. Sing to me, dearest."

So she poured out the liquid music of her voice to quench the thirst of his spirit. He then took his leave with a boyish exuberance of gayety, assuring her that her seclusion would endure but a little longer, and that the result was already certain. Scarcely had he departed when Georgiana felt irresistibly impelled to follow him. She had forgotten to inform Aylmer of a symptom which for two or three hours past had begun to excite her attention. It was a sensation in the fatal birthmark, not painful, but which induced a restlessness throughout her system. Hastening after her husband, she intruded for the first time into the laboratory.

The first thing that struck her eye was the furnace, that hot and feverish worker, with the intense glow of its fire, which by the quantities of soot clustered above it seemed to have been burning for ages. There was a distilling apparatus in full operation. Around the room were retorts, tubes, cylinders, crucibles, and other apparatus of chemical research. An electrical machine stood ready for immediate use. The atmosphere felt oppressively close, and was tainted with gaseous odors which had been tormented forth by the processes of science. The severe and homely simplicity of the apartment, with its naked walls and brick pavement, looked strange, accustomed as Georgiana had become to the fantastic elegance of her boudoir. But what chiefly, indeed almost solely, drew her attention, was the aspect of Aylmer himself.

He was pale as death, anxious and absorbed, and hung over the furnace as if it depended upon his utmost watchfulness whether the liquid which it was distilling should be the draught of immortal happiness or misery. How different from the sanguine and joyous mien that he had assumed for Georgiana's encouragement!

"Carefully now, Aminadab; carefully, thou human machine; carefully, thou man of clay!" muttered Aylmer, more to himself than his assistant. "Now, if there be a thought too much or too little, it is all over."

"Ho! ho!" mumbled Aminadab. "Look, master! look!"

Aylmer raised his eyes hastily, and at first reddened, then grew paler than ever, on beholding Georgiana. He rushed towards her and seized her arm with a gripe that left the print of his fingers upon it.

"Why do you come hither? Have you no trust in your husband?" cried he impetuously. "Would you throw the blight of that fatal birthmark over my labors? It is not well done. Go, prying woman, go!"

"Nay, Aylmer," said Georgiana with the firmness of which she possessed no stinted endowment, "it is not you that have a right to complain. You mistrust your wife; you have concealed the anxiety with which you watch the development of this experiment. Think not so unworthily of me, my husband. Tell me all the risk we run, and fear not that I shall shrink; for my share in it is far less than your own."

"No, no, Georgiana!" said Aylmer impatiently; "it must not be."

"I submit," replied she calmly. "And, Aylmer, I shall quaff whatever draught you bring me; but it will be on the same principle that would induce me to take a dose of poison if offered by your hand."

"My noble wife," said Aylmer, deeply moved, "I knew not the height and depth of your nature until now. Nothing shall be concealed. Know, then, that this crimson hand, superficial as it seems, has clutched its grasp into your being with a strength of which I had no previous conception. I have already administered agents powerful enough to do aught except to change your entire physical system. Only one thing remains to be tried. If that fail us we are ruined."

"Why did you hesitate to tell me this?" asked she.

"Because, Georgiana," said Aylmer in a low voice, "there is danger."

"Danger? There is but one danger — that this horrible stigma shall be left upon my cheek!" cried Georgiana. "Remove it, remove it, whatever be the cost, or we shall both go mad!"

"Heaven knows your words are too true," said Aylmer sadly. "And now, dearest, return to your boudoir. In a little while all will be tested."

He conducted her back and took leave of her with a solemn tenderness which spoke far more than his words how much was now at stake. After his departure Georgiana became rapt in musings. She considered the character of Aylmer, and did it completer justice than at any previous moment. Her heart exulted, while it trembled, at his honorable love—so pure and lofty that it would accept nothing less than perfection nor miserably make itself contented with an earthier nature than he had dreamed of. She felt how much more precious was such a sentiment than that meaner kind which would have borne with the imperfection for her sake, and have been guilty of treason to holy love by degrading its perfect idea to the level of the actual; and with her whole spirit she prayed that, for a single moment, she might satisfy his highest and deepest conception. Longer than one moment she well knew it could not be; for his spirit was ever on the march, ever ascending, and each instant required something that was beyond the scope of the instant before.

The sound of her husband's footsteps aroused her. He bore a crystal goblet containing a liquor colorless as water, but bright enough to be the draught of immortality. Aylmer was pale; but it seemed rather the consequence of a highly wrought state of mind and tension of spirit than of fear or doubt.

"The concoction of the draught has been perfect," said he, in answer to Georgiana's look. "Unless all my science have deceived me, it cannot fail."

"Save on your account, my dearest Alymer," observed his wife, "I might wish to put off this birthmark of mortality by relinquishing mortality itself in preference to any other mode. Life is but a sad possession to those who have attained precisely the degree of moral advancement at which I stand. Were I weaker and blinder it might be happiness. Were I stronger, it might be endured hopefully. But, being what I find myself, methinks I am of all mortals the most fit to die."

"You are fit for heaven without tasting death!" replied her husband. "But why do we speak of dying? The draught cannot fail. Behold its effect upon this plant."

On the window seat there stood a geranium diseased with yellow blotches, which had overspread all its leaves. Aylmer poured a small quantity of the liquid upon the soil in which it grew. In a little time, when the roots of the plant had taken up the moisture, the unsightly blotches began to be extinguished in a living verdure.

"There needed no proof," said Georgiana quietly. "Give me the goblet. I joyfully stake all upon your word."

"Drink, then, thou lofty creature!" exclaimed Aylmer, with fervid admiration. "There is no taint of imperfection on thy spirit. Thy sensible frame, too, shall soon be all perfect."

She quaffed the liquid and returned the goblet to his hand.

"It is grateful," said she, with a placid smile. "Methinks it is like water from a heavenly fountain; for it contains I know not what of unobtrusive fragrance and deliciousness. It allays a feverish thirst that had parched me for many days. Now, dearest, let me sleep. My earthly sense are closing over my spirit like the leaves around the heart of a rose at sunset."

She spoke the last words with a gentle reluctance, as if it required almost more energy than she could command to pronounce the faint and lingering syllables. Scarcely had they loitered through her lips ere she was lost in slumber. Aylmer sat by her side, watching her aspect with the emotions proper to a man the whole value of whose existence was involved in the process now to be tested. Mingled with this mood, however, was the philosophic investigation characteristic of the man of science. Not the minutest symptom escaped him. A heightened flush of the cheek, a slight irregularity of breath, a quiver of the eyelid, a hardly perceptible tremor through the frame,—such were the details which, as the moments passed, he wrote down in his folio volume. Intense thought had set its stamp upon every previous page of that volume, but the thoughts of years were all concentrated upon the last.

While thus employed, he failed not to gaze often at the fatal hand, and not without a shudder. Yet once, by a strange and unaccountable impulse, he pressed it with his lips. His spirit recoiled, however, in the very act; and Georgiana, out of the midst of her deep sleep, moved uneasily and murmured as if in remonstrance. Again Aylmer resumed his watch. Nor was it without avail. The crimson hand, which at first had been strongly visible upon the marble paleness of Georgiana's cheek, now grew more faintly outlined. She remained not less pale than ever; but the birthmark, with every breath that came and went, lost somewhat of its former distinctness. Its presence had been awful; its departure was more awful still. Watch the stain of the rainbow fading out of the sky, and you will know how that mysterious symbol passed away.

"By Heaven! it is well-nigh gone!" said Aylmer to himself, in almost irrepressible ecstasy. "I can scarcely trace it now. Success! success! And now it is like the faintest rose color. The lightest flush of blood across her cheek would overcome it. But she is so pale!"

He drew aside the window curtain and suffered the light of natural day to fall into the room and rest upon her cheek. At the same time he heard a gross, hoarse chuckle, which he had long known as his servant Aminadab's expression of delight.

"Ah, clod! ah, earthly mass!" cried Aylmer, laughing in a sort of frenzy, "you have served me well! Matter and spirit—earth and heaven—have both done their part in this! Laugh, thing of the sehses! You have earned the right to laugh."

These exclamations broke Georgiana's sleep. She slowly unclosed her eyes and gazed into the mirror which her husband had arranged for that purpose. A faint smile flitted over her lips when she recognized how barely perceptible was now that crimson hand which had once blazed forth with such disastrous brilliancy as to scare away all their happiness. But then her eyes sought Aylmer's face with a trouble and anxiety that he could by no means account for.

"My poor Aylmer!" murmured she.

"Poor? Nay, richest, happiest, most favored!" exclaimed he. "My peerless bride, it is successful! You are perfect!"

"My poor Aylmer," she repeated, with a more than human tenderness, "you have aimed loftily; you have done nobly. Do not repent that with so high and pure a feeling, you have rejected the best the earth could offer. Aylmer, dearest Aylmer, I am dying.!"

Alas! it was too true! The fatal hand had grappled with the mystery of life, and was the bond by which an angelic spirit kept itself in union with a mortal frame. As the last crimson tint of the birthmark— that sole token of human imperfection—faded from her cheek, the parting breath of the now perfect woman passed into the atmosphere, and her soul, lingering a moment near her husband, took its heavenward flight. Then a hoarse, chuckling laugh was heard again! Thus ever does the gross fatality of earth exult in its invariable triumph over the immortal essence which, in this dim sphere of half development, demands the completeness of a higher state. Yet, had Aylmer reached a profounder wisdom, he need not thus have flung away the happiness which would have woven his mortal life of the selfsame texture with the celestial. The momentary circumstance was too strong for him; he failed to look beyond the shadowy scope of time, and, living once for all in eternity, to find the perfect future in the present.

Poe

1809 January 19. Edgar Allan Poe born in Boston, Massachusetts.

1811 Parents die. Becomes the foster child of John and Frances Allan, a wealthy couple from Virginia.

1815–20 The Allans live in England for five years. Poe attends private school.

1826–29 Enters the University of Virginia. Debts force him to drop out, and he joins the army in 1827. He is honorably discharged in 1829. *Tamerlane and Other Poems* (1827) and *Al Araaf, Tamerlane, and Minor Poems* (1829) appear.

1830–33 Enters the military academy at West Point in 1830 but arranges for his expulsion the following year. *Poems* appear in 1831. "MS. Found in Bottle" wins a prize in 1833, and Poe becomes editor of the *Southern Literary Messenger*.

1836–40 Marries his young cousin, Virginia Clemm. *The Narrative of Arthur Gordon Pym,* his only novel, appears in 1838. *Tales of the Grotesque and Arabesque* appears in 1840.

1841–45 Edits *Graham's Magazine* (1841–42) in which he publishes "The Murders in the Rue Morgue," the first detective story. "The Gold Bug" appears in 1843 and sells 300,000 copies. In 1845, both *Tales* and *The Raven and Other Poems* appear, and James Russell Lowell writes the first critical appreciation of Poe as a writer and critic.

1847–49 Virginia Poe dies after a five year struggle with tuberculosis. "Ulalume" is written in 1847. Between 1848 and 49 "The Bells," "For Annie," "Annabel Lee," "Eldorado," and "Von Kempelen and His Discovery" are written, and Poe is engaged twice. Poe dies on October 7, 1849.

Edgar Allan Poe

Poe is the necromancer of American literature. Read his prose and you crown him as the king of terror. Read his poetry and you concede a witchery of words found in no other of our American poets. There have been those who denied him a place among our greatest prose writers as well as our greatest poets; but no one has denied his power, his ability to reach the hidden places of the soul, his unique position in literature. No other poet has ever written so little and yet lodged so much in the memory as Poe. The emotions to which he appeals are neither many nor varied, but they are elemental and universal; and he appeals to them with a directness, with a weird vividness, with an impassioned intensity that have made him—though dead—a living force.

But the popular conception of the man's real service remains strangely vague. As a poet there are thousands of Americans who still think of him only as "the jingle man"; and as a prose writer they consider him chiefly a "manufacturer of cold creeps and maker of shivers." If this were all, his international fame would be not only hard to explain, but a stinging indictment of the literary taste of two worlds.

As I see it, Poe has influenced world literature in several definite ways. He had his weaknesses both of character and of genius. But America has produced no other genius whose life has been so mercilessly probed, whose every word and act has been so publicly blazoned, or whose motives have been so relentlessly scrutinized.

Poe has been a discoverer in the realm of meter and rhythm. I say "discoverer" advisedly, not "inventor." Men do not invent new rhyme combinations or new stanza forms. These forms were already existent, waiting for someone to call them into service. Now, Poe was a ceaseless experimenter in sound combinations, line combinations, and stanza combinations. His mastery of the technical devices of "repetition" and "parallelism" has permanently enriched the resources of English poetry. Take also the matter of new stanza forms. So far as I know, no new stanza had been coined in English literature since Spenser's time, till Poe appeared. The stanza structure of "The Raven," of "To Helen," and of "Ulalume" are altogether new creations. It was instantly recognized that Poe had done a new thing in these poems. Indeed, Poe gave such flexibility and malleableness to stanza structure as to justify us in saying of him that he found the stanza a *solid*, but left it a *liquid*.

Both in theory and practice Poe is the founder of the American short story as distinguished from the story that is merely short. His constructive leadership in this realm is recognized both at home and abroad. Washington Irving may be said to have legendized the short story, making it a means of storing legendary material in more enduring and attractive form. Hawthorne allegorized it, converting it into a sort of miniature *Pilgrim's Progress*. Bret Harte localized it, and California became the first romantic region that was lifted into literature on the shoulders of the short story. Joel Chandler Harris folklorized it with the Uncle Remus stories. O. Henry socialized it, leaving it the most flexible and responsive medium of expression of every day life and the social reaction that American literature has to its credit. Poe's contribution was unlike any of these. He retold no legends, he looked askance at allegory, he brought no locality into literature, he saw no career for art in folklore, and he found his creative inspiration not in the changing moods and whims of society about him, but in the visions and questionings deep within the human consciousness. His central contribution to the new form was not content, but structure. Poe *standardized* the short story; that is, he formulated a code for short story writing that has been followed consciously or unconsciously in all lands. The old way was to begin with your chief character or your plot or your background, and to make one of these central and distinctive. But Poe declared that all of these should be made dependent upon and convergent upon the effect that you wish to produce—the *effect*, that was the chief thing.

Begin with this predetermined effect—that should be your real and only goal. Character, plot, and background have no reason for existence except as they contribute to this central and controlling purpose.

Poe's phrase, "totality of effect," sums up admirably his point of view. It was a formula from which he never swerved a hair's breadth. There are no unnecessary phrases or lines in his best stories. From the first word the lines begin to converge toward the predetermined and prearranged effect. In all lands his stories have been fruitful of suggestion, not because they brought a new message, but because they showed a faultless method of expressing whatever a writer of narrative had to say. There is no better model than that established by Poe. His motto was not merely brevity, but brevity plus effectiveness.

An old question, and a large one, in art is: Does genius act spontaneously or self-consciously? Poe stands for conscious and painstaking craftsmanship. Kant said that genius is wholly unconscious of its own operations. My own opinion is that Poe is much nearer the ultimate truth in this matter than Kant. At any rate, when Poe wrote his *Philosophy of Composition* (1846), telling just how he composed "The Raven," he touched a big thought in a vital way and furnished the chief whetstone on which foreign critics, whether with him or against him, have sharpened their critical knives. He was thus a constructive force not only by what he did, *but by what he said as to how he did it.* He once called this self-attentiveness "a curse"; but, if it was a curse to him, it has been a blessing to other craftsmen. Poe wrote with a freedom and minuteness of detail about the composition of his own work, that have made him preeminently the spokesman of those who believe that genius, whether in literature, painting, sculpture, or music, must toil painstakingly and self-consciously to bridge the chasm between the first rapture and the well-ordered expression of the rapture in concrete form.

—*from* Southern Literary Studies *by Charles Alphonso Smith*

MS. Found in a Bottle

> Qui n'a plus qu'un moment à vivre
> N'a plus rien à dissimuler.
>
> QUINAULT, *Atys*.

Of my country and of my family I have little to say. Ill usage and length of years have driven me from the one, and estranged me from the other. Hereditary wealth afforded me an education of no common order, and a contemplative turn of mind enabled me to methodize the stores which early study very diligently garnered up. — Beyond all things, the study of the German moralists gave me great delight; not from any ill-advised admiration of their eloquent madness, but from the ease with which my habits of rigid thought enabled me to detect their falsities. I have often been reproached with the aridity of my genius; a deficiency of imagination has been imputed to me as a crime; and the Pyrrhonism of my opinions has at all times rendered me notorious. Indeed, a strong relish for physical philosophy has, I fear, tinctured my mind with a very common error of this age — I mean the habit of referring occurrences, even the least susceptible of such reference, to the principles of that science. Upon the whole, no person could be less liable than myself to be led away from the severe precincts of truth by the *ignes fatui* of superstition. I have thought proper to premise thus much, lest the incredible tale I have to tell should be considered rather the raving of a crude imagination, than the positive experience of a mind to which the reveries of fancy have been a dead letter and a nullity.

After many years spent in foreign travel, I sailed in the year 18—, from the port of Batavia, in the rich and populous island of Java, on a voyage to the Archipelago of the Sunda islands. I went as passenger — having no other inducement than a kind of nervous restlessness which haunted me as a fiend.

Our vessel was a beautiful ship of about four hundred tons, copper-fastened, and built at Bombay of Malabar teak. She was freighted with cotton wool and oil, from the Laccadive islands. We had also on board coir, jaggeree, ghee, cocoanuts, and a few cases of opium. The stowage was clumsily done, and the vessel consequently crank.

We got under way with a mere breath of wind, and for many days stood along the eastern coast of Java, without any other incident to beguile the monotony of our course than the ocassional meeting with some of the small grabs of the Archipelago to which we were bound.

One evening, leaning over the taffrail, I observed a very singular, isolated cloud, to the N. W. It was remarkable, as well for its color, as from its being the first we had seen since our departure from Batavia. I watched it attentively until sunset, when it spread all at once to the eastward and westward, girting in the horizon with a narrow strip of vapor, and looking like a long line of low beach. My notice was soon afterwards attracted by the dusky-red appearance of the moon, and the peculiar character of the sea. The latter was undergoing a rapid change, and the water seemed more than usually transparent. Although I could distinctly see the bottom, yet, heaving the lead, I found the ship in fifteen fathoms. The air now became intolerably hot, and was loaded with spiral exhalations similar to those arising from heated iron. As night came on, every breath of wind died away, and a more entire calm it is impossible to conceive. The flame of a candle burned upon the poop without the least perceptible motion, and a long hair, held between the finger and thumb, hung without the possibility of detecting a vibration. However, as the captain said he could perceive no indication of danger, and as we were drifting in bodily to shore, he ordered the sails to be furled, and the anchor let go. No watch was set, and the crew, consisting principally of Malays, stretched themselves deliberately upon deck. I went below—not without a full presentiment of evil. Indeed, every appearance warranted me in apprehending a simoom. I told the captain my fears; but he paid no attention to what I said, and left me without deigning to give a reply. My uneasiness, however, prevented me from sleeping, and about midnight I went upon deck. — As I placed my foot upon the upper step of the companion ladder, I was startled by a loud, humming noise, like that occasioned by the rapid revolution of a mill-wheel, and before I could ascertain its meaning, I found the ship quivering to its center. In the next instant, a wilderness of foam hurled us upon our beam-ends, and, rushing over us fore and aft, swept the entire decks from stem to stern.

The extreme fury of the blast proved, in a great measure, the salvation of the ship. Although completely waterlogged, yet, as her masts had gone by the board, she rose, after a minute, heavily from the sea, and, staggering awhile beneath the immense pressure of the tempest, finally righted.

By what miracle I escaped destruction, it is impossible to say. Stunned by the shock of the water, I found myself, upon recovery, jammed in between the sternpost and rudder. With great difficulty I gained my feet, and looking dizzily around, was, at first struck with the idea of our being among breakers; so terrific, beyond the wildest imagination, was the whirlpool of mountainous and foaming ocean within which we were engulfed. After a while, I heard the voice of an old Swede, who had shipped with us at the moment of our leaving port. I hallooed to him with all my strength, and presently he came reeling aft. We soon discovered that we were the sole survivors of the accident. All on deck, with the exception of ourselves, had been swept overboard; — the captain and mates must have perished as they slept, for the cabins were deluged with water. Without assistance, we could expect to do little for the security of the ship, and our exertions were at first paralyzed by the momentary expectation of going down. Our cable had, of course, parted like packthread, at the first breath of the hurricane, or we should have been instantaneously overwhelmed. We scudded with frightful velocity before the sea, and the water made clear breaches over us. The framework of our stern was shattered excessively, and, in almost every respect, we had received considerable injury; but to our extreme joy we found the pumps unchoked, and that we had made no great shifting of our ballast. The main fury of the blast had already blown over, and we apprehended little danger from the violence of the wind; but we looked forward to its total cessation with dismay; well believing, that, in our shattered condition, we should inevitably perish in the tremendous swell which would ensue. But this very just apprehension seemed by no means likely to be soon verified. For five entire days and nights — during which our only subsistence was a small quantity of jaggeree, procured with great difficulty from the forecastle — the hulk flew at a rate defying computation, before rapidly succeeding flaws of wind, which, without equalling the first violence of the simoom, were still more terrific than any tempest I had before encountered. Our course for the first four days was, with trifling variations, S. E. and by S.; and we must have run down the coast of New Holland. — On the fifth day the cold became extreme, although the wind had hauled round a point more to the northward. — The sun arose with a sickly yellow luster, and clambered a very few degrees above the horizon — emitting no decisive light. — There were no clouds apparent, yet the wind was upon the increase, and blew with a fitful and unsteady fury. About noon, as nearly as we could guess, our attention was again arrested by the appearance of the sun. It gave out no light, properly so called, but a dull and sullen glow without reflection, as if all its rays were polarized. Just before sinking within the turgid sea, its central fires suddenly went out, as if hurriedly extinguished by some unaccountable power. It was a dim, silver-like rim, alone, as it rushed down the unfathomable ocean.

We waited in vain for the arrival of the sixth day—that day to me has not arrived—to the Swede, never did arrive. Thenceforward we were enshrouded in pitchy darkness, so that we could not have seen an object at twenty paces from the ship. Eternal night continued to envelop us, all unrelieved by the phosphoric sea-brilliancy to which we had been accustomed in the tropics. We observed too, that, although the tempest continued to rage with unabated violence, there was no longer to be discovered the usual appearance of surf, or foam, which had hitherto attended us. All around were horror, and thick gloom, and a black sweltering desert of ebony.—Superstitious terror crept by degrees into the spirit of the old Swede, and my own soul was wrapped up in silent wonder. We neglected all care of the ship, as worse than useless, and securing ourselves, as well as possible, to the stump of the mizzenmast, looked out bitterly into the world of ocean. We had no means of calculating time, nor could we form any guess of our situation. We were, however, well aware of having made farther to the southward than any previous navigators and felt great amazement at not meeting with the usual impediments of ice. In the meantime every moment threatened to be our last—every mountainous billow hurried to overwhelm us. The swell surpassed anything I had imagined possible, and that we were not instantly buried is a miracle. My companion spoke of the lightness of our cargo, and reminded me of the excellent qualities of our ship; but I could not help feeling the utter hopelessness of hope itself, and prepared myself gloomily for that death which I thought nothing could defer beyond an hour, as, with every knot of way the ship made, the swelling of the black stupendous seas became more dismally appalling. At times we gasped for breath at an elevation beyond the albatross—at times became dizzy with the velocity of our descent into some watery hell, where the air grew stagnant, and no sound disturbed the slumbers of the kraken.

We were at the bottom of one of these abysses, when a quick scream from my companion broke fearfully upon the night. "See! see!" cried he, shrieking in my ears, "Almighty God! see! see!" As he spoke, I became aware of dull, sullen glare of red light which streamed down the sides of the vast chasm where we lay, and threw a fitful brilliancy upon our deck. Casting my eyes upwards, I beheld a spectacle which froze the current of my blood. At a terrific height directly above us, and upon the very verge of the precipitous descent, hovered a gigantic ship of, perhaps, four thousand tons. Although upreared upon the summit of a wave more than a hundred times her own altitude, her apparent size still exceeded that of any ship of the line or East Indiaman in existence. Her huge hull was of a deep dingy black, unrelieved by any of the customary carvings of a ship. A single row of brass cannon protruded from her open ports, and dashed from their polished surfaces the fires of innumerable battle-lanterns, which swung to and fro about her rigging. But what mainly inspired us with horror and astonishment, was that she bore up under a press of sail in the very teeth of that supernatural sea, and of that ungovernable hurricane. When we first discovered her, her bows were alone to be seen, as she rose slowly from the dim and horrible gulf beyond her. For a moment of intense terror she paused upon the giddy pinnacle, as if in contemplation of her own sublimity, then trembled and tottered, and—came down.

At this instant, I know not what sudden self-possession came over my spirit. Staggering as far aft as I could, I awaited fearlessly the ruin that was to overwhelm. Our own vessel was at length ceasing from her struggles, and sinking with her head to the sea. The shock of the descending mass struck her, consequently, in that portion of her frame which was already under water, and the inevitable result was to hurl me, with irresistible violence, upon the rigging of the stranger.

As I fell, the ship hove in stays, and went about; and to the confusion ensuing I attributed my escape from the notice of the crew. With little difficulty I made my way unperceived to the main hatchway, which was partially open, and soon found an opportunity of secreting myself in the hold. Why I did so I can hardly tell. An indefinite sense of awe, which at first sight of the navigators of the ship had taken hold of my mind, was perhaps the principle of my concealment. I was unwilling to trust myself with a race of people who had offered, to the cursory glance I had taken, so many points of vague novelty, doubt, and apprehension. I therefore thought proper to contrive a hiding place in the hold. This I did by removing a small portion of the shifting-boards, in such a manner as to afford me a convenient retreat between the huge timbers of the ship.

I had scarcely completed my work, when a footstep in the hold forced me to make use of it. A man passed by my place of concealment with a feeble and unsteady gait. I could not see his face, but had an opportunity of observing his general appearance. There was about it an evidence of great age and infirmity. His knees tottered beneath a load of years, and his entire frame quivered under the burthen. He muttered to himself, in a low broken tone, some words of a language which I could not understand, and groped in a corner among a pile of singular-looking instruments, and decayed charts of navigation. His manner was a wild mixture of the peevishness of second childhood, and the solemn dignity of a God. He at length went on deck, and I saw him no more.

A feeling, for which I have no name, has taken possession of my soul—a sensation which will admit of no analysis, to which the lessons of bygone times are inadequate, and for which I fear futurity itself will offer me no key. To a mind constituted like my own, the latter consideration is an evil. I shall never—I know that I shall never—be satisfied with regard to the nature of my conceptions. Yet it is not wonderful that these conceptions are indefinite, since they have their origin in sources so utterly novel. A new sense—a new entity is added to my soul.

It is long since I first trod the deck of this terrible ship, and the rays of my destiny are, I think, gathering to a focus. Incomprehensible men! Wrapped up in meditations of a kind which I cannot divine, they pass me by unnoticed. Concealment is utter folly on my part, for the people *will not* see. It was but just now that I passed directly before the eyes of the mate—it was no long while ago that I ventured into the captain's own private cabin, and took thence the materials with which I write, and have written. I shall from time to time continue this journal. It is true that I may not find an opportunity of transmitting it to the world, but I will not fail to make the endeavor. At the last moment I will enclose the MS. in a bottle, and cast it within the sea.

An incident has occurred which has given me new room for meditation. Are such things the operation of ungoverned Chance? I had ventured upon deck and thrown myself down, without attracting any notice, among a pile of ratlin-stuff and old sails, in the bottom of the yawl. While musing upon the singularity of my fate, I unwittingly daubed with a tar brush the edges of a neatly folded studdingsail which lay near me on a barrel. The studdingsail is now bent upon the ship, and the thoughtless touches of the brush are spread out into the word DISCOVERY . . . .

I have made many observations lately upon the structure of the vessel. Although well armed, she is not, I think, a ship of war. Her rigging, build, and general equipment, all negative a supposition of this kind. What she *is not*, I can easily perceive—what she *is* I fear it is impossible to say. I know not how it is, but in scrutinizing her strange model and singular cast of spars, her huge size and overgrown suits of canvas, her severely simple bow and antiquated stern, there will occasionally flash across my mind a sensation of familiar things, and there is always mixed up with such indistinct shadows of recollection, an unaccountable memory of old foreign chronicles and ages long ago . . . .

I have been looking at the timbers of the ship. She is built of a material to which I am a stranger. There is a peculiar character about the wood which strikes me as rendering it unfit for the purpose to which it has been applied. I mean its extreme *porousness*, considered independently of the worm-eaten condition which is a consequence of navigation in these seas and apart from the rottenness attendant upon age. It will appear perhaps an observation somewhat overcurious, but this wood would have every characteristic of Spanish oak, if Spanish oak were distended by any unnatural means.

In reading the above sentence a curious apothegm of an old weather-beaten Dutch navigator comes full upon my recollection. "It is as sure," he was wont to say, when any doubt was entertained of his veracity, "as sure as there is a sea where the ship itself will grow in bulk like the living body of the seaman" . . . .

About an hour ago, I made bold to thrust myself among a group of the crew. They paid me no manner of attention, and, although I stood in the very midst of them all, seemed utterly unconscious of my presence. Like the one I had at first seen in the hold, they all bore about them the marks of a hoary old age. Their knees trembled with infirmity; their shoulders were bent double with decrepitude; their shrivelled skins rattled in the wind; their voices were low, tremulous and broken; their eyes glistened with the rheum of years; and their grey hairs streamed terribly in the tempest. Around them,

MS. Found in a Bottle 239

on every part of the deck, lay scattered mathematical instruments of the most quaint and obsolete construction . . . .

I mentioned some time ago the bending of a studdingsail. From that period the ship, being thrown dead off the wind, has continued her terrific course due south, with every rag of canvas packed upon her, from her trucks to her lower studdingsail booms, and rolling every moment her topgallant yardarms into the most appalling hell of water which it can enter into the mind of man to imagine. I have just left the deck, where I find it impossible to maintain a footing, although the crew seem to experience little inconvenience. It appears to me a miracle of miracles that our enormous bulk is not swallowed up at once and forever. We are surely doomed to hover continually upon the brink of Eternity, without taking a final plunge into the abyss. From billows a thousand times more stupendous than any I have ever seen, we glide away with the facility of the arrowy seagull; and the colossal waters rear their heads above us like demons of the deep, but like demons confined to simple threats and forbidden to destroy. I am led to attribute these frequent escapes to the only natural cause which can account for such effect. — I must suppose the ship to be within the influence of some strong current, or impetuous undertow . . . .

I have seen the captain face to face, and in his own cabin — but, as I expected, he paid me no attention. Although in his appearance there is, to a casual observer, nothing which might bespeak him more or less than man — still a feeling of irrepressible reverence and awe mingled with the sensation of wonder with which I regarded him. In stature he is nearly my own height; that is, about five feet eight inches. He is of a well-knit and compact frame of body, neither robust nor remarkably otherwise. But it is the singularity of the expression which reigns upon the face — it is the intense, the wonderful, the thrilling evidence of old age, so utter, so extreme, which excites within my spirit a sense — a sentiment ineffable. His forehead, although little wrinkled, seems to bear upon it the stamp of a myriad of years. — His grey hairs are records of the past, and his greyer eyes are Sibyls of the future. The cabin floor was thickly strewn with strange, iron-clasped folios, and moldering instruments of science, and obsolete long-forgotten charts. His head was bowed down upon his hands, and he pored, with a fiery unquiet eye, over a paper which I took to be a commission, and which, at all events, bore the signature of a monarch. He muttered to himself, as did the first seaman whom I saw in the hold, some low peevish syllables of a

foreign tongue, and although the speaker was close at my elbow, his voice seemed to reach my ears from the distance of a mile . . . .
The ship and all in it are imbued with the spirit of Eld. The crew glide to and fro like the ghosts of buried centuries; their eyes have an eager and uneasy meaning; and when their fingers fall athwart my path in the wild glare of the battle-lanterns, I feel as I have never felt before, although I have been all my life a dealer in antiquities, and have imbibed the shadows of fallen columns at Balbec, and Tadmor, and Persepolis, until my very soul has become a ruin . . . .
When I look around me I feel ashamed of my former apprehensions. If I trembled at the blast which has hitherto attended us, shall I not stand aghast at a warring of wind and ocean, to convey any idea of which the words tornado and simoom are trivial and ineffective? All in the immediate vicinity of the ship is the blackness of eternal night, and a chaos of foamless water; but, about a league on either side of us, may be seen, indistinctly and at intervals, stupendous ramparts of ice, towering away into the desolate sky, and looking like the walls of the universe . . . .
As I imagined, the ship proves to be in a current; if that appellation can properly be given to a tide which, howling and shrieking by the white ice, thunders on to the southward with a velocity like the headlong dashing of a cataract . . . .
To conceive the horror of my sensations is, I presume, utterly impossible; yet a curiosity to penetrate the mysteries of these awful regions, predominates even over my despair, and will reconcile me to the most hideous aspect of death. It is evident that we are hurrying onwards to some exciting knowledge—some never to-be-imparted secret, whose attainment is destruction. Perhaps this current leads us to the southern pole itself. It must be confessed that a supposition apparently so wild has every probability in its favor . . . .
The crew pace the deck with unquiet and tremulous step; but there is upon their countenances an expression more of the eagerness of hope than of the apathy of despair.
In the meantime the wind is still in our poop, and, as we carry a crowd of canvas, the ship is at times lifted bodily from out the sea— Oh, horror upon horror! the ice opens suddenly to the right, and to the left, and we are whirling dizzily, in immense concentric circles, round and round the borders of a gigantic amphitheater, the summit of whose walls is lost in the darkness and the distance. But little time will be left me to ponder upon my destiny—the circles rapidly grow small—we are plunging madly within the grasp of the whirlpool—

and amid a roaring, and bellowing, and thundering of ocean and of tempest, the ship is quivering, oh God! and—going down.

William Wilson

> What say of it? what say of CONSCIENCE grim,
> That spectre in my path?
>
> CHAMBERLAYNE'S *Pharronida*.

Let me call myself, for the present, William Wilson. The fair page now lying before me need not be sullied with my real appellation. This has been already too much an object for the scorn—for the horror—for the detestation of my race. To the uttermost regions of the globe have not the indignant winds bruited its unparalleled infamy? Oh, outcast of all outcasts most abandoned!—to the earth art thou not forever dead? to its honors, to its flowers, to its golden aspirations?—and a cloud, dense, dismal, and limitless, does it not hang eternally between thy hopes and heaven?

I would not, if I could, here or today, embody a record of my later years of unspeakable misery, and unpardonable crime. This epoch— these later years—took unto themselves a sudden elevation in turpitude, whose origin alone it is my present purpose to assign. Men usually grow base by degrees. From me, in an instant, all virtue dropped bodily as a mantle. From comparatively trivial wickedness I passed, with the stride of a giant, into more than the enormities of an Elah-Gabalus. What chance—what one event brought this evil thing to pass, bear with me while I relate. Death approaches; and the shadow which foreruns him has thrown a softening influence over my spirit. I long, in passing through the dim valley, for the sympathy— I had nearly said for the pity—of my fellow men. I would fain have them believe that I have been, in some measure, the slave of circumstances beyond human control. I would wish them to seek out for me, in the details I am about to give, some little oasis of *fatality* amid a wilderness of error, I would have them allow—what they cannot refrain from allowing—that, although temptation may have erewhile existed as great, man was never *thus*, at least, tempted before—certainly, never *thus* fell. And is it therefore that he has never thus suffered? Have I not indeed been living in a dream? And am I not now dying a victim to the horror and the mystery of the wildest of all sublunary visions?

I am the descendant of a race whose imaginative and easily excitable temperament has at all times rendered them remarkable; and, in my earliest infancy, I gave evidence of having fully inherited the family character. As I advanced in years it was more strongly developed; becoming, for many reasons, a cause of serious disquietude to my friends, and of positive injury to myself. I grew self-willed, addicted to the wildest caprices, and a prey to the most ungovernable passions. Weak-minded, and beset with constitutional infirmities akin to my own, my parents could do but little to check the evil propensities which distinguished me. Some feeble and ill-directed efforts resulted in complete failure on their part, and, of course, in total triumph on mine. Thenceforward my voice was a household law; and at an age when few children have abandoned their leading-strings, I was left to the guidance of my own will, and became, in all but name, the master of my own actions.

My earliest recollections of a school life, are connected with a large, rambling, Elizabethan house, in a misty-looking village of England, where were a vast number of gigantic and gnarled trees, and where all the houses were excessively ancient. In truth, it was a dreamlike and spirit-soothing place, that venerable old town. At this moment, in fancy, I feel the refreshing chilliness of its deeply-shadowed avenues, inhale the fragrance of its thousand shrubberies, and thrill anew with undefinable delight, at the deep hollow note of the church bell, breaking, each hour, with sullen and sudden roar, upon the stillness of the dusky atmosphere in which the fretted Gothic steeple lay imbedded and asleep.

It gives me, perhaps, as much of pleasure as I can now in any manner experience, to dwell upon minute recollections of the school and its concerns. Steeped in misery as I am—misery, alas! only too real—I shall be pardoned for seeking relief, however slight and temporary, in the weakness of a few rambling details. These, moreover, utterly trivial, and even ridiculous in themselves, assume, to my fancy, adventitious importance, as connected with a period and a locality when and where I recognize the first ambiguous monitions of the destiny which afterwards so fully overshadowed me. Let me then remember.

The house, I have said, was old and irregular. The grounds were extensive, and a high and solid brick wall, topped with a bed of mortar and broken glass, encompassed the whole. This prison-like rampart formed the limit of our domain; beyond it we saw but thrice a week—once every Saturday afternoon, when, attended by two ushers, we were permitted to take brief walks in a body through some of the neighboring fields—and twice during Sunday, when we were paraded in the same formal manner to the morning and evening service in the one church of the village. Of this church the principal of our school was pastor. With how deep a spirit of wonder and perplexity was I wont to regard him from our remote pew in the gallery, as, with step solemn and slow, he ascended the pulpit! This reverend man, with countenance so demurely benign, with robes so glossy and so clerically flowing, with wig so minutely powdered, so rigid and so vast,—could this be he who, of late, with sour visage, and in snuffy habiliments, administered, ferule in hand, the Draconian laws of the academy? Oh, gigantic paradox, too utterly monstrous for solution!

At an angle of the ponderous wall frowned a more ponderous gate. It was riveted and studded with iron bolts, and surmounted with jagged iron spikes. What impressions of deep awe did it inspire! It was never opened save for the three periodical egressions and ingressions already mentioned; then, in every creak of its mighty hinges, we found a plenitude of mystery—a world of matter for solemn remark, or for more solemn meditation.

The extensive enclosure was irregular in form, having many capacious recesses. Of these, three or four of the largest constituted the playground. It was level, and covered with fine hard gravel. I well remember it had no trees, nor benches, nor any thing similar within it. Of course it was in the rear of the house. In front lay a small parterre, planted with box and other shrubs; but through this sacred division we passed only upon rare occasions indeed—such as a first advent to school or final departure thence, or perhaps, when a parent or friend having called for us, we joyfully took our way home for the Christmas or Midsummer holidays.

But the house!—how quaint an old building was this!—to me how veritably a palace of enchantment! There was really no end to its windings—to its incomprehensible subdivisions. It was difficult, at any given time, to say with certainty upon which of its two stories one happened to be. From each room to every other there were sure to be found three or four steps either in ascent or descent. Then the lateral branches were innumerable—inconceivable—and so returning in upon themselves, that our most exact ideas in regard to the whole mansion were not very far different from those with which we pondered upon infinity. During the five years of my residence here, I was never able to ascertain with precision, in what remote locality lay the little sleeping apartment assigned to myself and some eighteen or twenty other scholars.

The schoolroom was the largest in the house—I could not help thinking, in the world. It was very long, narrow, and dismally low, with pointed Gothic windows and a ceiling of oak. In a remote and terror-inspiring angle was a square enclosure of eight or ten feet, comprising the *sanctum*, "during hours," of our principal, the Reverend Dr. Bransby. It was a solid structure, with massy door, sooner than open which in the absence of the "Dominie," we would all have willingly perished by the *peine forte et dure*. In other angles were two other similar boxes, far less reverenced, indeed, but still greatly matters of awe. One of these was the pulpit of the "classical" usher, one of the "English and mathematical." Interspersed about the room, crossing and recrossing in endless irregularity, were innumerable benches and desks, black, ancient, and timeworn, piled desperately with much-bethumbed books, and so beseamed with initial letters, names at full length, grotesque figures, and other multiplied efforts of the knife, as to have entirely lost what little of original form might have been their portion in days long departed. A huge bucket with water stood at one extremity of the room, and a clock of stupendous dimensions at the other.

Encompassed by the massy walls of this venerable academy, I passed, yet not in tedium or disgust, the years of the third lustrum of my life. The teeming brain of childhood requires no external world of incident to occupy or amuse it; and the apparently dismal monotony of a school was replete with more intense excitement than my riper youth has derived from luxury, or my full manhood from crime. Yet I must believe that my first mental development had in it much of the uncommon—even much of the *outré*. Upon mankind at large the events of very early existence rarely leave in mature age any definite impression. All is grey shadow—a weak and irregular remembrance—an indistinct regathering of feeble pleasures and phantasmagoric pains. With me this is not so. In childhood I must have felt with the energy of a man what I now find stamped upon memory in lines as vivid, as deep, and as durable as the *exergues* of the Carthaginian medals.

Yet in fact—in the fact of the world's view—how little was there to remember! The morning's awakening, the nightly summons to bed; the connings, the recitations; the periodical half-holidays, and perambulations; the playground, with its broils, its pastimes, its intrigues; — these, by a mental sorcery long forgotten, were made to involve a wilderness of sensation, a world of rich incident, an universe of varied emotion, of excitement the most passionate and spirit-stirring. *"Oh, le bon temps, que ce siècle de fer!"*

In truth, the ardor, the enthusiasm, and the imperiousness of my disposition, soon rendered me a marked character among my schoolmates, and by slow, but natural gradations, gave me an ascendancy over all not greatly older than myself; — over all with a single exception. This exception was found in the person of a scholar, who, although no relation, bore the same Christian and surname as myself; — a circumstance, in fact, little remarkable; for, notwithstanding a noble descent, mine was one of those everyday appellations which seem, by prescriptive right, to have been, time out of mind, the common property of the mob. In this narrative I have therefore designated myself as William Wilson, — a fictitious title not very dissimilar to the real. My namesake alone, of those who in school phraseology constituted "our set," presumed to compete with me in the studies of the class — in the sports and broils of the playground — to refuse implicit belief in my assertions, and submission to my will — indeed, to interfere with my arbitrary dictation in any respect whatsoever. If there is on earth a supreme and unqualified despotism, it is the despotism of a mastermind in boyhood over the less energetic spirits of its companions.

Wilson's rebellion was to me a source of the greatest embarrassment; — the more so as, in spite of the bravado with which in public I made a point of treating him and his pretensions, I secretly felt that I feared him, and could not help thinking the equality which he maintained so easily with myself, a proof of his true superiority; since not to be overcome cost me a perpetual struggle. Yet this superiority — even this equality — was in truth acknowledged by no one but myself; our associates, by some unaccountable blindness, seemed not even to suspect it. Indeed, his competition, his resistance, and especially his impertinent and dogged interference with my purposes, were not more pointed than private. He appeared to be destitute alike of the ambition which urged, and of the passionate energy of mind which enabled me to excel. In his rivalry he might have been supposed actuated solely by a whimsical desire to thwart, astonish, or mortify myself; although there were times when I could not help observing, with a feeling made up of wonder, abasement, and pique, that he mingled with his injuries, his insults, or his contradictions, a certain most inappropriate, and assuredly most unwelcome *affectionateness* of manner. I could only conceive this singular behavior to arise from a consummate self-conceit assuming the vulgar airs of patronage and protection.

Perhaps it was this latter trait in Wilson's conduct, conjoined with our identity of name, and the mere accident of our having entered the school upon the same day, which set afloat the notion that we were brothers, among the senior classes in the academy. These do not usually inquire with much strictness into the affairs of their juniors. I have before said, or should have said, that Wilson was not, in the most remote degree, connected with my family. But assuredly if we *had* been brothers we must have been twins; for, after leaving Dr. Bransby's, I casually learned that my namesake was born on the nineteenth of January, 1813—and this is a somewhat remarkable coincidence; for the day is precisely that of my own nativity.

It may seem strange that in spite of the continual anxiety occasioned me by the rivalry of Wilson, and his intolerable spirit of contradiction, I could not bring myself to hate him altogether. We had, to be sure, nearly every day a quarrel in which, yielding me publicly the palm of victory, he, in some manner, contrived to make me feel that it was he who had deserved it; yet a sense of pride on my part, and a veritable dignity on his own, kept us always upon what are called "speaking terms," while there were many points of strong congeniality in our tempers, operating to awake in me a sentiment which our position alone, perhaps, prevented from ripening into friendship. It is difficult, indeed, to define, or even to describe, my real feelings towards him. They formed a motley and heterogeneous admixture;— some petulant animosity, which was not yet hatred, some esteem, more respect, much fear, with a world of uneasy curiosity. To the moralist it will be unnecessary to say, in addition, that Wilson and myself were the most inseparable of companions.

It was no doubt the anomalous state of affairs existing between us, which turned all my attacks upon him (and they were many, either open or covert) into the channel of banter or practical joke (giving pain while assuming the aspect of mere fun) rather than into a more serious and determined hostility. But my endeavors on this head were by no means uniformly successful, even when my plans were the most wittily concocted; for my namesake had much about him, in character, of that unassuming and quiet austerity which, while enjoying the poignancy of its own jokes, has no heel of Achilles in itself, and absolutely refuses to be laughed at. I could find, indeed, but one vulnerable point, and that, lying in a personal peculiarity, arising, perhaps, from constitutional disease, would have been spared by any antagonist less at his wit's end than myself;—my rival had a weakness in the facial or guttural organs, which precluded him from raising his voice at any time *above a very low whisper*. Of this defect I did not fail to take what poor advantage lay in my power.

Wilson's retaliations in kind were many; and there was one form of his practical wit that disturbed me beyond measure. How his sagacity first discovered at all that so petty a thing would vex me, is a question I never could solve; but, having discovered, he habitually practiced the annoyance. I had always felt aversion to my uncourtly patronymic, and its very common, if not plebeian praenomen. The words were venom in my ears; and when, upon the day of my arrival, a second William Wilson came also to the academy, I felt angry with him for bearing the name, and doubly disgusted with the name because a stranger bore it, who would be the cause of its twofold repetition, who would be constantly in my presence, and whose concerns, in the ordinary routine of the school business, must inevitably, on account of the detestable coincidence, be often confounded with my own.

The feeling of vexation thus engendered grew stronger with every circumstance tending to show resemblance, moral or physical, between my rival and myself. I had not then discovered the remarkable fact that we were of the same age; but I saw that we were of the same height, and I perceived that we were even singularly alike in general contour of person and outline of feature. I was galled, too, by the rumor touching a relationship, which had grown current in the upper forms. In a word, nothing could more seriously disturb me (although I scrupulously concealed such disturbance), than any allusion to a similarity of mind, person, or condition existing between us. But, in truth, I had no reason to believe that (with the exception of the matter of relationship, and in the case of Wilson himself) this similarity had ever been made a subject of comment, or even observed at all by our schoolfellows. That *he* observed it in all its bearings, and as fixedly as I, was apparent; but that he could discover in such circumstances so fruitful a field of annoyance, can only be attributed, as I said before, to his more than ordinary penetration.

His cue, which was to perfect an imitation of myself, lay both in words and in actions; and most admirably did he play his part. My dress it was an easy matter to copy; my gait and general manner were, without difficulty, appropriated; in spite of his constitutional defect, even my voice did not escape him. My louder tones were, of course, unattempted, but then the key, it was identical; *and his singular whisper, it grew the very echo of my own.*

How greatly this most exquisite portraiture harassed me (for it could not justly be termed a caricature), I will not now venture to describe. I had but one consolation—in the fact that the imitation, apparently, was noticed by myself alone, and that I had to endure only the knowing and strangely sarcastic smiles of my namesake himself. Satisfied with having produced in my bosom the intended effect, he seemed to chuckle in secret over the sting he had inflicted, and was characteristically disregardful of the public applause which the success of his witty endeavors might have so easily elicited. That the school, indeed, did not feel his design, perceive its accomplishment, and participate in his sneer, was, for many anxious months, a riddle I could not resolve. Perhaps the *gradation* of his copy rendered it not so readily perceptible; or, more possibly, I owed my security to the masterly air of the copyist, who, disdaining the letter (which in a painting is all the obtuse can see), gave but the full spirit of his original for my individual contemplation and chagrin.

I have already more than once spoken of the disgusting air of patronage which he assumed toward me, and of his frequent officious interference with my will. This interference often took the ungracious character of advice; advice not openly given, but hinted or insinuated. I received it with a repugnance which gained strength as I grew in years. Yet, at this distant day, let me do him the simple justice to acknowledge that I can recall no occasion when the suggestions of my rival were on the side of those errors or follies so usual to his immature age and seeming inexperience; that his moral sense, at least, if not his general talents and worldly wisdom, was far keener than my own; and that I might, today, have been a better, and thus a happier man, had I less frequently rejected the counsels embodied in those meaning whispers which I then but too cordially hated and too bitterly despised.

As it was, I at length grew restive in the extreme under his distasteful supervision, and daily resented more and more openly what I considered his intolerable arrogance. I have said that, in the first years of our connection as schoolmates, my feelings in regard to him might have been easily ripened into friendship: but, in the latter months of my residence at the academy, although the intrusion of his ordinary manner had, beyond doubt, in some measure, abated, my sentiments, in nearly similar proportion, partook very much of positive hatred. Upon one occasion he saw this, I think, and afterwards avoided, or made a show of avoiding me.

It was about the same period, if I remember aright, that, in an altercation of violence with him, in which he was more than usually thrown off his guard, and spoke and acted with an openness of demeanor rather foreign to his nature, I discovered, or fancied I discovered, in his accent, his air, and general appearance, a something which first startled, and then deeply interested me, by bringing to mind dim visions of my earliest infancy—wild, confused and thronging memories of a time when memory herself was yet unborn. I cannot better describe the sensation which oppressed me than by saying that I could with difficulty shake off the belief of my having been acquainted with the being who stood before me, at some epoch very long ago—some point of the past even infinitely remote. The delusion, however, faded rapidly as it came; and I mention it at all but to define the day of the last conversation I there held with my singular namesake.

The huge old house, with its countless subdivisions, had several large chambers communicating with each other, where slept the greater number of the students. There were, however, (as must necessarily happen in a building so awkwardly planned) many little nooks or recesses, the odds and ends of the structure; and these the economic ingenuity of Dr. Bransby had also fitted up as dormitories; although, being the merest closets, they were capable of accommodating but a single individual. One of these small apartments was occupied by Wilson.

One night, about the close of my fifth year at the school, and immediately after the altercation just mentioned, finding every one wrapped in sleep, I arose from bed, and, lamp in hand, stole through a wilderness of narrow passages from my own bedroom to that of my rival. I had long been plotting one of those ill-natured pieces of practical wit at his expense in which I had hitherto been so uniformly unsuccessful. It was my intention, now, to put my scheme in operation, and I resolved to make him feel the whole extent of the malice with which I was imbued. Having reached his closet, I noiselessly entered, leaving the lamp, with a shade over it, on the outside. I advanced a step, and listened to the sound of his tranquil breathing. Assured of his being asleep, I returned, took the light, and with it again approached the bed. Close curtains were around it, which, in the prosecution of my plan, I slowly and quietly withdrew, when the bright rays fell vividly upon the sleeper, and my eyes, at the same moment, upon his countenance. I looked;—and a numbness, an iciness of feeling instantly pervaded my frame. My breast heaved, my knees tottered, my whole spirit became possessed with an objectless yet intolerable horror. Gasping for breath, I lowered the lamp in still nearer proximity to the face. Were these—*these* the lineaments of William Wilson? I saw, indeed, that they were his, but I shook as if with a fit of the argue in fancying they were not. What *was* there about them to confound me in this manner? I gazed;—while my brain reeled with a multitude of incoherent thoughts. Not thus he appeared—assuredly not *thus*—in the vivacity of his waking hours. The same name! the same contour of person! the same day of arrival at the academy! And then his dogged and meaningless imitation of my gait, my voice, my habits, and my manner! Was it, in truth, within the bounds of human possibility, that *what I now saw* was the result, merely, of the habitual practice of this sarcastic imitation? Awe-stricken, and with a creeping shudder, I extinguished the lamp, passed silently from the chamber, and left, at once, the halls of that old academy, never to enter them again.

After a lapse of some months, spent at home in mere idleness, I found myself a student at Eton. The brief interval had been sufficient to enfeeble my remembrance of the events at Dr. Bransby's, or at least to effect a material change in the nature of the feelings with which I remembered them. The truth—the tragedy—of the drama was no more. I could now find room to doubt the evidence of my senses; and seldom called up the subject at all but with wonder at the extent of human credulity, and a smile at the vivid force of the imagination which I hereditarily possessed. Neither was this species of scepticism likely to be diminished by the character of the life I led at Eton. The vortex of thoughtless folly into which I there so immediately and so recklessly plunged, washed away all but the froth of my past hours, engulfed at once every solid or serious impression, and left to memory only the veriest levities of a former existence.

I do not wish, however, to trace the course of my miserable profligacy here—a profligacy which set at defiance the laws, while it eluded the vigilance of the institution. Three years of folly, passed without profit, had but given me rooted habits of vice, and added, in a somewhat unusual degree, to my bodily stature, when, after a week of soulless dissipation, I invited a small party of the most dissolute students to a secret carousal in my chambers. We met at a late hour of the night; for our debaucheries were to be faithfully protracted until morning. The wine flowed freely, and there were not wanting other and perhaps more dangerous seductions; so that the grey dawn had already faintly appeared in the east, while our delirious extravagance was at its height. Madly flushed with cards and intoxication, I was in the act of insisting upon a toast of more than wonted profanity, when my attention was suddenly diverted by the violent, although partial unclosing of the door of the apartment, and by the eager voice of a servant from without. He said that some person, apparently in great haste, demanded to speak with me in the hall.

Wildly excited with wine, the unexpected interruption rather delighted than surprised me. I staggered forward at once, and a few steps brought me to the vestibule of the building. In this low and small room there hung no lamp; and now no light at all was admitted, save that of the exceedingly feeble dawn which made its way through the semicircular window. As I put my foot over the threshold, I became aware of the figure of a youth about my own height, and habited in a white kerseymere morning frock, cut in the novel fashion of the one I myself wore at the moment. This the faint light enabled me to perceive; but the features of his face I could not distinguish. Upon my entering he strode hurriedly up to me, and, seizing me by the arm with a gesture of petulant impatience, whispered the words "William Wilson!" in my ear.

I grew perfectly sober in an instant.

There was that in the manner of the stranger, and in the tremulous shake of his uplifted finger, as he held it between my eyes and the light, which filled me with unqualified amazement; but it was not this which had so violently moved me. It was the pregnancy of solemn admonition in the singular, low, hissing utterance; and, above all, it was the character, the tone, *the key*, of those few simple, and familiar, yet *whispered* syllables, which came with a thousand thronging memories of bygone days, and struck upon my soul with the shock of a galvanic battery. Ere I could recover the use of my senses he was gone.

Although this event failed not of a vivid effect upon my disordered imagination, yet was it evanescent as vivid. For some weeks, indeed, I busied myself in earnest inquiry, or was wrapped in a cloud of morbid speculation. I did not pretend to disguise from my perception the identity of the singular individual who thus perseveringly interfered with my affairs, and harassed me with his insinuated counsel. But who and what was this Wilson? — and whence came he? — and what were his purposes? Upon neither of these points could I be satisfied;

merely ascertaining, in regard to him, that a sudden accident in his family had caused his removal from Dr. Bransby's academy on the afternoon of the day in which I myself had eloped. But in a brief period I ceased to think upon the subject; my attention being all absorbed in a contemplated departure for Oxford. Thither I soon went; the uncalculating vanity of my parents furnishing me with an outfit and annual establishment, which would enable me to indulge at will in the luxury already so dear to my heart,—to vie in profuseness of expenditure with the haughtiest heirs of the wealthiest earldoms in Great Britain.

Excited by such appliances to vice, my constitutional temperament broke forth with redoubled ardor, and I spurned even the common restraints of decency in the mad infatuation of my revels. But it were absurd to pause in the detail of my extravagance. Let it suffice, that among spendthrifts I out-Heroded Herod, and that, giving name to a multitude of novel follies, I added no brief appendix to the long catalogue of vices then usual in the most dissolute university of Europe.

It could hardly be credited, however, that I had, even here, so utterly fallen from the gentlemanly estate, as to seek acquaintance with the vilest arts of the gambler by profession, and, having become an adept in his despicable science, to practice it habitually as a means of increasing my already enormous income at the expense of the weakminded among my fellow collegians. Such, nevertheless, was the fact. And the very enormity of this offense against all manly and honourable sentiment proved, beyond doubt, the main if not the sole reason of the impunity with which it was committed. Who, indeed, among my most abandoned associates, would not rather have disputed the clearest evidence of his senses, than have suspected of such courses, the gay, the frank, the generous William Wilson—the noblest and most liberal commoner at Oxford—him whose follies (said his parasites) were but the follies of youth and unbridled fancy—whose errors but inimitable whim—whose darkest vice but a careless and dashing extravagance?

I had been now two years successfully busied in this way, when there came to the university a young *parvenu* nobleman, Glendinning—rich, said report, as Herodes Atticus—his riches, too, as easily acquired. I soon found him of weak intellect, and, of course, marked him as a fitting subject for my skill. I frequently engaged him in play, and contrived, with the gambler's usual art, to let him win considerable sums, the more effectually to entangle him in my snares. At length, my schemes being ripe, I met him (with the full intention that this meeting should be final and decisive) at the chambers of a fellow commoner (Mr. Preston), equally intimate with both, but who, to do him justice, entertained not even a remote suspicion of my design. To give to this a better coloring, I had contrived to have assembled a party of some eight or ten, and was solicitously careful that the introduction of cards should appear accidental, and originate in the proposal of my contemplated dupe himself. To be brief upon a vile topic, none of the low finesse was omitted, so customary upon similar occasions that it is a just matter for wonder how any are still found so besotted as to fall its victim.

We had protracted our sitting far into the night, and I had at length effected the manœuvre of getting Glendinning as my sole antagonist. The game, too, was my favorite *écarté*. The rest of the company, interested in the extent of our play, had abandoned their own cards, and were standing around us as spectators. The *parvenu*, who had been induced by my artifices in the early part of the evening, to drink deeply, now shuffled, dealt, or played, with a wild nervousness of manner for which his intoxication, I thought, might partially, but could not altogether account. In a very short period he had become my debtor to a large amount, when, having taken a long draught of port, he did precisely what I had been coolly anticipating— he proposed to double our already extravagant stakes. With a well-feigned show of reluctance, and not until after my repeated refusal had seduced him into some angry words which gave a color of *pique* to my compliance, did I finally comply. The result, of course, did but prove how entirely the prey was in my toils; in less than an hour he had quadrupled his debt. For some time his countenance had been losing the florid tinge lent it by the wine; but now, to my astonishment, I perceived that it had grown to a pallor truly fearful. I say to my astonishment. Glendinning had been represented to my eager inquiries as immeasurably wealthy; and the sums which he had as yet lost, although in themselves vast, could not, I supposed, very seriously annoy, much less so violently affect him. That he was overcome by the wine just swallowed, was the idea which most readily presented itself; and, rather with a view to the preservation of my own character in the eyes of my associates, than from any less interested motive, I was about to insist, peremptorily, upon a discontinuance of the play, when some expressions at my elbow from among the company, and an ejaculation evincing utter despair on the part of Glendinning, gave me to understand that I had effected his total ruin under circumstances which, rendering him an object for the pity of all, should have protected him from the ill offices even of a fiend.

What now might have been my conduct it is difficult to say. The pitiable condition of my dupe had thrown an air of embarrassed gloom over all; and, for some moments, a profound silence was maintained, during which I could not help feeling my cheeks tingle with the many burning glances of scorn or reproach cast upon me by the less abandoned of the party. I will even own that an intolerable weight of anxiety was for a brief instant lifted from my bosom by the sudden and extraordinary interruption which ensued. The wide, heavy folding doors of the apartment were all at once thrown open, to their full extent, with a vigorous and rushing impetuosity that extinguished, as if by magic, every candle in the room. Their light, in dying, enabled us just to perceive that a stranger had entered, about my own height, and closely muffled in a cloak. The darkness, however, was now total; and we could only *feel* that he was standing in our midst. Before any one of us could recover from the extreme astonishment into which this rudeness had thrown all, we heard the voice of the intruder.

"Gentlemen," he said, in a low, distinct, and never-to-be-forgotten *whisper* which thrilled to the very marrow of my bones, "Gentlemen, I make no apology for this behavior, because in thus behaving, I am but fulfilling a duty. You are, beyond doubt, uninformed of the true character of the person who has tonight won at *écarté* a large sum of money from Lord Glendinning. I will therefore put you upon an expeditious and decisive plan of obtaining this very necessary information. Please to examine, at your leisure, the inner linings of the cuff of his left sleeve, and the several little packages which may be found in the somewhat capacious pockets of his embroidered morning wrapper."

While he spoke, so profound was the stillness that one might have heard a pin drop upon the floor. In ceasing, he departed at once, and as abruptly as he had entered. Can I—shall I describe my sensations?—must I say that I felt all the horrors of the dammed? Most assuredly I had little time given for reflection. Many hands roughly seized me upon the spot, and lights were immediately reprocured. A search ensued. In the lining of my sleeve were found all the court cards essential in *écarté*, and, in the pockets of my wrapper, a number of packs, facsimiles of those used at our sittings, with the single exception that mine were of the species called, technically, *arrondées*; the honors being slightly convex at the ends, the lower cards slightly convex at the sides. In this disposition, the dupe who cuts, as customary, at the length of the pack, will invariably find that he cuts his antagonist an honor; while the gambler, cutting at the breadth, will, as certainly, cut nothing for his victim which may count in the records of the game.

Any burst of indignation upon this discovery would have affected me less than the silent contempt, or the sarcastic composure, with which it was received.

"Mr. Wilson," said our host, stooping to remove from beneath his feet an exceedingly luxurious cloak of rare furs, "Mr. Wilson, this is your property." (The weather was cold; and, upon quitting my own room, I had thrown a cloak over my dressing-wrapper, putting it off upon reaching the scene of play.) "I presume it is supererogatory to seek here" (eyeing the folds of the garment with a bitter smile) "for any farther evidence of your skill. Indeed, we have had enough. You will see the necessity, I hope, of quitting Oxford—at all events, of quitting instantly my chambers."

Abased, humbled to the dust as I then was, it is probable that I should have resented this galling language by immediate personal violence, had not my whole attention been at the moment arrested by a fact of almost startling character. The cloak which I had worn was of a rare description of fur; how rare, how extravagantly costly, I shall not venture to say. Its fashion, too, was of my own fantastic invention; for I was fastidious to an absurd degree of coxcombry, in matters of this frivolous nature. When, therefore, Mr. Preston reached me that which he had picked up upon the floor, and near the folding doors of the apartment, it was with an astonishment nearly bordering upon terror, that I perceived my own already hanging on my arm (where I had no doubt unwittingly placed it), and that the one presented me was but its exact counterpart in every, in even the minutest possible particular. The singular being who had so disastrously exposed me, had been muffled, I remembered, in a cloak; and none had been worn at all by any of the members of our party with the exception of myself. Retaining some presence of mind, I took the one offered me by Preston; placed it, unnoticed, over my own; left the apartment with a resolute scowl of defiance; and, next morning ere dawn of day, commenced a hurried journey from Oxford to the continent, in a perfect agony of horror and of shame.

I fled in vain. My evil destiny pursued me as if in exultation, and proved, indeed, that the exercise of its mysterious dominion had as yet only begun. Scarcely had I set foot in Paris ere I had fresh evidence of the detestable interest taken by this Wilson in my concerns. Years flew, while I experienced no relief. Villain!—at Rome, with how untimely, yet with how spectral an officiousness, stepped he in between me and my ambition! At Vienna, too—at Berlin—and at Moscow! Where, in truth, had I *not* bitter cause to curse him within my heart? From his inscrutable tyranny did I at length flee, panic-stricken, as from a pestilence; and to the very ends of the earth *I fled in vain.*

And again, and again, in secret communion with my own spirit, would I demand the questions "Who is he?—whence came he?—and what are his objects?" But no answer was there found. And then I scrutinized, with a minute scrutiny, the forms, and the methods, and the leading traits of his impertinent supervision. But even here there was very little upon which to base a conjecture. It was noticeable, indeed, that, in no one of the multiplied instances in which he had of late crossed my path, had he so crossed it except to frustrate those schemes, or to disturb those actions, which, if fully carried out, might have resulted in bitter mischief. Poor justification this, in truth, for an authority so imperiously assumed! Poor indemnity for natural rights of self-agency so pertinaciously, so insultingly denied!

I had also been forced to notice that my tormentor, for a very long period of time (while scrupulously and with miraculous dexterity maintaining his whim of an identity of apparel with myself), had so contrived it, in the execution of his varied interference with my will, that I saw not, at any moment, the features of his face. Be Wilson what he might, *this*, at least, was but the veriest of affectation, or of folly. Could he, for an instant, have supposed that, in my admonisher at Eton—in the destroyer of my honor at Oxford,—in him who thwarted my ambition at Rome, my revenge at Paris, my passionate love at Naples, or what he falsely termed my avarice in Egypt,—that in this, my archenemy and evil genius, I could fail to recognize the William Wilson of my schoolboy days,—the namesake, the companion, the rival,—the hated and dreaded rival at Dr. Bransby's? Impossible!—But let me hasten to the last eventful scene of the drama.

Thus far I had succumbed supinely to this imperious domination. The sentiment of deep awe with which I habitually regarded the elevated character, the majestic wisdom, the apparent omnipresence and omnipotence of Wilson, added to a feeling of even terror, with which certain other traits in his nature and assumptions inspired me, had operated, hitherto, to impress me with an idea of my own utter weakness and helplessness, and to suggest an implicit, although bitterly reluctant submission to his arbitrary will. But, of late days, I had given myself up entirely to wine; and its maddening influence upon my hereditary temper rendered me more and more impatient of control. I began to murmur,—to hesitate,—to resist. And was it only fancy which induced me to believe that, with the increase of my own firmness, that of my tormentor underwent a proportional diminution? Be this as it may, I now began to feel the inspiration of a burning hope, and at length nurtured in my secret thoughts a stern and desperate resolution that I would submit no longer to be enslaved.

It was at Rome, during the Carnival of 18—, that I attended a masquerade in the palazzo of the Neapolitan Duke Di Broglio. I had indulged more freely than usual in the excesses of the wine-table; and now the suffocating atmosphere of the crowded rooms irritated me beyond endurance. The difficulty, too, of forcing my way through the mazes of the company contributed not a little to the ruffling of my temper; for I was anxiously seeking (let me not say with what unworthy motive) the young, the gay, the beautiful wife of the aged and doting Di Broglio. With a too unscrupulous confidence she had previously communicated to me the secret of the costume in which she would be habited, and now, having caught a glimpse of her person, I was hurrying to make my way into her presence.—At this moment I felt a light hand placed upon my shoulder, and that ever-remembered, low, damnable *whisper* within my ear.

In an absolute phrenzy of wrath, I turned at once upon him who had thus interrupted me, and seized him violently by the collar. He was attired, as I had expected, in a costume altogether similar to my own; wearing a Spanish cloak of blue velvet, begirt about the waist with a crimson belt sustaining a rapier. A mask of black silk entirely covered his face.

"Scoundrel!" I said, in a voice husky with rage, while every syllable I uttered seemed as new fuel to my fury, "scoundrel! impostor! accursed villain! you shall not—you *shall not* dog me unto death! Follow me, or I stab you where you stand!"—and I broke my way from the ballroom into a small antechamber adjoining—dragging him unresistingly with me as I went.

Upon entering I thrust him furiously from me. He staggered against the wall, while I closed the door with an oath, and commanded him to draw. He hesitated but for an instant; then, with a slight sigh, drew in silence, and put himself upon his defense.

The contest was brief indeed. I was frantic with every species of wild excitement, and felt within my single arm the energy and power of a multitude. In a few seconds I forced him by sheer strength against the wainscoting, and thus, getting him at mercy, plunged my sword, with brute ferocity repeatedly through and through his bosom.

At that instant some person tried the latch of the door. I hastened to prevent an intrusion, and then immediately returned to my dying antagonist. But what human language can adequately portray *that* astonishment, *that* horror which possessed me at the spectacle then presented to view? The brief moment in which I averted my eyes had been sufficient to produce, apparently, a material change in the arrangements at the upper or farther end of the room. A large mirror,—so at first it seemed to me in my confusion—now stood where none had been perceptible before; and, as I stepped up to it in extremity of terror, mine own image, but with features all pale and dabbled in blood, advanced to meet me with a feeble and tottering gait.

Thus it appeared, I say, but was not. It was my antagonist—it was Wilson, who then stood before me in the agonies of his dissolution. His mask and cloak lay, where he had thrown them, upon the floor. Not a thread in all his raiment—not a line in all the marked and singular lineaments of his face which was not, even in the most absolute identity, *mine own!*

It was Wilson; but he spoke no longer in a whisper, and I could have fancied that I myself was speaking while he said:

"*You have conquered, and I yield. Yet, henceforward art thou also dead—dead to the World, to Heaven and to Hope! In me didst thou exist— and, in my death, see by this image, which is thine own, how utterly thou hast murdered himself.*"

Hop-Frog

I never knew any one so keenly alive to a joke as the king was. He seemed to live only for joking. To tell a good story of the joke kind, and to tell it well, was the surest road to his favor. Thus it happened that his seven ministers were all noted for their accomplishments as jokers. They all took after the king, too, in being large, corpulent, oily men, as well as inimitable jokers. Whether people grow fat by joking, or whether there is something in fat itself which predisposes to a joke, I have never been quite able to determine; but certain it is that a lean joker is a *rara avis in terris*.

About the refinements, or, as he called them, the "ghosts" of wit, the king troubled himself very little. He had an especial admiration for *breadth* in a jest, and would often put up with *length*, for the sake of it. Over-niceties wearied him. He would have preferred Rabelais's "Gargantua," to the "Zadig" of Voltaire: and, upon the whole, practical jokes suited his taste far better than verbal ones.

At the date of my narrative, professing jesters had not altogether gone out of fashion at court. Several of the great continental "powers" still retained their "fools," who wore motley, with caps and bells, and who were expected to be always ready with sharp witticisms, at a moment's notice, in consideration of the crumbs that fell from the royal table.

Our king, as a matter of course, retained his "fool." The fact is, he *required* something in the way of folly—if only to counterbalance the heavy wisdom of the seven wise men who were his ministers—not to mention himself.

His fool, or professional jester, was not *only* a fool, however. His value was trebled in the eyes of the king, by the fact of his being also a dwarf and a cripple. Dwarfs were as common at court, in those days, as fools; and many monarchs would have found it difficult to get through their days (days are rather longer at court than elsewhere) without both a jester to laugh *with*, and a dwarf to laugh *at*. But, as I have already observed, your jesters, in ninety-nine cases out of a hundred, are fat, round and unwieldy—so that it was no small source of self-gratulation with our king that, in Hop-Frog (this was the fool's name) he possessed a triplicate treasure in one person.

I believe the name "Hop-Frog" was *not* that given to the dwarf by his sponsors at baptism, but it was conferred upon him, by general consent of the seven ministers, on account of his inability to walk as other men do. In fact, Hop-Frog could only get along by a sort of interjectional gait—something between a leap and a wriggle—a movement that afforded illimitable amusement, and of course consolation, to the king, for (notwithstanding the protuberance of his stomach and a constitutional swelling of the head) the king, by his whole court, was accounted a capital figure.

But although Hop-Frog, through the distortion of his legs, could move only with great pain and difficulty along a road or floor, the prodigious muscular power which nature seemed to have bestowed upon his arms, by way of compensation for deficiency in the lower limbs, enabled him to perform many feats of wonderful dexterity, where trees or ropes were in question, or any thing else to climb. At such exercises he certainly much more resembled a squirrel, or a small monkey, than a frog.

I am not able to say, with precision, from what country Hop-Frog originally came. It was from some barbarous region, however, that no person ever heard of—a vast distance from the court of our king. Hop-Frog, and a young girl very little less dwarfish than himself (although of exquisite proportions, and a marvellous dancer), had been forcibly carried off from their respective homes in adjoining provinces, and sent as presents to the king, by one of his ever-victorious generals.

Under these circumstances, it is not to be wondered at that a close intimacy arose between the two little captives. Indeed, they soon became sworn friends. Hop-Frog, who, although he made a great deal of sport, was by no means popular, had it not in his power to render Trippetta many services; but *she*, on account of her grace and exquisite beauty (although a dwarf), was universally admired and petted: so she possessed much influence; and never failed to use it, whenever she could, for the benefit of Hop-Frog.

On some grand state occasion—I forget what—the king determined to have a masquerade; and whenever a masquerade, or any thing of that kind, occurred at our court, then the talents both of Hop-Frog and Trippetta were sure to be called in play. Hop-Frog, in especial, was so inventive in the way of getting up pageants, suggesting novel characters and arranging costume for masked balls, that nothing could be done, it seems, without his assistance.

The night appointed for the *fête* had arrived. A gorgeous hall had been fitted up, under Trippetta's eye, with every kind of device which could possibly give *éclat* to a masquerade. The whole court was in a fever of expectation. As for costumes and characters, it might well be supposed that everybody had come to a decision on such points. Many had made up their minds as to what *rôles* they should assume, a week, or even a month, in advance; and, in fact, there was not a particle of indecision anywhere—except in the case of the king and his seven ministers. Why *they* hesitated I never could tell, unless they did it by way of a joke. More probably, they found it difficult, on account of being so fat, to make up their minds. At all events, time flew; and, as a last resource, they sent for Trippetta and Hop-Frog.

When the two little friends obeyed the summons of the king, they found him sitting at his wine with the seven members of his cabinet council; but the monarch appeared to be in a very ill humor. He knew that Hop-Frog was not fond of wine; for it excited the poor cripple almost to madness; and madness is no comfortable feeling. But the king loved his practical jokes, and took pleasure in forcing Hop-Frog to drink and (as the king called it) "to be merry."

"Come here, Hop-Frog," said he, as the jester and his friend entered the room: "swallow this bumper to the health of your absent friends" (here Hop-Frog sighed), "and then let us have the benefit of your invention. We want characters—*characters*, man—something novel—out of the way. We are wearied with this everlasting sameness. Come, drink! the wine will brighten your wits."

Hop-Frog endeavored, as usual, to get up a jest in reply to these advances from the king; but the effort was too much. It happened to be the poor dwarf's birthday, and the command to drink to his "absent friends" forced the tears to his eyes. Many large, bitter drops fell into the goblet as he took it, humbly from the land of the tyrant.

"Ah! ha! ha! ha!" roared the latter, as the dwarf reluctantly drained the beaker. "See what a glass of good wine can do! Why, your eyes are shinning already!"

Poor fellow! his large eyes *gleamed* rather than shone, for the effect of wine on his excitable brain was not more powerful than instantaneous. He placed the goblet nervously on the table, and looked round upon the company with a half-insane stare. They all seemed highly amused at the success of the king's "*joke.*"

"And now to business," said the prime minister, a *very* fat man.

"Yes," said the king; "come, Hop-Frog, lend us your assistance. Characters, my fine fellow; we stand in need of characters—all of us—ha! ha! ha!" and as this was seriously meant for a joke, his laugh was chorused by the seven.

Hop-Frog also laughed, although feebly and somewhat vacantly.

"Come, come," said the king, impatiently, "have you nothing to suggest?"

"I am endeavoring to think of something *novel*," replied the dwarf, abstractedly, for he was quite bewildered by the wine.

"Endeavoring!" cried the tyrant, fiercely; "what do you mean by *that*? Ah, I perceive. You are sulky, and want more wine. Here, drink this!" and he poured out another gobletful and offered it to the cripple, who merely gazed at it, gasping for breath.

"Drink, I say!" shouted the monster, "or by the fiends—"

The dwarf hesitated. The king grew purple with rage. The courtiers smirked. Trippetta, pale as a corpse, advanced to the monarch's seat, and, falling on her knees before him, implored him to spare her friend.

The tyrant regarded her, for some moments, in evident wonder at her audacity. He seemed quite at a loss what to do or say—how most becomingly to express his indignation. At last, without uttering a syllable, he pushed her violently from him, and threw the contents of the brimming goblet in her face.

The poor girl got up as best she could, and, not daring even to sigh, resumed her position at the foot of the table.

There was a dead silence for about half a minute during which the falling of a leaf, or of a feather, might have been heard. It was interrupted by a low, but harsh and protracted *grating* sound which seemed to come at once from every corner of the room.

"What—what—*what* are you making that noise for?" demanded the king, turning furiously to the dwarf.

The latter seemed to have recovered, in great measure, from his intoxication, and looking fixedly but quietly into the tyrant's face, merely ejaculated:

"I—I? How could it have been me?"

"The sound appeared to come from without," observed one of the courtiers. "I fancy it was the parrot at the window, whetting his bill upon his cage wires."

"True," replied the monarch, as if much relieved by the suggestion; "but, on the honor of a knight, I could have sworn that it was gritting of this vagabond's teeth."

Hereupon the dwarf laughed (the king was too confirmed a joker to object to any one's laughing), and display a set of large, powerful, and very repulsive teeth. Moreover, he avowed his perfect willingness to swallow as much wine as desired. The monarch was pacified; and having drained another bumper with no very perceptible ill effect, Hop-Frog entered at once, and with spirit, into the plans for the masquerade.

"I cannot tell what was the association of idea," observed he, very tranquilly, and as if he had never tasted wine in his life, "but *just after* your majesty had struck the girl and thrown the wine in her face—*just after* your majesty had done this, and while the parrot was making that odd noise outside the window, there came into my mind a capital diversion—one of my own country frolics—often enacted among us, at our masquerades: but here it will be new altogether. Unfortunately, however, it requires a company of eight persons, and—"

"Here we *are*!" cried the king, laughing at his acute discovery of the coincidence; "eight to a fraction—I and my seven ministers. Come! what is the diversion?"

"We call it," replied the cripple, "the Eight Chained Ourang-Outangs, and it really is excellent sport if well enacted."

"*We* will enact it," remarked the king, drawing himself up, and lowering his eyelids.

"The beauty of the game," continued Hop-Frog, "lies in the fright it occasions among the women,"

"Capital!" roared in chorus the monarch and his ministry.

"*I* will equip you as ourang-outangs," proceeded the dwarf; "leave all that to me. The resemblance shall be so striking that the company of masqueraders will take you for real beasts—and, of course, they will be as much terrified as astonished."

"Oh, this is exquisite!" exclaimed the king. "Hop-Frog! I will make a man of you."

"The chains are for the purpose of increasing the confusion by their jangling. You are supposed to have escaped, *en masse*, from your keepers. Your majesty cannot conceive the *effect* produced, at a masquerade, by eight chained ourang-outangs, imagined to be real ones by most of the company, and rushing in with savage cries among the crowd of delicately and gorgeously habited men and women. The *contrast* is inimitable."

"It *must* be," said the king: and the council arose hurriedly (as it was growing late), to put in execution the scheme of Hop-Frog.

His mode of equipping the party as ourang-outangs was very simple, but effective enough for his purposes. The animals in question had, at the epoch of my story, very rarely been seen in any part of the civilized world; and as the imitations made by the dwarf were sufficiently beast-like and more than sufficiently hideous, their truthfulness to nature was thus thought to be secured.

The king and his ministers were first encased in tight-fitting stockinet shirts and drawers. They were then saturated with tar. At this stage of the process some one of the party suggested feathers; but the suggestion was at once overruled by the dwarf, who soon convinced the eight, by ocular demonstration, that the hair of such a brute as the ourang-outang was much more efficiently represented by *flax*. A thick coating of tar. A long chain was now procured. First, it was passed about the waist of the king, *and tied*; then about another of the party, and also tied; then about all successively, in the same manner. When this chaining arrangement was complete, and the party stood as far apart from each other as possible, they formed a circle; and to make all things appear natural, Hop-Frog passed the residue of the chain, in two diameters, at right angles, across the circle, after the fashion adopted, at the present day, by those who capture Chimpanzees, or other large apes, in Borneo.

The grand saloon in which the masquerade was to take place, was a circular room, very lofty, and receiving the light of the sun only through a single window at top. At night (the season for which the apartment was especially designed), it was illuminated principally by a large chandelier, depending by a chain from the center of the skylight, and lowered, or elevated, by means of a counterbalance as usual; but (in order not to look unsightly) this latter passed outside the cupola and over the roof.

The arrangements of the room had been left to Trippetta's superintendence; but, in some particulars, it seems, she had guided by the calmer judgment of her friend the dwarf. At his suggestion it was that, on this occasion the chandelier was removed. Its waxen drippings (which, in weather so warm, it was quite impossible to prevent) would have been seriously detrimental to the rich dresses of the guests, who, on account of the crowded state of the saloon, could not *all* be expected to keep from out its center—that is to say, from under the chandelier. Additional sconces were set in various parts of the hall, out of the way; and a flambeau, emitting sweet odor, was placed in the right hand of each of the Caryatides that stood against the wall—some fifty or sixty altogether.

The eight ourang-outangs, taking Hop-Frog's advice, waited patiently until midnight (when the room was thoroughly filled with masqueraders) before making their appearance. No sooner had the clock ceased striking, however, than they rushed, or rather rolled in, all together—for the impediment of their chains caused most of the party to fall, and all to stumble as they entered.

The excitement among the masqueraders was prodigious, and filled the heart of the king with glee. As had been anticipated, there were not a few of the guests who supposed the ferocious-looking creatures to be beasts of *some* kind in reality, if not precisely ourang-outangs. Many of the women swooned with affright; and had not the king taken the precaution to exclude all weapons from the saloon, his party might soon have expiated their frolic in their blood. As it was, a general rush was made for the doors; but the king had ordered them to be locked immediately upon his entrance; and, at the dwarf's suggestion, the keys had been deposited with *him*.

While the tumult was at its height, and each masquerader attentive only to his own safety (for, in fact, there was much *real* danger from the pressure of the excited crowd), the chain by which the chandelier ordinarily hung, and which had been drawn up on its removal, might have been seen very gradually to descend, until its hooked extremity came within three feet of the floor.

Soon after this, the king and his seven friends, having reeled about the hall in all directions, found themselves, at length, in its center and, of course, in immediate contact with the chain. While they were thus situated, the dwarf, who had followed closely at their heels, inciting them to keep up the commotion, took hold of their own chain at the intersection of the two portions which crossed the circle diametrically and at right angles. Here, with the rapidity of thought, he inserted the hook from which the chandelier had been wont to depend; and, in an instant, by some unseen agency, the chandelier-chain was drawn so far upward as to take the hook out of reach, and, as an inevitable consequence, to drag the ourang-outangs together in close connection, and face to face.

The masqueraders, by this time, had recovered, in some measure, from their alarm; and, beginning to regard the whole matter as a well-contrived pleasantry, set up a loud shout of laughter at the predicament of the apes.

"Leave them to *me*!" now screamed Hop-Frog, his shrill voice making itself easily heard through all the din. "Leave them to *me*. I fancy *I* know them. If I can only get a good look at them, *I* can soon tell who they are."

Here, scrambling over the heads of the crowd, he managed to get to the wall; when, seizing a flambeau from one of the Caryatides, he returned, as he went, to the center of the room—leaped, with the agility of a monkey, upon the king's head—and thence clambered a few feet up the chain—holding down the torch to examine the group of ourang-outangs, and still screaming, "*I* shall soon find out who they are!"

And now, while the whole assembly (the apes included) were convulsed with laughter, the jester suddenly uttered a shrill whistle; when the chain flew violently up for about thirty feet—dragging with it the dismayed and struggling ourang-outangs, and leaving them suspended in mid-air between the skylight and the floor. Hop-Frog, clinging to the chain as it rose, still maintained his relative position in respect to the eight maskers, and still (as if nothing were the matter) continued to thrust his torch down towards them, as though endeavoring to discover who they were.

So thoroughly astonished were the whole company at this ascent, that a dead silence, of about a minute's duration, ensued. It was broken by just such a low, harsh, *grating* sound, as had before attracted the attention of the king and his councillors, when the former threw the wine in the face of Trippetta. But, on the present occasion, there could be no question as to *whence* the sound issued. It came from the fang-like teeth of the dwarf, who ground them and gnashed them as he foamed at the mouth, and glared, with an expression of maniacal rage, into the upturned countenances of the king and his seven companions.

"Ah, ha!" said at length the infuriated jester. "Ah, ha! I begin to see who these people *are*, now!" Here, pretending to scrutinize the king more closely, he held the flambeau to the flaxen coat which enveloped him, and which instantly burst into a sheet of vivid flame. In less than half a minute the whole eight ourang-outangs were blazing fiercely, amid the shrieks of the multitude who gazed at them from below, horror-stricken, and without the power to render them the slightest assistance.

At length the flames, suddenly increasing in virulence, forced the jester to climb higher up the chain, to be out of their reach; and, as he made this movement, the crowd again sank, for a brief instant, into silence. The dwarf seized his opportunity, and once more spoke:

"I now see *distinctly*," he said, "what manner of people these maskers are. They are a great king and his seven privy-councillors — a king who does not scruple to strike a defenseless girl, and his seven councillors who abet him in the outrage. As for myself, I am simply Hop-Frog, the jester — and *this is my last jest*."

Owing to the high combustibility of both the flax and the tar to which it adhered, the dwarf had scarcely made an end of his brief speech before the work of vengeance was complete. The eight corpses swung in their chains, a fetid, blackened, hideous, and indistinguishable mass. The cripple hurled his torch at them, clambered leisurely to the ceiling, and disappeared through the skylight.

It is supposed that Trippetta, stationed on the roof of the saloon, had been the accomplice of her friend in his fiery revenge, and that, together, they effected their escape to their own country: for neither was seen again.

The Purloined Letter

Nil sapientiæ odiosius acumine nimie

SENECA.

At Paris, just after dark one gusty evening in the autumn of 18—, I was enjoying the twofold luxury of meditation and a meerschaum, in company with my friend C. Auguste Dupin, in his little back library, or book-closet, *au troisième, No. 33, Rue Dunôt, Faubourg St. Germain*. For one hour at least we had maintained a profound silence; while each, to any casual observer, might have seemed intently and exclusively occupied with the curling eddies of smoke that oppressed the atmosphere of the chamber. For myself, however, I was mentally discussing certain topics which had formed matter for conversation between us at an earlier period of the evening; I mean the affair of the Rue Morgue, and the mystery attending the murder of Marie Rogêt. I looked upon it, therefore, as something of a coincidence, when the door of our apartment was thrown open and admitted our old acquaintance, Monsieur G—, the Prefect of the Parisian police.

We gave him a hearty welcome; for there was nearly half as much of the entertaining as of the contemptible about the man, and we had not seen him for several years. We had been sitting in the dark, and Dupin now arose for the purpose of lighting a lamp, but sat down again, without doing so, upon G—'s saying that he had called to consult us, or rather to ask the opinion of my friend, about some official business which had occasioned a great deal of trouble.

"If it is any point requiring reflection," observed Dupin, as he forbore to enkindle the wick, "we shall examine it to better purpose in the dark."

"That is another of your odd notions," said the Prefect, who had a fashion of calling every thing "odd" that was beyond his comprehension, and thus lived amid an absolute legion of "oddities."

"Very true," said Dupin, as he supplied his visitor with a pipe, and rolled towards him a comfortable chair.

"And what is the difficulty now?" I asked. "Nothing more in the assassination way, I hope?"

"Oh no; nothing of that nature. The fact is, the business is *very* simple indeed, and I make no doubt that we can manage it sufficiently well ourselves; but then I thought Dupin would like to hear the details of it, because it is so excessively *odd*."

"Simple and odd," said Dupin.

"Why, yes; and not exactly that, either. The fact is, we have all been a good deal puzzled because the affair *is* so simple, and yet baffles us altogether."

"Perhaps it is the very simplicity of the thing which puts you at fault," said my friend.

"What nonsense you *do* talk!" replied the Prefect, laughing heartily.

"Perhaps the mystery is a little *too* plain," said Dupin.

"Oh, good heavens! who ever heard of such an idea?"

"A little *too* self-evident."

"Ha! ha! ha!—ha! ha! ha!—ho! ho! ho!"—roared our visitor, profoundly amused, "oh, Dupin, you will be the death of me yet!"

"And what, after all, *is* the matter on hand?" I asked.

"Why, I will tell you," replied the Prefect, as he gave a long, steady, and contemplative puff, and settled himself in his chair. "I will tell you in a few words; but, before I begin, let me caution you that this is an affair demanding the greatest secrecy, and that I should most probably lose the position I now hold, were it known that I confided it to any one."

"Proceed," said I.

"Or not," said Dupin.

"Well, then; I have received personal information, from a very high quarter, that a certain document of the last importance, has been purloined from the royal apartments. The individual who purloined it is known; this beyond a doubt; he was seen to take it. It is known, also, that it still remains in his possession."

"How is this known?" asked Dupin.

"It is clearly inferred," replied the Prefect, "from the nature of the document, and from the non-appearance of certain results which would at once arise from its passing *out* of the robber's possession;—that is to say, from his employing it as he must design in the end to employ it."

"Be a little more explicit," I said.

"Well, I may venture so far as to say that the paper gives its holder a certain power in a certain quarter where such power is immensely valuable." The Prefect was fond of the cant of diplomacy.

"Still I do not quite understand," said Dupin.

"No? Well; the disclosure of the document to a third person, who shall be nameless, would bring in question the honor of a personage of most exalted station; and this fact gives the holder of the document an ascendancy over the illustrious personage whose honor and peace are so jeopardized."

"But this ascendancy," I interposed, "would depend upon the robber's knowledge of the loser's knowledge of the robber. Who would dare—"

"The thief," said G—, "is the Minister D—, who dares all things, those unbecoming as well as those becoming a man. The method of the theft was not less ingenious than bold. The document in question—a letter, to be frank—had been received by the personage robbed while alone in the royal *boudoir*. During its perusal she was suddenly interrupted by the entrance of the other exalted personage from whom especially it was her wish to conceal it. After a hurried and vain endeavor to thrust it in a drawer, she was forced to place it, open as it was, upon a table. The address, however, was uppermost, and, the contents thus unexposed, the letter escaped notice. At this juncture enters the Minister D—. His lynx eye immediately perceives the paper, recognizes the handwriting of the address, observes the confusion of the personage addressed, and fathoms her secret. After some business transactions, hurried through in his ordinary manner, he produces a letter somewhat similar to the one in question, opens it, pretends to read it, and then places it in close juxtaposition to the other. Again he converses, for some fifteen minutes, upon the public affairs. At length, in taking leave, he takes also from the table the letter to which he had no claim. Its rightful owner saw, but, of course, dared not call attention to the act, in the presence of the third personage who stood at her elbow. The minister decamped; leaving his own letter—one of no importance—upon the table."

"Here, then," said Dupin to me, "you have precisely what you demand to make the ascendancy complete—the robber's knowledge of the loser's knowledge of the robber."

"Yes," replied the Prefect; "and the power thus attained has, for some months past, been wielded, for political purposes, to a very dangerous extent. The personage robbed is more thoroughly convinced, every day, of the necessity of reclaiming her letter. But this, of course, cannot be done openly. In fine, driven to despair, she has committed the matter to me."

"Than whom," said Dupin, amid a perfect whirlwind of smoke, "no more sagacious agent could, I suppose, be desired, or even imagined."

"You flatter me," replied the Prefect; "but it is possible that some such opinion may have been entertained."

"It is clear," said I, "as you observe, that the letter is still in possession of the minister; since it is this possession, and not any employment of the letter, which bestows the power. With the employment the power departs."

"True," said G—; "and upon this conviction I proceeded. My first care was to make thorough search of the minister's hotel; and here my chief embarrassment lay in the necessity of searching without his knowledge. Beyond all things, I have been warned of the danger which would result from giving him reason to suspect our design."

"But," said I, "you are quite *au fait* in these investigations. The Parisian police have done this thing often before."

"Oh yes; and for this reason I did not despair. The habits of the minister gave me, too, a great advantage. He is frequently absent from home all night. His servants are by no means numerous. They sleep at a distance from their master's apartment, and, being chiefly Neapolitans, are readily made drunk. I have keys, as you know, with which I can open any chamber or cabinet in Paris. For three months a night has not passed, during the greater part of which I have not been engaged, personally, in ransacking the D— hotel. My honor is interested, and, to mention a great secret, the reward is enormous. So I did not abandon the search until I had become fully satisfied that the thief is a more astute man than myself. I fancy that I have investigated every nook and corner of the premises in which it is possible that the paper can be concealed."

"But is it not possible," I suggested, "that although the letter may be in possession of the minister, as it unquestionably is, he may have concealed it elsewhere than upon his own premises?"

"This is barely possible," said Dupin. "The present peculiar condition of affairs at court, and especially of those intrigues in which D— is known to be involved, would render the instant availability of the document—its susceptibility of being produced at a moment's notice—a point of nearly equal importance with its possession."

"Its susceptibility of being produced?" said I.

"That is to say, of being *destroyed*," said Dupin.

"True," I observed; "the paper is clearly then upon the premises. As for its being upon the person of the minister, we may consider that as out of the question."

"Entirely," said the Prefect. "He has been twice waylaid, as if by footpads, and his person rigorously searched under my own inspection."

"You might have spared yourself this trouble," said Dupin. "D—,

I presume, is not altogether a fool, and, if not, must have anticipated these waylayings, as a matter of course."

"Not *altogether* a fool," said G—, "but then he's a poet, which I take to be only one remove from a fool."

"True," said Dupin, after a long and thoughtful whiff from his meerschaum, "although I have been guilty of certain doggerel myself."

"Suppose you detail," said I, "the particulars of your search."

"Why, the fact is, we took our time, and we searched *everywhere*. I have had long experience in these affairs. I took the entire building, room by room; devoting the nights of a whole week to each. We examined, first, the furniture of each apartment. We opened every possible drawer; and I presume you know that, to a properly trained police agent, such a thing as a *secret* drawer is impossible. Any man is a dolt who permits a 'secret' drawer to escape him in a search of this kind. The thing is *so* plain. There is a certain amount of bulk — of space — to be accounted for in every cabinet. Then we have accurate rules. The fiftieth part of a line could not escape us. After the cabinets we took the chairs. The cushions we probed with the fine long needles you have seen me employ. From the tables we removed the tops."

"Why so?"

"Sometimes the top of a table, or other similarly arranged piece of furniture, is removed by the person wishing to conceal an article; then the leg is excavated, the article deposited within the cavity, and the top replaced. The bottoms and tops of bedposts are employed in the same way."

"But could not the cavity be detected by sounding?" I asked.

"By no means, if, when the article is deposited, a sufficient wadding of cotton be placed around it. Besides, in our case, we were obliged to proceed without noise."

"But you could not have removed — you could not have taken to pieces *all* articles of furniture in which it would have been possible to make a deposit in the manner you mention. A letter may be compressed into a thin spiral roll, not differing much in shape or bulk from a large knitting-needle, and in this form it might be inserted into the rung of a chair, for example. You did not take to pieces all the chairs?"

"Certainly not; but we did better — we examined the rungs of every chair in the hotel, and, indeed, the jointings of every description of furniture, by the aid of a most powerful microscope. Had there been any traces of recent disturbance we should not have failed to detect it instantly. A single grain of gimlet dust, for example, would have been as obvious as an apple. Any disorder in the glueing—any unusual gaping in the joints—would have sufficed to insure detection."

"I presume you looked to the mirrors, between the boards and the plates, and you probed the beds and the bedclothes, as well as the curtains and carpets."

"That of course; and when we had absolutely completed every particle of the furniture in this way, then we examined the house itself. We divided its entire surface into compartments, which we numbered, so that none might be missed; then we scrutinized each individual square inch throughout the premises, including the two houses immediately adjoining, with the microscope, as before."

"The two houses adjoining!" I exclaimed; "you must have had a great deal of trouble."

"We had; but the reward offered is prodigious."

"You include the *grounds* about the houses?"

"All the grounds are paved with brick. They gave us comparatively little trouble. We examined the moss between the bricks, and found it undisturbed."

"You looked among D—'s papers, of course, and into the books of the library?"

"Certainly; we opened every package and parcel; we not only opened every book, but we turned over every leaf in each volume, not contenting ourselves with a mere shake, according to the fashion of some of our police officers. We also measured the thickness of every book-*cover*, with the most accurate admeasurement, and applied to each the most jealous scrutiny of the microscope. Had any of the bindings been recently meddled with, it would have been utterly impossible that the fact should have escaped observation. Some five or six volumes, just from the hands of the binder, we carefully probed, longitudinally, with the needles."

"You explored the floors beneath the carpets?"

"Beyond doubt. We removed every carpet, and examined the boards with the microscope."

"And the paper on the walls?"

"Yes."

"You looked into the cellars?"

"We did."

"Then," I said, "you have been making a miscalculation, and the letter is *not* upon the premises, as you suppose."

"I fear you are right there," said the Prefect. "And now, Dupin, what would you advise me to do?"

"To make a thorough re-search of the premises."

"That is absolutely needless," replied G—. "I am not more sure that I breathe than I am that the letter is not at the hotel."

"I have no better advice to give you," said Dupin. "You have, of course, an accurate description of the letter?"

"Oh yes!"— And here the Prefect, producing a memorandum book, proceeded to read aloud a minute account of the internal, and especially of the external appearance of the missing document. Soon after finishing the perusal of this description, he took his departure, more entirely depressed in spirits than I had ever known the good gentleman before.

In about a month afterwards he paid us another visit, and found us occupied very nearly as before. He took a pipe and a chair and entered into some ordinary conversation. At length I said,—

"Well, but G—, what of the purloined letter? I presume you have at last made up your mind that there is no such thing as overreaching the minister?"

"Confound him, say I—yes; I made the re-examination, however, as Dupin suggested—but it was all labor lost, as I knew it would be."

"How much was the reward offered, did you say?" asked Dupin.

"Why, a very great deal—a *very* liberal reward—I don't like to say how much, precisely; but one thing I *will* say, that I wouldn't mind giving my individual check for fifty thousand francs to any one who could obtain me that letter. The fact is, it is becoming of more and more importance every day; and the reward has been lately doubled. If it were trebled, however, I could do no more than I have done."

"Why, yes," said Dupin, drawlingly, between the whiffs of his meerschaum, "I really—think, G—, you have not exerted yourself—to the utmost in this matter. You might—do a little more, I think, eh?"

"How?—in what way?"

"Why—puff, puff—you might—puff, puff—employ counsel in the matter, eh?—puff, puff, puff. Do you remember the story they tell of Abernethy?"

"No; hang Abernethy!"

"To be sure! hang him and welcome. But, once upon a time, a certain rich miser conceived the design of spunging upon this Abernethy for a medical opinion. Getting up, for this purpose, an ordinary conversation in a private company, he insinuated his case to the physician, as that of an imaginary individual.

"'We will suppose,' said the miser, 'that his symptoms are such and such; now, doctor, what would *you* have directed him to take?'"

"'Take!' said Abernethy, 'why, take *advice*, to be sure.'"

"But," said the Prefect, a little discomposed, "I am *perfectly* willing to take advice, and to pay for it. I would *really* give fifty thousand francs to any one who would aid me in the matter."

"In that case," replied Dupin, opening a drawer, and producing a checkbook, "you may as well fill me up a check for the amount mentioned. When you have signed it, I will hand you the letter."

I was astounded. The Prefect appeared absolutely thunderstricken. For some minutes he remained speechless and motionless, looking incredulously at my friend with open mouth, and eyes that seemed starting from their sockets; then, apparently recovering himself in some measure, he seized a pen, and after several pauses and vacant stares, finally filled up and signed a check for fifty thousand francs, and handed it across the table to Dupin. The latter examined it carefully and deposited it in his pocketbook; then, unlocking an *escritoire*, took thence a letter and gave it to the Prefect. This functionary grasped it in a perfect agony of joy, opened it with a trembling hand, cast a rapid glance at its contents, and then, scrambling and struggling to the door, rushed at length unceremoniously from the room and from the house, without having uttered a syllable since Dupin had requested him to fill up the check.

When he had gone, my friend entered into some explanations.

"The Parisian police," he said, "are exceedingly able in their way. They are persevering, ingenious, cunning, and thoroughly versed in the knowledge which their duties seem chiefly to demand. Thus, when G— detailed to us his mode of searching the premises at the Hotel D—, I felt entire confidence in his having made a satisfactory investigation—so far as his labors extended."

"So far as his labors extended?" said I.

"Yes," said Dupin. "The measures adopted were not only the best of their kind, but carried out to absolute perfection. Had the letter been deposited within the range of their search, these fellows would, beyond a question, have found it."

I merely laughed—but he seemed quite serious in all that he said.

The Purloined Letter 275

"The measures, then," he continued, "were good in their kind, and well executed; their defect lay in their being inapplicable to the case, and to the man. A certain set of highly ingenious resources are, with the Prefect, a sort of Procrustean bed, to which he forcibly adapts his designs. But he perpetually errs by being too deep or too shallow for the matter in hand; and many a schoolboy is a better reasoner than he. I knew one about eight years of age whose success at guessing in the game of 'even and odd' attracted universal admiration. This game is simple, and is played with marbles. One player holds in his hand a number of these toys, and demands of another whether that number is even or odd. If the guess is right, the guesser wins one; if wrong, he loses one. The boy to whom I allude won all the marbles of the school. Of course he had some principle of guessing; and this lay in mere observation and admeasurement of the astuteness of his opponents. For example, an arrant simpleton is his opponent, and, holding up his closed hand, asks, 'Are they even or odd?' Our schoolboy replies, 'odd,' and loses; but upon the second trial he wins, for he then says to himself, 'the simpleton had them even upon the first trial, and his amount of cunning is just sufficient to make him have them odd upon the second; I will therefore guess odd';—he guesses odd, and wins. Now, with a simpleton a degree above the first, he would have reasoned thus: 'This fellow finds that in the first instance I guessed odd, and, in the second, he will propose to himself upon the first impulse, a simple variation from even to odd, as did the first simpleton; but then a second thought will suggest that this is too simple a variation, and finally he will decide upon putting it even as before. I will therefore guess even';—he guesses even, and wins. Now this mode of reasoning in the schoolboy, whom his fellows termed 'lucky,'—what, in its last analysis, is it?"

"It is merely," I said, "an identification of the reasoner's intellect with that of his opponent."

"It is," said Dupin; "and, upon inquiring of the boy by what means he effected the *thorough* identification in which his success consisted, I received answer as follows: 'When I wish to find out how wise, or how stupid, or how good, or how wicked is any one, or what are his thoughts at the moment, I fashion the expression of my face, as accurately as possible, in accordance with the expression of his, and then wait to see what thoughts or sentiments arise in my mind or heart, as if to match or correspond with the expression.' This response of the schoolboy lies at the bottom of all the spurious profundity which has been attributed to Rochefoucauld, to La Bougive, to Machiavelli, and to Campanella."

"And the identification," I said, "of the reasoner's intellect with that of his opponent, depends, if I understand you aright, upon the accuracy with which the opponent's intellect is admeasured."

"For its practical value it depends upon this," replied Dupin; "and the Prefect and his cohort fail so frequently, first, by default of this identification, and, secondly, by ill-admeasurement, or rather through non-admeasurement, of the intellect with which they are engaged. They consider only their *own* ideas of ingenuity; and, in searching for any thing hidden, advert only to the modes in which *they* would have hidden it. They are right in this much—that their own ingenuity is a faithful representative of that of *the mass*; but when the cunning of the individual felon is diverse in character from their own, the felon foils them, of course. This always happens when it is above their own, and very usually when it is below. They have no variation of principle in their investigations; at best, when urged by some unusual emergency—by some extraordinary reward—they extend or exaggerate their old modes of *practice*, without touching their principles. What, for example, in this case of D—, has been done to vary the principle of action? What is all this boring, and probing, and sounding, and scrutinizing with the microscope, and dividing the surface of the building into registered square inches— what is it all but an exaggeration *of the application* of the one principle or set of principles of search, which are based upon the one set of notions regarding human ingenuity, to which the Prefect, in the long routine of his duty, has been accustomed? Do you not see he has taken it for granted that *all* men proceed to conceal a letter,—not exactly in a gimlet-hole bored in a chair leg—but, at least, in *some* out-of-the-way hole or corner suggested by the same tenor of thought which would urge a man to secret a letter in a gimlet-hole bored in a chair leg? And do you not see also, that such *recherchés* nooks for concealment are adapted only for ordinary occasions, and would be adopted only by ordinary intellects; for, in all cases of concealment, a disposal of the article concealed—a disposal of it in this *recherché* manner,—is, in the very first instance, presumable and presumed; and thus its discovery depends, not at all upon the acumen, but altogether upon the mere care, patience, and determination of the seekers; and where the case is of importance—or, what amounts to the same thing in the policial eyes, when the reward is of magnitude, — the qualities in question have *never* been known to fail. You will now understand what I mean in suggesting that, had the purloined letter been hidden anywhere within the limits of the Prefect's examination—in other words, had the principle of its concealment been comprehended within the principles of the Prefect—its discovery would have been a matter altogether beyond question. This functionary, however, has been thoroughly mystified; and the remote source of his defeat lies in the supposition that the minister is a fool, because he has acquired renown as a poet. All fools are poets; this the Prefect *feels*; and he is merely guilty of a *non distributio medii* in thence inferring that all poets are fools."

"But is this really the poet?" I asked. "There are two brothers, I know; and both have attained reputation in letters. The minister I believe has written learnedly on the Differential Calculus. He is a mathematician, and no poet."

"You are mistaken; I know him well; he is both. As poet *and* mathematician, he would reason well; as mere mathematician, he could not have reasoned at all, and thus would have been at the mercy of the Prefect."

"You surprise me," I said, "by these opinions, which have been contradicted by the voice of the world. You do not mean to set at naught the well-digested idea of centuries. The mathematical reason has long been regarded as *the* reason *par excellence*."

"'*Il y à parier*,'" replied Dupin, quoting from Chamfort, "'*que toute idée publique, toute convention reçue, est une sottise, car elle a convenu au plus grand nombre.*' The mathematicians, I grant you, have done their best to promulgate the popular error to which you allude, and which is none the less an error for its promulgation as truth. With an art worthy a better cause, for example, they have insinuated the term 'analysis' into application to algebra. The French are the originators of this particular deception; but if a term is of any importance—if words derive any value from applicability—then 'analysis' conveys 'algebra' about as much as, in Latin, 'ambitus' implies 'ambition,' '*religio*' 'religion,' or '*homines honesti*,' a set of *honorable* men."

"You have a quarrel on hand, I see," said I, "with some of the algebraists of Paris; but proceed."

"I dispute the availability, and thus the value, of that reason which is cultivated in any special form other than the abstractly logical. I dispute, in particular, the reason educed by mathematical study. The mathematics are the science of form and quantity; mathematical reasoning is merely logic applied to observation upon form and quantity. The great error lies in supposing that even the truths of what is called *pure* algebra, are abstract or general truths. And this error is so egregious that I am confounded at the universality with which it has been received. Mathematical axioms are *not* axioms of general truth. What is true of *relation*—of form and quantity—is often grossly false in regard to morals, for example. In this latter science it is very usually *un*true that the aggregated parts are equal to the whole. In chemistry also the axiom fails. In the consideration of motive it fails; for two motives, each of a given value, have not, necessarily, a value when united, equal to the sum of their values apart. There are numerous other mathematical truths which are only truths within the limits of *relation*. But the mathematician argues, from his *finite truths*, through habit, as if they were of an absolutely general applicability—as the world indeed imagines them to be. Bryant, in his very learned 'Mythology,' mentions an analogous source of error, when he says that 'although the Pagan fables are not believed, yet we forget ourselves continually, and make inferences from them as existing realities.' With the algebraists, however, who are Pagans themselves, the 'Pagan fables' *are* believed, and the inferences are made, not so much through lapse of memory, as through an unaccountable addling of the brains. In short, I never yet encountered the mere mathematician who could be trusted out of equal roots, or one who did not clandestinely hold it as a point of his faith that $x^2 + px$ was absolutely and unconditionally equal to q. Say to one of these gentlemen, by way of experiment, if you please, that you believe occasions may occur where $x^2 + px$ is *not* altogether equal to q, and, having made him understand what you mean, get out of his reach as speedily as convenient, for, beyond doubt, he will endeavor to knock you down.

"I mean to say," continued Dupin, while I merely laughed at his last observations, "that if the minister had been no more than a mathematician, the Prefect would have been under no necessity of giving me this check. I knew him, however, as both mathematician and poet, and my measures were adapted to his capacity, with reference to the circumstances by which he was surrounded. I knew him as a courtier, too, and as a bold *intrigant*. Such a man, I considered, could not fail to be aware of the ordinary political modes of action. He could not have failed to anticipate—and events have proved that he did not fail to anticipate—the waylayings to which he was subjected. He must have foreseen, I reflected, the secret investigations of his premises. His frequent absences from home at night, which were hailed by the Prefect as certain aids to his success, I regarded only as *ruses*, to afford opportunity for thorough search to the police, and thus the sooner to impress them with the conviction to which G—, in fact, did finally arrive—the conviction that the letter was not upon the premises. I felt, also, that the whole train of thought, which I was at some pains in detailing to you just now, concerning the invariable principle of policial action in searches for articles concealed—I felt that this whole train of thought would necessarily pass through the mind of the minister. It would imperatively lead him to despise all the ordinary *nooks* of concealment. *He* could not, I reflected, be so weak as not to see that the most intricate and remote recess of his hotel would be as open as his commonest closets to the eyes, to the probes, to the gimlets, and to the microscopes of the Prefect. I saw, in fine, that he would be driven, as a matter of course, to *simplicity*, if not deliberately induced to it as a matter of choice. You will remember, perhaps, how desperately the Prefect laughed when I suggested, upon our first interview, that it was just possible this mystery troubled him so much on account of its being so *very* self-evident."

"Yes," said I, "I remember his merriment well. I really thought he would have fallen into convulsions."

"The material world," continued Dupin, "abounds with very strict analogies to the immaterial; and thus some color of truth has been given to the rhetorical dogma, that metaphor, or simile, may be made to strengthen an argument, as well as to embellish a description. The principle of the *vis inertiæ*, for example, seems to be identical in physics and metaphysics. It is not more true in the former, that a large body is with more difficulty set in motion than a smaller one, and that its subsequent *momentum* is commensurate with this difficulty, than it is, in the latter, that intellects of the vaster capacity, while more forcible, more constant, and more eventful in their movements than those of inferior grade, are yet the less readily moved, and more embarrassed and full of hesitation in the first few steps of their progress. Again: have you ever noticed which of the street signs, over the shop doors, are the most attractive of attention?"

"I have never given the matter a thought," I said.

"There is a game of puzzles," he resumed, "which is played upon a map. One party playing requires another to find a given word—the name of town, river, state or empire—any word, in short, upon the motley and perplexed surface of the chart. A novice in the game generally seeks to embarrass his opponents by giving them the most minutely-lettered names; but the adept selects such words as stretch, in large characters, from one end of the chart to the other. These, like the over-largely lettered signs and placards of the street, escape observation by dint of being excessively obvious; and here the physical oversight is precisely analogous with the moral inapprehension by which the intellect suffers to pass unnoticed those considerations which are too obtrusively and too palpably self-evident. But this is a point, it appears, somewhat above or beneath the understanding of the Prefect. He never once thought it probable, or possible, that the minister had deposited the letter immediately beneath the nose of the whole world, by way of best preventing any portion of that world from perceiving it.

"But the more I reflected upon the daring, dashing, and discriminating ingenuity of D—; upon the fact that the document must always have been *at hand*, if he intended to use it to good purpose; and upon the decisive evidence, obtained by the Prefect, that it was not hidden within the limits of that dignitary's ordinary search — the more satisfied I became that, to conceal this letter, the minister had resorted to the comprehensive and sagacious expedient of not attempting to conceal it at all.

"Full of these ideas, I prepared myself with a pair of green spectacles, and called one fine morning, quite by accident, at the ministerial hotel. I found D— at home, yawning, lounging, and dawdling, as usual, and pretending to be in the last extremity of *ennui*. He is, perhaps, the most really energetic human being now alive — but that is only when nobody sees him.

"To be even with him, I complained of my weak eyes, and lamented the necessity of the spectacles, under cover of which I cautiously and thoroughly surveyed the apartment, while seemingly intent only upon the conversation of my host.

"I paid special attention to a large writing table near which he sat, and upon which lay confusedly, some miscellaneous letters and other papers, with one or two musical instruments and a few books. Here, however, after a long and very deliberate scrutiny, I saw nothing to excite particular suspicion.

"At length my eyes, in going the circuit of the room, fell upon a trumpery filigree cardrack of pasteboard, that hung dangling by a dirty blue ribbon, from a little brass knob just beneath the middle of the mantelpiece. In this rack, which had three or four compartments, were five or six visiting cards and a solitary letter. This last was much soiled and crumpled. It was torn nearly in two, across the middle —

as if a design, in the first instance, to tear it entirely up as worthless, had been altered, or stayed, in the second. It had a large black seal, bearing the D— cipher *very* conspicuously, and was addressed, in a diminutive female hand, to D—, the minister, himself. It was thrust carelessly, and even, as it seemed, contemptuously, into one of the upper divisions of the rack.

"No sooner had I glanced at this letter, than I concluded it to be that of which I was in search. To be sure, it was, to all appearance, radically different from the one of which the Prefect had read us so minute a description. Here the seal was large and black, with the D— cipher; there it was small and red, with the ducal arms of the S— family. Here, the address, to the minister, was diminutive and feminine; there the superscription, to a certain royal personage, was markedly bold and decided; the size alone formed a point of correspondence. But, then, the *radicalness* of these differences, which was excessive; the dirt; the soiled and torn condition of the paper, so inconsistent with the *true* methodical habits of D—, and so suggestive of a design to delude the beholder into an idea of the worthlessness of the document; these things, together with the hyperobtrusive situation of this document, full in the view of every visitor, and thus exactly in accordance with the conclusions to which I had previously arrived; these things, I say, were strongly corroborative of suspicion, in one who came with the intention to suspect.

"I protracted my visit as long as possible, and, while I maintained a most animated discussion with the minister, on a topic which I knew well had never failed to interest and excite him, I kept my attention really riveted upon the letter. In this examination, I committed to memory its external appearance and arrangement in the rack; and also fell, at length, upon a discovery which set at rest whatever trivial doubt I might have entertained. In scrutinizing the edges of the paper, I observed them to be more *chafed* than seemed necessary. They presented the *broken* appearance, which is manifested when a stiff paper, having been once folded and pressed with a folder, is refolded in a reversed direction, in the same creases or edges which had formed the original fold. This discovery was sufficient. It was clear to me that the letter had been turned, as a glove, inside out, re-directed, and resealed. I bade the minister good morning, and took my departure at once, leaving a gold snuffbox upon the table.

"The next morning I called for the snuffbox, when we resumed, quite eagerly, the conversation of the preceding day. While thus engaged, however, a loud report, as if of a pistol, was heard immediately beneath the windows of the hotel, and was succeeded by a series of fearful screams, and the shoutings of a mob. D— rushed to a casement, threw it open, and looked out. In the mean time, I stepped to the cardrack, took the letter, put it in my pocket, and replaced it by a *facsimile* (so far as regards externals), which I had carefully prepared at my lodgings; imitating the D— cipher, very readily, by means of a seal formed of bread.

"The disturbance in the street had been occasioned by the frantic behavior of a man with a musket. He had fired it among a crowd of women and children. It proved, however, to have been without ball, and the fellow was suffered to go his way as a lunatic or a drunkard. When he had gone, D— came from the window, whither I had followed him immediately upon securing the object in view. Soon afterwards I bade him farewell. The pretended lunatic was a man in my own pay."

"But what purpose had you," I asked, "in replacing the letter by a *facsimile*? Would it not have been better, at the first visit, to have seized it openly, and departed?"

"D—," replied Dupin, "is a desperate man, and a man of nerve. His hotel, too, is not without attendants devoted to his interests. Had I made the wild attempt you suggest, I might never have left the ministerial presence alive. The good people of Paris might have heard of me no more. But I had an object apart from these considerations. You know my political prepossessions. In this matter, I act as a partisan of the lady concerned. For eighteen months the minister has had her in his power. She has now him in hers; since, being unaware that the letter is not in his possession, he will proceed with his exactions as if it was. Thus will he inevitably commit himself, at once, to his political destruction. His downfall, too, will not be more precipitate than awkward. It is all very well to talk about the *facilis descensus Averni*; but in all kinds of climbing, as Catalani said of singing, it is far more easy to get up than to come down. In the present instance I have no sympathy—at least no pity—for him who descends. He is that *monstrum horrendum*, an unprincipled man of genius. I confess, however, that I should like very well to know the precise character of his thoughts, when, being defied by her whom the Prefect terms 'a certain personage,' he is reduced to opening the letter which I left for him in the cardrack."

"How? did you put any thing particular in it?"

"Why—it did not seem altogether right to leave the interior blank—

that would have been insulting. D—, at Vienna once, did me an evil turn, which I told him, quite good-humoredly, that I should remember, So, as I knew he would feel some curiosity in regard to the identity of the person who had outwitted him, I thought it a pity not to give him a clue. He is well acquainted with my MS., and I just copied into the middle of the blank sheet the words—

>—Un dessein si funeste,
>S'il n'est digne d'Atrée, est digne de Thyeste.

They are to be found in Crébillon's 'Atrée.'"

Gogol

1809	March 31. Nikolai Gogol born in the Ukrainian province of Poltava, Russia.
1828−31	Moves to St. Petersburg. Publishes *Hans Kuchelgarten* under the pseudonym V. Alov in 1829. Burns almost all copies of the poem due to angry reviews and leaves Russia—only to return later that year. In 1831 a book of stories, *Evenings on a Farm Near Dikanka*, appears to favorable reviews. Meets Pushkin who encourages him in his literary career.
1833−35	Devotes himself to study and, in 1834, is appointed professor of world history at the University of St. Petersburg. His research of Ukrainian history informs such stories as *Taras Bulbas*. In 1835 *Mirogorod*, two volumes of stories, and *Arabesques*, two volumes of prose and tales, appear. Gogol resigns from his academic position.
1836−47	The *Inspector-General* is first performed and opens to negative reviews. Gogol again leaves Russia and settles in Rome for 12 years. In 1836 "The Nose" is published in Pushkin's magazine, *Contemporary*. "The Overcoat" appears in 1841. In 1842 the first part of *Dead Souls* is published, but in 1845, Gogol burns the manuscript for part two. The reactionary *Selected Passages from Correspondence with Friends* is published in 1847 and alienates many readers.
1848−52	Makes a pilgrimage to Palestine and returns to Russia. Begins revising previous works to conform to his current moral and religious leanings. Works on another draft of *Dead Souls*, part two, and again burns a major portion of it. Gogol dies on March 4, 1852.

Nikolai Gogol

Nikolai Vassilievich Gogol was born at Sorotchinetz, in Little Russia, in March, 1809. The year in which he appeared on the planet proved to be the literary *annus mirabilis* of the century; for in that same twelvemonth were born Charles Darwin, Alfred Tennyson, Abraham Lincoln, Poe, Gladstone, and Oliver Wendell Holmes. His father was a lover of literature, who wrote dramatic pieces for his own amusement, and who spent his time on the old family estates, not in managing the farms, but in wandering about the fields, and beholding the fowls of the air. The boy inherited much from his father; but, unlike Turgenev, he had the best of all private tutors and a good mother.

At the age of twelve, Nikolai was sent away to the high school at Nezhin, a town near Kiev. There he remained from 1821 to 1828. He was an unpromising student, having no enthusiasm for his lessons, and showing no distinction either in scholarship or deportment. Fortunately, however, the school had a little theater of its own, and Gogol, who hated mathematics, and cared little for the study of modern language, here found an outlet for all his mental energy. He soon became the acknowledged leader of the school in matters dramatic, and unconsciously prepared himself for his future career. Like Schiller, he wrote a tragedy, and called it *The Robbers*.

In December, 1828, Gogol took up his residence in St. Petersburg, bringing with him some manuscripts that he had written while at school. He had temerity to publish one, which was so brutally ridiculed by the critics, that the young genius, in despair, burned all the unsold copies — as unwitting prophecy of a later and more lamentable conflagration. Then he vainly tried various means of subsistence. Suddenly he decided to seek his fortune in America, but he was both homesick and seasick before the ship emerged from the Baltic, and from Lübeck he fled incontinently back to Petersburg. Then he tried to become an actor, but lacked the necessary strength of voice. For a short time he held a minor official position, and a little later was professor of history, an occupation he did not enjoy, saying after his resignation, "Now I am a free Cossack again." Meanwhile his pen was steadily busy, and his sketches of farm life in the Ukraine attracted considerable attention among literary circles in the capital.

Gogol suffered from nostalgia all the time he lived at St. Petersburg; he did not care for that form of society, and the people, he said, did not seem like real Russians. He was thoroughly homesick for his beloved Ukraine; and it is significant that his short stories of life in Little Russia, truthfully depicting the country customs, were written far off in a strange and uncongenial environment.

In 1831 he had the good fortune to meet the poet Pushkin, and a few months later in the same year he was presented to Madame Smirnova; these friends gave him the *entrée* to the literary salons, and the young author, lonesome as he was, found the intellectual stimulation he needed. It was Pushkin who suggested to him the subjects for two of his most famous works, *The Inspector-General* and *Dead Souls*. Another friend, Jukovski, exercised a powerful influence, and gave invaluable aid at several crises of his career. Jukovski had translated the *Iliad* and the *Odyssey*; his enthusiasm for Hellenic poetry was contagious; and under this inspiration Gogol proceeded to write the most Homeric romance in Russian literature, *Taras Bulba*. This story gave the first indubitable proof of its author's genius, and today in the world's fiction it holds an unassailable place in the front rank. The book is so short that it can be read through in less than two hours; but it gives the same impression of vastness and immensity as the huge volumes of Sienkiewicz.

From 1836 until his death in 1852, Gogol lived mainly abroad, and spent much time in travel. His favorite place of residence was Rome, to which city he repeatedly returned with increasing affection. In 1848 he made a pilgrimage to the Holy Land, for Gogol never departed from the pious Christian faith taught him by his mother; in fact, toward the end of his life, he became an ascetic and a mystic. The last years were shadowed by illness and — a common thing among Russian writers — by intense nervous depression. He died at Moscow, 21 February 1852. His last words were the old saying, "And I shall laugh with a bitter laugh." These words were placed on his tomb.

His first book, *Evenings on a Farm near the Dikanka* (*Veillées de l'Ukraine*), appeared early in the thirties, and, with all its crudity and excrescences, was a literary sunrise. It attracted immediate and widespread attention, and the wits of Petersburg knew that Russia had an original novelist. The work is a collection of short stories or sketches, introduced with a rollicking humorous preface, in which the author announces himself as Rudii Panko, raiser of bees. Into this book the exile in the city of the North poured out all his love for the country and the village customs of his own Little Russia. He gives us great pictures of Nature, and little pictures of social life. He describes with the utmost detail a country fair at the place of his birth, Sorotchinetz. His descriptions of the simple folk, the beasts, and the bargainings seem as true as those in *Madame Bovary* — the difference is in the attitude of the author toward his work. Gogol has nothing of the aloofness, nothing of the scorn of Flaubert; he himself loves the revelry and the superstitions he pictures, loves above all the people. Superstition plays a prominent role in these sketches; the unseen world of ghosts and apparitions has an enormous influence on the daily life of the peasants. The love of fun is everywhere in evidence; these people cannot live without practical jokes, violent dances, and horseplay. Shadowy forms of amorous couples move silent in the warm summer night, and the stillness is broken by silver laughter. Far away, in his room at St. Petersburg, shut in by the long winter darkness, the homesick man dreamed of the vast landscape he loved, in the warm embrace of the sky at noon, or asleep in the pale moonlight. The first sentence of the book is a cry of longing. "What ecstasy; what splendor has a summer day in Little Russia!" Pushkin used to say that the Northern summer was a caricature of the Southern winter.

Gogol followed up the *Evenings on a Farm near the Dikanka* with two other volumes of stories and sketches, of which the immortal *Taras Bulba* was included in one. Those other tales show an astonishing advance in power of conception and mastery of style. I do not share the general enthusiasm for the narrative of the comically grotesque quarrel between the two Ivans; but the three stories, *Old-Fashioned Farmers*, *The Portrait*, and *The Overcoat*, show to a high degree that mingling of Fantasy with Reality that is so characteristic of this author. The obsolete old pair of lovers in *Old-Fashioned Farmers* is one of the most charming and winsome things that Gogol wrote at this period: It came straight from the depths of his immeasurable tenderness. It appealed to that Pity which, as every one has noticed, is a fundamental attribute of the national Russian character. In *The Portrait*, which is partly written in the minute manner of Balzac, and partly with the imaginative fantastic horror of Poe and Hoffmann, we have the two sides of Gogol's nature clearly reflected. Into this strange story he has also indicated two of the great guiding principles of his life; his intense democratic sympathies, and his devotion to the highest ideals in Art. When the young painter forsakes poverty and sincerity for wealth and popularity, he steadily degenerates as an artist and eventually loses his soul. The ending of the story, with the disappearance of the portrait, is remarkably clever. The brief tale called *The Overcoat* has great significance in the history of Russian fiction, for all Russian novelists have been more or less influenced by it. Its realism is so obviously and emphatically realistic that it becomes exaggeration, but this does not lessen its tremendous power; then suddenly at the very end, it leaves the ground, even the air, and soars away into the ether of Romance.

Gogol's realism differs in two important aspects from the realism of the French school, whether represented by Balzac, Flaubert, Guy de Maupassant, or Zola. He had all the French love of veracity, and could have honestly said with the author of *Une Vie* that he painted *l'humble vérité*. But there are two ground qualities in his realistic method absent in the four Frenchmen: humor and moral force. Gogol could not repress the fun that is so essential an element in human life, any more than he could stop the beating of his heart; he saw men and women with the eyes of a natural born humorist, to whom the utter absurdity of humanity and human relations was enormously salient. And he could not help preaching, because he had boundless sympathy with the weakness and suffering of his fellow creatures, and because he believed with all the tremendous force of his character in the Christian religion. His main endeavor was to sharpen the sight of his readers, whether they looked without or within; for not even the greatest physician can remedy an evil, unless he knows what the evil is.

—*from* Essays on Russian Novelists *by William Lyon Phelps*

Ivan Fyodorovich Shponka and His Aunt

There is a story about this story; we were told it by Stepan Ivanovich Kurochka, who came over from Gadyach. You must know that my memory is incredibly poor: you may tell me a thing or not tell it, it is all the same. It is like pouring water into a sieve. Being aware of this failing, I purposely begged him to write the story down in a notebook. Well, God give him good health, he was always kind to me; he set to work and wrote it down. I put it in the little table; I expect you know it; it stands in the corner as you come in by the door. But there, I forgot that you had never been in my house. My old woman, with whom I have lived thirty years, has never learnt to read—no use hiding it. Well, I noticed that she baked the pies on paper of some sort. She bakes pies beautifully, dear readers; you will never taste better pies anywhere. I happened to look at the underside of a pie—and what do I see? Written words! I went to the table as though my heart had told me to do so; only half the book was there! All the other pages she had carried off for the pies! What could I do? It would be silly to fight at our age!

Last year I happened to be passing through Gadyach. Before I reached the town I purposely tied a knot in my handkerchief that I might not forget to ask Stepan Ivanovich about it. That was not all; I vowed to myself that as soon as ever I sneezed in the town I would be sure to think of it. It was all no use. I drove through the town and sneezed and blew my nose, too, but still I forgot it; and I only thought of it about six versts after I had passed through the towngate. There was no help for it, I had to print it without the end. However, if anyone particularly wants to know what happened later on in the story, he need only go to Gadyach and ask Stepan Ivanovich. He will be glad to tell the story, I daresay, all over again from the beginning. He lives not far from the brick church. There is a little lane close by, and as soon as you turn into the lane it is the second or third gate. Or better still, his yard is where you will see a big pole with a quail on it and where a stout peasant woman in a green skirt (it may be as well to mention that he is a bachelor) will come out to meet you. However, you may meet him in the market, where he is to be seen every morning before nine o'clock, choosing fish and vegetables for his table and talking to Father Antip or the Jewish contractor. You will know him at once, for no one else has trousers of colored linen or a yellow cotton coat. And another thing you may know him by— he always swings his arms as he walks. Denis Petrovich, the late assessor, used to say when he saw him in the distance, "Look, here comes our windmill!"

I

Ivan Fyodorovich Shponka

It is four years since Ivan Fyodorovich retired from the army and came to live on his Vitrebenki farmstead. When he was still a boy and was accordingly called Vanyusha, he went to the Gadyach district school, and I must say he was a very well-behaved and industrious boy. Nikifor Timofeyevich Deyeprichastiye, the teacher of Russian grammar, used to say that if all the boys had been as anxious to do their best as Shponka, he would not have brought into the classroom the maple-wood ruler with which, as he owned himself, he was tired of hitting the lazy and mischievous boys' hands. His exercise book was always neat, with a ruled margin, and not the tiniest blot anywhere. He always sat quietly, with his arms folded and his eyes fixed on the teacher, and he never used to stick scraps of paper on the back of the boy sitting in front of him, never cut the form, and never played at shoving the other boys off the form before the master came in. If anyone wanted a penknife to sharpen his pen, he immediately applied to Ivan Fyodorovich, knowing that he always had a penknife, and Ivan Fyodorovich—at that time simply Vanyusha—would take it out of a little leather case attached to a buttonhole of his grey coat, and would only request that the sharp edge should not be used for scraping the pen, pointing out that there was a blunt side for the purpose. Such good conduct soon attracted the attention of the Latin master himself, whose cough in the passage was enough to reduce the class to terror, even before his frieze coat and pockmarked countenance had appeared in the doorway. This terrible master, who always had two bundles of birch lying on his desk and half of whose pupils were always on their knees, made Ivan Fyodorovich monitor, although there were many boys in the class of much greater ability.

At this point I cannot omit an incident which had an influence on the whole of his future life. One of the boys entrusted to his charge tried to induce his monitor to write *scit* on his report, though he had not learnt his lesson, by bringing into class a pancake soaked in butter and wrapped in paper. Though Ivan Fyodorovich was usually conscientious, on this occasion he was hungry and could not resist the temptation; he took the pancake, and holding a book up before him, began eating it, and he was so absorbed in this occupation that he did not observe that a deathly silence had fallen upon the classroom. He only came to with horror when a terrible hand reaching from a frieze overcoat seized him by the ear and dragged him into the middle of the room. "Hand over that pancake! Hand it over, I tell you, you rascal!" said the terrible master; he seized the buttery pancake in his fingers and flung it out of the window, sternly forbidding the boys running about in the yard to pick it up. Then he proceeded to whack Ivan Fyodorovich very painfully on the hands; and quite rightly: the hands were responsible for taking the pancake and no other part of the body. Anyway, the timidity which had always been characteristic of him was more marked from then on. Possibly the same incident was the reason why he never felt a desire to enter the civil service, having learnt by experience that one is not always successful in covering up one's misdeeds.

He was very nearly fifteen when he moved up into the second form, where instead of the four rules of arithmetic and the abridged catechism, he went on to the longer one, the book on the duties of man, and fractions. But seeing, as they say, that the further you went into the forest the thicker the wood became, and receiving the news that his father had departed this life, he stayed only two years longer at school, and with his mother's consent joined an infantry regiment.

The regiment in question was not at all of the class to which many infantry regiments belong, and although it was for the most part stationed in country places, it was in no way inferior to many cavalry regiments. Most of the officers drank neat spirit and were quite as good at dragging about Jews by their curls as the hussars; some of them even danced the mazurka, and the colonel of the regiment never missed an opportunity of mentioning the fact when he was talking to anyone in society. "Among my officers," he used to say, patting himself on the belly after every word, "a number dance the mazurka, quite a number of them, a very great number of them." To show our readers the degree of culture of the regiment, we must add that two of the officers were passionately fond of playing cards and used to gamble away their uniforms, caps, overcoats, swordknots, and even their underclothes, which is more than you could find even in a cavalry regiment.

Contact with such comrades did not, however, diminish Ivan Fyodorovich's timidity; and as he did not drink neat spirit, preferring to it a glassful of ordinary vodka before dinner and supper, did not dance the mazurka or play cards, he was naturally bound to be always left alone. And so it came to pass that while the others were driving about on hired horses and visiting the less important landowners, he sat at home and spent his time in pursuits peculiar to a mild and gentle soul: he either polished his buttons, or read a fortuneteller's book, or set mousetraps in the corners of his room, or he took off his uniform and lay on his bed.

On the other hand, no one in the regiment was more punctual in his duties than Ivan Fyodorovich, and he drilled his platoon in such a way that the commander of the company always held him up as a model to the others. Consequently in a short time — eleven years after becoming an ensign — he was promoted to be a second lieutenant.

During that time he had received the news that his mother was dead, and his aunt, his mother's sister, whom he only knew from her bringing him in his childhood — and even sending him when he was at Gadyach — dried pears and extremely nice honey cakes which she made herself (she was no bad terms with his mother and so Ivan Fyodorovich had not seen her in later years), this aunt, in the goodness of her heart, undertook to look after his little estate and in due time informed him of the fact by letter.

Ivan Fyodorovich, having the fullest confidence in his aunt's good sense, continued to perform his duties as before. Some men in his position would have grown conceited at such promotion, but pride was a feeling of which he knew nothing, and as a lieutenant he was the same Ivan Fyodorovich as he had been when an ensign. He spent another four years in the regiment after the event of so much consequence to him, and was about to leave Mogilyov Province for Great Russia with his regiment when he received a letter as follows:

"My dear Nephew, Ivan Fyodorovich,
I am sending you some linen: five pairs of thread socks and four shirts of fine linen; and what is more, I want to talk to you of something serious; since you have already a rank of some importance, as I suppose you are aware, and have reached a time of life when it is fitting to take up the management of your land, there is no reason for you to remain any longer in military service. I am getting old and can no longer see to everything on your farm; and in fact there is a great deal that I want to talk to you about in person.

"Come, Vanyusha! Looking forward to the real pleasure of seeing you, I remain your very affectionate aunt,
"Vasilisa Tsupchevska."

"P.S.—There are wonderful turnips in our kitchen garden, they look very strange, more like potatoes than turnips."

A week after receiving this letter Ivan Fyodorovich wrote an answer as follows:

"Honored Madam, Auntie Vasilisa Kashporovna,
Thank you very much for sending the linen. My socks especially were very old; my orderly had darned them four times and that had made them very tight. As to your views in regard to my service in the army, I completely agree with you, and the other day I sent in my papers. As soon as I get my discharge I will engage a chaise. As to your commission in regard to the seed wheat of the Siberian variety, I cannot carry it out; there is none in all Mogilyov Province. As regards pigs here, they are mostly fed on brewers' mash together with a little beer when it has grown flat.

"With the greatest respect, honored Madam and Auntie, I remain your nephew,
"Ivan Shponka."

At last Ivan Fyodorovich received his discharge with the rank of lieutenant, hired for forty rubles a Jew to drive from Mogilyov to Gadyach, and set off in the chaise just at the time when the trees were clothed with young and still scanty leaves, the whole earth was bright with fresh green, and there was the fragrance of spring in the fields.

II
The Journey

Nothing of great interest occurred on the journey. They were travelling a little over a fortnight. Ivan Fyodorovich might have arrived a little sooner than that, but the devout Jew kept the Sabbath on the Saturdays and, putting his horsecloth over his head, prayed the whole day. Ivan Fyodorovich, however, as I have already had occasion to mention, was a man who did not give way to being bored. During these intervals he undid his trunk, took out his underclothes, inspected them thoroughly to see whether they were properly washed and folded; carefully removed fluff from his new uniform, which had been made without epaulettes, and repacked it all in the best possible way. He was not fond of reading; and if he did sometimes look into a fortuneteller's book, it was because he liked to meet again what he had already read several times. In the same way one who lives in the town goes every day to the club, not for the sake of hearing anything new there, but in order to meet there friends with whom it has been one's habit to chat at the club from time immemorial. In the same way a government clerk will read a directory of addresses with immense satisfaction several times a day with no ulterior object but merely because he is entertained by the printed list of names. "Ah! Ivan Gavrilovich So-and-so!" he murmurs to himself. "And here am I! H'm!" And next time he reads it over again with exactly the same exclamations.

After a fortnight's journey Ivan Fyodorovich reached a little village about a hundred versts from Gadyach. This was on a Friday. The sun had long set when with the chaise and the Jew he reached an inn.

The inn differed in no respect from other little village inns. As a rule the traveller is zealously regaled in them with hay and oats, as though he were a post-horse. But should he want to lunch as decent people do lunch, he would keep his appetite intact for some future opportunity. Ivan Fyodorovich, knowing all this, had provided himself beforehand with two bundles of bread rings and a sausage, and asking for a glass of vodka, of which there is never a shortage in any inn, he began his supper, sitting down on a bench before an oak table which was fixed immovably in the clay floor.

Meanwhile he heard the rattle of a chaise. The gates creaked, but it was a long while before the chaise drove into the yard. A loud voice was engaged in scolding the old woman who kept the inn. "I will drive in," Ivan Fyodorovich heard someone say, "but if I am bitten by a single bug in your inn, I will beat you, on my soul I will, you old witch! And I will give you nothing for your hay!"

A minute later the door opened and there walked, or rather squeezed himself in a stout man in a green frockcoat. His head rested immovably on his short neck, which seemed even thicker because of the double chin. To judge from his appearance, he belonged to that class of men who have never bothered about trifles and whose whole life has passed easily.

"I wish you good day, sir!" he pronounced on seeing Ivan Fyodorovich.

Ivan Fyodorovich bowed in silence.

"May I ask to whom I have the honor of speaking?" the stout newcomer continued.

At this Ivan Fyodorovich involuntarily got up and stood at attention, as he usually did when the colonel asked him a question.

"Retired Lieutenant Ivan Fyodorovich Shponka," he answered.

"And may I ask what place you are bound for?"

"My own farm, Vitrebenki."

"Vitrebenki!" cried the stern interrogator. "Allow me, sir, allow me!" he said, going towards him and waving his arms as though someone were hindering him, or as though he were making his way through a crowd; coming up to Ivan Fyodorovich, he folded him in an embrace and kissed him first on the right cheek and then on the left and then on the right again. Ivan Fyodorovich greatly enjoyed the osculation, for the stranger's large cheeks felt like soft cushions to his lips.

"Allow me to introduce myself, sir!" the stout man continued: "I am a landowner of the same district of Gadyach and your neighbor. I live not more than five versts from your Vitrebenki, in the village of Khorstishche; and my name is Grigory Grigoryevich Storchenko. You really must, sir, you really must pay me a visit at Khortishche. I won't speak to you if you don't. I am in haste now on business. Why, what's this?" he said in a mild voice to his postilion, a boy in a Cossack jacket with patched elbows and a bewildered expression, who came in and put bags and boxes on the table. "What's this, what's the meaning of it?" And by degrees Grigory Grigoryevich's voice grew more and more threatening. "Did I tell you to put them here, my good lad? Did I tell you to put them here, you rascal? Didn't I tell you to heat the chicken up first, you scoundrel? Get out!" he shouted, stamping. "Wait, you monkey face! Where's the basket with the bottles? Ivan Fyodorovich!" he said, pouring out a glass of liqueur, "I humbly beg you to take some cordial!"

"Oh, really, I cannot—I have already had occasion—" Ivan Fyodorovich began hesitatingly.

"I won't hear a word, sir!" The landowner raised his voice. "I won't hear a word! I won't budge till you take it!"

Ivan Fyodorovich, seeing that it was impossible to refuse, emptied the glass not without pleasure.

"This is a fowl, sir," said the fat Grigory Grigoryevich, carving it in a wooden box. "I must tell you that my cook Yavdokha is fond of a drop at times and so she often dries up things. Hey, lad!" He turned to the boy in the Cossack jacket, who was bringing in a feather bed and pillows. "Make my bed on the floor in the middle of the room! Mind you put plenty of hay under the pillow! And pull a bit of hemp from the woman's distaff to stop up my ears for the night. I must tell you, sir, that I have the habit of stopping up my ears at night ever since the damnable occasion when a cockroach crawled into my left ear in a Russian inn. The confounded longbeards, as I found out afterwards, even eat their soup with cockroaches in it. Impossible to describe what happened to me; there was such a tickling, such a tickling in my ear—it almost drove me crazy! I was cured by a simple old woman in our parts, and can you imagine how she did it? She charmed it out simply by whispering. What do you think, sir, about doctors? I think they just hoax us and make fools of us. Sometimes an old woman knows a dozen times as much as all those doctors."

"Indeed, what you say is perfectly true, sir. There certainly are cases—" Here Ivan Fyodorovich paused as though he could not find the right word.

It may not be amiss to mention here that he was at no time lavish of words. This may have been due to timidity, or to a desire to express himself elegantly.

"Shake up the hay properly, shake it up properly!" said Grigory Grigoryevich to his servant. "The hay is so bad about here that you may come upon a twig in it any minute. Allow me, sir, to wish you a good night! We shall not see each other tomorrow. I am setting off before dawn. Your Jew will keep the Sabbath because tomorrow is Saturday, so you need not get up early. Don't forget my invitation; I won't speak to you if you don't come to see me at Khortishche."

At this point Grigory Grigoryevich's servant pulled off his coat and high boots and pulled his dressing gown on him instead, and Grigory Grigoryevich stretched on his bed, and it looked as though one huge feather bed were lying on another.

"Hey, lad! Where are you, rascal? Come here and arrange my quilt. Hey, lad, prop up my head with hay! Have you watered the horses yet? Some more hay! Here, under this side! And arrange the quilt properly, you rascal! That's right, more! Oof!"

Then Grigory Grigoryevich heaved two sighs and filled the whole room with a terrible whistling through his nose, snoring so loudly at times that the old woman, who was snoozing on the stove-couch, suddenly woke up and stared about her wide-eyed, but seeing nothing, subsided and went to sleep again.

When Ivan Fyodorovich woke up next morning, the stout landowner was gone. That was the only noteworthy incident that occurred on the journey. Two days later he drew near his little farm.

He felt his heart begin to throb when the windmill waving its sails peeped out and, as the Jew drove his hacks uphill, the row of willows came in sight below. The pond shone brightly through them and a breath of freshness rose from it. Here he used to bathe in old days; in this pond he used to wade with the peasant lads up to his neck after crayfish. The chaise mounted the dam and Ivan Fyodorovich saw the little old-fashioned house thatched with reeds, and the apple and cherry trees which he used to climb on the sly. He had no sooner driven into the yard than dogs of all kinds—brown, black, grey, spotted—ran up from every side. Some flew under the horse's hoofs, barking, others ran behind the cart, discovering that the axle was smeared with bacon fat; one, standing near the kitchen and keeping his foot on a bone, uttered a volley of shrill barks; and another gave tongue in the distance, running to and fro, wagging his tail, and seeming to say: "Look, good Christians, what a fine young fellow I am!" Boys in grubby shirts ran out to stare. A sow who was strolling in the yard with sixteen little pigs lifted her snout with an inquisitive air and grunted louder than usual. In the yard a number of hempen sheets were lying on the ground, covered with wheat, millet, and barley drying in the sun. A good many different kinds of herbs, such as wild chicory and swine-herb, were drying on the roof.

Ivan Fyodorovich was so occupied in scrutinizing all this that he was roused only when a spotted dog bit the Jew on the calf of his leg as he was getting down from the box. The servants, that is, the cook and another woman and two girls in woollen petticoats, ran out and after the first exclamations: "Why, it's our young master!" informed him that his aunt was sowing sweet corn together with the girl Palashka and Omelko the coachman, who also often performed the duties of a gardener and watchman. But his aunt, who had seen the chaise in the distance, was already on the spot. And Ivan Fyodorovich was astonished when she almost lifted him from the ground in her arms, hardly able to believe that this could be the aunt who had written to him of her old age and infirmities.

III
Auntie

Auntie Vasilisa Kashporovna was at this time about fifty. She had never been married, and usually declared that she valued her maiden state above everything. However, to the best of my memory, no one had ever courted her. This was due to the fact that all men felt a certain timidity in her presence, and never had the spirit to propose to her. "A girl of great character, is Vasilisa Kashporovna!" all the young men used to say, and they were quite right, too, for there was no one Vasilisa Kashporovna could not get the whip hand of. With her own manly hand, tugging every day at his scalp-lock, she could, unaided, turn the drunken miller, a worthless fellow, into a perfect treasure. She was of almost gigantic stature and her corpulence and strength were fully in proportion. It seemed as though nature had made an unpardonable mistake in condemning her to wear a dark brown gown with little flounces on weekdays and a red cashmere shawl on Easter Sunday and on her name-day, though a dragoon's moustaches and top-boots would have suited her better than anything. On the other hand, her pursuits completely corresponded to her appearance: she rowed the boat herself and was more skilful with the oars than any fisherman; shot game; supervised the mowers all the while they were at work; knew the exact number of the melons in the kitchen garden; took a toll of five kopeks from every wagon that crossed her dam; climbed the trees and shook down the pears; beat lazy vassals with her terrible hand and with the same formidable hand bestowed a glass of vodka on the deserving. Almost at the same moment she was scolding, dyeing yarn, racing to the kitchen, brewing kvass, making jam with honey; she was busy all day long and managed to get everything done on time. The result of all this was that Ivan Fyodorovich's little estate, which had consisted of eighteen souls at the last census, was flourishing in the fullest sense of the word. Moreover, she had a very warm affection for her nephew and carefully accumulated kopeks for him.

From the time of his arrival at his home Ivan Fyodorovich's life was completely transformed and took an entirely different turn. It seemed as though nature had designed him expressly for looking after an estate of eighteen souls. Auntie herself observed that he would make an excellent farmer, though she did not yet permit him to meddle in every branch of the management. "He's but a child yet," she used to say, though Ivan Fyodorovich was, as a matter of fact, not far off forty, "How should he know it all!"

However, he was always in the fields with the reapers and mowers, and this was a source of unutterable pleasure to his gentle heart. The sweep of a dozen or more gleaming scythes in unison; the sound of the grass falling in even swathes; the occasional carolling songs of the reapers, now joyous as the welcoming of a guest, now mournful as parting; the calm pure evening—and what an evening! How free and fresh the air was! How everything revived: the steppe flushed red, then turned dark blue and glowed with colors; quails, bustards, gulls, grasshoppers, thousands of insects whistling, buzzing, chirring, calling, and all of it suddenly blending into a harmonious chorus; nothing silent for an instant. Meanwhile the sun set and disappeared. Oh, how fresh and delightful it was! Here and there in the fields fires were built and cauldrons set over them, and round the fires the moustached mowers sat down; the steam from the dumplings floated upwards; the twilight turned greyer . . . It is hard to say what passed in Ivan Fyodorovich at such times. When he joined the mowers, he forgot to try their dumplings, though he liked them immensely, and stood motionless, watching a gull drop out of sight in the sky, or counting the sheaves of corn dotting the field.

Before long Ivan Fyodorovich was spoken of as a great farmer. Auntie was never tired of rejoicing over her nephew and never missed an opportunity of boasting of him. One day—it was just after the end of the harvest, that is, late in July—Vasilisa Kashporovna took Ivan Fyodorovich by the arm with a mysterious air, and said she wanted to speak to him of a matter which had long been on her mind.

"You are aware, dear Ivan Fyodorovich," she began "that there are eighteen souls on your farm, though, indeed, that is by the census register, and in reality they may reckon up to more; there may be twenty-four. But that is not the point. You know the copse that lies beyond our estate, and no doubt you know the broad meadow beyond it; there are very nearly twenty dessiatines in it; and the grass is so good that it is worth a hundred rubles every year, especially if, as they say, a cavalry regiment is to be stationed at Gadyach."

"To be sure, Auntie, I know: the grass is very good."

"You needn't tell me the grass is very good, I know it; but do you know that all that land is by rights yours? Why do you stare like that? Listen, Ivan Fyodorovich! You remember Stepan Kuzmich? But how can I ask? You were so little then that you couldn't even pronounce his name. Yes, indeed! When I came on the very eve of Christmas Fast and took you in my arms, you almost ruined my dress; luckily I was just in time to hand you to your nurse, Matryona; you were such a horrid little thing then! But that is not the point. All the land beyond our farm, and the village of Khortishche itself belonged to Stepan Kuzmich. I must tell you that before you were in this world he used to visit your mamma—though, indeed, only when your father was not at home. Not that I say it in blame of her—God rest her soul!—though your poor mother was always unfair to me. But that is not the point. Be that as it may, Stepan Kuzmich made a deed of gift to you of the estate I am speaking about. But your poor mamma, between you and me, was a very strange character. The devil himself—God forgive me for the nasty word!—would have been unable to make her out. What she did with that deed of gift God only knows. I think it must be in the hands of that old bachelor, Grigory Grigoryevich Storchenko. That potbellied rascal has got hold of the whole estate. I'd bet anything you like that he has hidden that deed."

"Allow me to ask, Auntie: isn't he the Storchenko whose acquaintance I made at the inn?"

Thereupon Ivan Fyodorovich described his meeting with Storchenko.

"Who knows," said his aunt after a moment's thought, "perhaps he is not a rascal. It's true that it's only six months since he came to live in these parts; you cannot come to know a man so soon. The old lady, his mother, is a very sensible woman, so I hear, and a great hand at pickling cucumbers. Her serf girls can make capital carpets. But as you say he gave you such a friendly welcome, you must go and see him—perhaps the old sinner will listen to his conscience and will give up what is not his. If you like you can go in the chaise, only those confounded brats have pulled out all the nails at the back. I must tell the coachman, Omelko, to nail the leather on better everywhere."

"What for, Auntie? I will take the trap that you sometimes go out shooting in."

There the conversation ended.

IV
The Dinner

It was about dinner time when Ivan Fyodorovich drove into the village of Khortishche, and he felt a little timid as he approached the manor-house. It was a long house, not thatched with reeds like the houses of many of the neighboring landowners, but with a wooden roof. Two barns in the yard also had wooden roofs: the gate was of oak. Ivan Fyodorovich felt like a dandy who, on arriving at a ball, sees everyone more smartly dressed than himself. He stopped his trap by a barn as a sign of respect and walked to the front door.

"Ah, Ivan Fyodorovich!" cried the fat man Grigory Grigoryevich, who was crossing the yard in his coat but without cravat, waistcoat and braces. But apparently even this attire weighed oppressively on his bulky person, for the perspiration was streaming down him. "Why, you said you would come as soon as you had seen your aunt, and all this time you have not been here!" After these words Ivan Fyodorovich's lips found themselves again in contact with the same cushions.

"Chiefly being busy looking after the farm—I have come just for a minute, as a matter of fact, on business."

"For a minute? Well, that won't do. Hey, lad!" shouted the fat gentleman, and the same boy in the Cossack jacket ran out of the kitchen. "Tell Kasyan to shut the gate tight—do you hear?—make it fast! And take this gentleman's horse out of the shafts this minute. Please come indoors; it is so hot out here that my shirt's soaked."

On going indoors Ivan Fyodorovich made up his mind to waste no time and in spite of his shyness to act with decision.

"My aunt had the honor—she told me a deed of gift of the late Stepan Kuzmich—"

It is difficult to describe the unpleasant grimace made by the broad countenance of Grigory Grigoryevich at these words.

"Oh dear, I can't hear anything!" he responded. "I must tell you that a cockroach got into my left ear. Those bearded Russians breed cockroaches in their huts. No pen can describe what agony it was, it kept tickling and tickling. An old woman cured me by the simplest means—"

"I meant to say," Ivan Fyodorovich ventured to interrupt, seeing that Grigory Grigoryevich was trying to change the subject, "that in the late Stepan Kuzmich's will mention is made, so to speak, of a deed of gift. According to it I ought—"

"I know; so your aunt has told you that story already. It's a lie, upon my soul it is! My uncle made no deed of gift. It is true, some such deed is referred to in the will, but where is it? No one has produced it. I tell you this because I sincerely wish you well. Upon my soul it is a lie!"

"Ivan Fyodorovich said nothing, thinking that his aunt really might be mistaken.

"Ah, here comes Mother with my sisters!" said Grigory Grigoryevich. "So dinner is ready. Let us go!"

Thereupon he drew Ivan Fyodorovich by the hand into a room in which vodka and savories were standing on the table.

At the same time a short old lady, a regular coffeepot in a cap, with two young ladies, one fair and dark, came in, Ivan Fyodorovich, like a wellbred gentleman, went up to kiss the old lady's hand and then the hands of the two young ladies.

"This is our neighbor, Ivan Fyodorovich Shponka, Mother," said Grigory Grigoryevich.

The old lady looked intently at Ivan Fyodorovich, or perhaps it only seemed so. She was goodnatured simplicity itself, though; she looked as though she would like to ask Ivan Fyodorovich: "How many cucumbers have you pickled for the winter?"

"Have you had some vodka?" the old lady asked.

"You mustn't have slept enough, Mother," said Grigory Grigoryevich. "Whoever asks a visitor whether he has had anything. You offer it to us, that's all: whether we've had any or not, that's our business. Ivan Fyodorovich, will you have centaury vodka or the Trofimov brand? Which do you prefer? And you, Ivan Ivanovich, why are you standing there?" said Grigory Grigoryevich, turning round, and Ivan Fyodorovich saw the gentleman so addressed approaching the vodka, in a frockcoat with long skirts and an immense stand-up collar, which covered the whole back of his head, so that his head sat in it, as though in a chaise.

Ivan Ivanovich went up to the vodka and rubbed his hands, carefully examined the wineglass, filled it, held it up to the light, and poured all the vodka at once into his mouth. He did not, however, swallow it at once, but rinsed his mouth thoroughly with it before finally swallowing it, and then, after eating some bread and pickled mushrooms, he turned to Ivan Fyodorovich.

"Is it not Ivan Fyodorovich Shponka I have the honor of addressing?"

"Yes, sir," answered Ivan Fyodorovich.

"You have changed a great deal since I saw you last. Why," he continued, "I remember you this high!" He held his hand a yard from the floor. "Your poor father, may he rest in peace, was a rare man. He used to have melons such as you never see anywhere now. Here, for instance," he went on, drawing him aside, "they'll set melons before you on the table—melons indeed! You won't care to look at them! Would you believe it, sir, he used to have watermelons," he pronounced with a mysterious air, flinging out his arms as if he were about to embrace a stout tree trunk, "as big as this, honest to God!"

"Come to dinner!" said Grigory Grigoryevich, taking Ivan Fyodorovich by the arm.

The company went to the dining room.

Grigory Grigoryevich sat down in his usual place at the end of the table, draped with an enormous table napkin which made him resemble the heroes depicted by barbers on their signs. Ivan Fyodorovich, blushing, sat down in the place assigned to him, facing the two young ladies; and Ivan Ivanovich did not let slip the chance of sitting down beside him, inwardly rejoicing that he had someone to whom he could impart his various items of information.

"You shouldn't take the bishop's nose, Ivan Fyodorovich! It's a turkey!" said the old lady, addressing Ivan Fyodorovich, to whom the rustic waiter in a grey swallowtail patched with black was offering a dish. "Take the back!"

"Mother! No one asked you to interfere!" commented Grigory Grigoryevich. "You may be sure our visitor knows what to take himself. Ivan Fyodorovich, take a wing, the other one there with the gizzard! But why have you taken so little? Take a leg! Why do you stand gaping with the dish? Ask him! Go down on your knees, rascal! Say, at once, 'Ivan Fyodorovich, take a leg!'"

"Ivan Fyodorovich, take a leg!" the waiter with the dish bawled, kneeling down.

"H'm! do you call this a turkey?" Ivan Ivanovich muttered in a low voice, turning to his neighbor with an air of disdain. "Is that what a turkey ought to look like? If you could see my turkeys! I assure you there is more fat on one of them than on a dozen of these. Would you believe me, sir, they look disgusting when they walk about my yard, they are so fat!"

"Ivan Ivanovich, you are lying!" said Grigory Grigoryevich, overhearing these remarks.

"I tell you," Ivan Ivanovich went on to tell his neighbor, affecting not to hear what Grigory Grigoryevich had said, "last year when I sent them to Gadyach, they offered me fifty kopeks apiece for them, and I wouldn't take even that."

"Ivan Ivanovich! You are lying, I tell you!" said Grigory Grigoryevich, stressing each syllable for greater distinctness, and speaking more loudly than before.

But Ivan Ivanovich behaved as though the words could not possibly refer to him; he went on as before, but in a much lower voice: "Yes, sir, I would not take it. There is not a gentleman in Gadyach—"

"Ivan Ivanovich, you are a fool, and that's the truth," Grigory Grigoryevich said in a loud voice. "Ivan Fyodorovich knows all about it better than you do, I'm sure he won't believe you."

At this Ivan Ivanovich was really offended; he said no more, but fell to stowing away the turkey, even though it was not so fat as those that looked disgusting.

For a while the clatter of knives, spoons, and plates took the place of conversation, but loudest of all was the sound made by Grigory Grigoryevich as he sucked the marrow out of the mutton bones.

"Have you," inquired Ivan Ivanovich after an interval of silence, poking his head out of his chaise-like collar, "read *Travels of Korobeinikov to the Holy Land*? It's a real delight to heart and soul! Such books aren't published nowadays. I very much regret that I did not notice in what year it was written."

Ivan Fyodorovich, hearing mention of a book, applied himself diligently to taking sauce.

"It is truly marvellous, sir, when you think that a humble townsman visited all those places: over three thousand versts, sir! over three thousand versts! Truly it was by divine grace that it was vouchsafed him to reach Palestine and Jerusalem."

"So you say," said Ivan Fyodorovich, who had heard a great deal about Jerusalem from his orderly, "that he visited Jerusalem?"

Ivan Fyodorovich Shponka and His Aunt 307

"What are you saying, Ivan Fyodorovich?" Grigory Grigoryevich inquired from the end of the table.

"I had occasion to observe what distant lands there are in the world!" said Ivan Fyodorovich, genuinely gratified that he had succeeded in uttering so long and difficult a sentence.

"Don't you believe him, Ivan Fyodorovich!" said Grigory Grigoryevich, who had not quite caught what was said. "He's always telling fibs!"

Meanwhile dinner was over. Grigory Grigoryevich went to his own room, as his habit was, for a little nap; and the visitors followed their aged hostess and the young ladies into the drawingroom, where the same table on which they had left vodka when they went out to dinner was now, as though by some magical transformation, covered with little saucers of jam of various sorts and dishes of cherries and different kinds of melons.

The absence of Grigory Grigoryevich was perceptible in everything: the old lady became more disposed to talk and, of her own accord, without being asked, revealed a great many secrets in regard to the making of apple cheese, and the drying of pears. Even the young ladies began talking; though the fair one, who looked some six years younger than her sister and who was apparently about five-and-twenty, was rather silent.

But Ivan Ivanovich was more talkative and active than anyone else. Feeling secure that no one would snub or contradict him, he talked of cucumbers and of planting potatoes and of how much more sensible people were in old days — no comparison with what people are now! — and of how as time goes on everything improves and the most intricate inventions are discovered. He was, indeed, one of those persons who take great pleasure in uplifting conversation and will talk of anything that possibly can be talked about. If the conversation touched upon grave and pious subjects, Ivan Ivanovich sighed after each word and nodded his head slightly; if the subject was of a more homely character, he would pop his head out of his chaise-like collar and make faces from which one could almost, it seemed, read how to make pear kvass, how large were the melons of which he was speaking and how fat were the geese that were running about in his yard.

At last, with great difficulty and not before evening, Ivan Fyodorovich succeeded in taking his leave, and although he was usually ready to give way and they almost kept him for the night by force, he persisted in his intention of going — and went.

V
Auntie's New Plan

"Well, did you get the deed of gift out of the old sinner?" Such was the question with which Ivan Fyodorovich was greeted by his aunt, who had been expecting him for some hours on the steps and had at last been unable to resist going out to the gate.

"No, Auntie," said Ivan Fyodorovich, getting out of the trap, "Grigory Grigoryevich has no deed of gift."

"And you believed him? He was lying, the confounded fellow! Some day I shall come across him and I will give him a drubbing with my own hands. Oh, I'd get rid of some of his fat for him! Though perhaps we ought first to consult our court assessor and see if we couldn't get the law on him. But that's not the point now. Was the dinner good?"

"Very—it was excellent, Auntie."

"Well, what did you have? Tell me. The old lady, I know, is a great hand at cooking."

"Curd fritters with sour cream, Auntie; stuffed pigeons in a sauce—"

"And a turkey with prunes?" asked his aunt, for she was herself very skilful in the preparation of that dish.

"Yes, there was a turkey, too! Very handsome young ladies— Grigory Grigoryevich's sisters—especially the fair one."

"Ah!" said Auntie, and she looked intently at Ivan Fyodorovich, who dropped his eyes, blushing. A new idea flashed upon her mind. "Come, tell me," she said eagerly and with curiosity, "what are her eyebrows like?"

It may not be amiss to observe that Auntie considered fine eyebrows the most important item in a woman's looks.

"Her eyebrows, Auntie, are exactly like what you said you had when you were young. And there are little freckles all over her face."

"Ah!" commented his aunt, well pleased with Ivan Fyodorovich's observation, though he had not at all meant to pay her a compliment. "What sort of dress was she wearing? Though, indeed, it's hard to get good material nowadays, such as I have here, for instance, in this gown. But that's not the point. Well, did you talk to her about anything?"

"Talk! How do you mean, Auntie? Perhaps you are imagining—"

"Well, what of it, there would be nothing strange in that. Such is

God's will! It may have been ordained at your birth that you should make a match of it."

"I don't understand how you can say such a thing, Auntie. That shows that you don't know me at all."

"Well, well, now he is offended," said his aunt. "He's still only a child!" she thought to herself. "He knows nothing. I must bring them together—let them get to know each other."

Thereupon Auntie went to have a look at the kitchen and left Ivan Fyodorovich alone. But from that time forward she thought of nothing but seeing her nephew married as soon as possible and fondling his little ones. Her mind was absorbed in making preparations for the wedding, and it was noticeable that she bustled about more busily than ever, though the work was the worse rather than the better for it. Often when she was making a cake, a job which she never left to the cook, she would forget everything, and imagining that a tiny grandnephew was standing by her asking for some cake, would absently hold out her hand with the nicest bit for him, and the yard-dog, taking advantage of this, would snatch the dainty morsel and by its loud munching rouse her from her reverie, for which it was always beaten with the poker. She even abandoned her favorite pursuits and did not go out shooting, especially after she shot a crow by mistake for a partridge, a thing which had never happened to her before.

At last, four days later, everyone saw the chaise brought out of the carriage house into the yard. The coachman Omelko—he was also the gardener and the watchman—had been hammering from early morning, nailing on the leather and continually chasing away the dogs which licked the wheels. I think it my duty to inform my readers that this was the very chaise in which Adam used to drive; and therefore, if anyone gives out that some other chaise was Adam's, it is an absolute lie, and his chaise is certainly not the genuine article. There is no telling how it survived the Deluge. It must be supposed that there was a special coach house for it in Noah's ark. I am very sorry that I cannot give a living picture of it for my readers.

Suffice it to say that Vasilisa Kashporovna was very well satisfied with its structure, and always expressed regret that the old style of carriages had gone out of fashion. The chaise had been constructed a little on one side, so that the right half stood much higher than the left, and this pleased her particularly, because, as she said, a short person could climb up on one side and a tall person on the other. Inside the chaise, however, there was room for five small persons or three such as Auntie herself.

About midday Omelko, having finished with the chaise, brought out of the stable three horses which were but a little younger than the chaise, and began harnessing them with cord to the magnificent vehicle. Ivan Fyodorovich and his aunt stepped in—he on the left side and she on the right—and the chaise drove off. The peasants they met on the road, seeing this sumptuous turnout (Vasilisa Kashporovna rarely drove out in it), stood respectfully, taking off their caps and bowing low.

Two hours later the chaise stopped at the front door—I think I need to say—of Storchenko's house. Grigory Grigoryevich was not at home. His old mother and the two young ladies came into the dining room to receive the visitors. Auntie walked in with a majestic step, with great skill put one foot forward, and said in a loud voice:

"I am delighted, Madam, to have the honor to offer you my respects in person, and at the same time to thank you for your hospitality to my nephew, who has been warm in his praises of it. Your buckwheat is very good, Madam—I saw it as we drove into the village. May I ask how many sheaves you get to the dessiatine?"

There followed kisses all round. As soon as everybody was seated in the drawing room, the old lady began:

"About the buckwheat I cannot tell you: that's Grigory Grigoryevich's department. It is long since I have had anything to do with that; indeed, I could not do it—I am old now. In old days I remember the buckwheat stood waist-high; now goodness knows what it is like, though they say everything is better now." The old lady heaved a sigh, and some observers would have heard in that sigh the sigh of a past age, of the eighteenth century.

"I have heard, my lady, that your maids can make excellent carpets," said Vasilisa Kashporovna, and with that touched on the old lady's most sensitive chord; at those words she seemed to brighten up, and she talked readily of the way to dye the yarn and prepare the thread.

From carpets the conversation drifted easily to the pickling of cucumbers and drying of pears. In short, before the end of an hour the two ladies were talking together as though they had known each other all their lives. Vasilisa Kashporovna had already said a great deal to her in such a low voice that Ivan Fyodorovich could not hear what she was saying.

"Yes, would not you like to have a look at them?" said the old lady, getting up.

The young ladies and Vasilisa Kashporovna also got up and all moved towards the maids' room. Auntie made a sign, however, to Ivan Fyodorovich to remain and said something in an undertone to the old lady.

"Mashenka," said the latter, addressing the fair-haired young lady, "stay with our visitor and talk with him, that he may not be dull!"

The fair-haired young lady sat down on the sofa. Ivan Fyodorovich sat on his chair as though on thorns, blushed and cast down his eyes; but the young lady appeared not to notice this and sat unconcernedly on the sofa, scanning the windows and the walls, or watching the cat running timorously round under the chairs.

Ivan Fyodorovich grew a little bolder and would have begun a conversation; but it seemed as though he had lost all his words on the way. Not a single idea occurred to him.

The silence lasted for nearly a quarter of an hour. The young lady went on sitting as before.

At last Ivan Fyodorovich plucked up his courage.

"There are a great many flies in summer, Madam!" he brought out in a half-trembling voice.

"A very great many!" answered the young lady. "My brother has made a flapper out of an old slipper of Mamma's to kill them, but there are lots of them still."

Here the conversation ran out, and Ivan Fyodorovich was utterly unable to find anything else to say.

At last the old lady came back with his aunt and the dark-haired young lady. After a little more conversation, Vasilisa Kashporovna took leave of the old lady and her daughters in spite of their entreaties that they should stay the night. The three ladies came out on the steps to see the visitors off, and continued for some time nodding to the aunt and the nephew, as they looked out of the chaise.

"Well, Ivan Fyodorovich, what did you talk about when you were alone with the young lady?" Auntie asked him on the way home.

"A very discreet and well-behaved young lady, is Marya Grigoryevna," said Ivan Fyodorovich.

"Listen, Ivan Fyodorovich, I want to talk seriously to you. Here you are over thirty-seven, thank God; you have obtained a good rank in the service—it's time to think about children. You must have a wife."

"What, Auntie!" cried Ivan Fyodorovich in fright. "A wife! No, Auntie, for goodness' sake! You make me quite ashamed. I've never had a wife. I shouldn't know what to do with her!"

"You'll find out, Ivan Fyodorovich, you will," said his aunt, smiling.

"Why, he is a perfect baby—he knows nothing!" she thought to herself. "Yes, Ivan Fyodorovich," she went on aloud, "we could not find a better wife for you than Marya Grigoryevna. Besides, you are very much attracted by her. I have had a good talk with the old lady about it; she'll be delighted to see you her son-in-law. It's true that we don't know what that reprobate Grigory Grigoryevich will say to it; but we won't consider him, and if he takes it into his head not to give her a dowry, we'll have the law on him."

At that moment the chaise drove into the yard and the ancient nags grew more lively, feeling that their stable was not far off.

"Mind, Omelko! Let the horses have a good rest first, and don't take them down to water the minute they are unharnessed—they are overheated."

"Well, Ivan Fyodorovich," his aunt went on as she got out of the chaise, "I advise you to think it over well. I must run to the kitchen: I forgot to tell Solokha what to get for supper, and I expect the wretched woman won't have thought of it herself."

But Ivan Fyodorovich stood as though thunderstruck. It was true that Marya Grigoryevna was a very nice-looking young lady; but to get married! It seemed to him so strange, so peculiar, he couldn't think of it without horror. Living with a wife! Unthinkable! He would not be alone in his own room, but they would always have to be two together! Perspiration came out on his face as he sank more deeply into meditation.

He went to bed earlier than usual, but in spite of all his efforts he could not go to sleep. But at last sleep, that universal comforter, came to him; but what sleep! He had never had such incoherent dreams. First he dreamed that everything was whirling with a noise around him, and he was running and running, as fast as his legs could carry him. Now he was at his last gasp. All at once someone caught him by the ear. "Ouch! Who is it?"

"It is me, your wife!" a voice resounded loudly in his ear, and he woke up. Then he imagined that he was married, that everything in their little house was so peculiar, so strange: a double bed stood in his room instead of a single one; his wife was sitting on a chair. He felt queer: he did not know how to approach her, what to say to her, and then he noticed that she had the face of a goose. He happened to turn aside and saw another wife, also with the face of a goose. Turning again, he saw yet another wife; and behind him was a fourth. Then he was seized by panic; he dashed away into the garden, but there it was hot; he took off his hat, and saw a wife sitting in his hat. Drops of sweat came out on his face. He put his hand in his pocket for his handkerchief and in his pocket, too, there was a wife; he took some cotton wool out of his ear—and there, too, sat a wife. Then he suddenly began hopping on one leg, and Auntie, looking at him, said with a dignified air: "Yes, you must hop on one leg now, for you are a married man." He went towards her, but his aunt was no longer an aunt but a belfry, and he felt that someone was dragging him by a rope up on the belfry. "Who is it pulling me?" Ivan Fyodorovich asked plaintively. "It is me, your wife. I am pulling you because you are a bell." "No, I am not a bell, I am Ivan Fyodorovich," he cried. "Yes, you are a bell," said the colonel of the infantry regiment, who happened to be passing. Then he suddenly dreamed that a wife was not a human being at all but a sort of woollen material; that he went into a shop in Mogilyov. "What sort of stuff would you like?" asked the shopkeeper. "You had better take a wife, that is the most fashionable material! It wears well! Everyone is having coats made of it now." The shopkeeper measured and cut off a wife. Ivan Fyodorovich put her under his arm and went off to a Jewish tailor. "No," said the Jew, "that is poor material. No one has coats made of that now."

Ivan Fyodorovich woke up in terror, not knowing where he was and dripping with cold perspiration.

As soon as he got up in the morning, he went at once to his fortuneteller's book, at the end of which a virtuous bookseller had in the goodness of his heart and disinterestedness inserted an abridged dream-book. But there was absolutely nothing in it that remotely resembled this incoherent dream.

Meanwhile a quite new design, of which you shall hear more in the following chapter, had taken shape in Auntie's brain.

The Overcoat

In the department of ... but I had better not mention in what department. There is nothing in the world more readily moved to wrath than a department, a regiment, a government office, and in fact any sort of official body. Nowadays every private individual considers all society insulted in his person. I have been told that very lately a petition was handed in from a police captain of what town I don't recollect, and that in this petition he set forth clearly that the institutions of the State were in danger and that its sacred name was being taken in vain; and, in proof thereof, he appended to his petition an enormously long volume of some work of romance in which a police captain appeared on every tenth page, occasionally, indeed, in an intoxicated condition. And so, to avoid any unpleasantness, we had better call the department of which we are speaking a certain department.

And so, in a certain department there was a government clerk; a clerk of whom it cannot be said that he was very remarkable; he was short, somewhat pockmarked, with rather reddish hair and rather dim, bleary eyes, with a small bald patch on the top of his head, with wrinkles on both sides of his cheeks and the sort of complexion which is usually associated with hemorrhoids ... no help for that, it is the Petersburg climate. As for his grade in the service (for among us the grade is what must be put first), he was what is called a perpetual titular councillor, a class at which, as we all know, various writers who indulge in the praiseworthy habit of attacking those who cannot defend themselves jeer and jibe to their hearts' content. This clerk's surname was Bashmatchkin. From the very name it is clear that it must have been derived from a shoe (*bashmak*); but when and under what circumstances it was derived from a shoe, it is impossible to say. Both his father and his grandfather and even his brother-in-law, and all the Bashmatchkins without exception wore boots, which they simply resoled two or three times a year. His name was Akaky Akakyevitch. Perhaps it may strike the reader as a rather strange and far-fetched name, but I can assure him that it was not far-fetched at all, that the circumstances were such that it was quite out of the question to give him any other name. Akaky Akakyevitch was born towards nightfall, if my memory does not deceive me, on the twenty-third of March. His mother, the wife of a government clerk, a very good woman, made arrangements in due course to christen the child. She was still lying in bed, facing the door, while on her right hand stood the godfather, an excellent man called Ivan Ivanovitch Yeroshkin, one of the head clerks in the Senate, and the godmother, the wife of a police official, and a woman of rare qualities, Arina Semyonovna Byelobryushkov. Three names were offered to the happy mother for selection—Moky, Sossy, or the name of the martyr Hozdazt. "No," thought the poor lady, "they are all such names!" To satisfy her, they opened the calendar at another place, and the names which turned up were: Trifily, Dula, Varahasy. "What an infliction!" said the mother. "What names they all are! I really never heard such names. Varadat or Varuh would be bad enough, but Trifily and Varahasy!" They turned over another page and the names were: Pavsikahy and Vahtisy. "Well, I see," said the mother, "it is clear that it is his fate. Since that is how it is, he had better be called after his father, his father is Akaky, let the son be Akaky, too." This was how he came to be Akaky Akakyevitch. The baby was christened and cried and made wry faces during the ceremony, as though he foresaw that he would be a titular councillor. So that was how it all came to pass. We have recalled it here so that the reader may see for himself that it happened quite inevitably and that to give him any other name was out of the question. No one has been able to remember when and how long ago he entered the department, nor who gave him the job. However many directors and higher officials of all sorts came and went, he was always seen in the same place, in the same position, at the very same duty, precisely the same copying clerk, so that they used to declare that he must have been born a copying clerk in uniform all complete and with a bald patch on his head. No respect at all was shown him in the department. The porters, far from getting up from their seats when he came in, took no more notice of him than if a simple fly had flown across the vestibule. His superiors treated him with a sort of domineering chilliness. The head clerk's assistant used to throw papers under his nose without even saying: "Copy this" or "Here is an interesting, nice little case" or some agreeable remark of the sort, as is usually done in well-behaved offices. And he would take it, gazing only at the paper without looking to see who had put it there and whether he had the right to do so; he would take it and at once set to work to copy it. The young clerks jeered and made jokes at him to the best of their clerkly wit, and told before his face all sorts of stories of their own invention about him; they would say of his landlady, an old woman of seventy, that she beat him, would enquire when the wedding was to take place, and would scatter bits of paper on his head, calling them snow. Akaky Akakyevitch never answered a word, however, but behaved as though there were no one there. It has no influence on his work even; in the midst of all this teasing, he never made a single mistake in his copying. Only when the jokes were too unbearable, when they jolted his arm and prevented him from going on with his work, he would bring out: "Leave me alone! Why do you insult me?" and there was something strange in the words and in the voice in which they were uttered. There was a note in it of something that aroused compassion, so that one young man, new to the office, who, following the example of the rest, had allowed himself to mock at him, suddenly stopped as though cut to the heart, and from that time forth, everything was, as it were, changed and appeared in a different light to him. Some unnatural force seemed to thrust him away from the companions with whom he had become acquainted, accepting them as well-bred, polished people. And long afterwards, at moments of the greatest gaiety, the figure of the humble little clerk with a bald patch on his head rose before him with his heart-rending words: "Leave me alone! Why do you insult me?" and in those heart-rending words he heard others: "I am your brother." And the poor young man hid his face in his hands, and many times afterwards in his life he shuddered, seeing how much inhumanity there is in man, how much savage brutality lies hidden under refined, cultured politeness, and, my God! even in a man whom the world accepts as a gentleman and a man of honor . . . .

It would be hard to find a man who lived in his work as did Akaky Akakyevitch. To say that he was zealous in his work is not enough; no, he loved his work. In it, in that copying, he found a varied and agreeable world of his own. There was a look of enjoyment on his face; certain letters were favorites with him, and when he came to them he was delighted; he chuckled to himself and winked and moved his lips, so that it seemed as though every letter his pen was forming could be read in his face. If rewards had been given according to the measure of zeal in the service, he might to his amazement have even found himself a civil councillor; but all he gained in the service, as the wits, his fellow clerks, expressed it, was a buckle in his buttonhole and a pain in his back. It cannot be said, however, that no notice had ever been taken of him. One director, being a goodnatured man and anxious to reward him for his long service, sent him something a little more important than his ordinary copying; he was instructed from a finished document to make some sort of report for another office; the work consisted only of altering the headings and in places changing the first person into the third. This cost him such an effort that it threw him into a regular perspiration: he mopped his brow and said at last, "No, better let me copy something."

From that time forth they left him to go on copying for ever. It seemed as though nothing in the world existed for him outside his copying. He gave no thought at all to his clothes; his uniform was — well, not green but some sort of rusty, muddy color. His collar was very short and narrow, so that, although his neck was not particularly long, yet, standing out of the collar, it looked as immensely long as those of the plaster kittens that wag their heads and are carried about on trays on the heads of dozens of foreigners living in Russia. And there were always things sticking to his uniform, either bits of hay or threads; moreover, he had a special art of passing under a window at the very moment when various rubbish was being flung out into the street, and so was continually carrying off bits of melon rind and similar litter on his hat. He had never once in his life noticed what was being done and going on in the streets, all those things at which, as we all know, his colleagues, the young clerks, always stare, carrying their sharp sight so far even as to notice any one on the other side of the pavement with a trouser strap hanging loose — a detail which always calls forth a sly grin. Whatever Akaky Akakyevitch looked at, he saw nothing anywhere but his clear, evenly written lines, and only perhaps when a horse's head suddenly appeared from nowhere just on his shoulder, and its nostrils blew a perfect gale upon his cheek, did he notice that he was not in the middle of his writing, but rather in the middle of the street.

On reaching home, he would sit down at once to the table, hurriedly sup his soup and eat a piece of beef with an onion; he did not notice the taste at all, but ate it all up together with the flies and anything else that Providence chanced to send him. When he felt that his stomach was beginning to be full, he would rise up from the table, get out a bottle of ink and set to copying the papers he had brought home with him. When he had none to do, he would make a copy expressly for his own pleasure, particularly if the document were remarkable not for the beauty of its style but for the fact of its being addressed to some new or important personage.

Even at those hours when the grey Petersburg sky is completely overcast and the whole population of clerks have dined and eaten their fill, each as best he can, according to the salary he receives and his personal tastes; when they are all resting after the scratching of pens and bustle of the office, their own necessary work and other people's, and all the tasks that an over-zealous man voluntarily sets himself even beyond what is necessary; when the clerks are hastening to devote what is left of their time to pleasure; some more enterprising are flying to the theater, others to the street to spend their leisure, staring at women's hats, some to spend the evening paying compliments to some attractive girl, the star of a little official circle, while some — and this is the most frequent of all — go simply to a fellow clerk's flat on the third or fourth storey, two little rooms with an entry or a kitchen, with some pretentions to style, with a lamp or some such article that has cost many sacrifices of dinners and excursions—at the time when all the clerks are scattered about the little flats of their friends, playing a tempestuous game of whist, sipping tea out of glasses to the accompaniment of farthing rusks, sucking in smoke from long pipes, telling, as the cards are dealt, some scandal that has floated down from higher circles, a pleasure which the Russian can never by any possibility deny himself, or, when there is nothing better to talk about, repeating the everlasting anecdote of the commanding officer who was told that the tail had been cut off the horse on the Falconet monument—in short, even when every one was eagerly seeking entertainment, Akaky Akakyevitch did not give himself up to any amusement. No one could say that they had ever seen him at an evening party. After working to his heart's content, he would go to bed, smiling at the thought of the next day and wondering what God would send him to copy. So flowed on the peaceful life of a man who knew how to be content with his fate on a salary of four hundred roubles, and so perhaps it would have flowed on to extreme old age, had it not been for the various calamities that bestrew the path through life, not only of titular, but even of privy, actual court, and all other councillors, even those who neither give council to others nor accept it themselves.

There is in Petersburg a mighty foe of all who receive a salary of four hundred roubles or about that sum. That foe is none other than our northern frost, although it is said to be very good for the health. Between eight and nine in the morning, precisely at the hour when the streets are full of clerks going to their departments, the frost begins giving such sharp and stinging flips at all their noses indiscriminately that the poor fellows don't know what to do with them. At that time, when even those in the higher grade have a pain in their brows and tears in their eyes from the frost, the poor titular councillors are sometimes almost defenseless. Their only protection lies in running as fast as they can through five or six streets in a wretched, thin little overcoat and then warming their feet thoroughly in the porter's room, till all their faculties and qualifications for their various duties thaw again after being frozen on the way. Akaky Akakyevitch had for some time been feeling that his back and shoulders were particularly nipped by the cold, although he did try to run the regular distance as fast as he could. He wondered at last whether there were any defects in his overcoat. After examining it thoroughly in the privacy of his home, he discovered that in two or three places, to wit on the back and the shoulders, it had become a regular sieve; the cloth was so worn that you could see through it and the lining was coming out. I must observe that Akaky Akakyevitch's overcoat had also served as a butt for the jibes of the clerks. It had even been deprived of the honorable name of overcoat and had been referred to as the "dressing jacket." It was indeed of rather a strange make. Its collar had been growing smaller year by year as it served to patch the other parts. The patches were not good specimens of the tailor's art, and they certainly looked clumsy and ugly. On seeing what was wrong, Akaky Akakyevitch decided that he would have to take the overcoat to Petrovitch, a tailor who lived on a fourth storey up a back staircase, and, in spite of having only one eye and being pockmarked all over his face, was rather successful in repairing the trousers and coats of clerks and others — that is, when he was sober, be it understood, and had no other enterprise in his mind. Of this tailor I ought not, of course, to say much, but since it is now the rule that the character of every person in a novel must be completely drawn, well, there is no help for it, here is Petrovitch too. At first he was called simply Grigory, and was a serf belonging to some gentleman or other. He began to be called Petrovitch from the time that he got his freedom and began to drink rather heavily on every holiday, at first only on the chief holidays, but afterwards on all church holidays indiscriminately, wherever there is a cross in the calendar. On that side he was true to the customs of his forefathers, and when he quarrelled with his wife used to call her "a worldly woman and a German." Since we have now mentioned the wife, it will be necessary to say a few words about her too, but unfortunately not much is known about her, except indeed that Petrovitch had a wife and that she wore a cap and not a kerchief, but apparently she could not boast of beauty; anyway, none but soldiers of the Guards peeped under her cap when they met her, and they twitched their moustaches and gave vent to a rather peculiar sound.

As he climbed the stairs, leading to Petrovitch's — which, to do them justice, were all soaked with water and slops and saturated through and through with that smell of spirits which makes the eyes smart, and is, as we all know, inseparable from the backstairs of Petersburg houses — Akaky Akakyevitch was already wondering how much Petrovitch would ask for the job, and inwardly resolving not to give more than two roubles. The door was open, for Petrovitch's wife was frying some fish and had so filled the kitchen with smoke that you could not even see the black beetles. Akaky Akakyevitch crossed the kitchen unnoticed by the good woman, and walked at last into a room where he saw Petrovitch sitting on a big, wooden, unpainted table with his legs tucked under him like a Turkish Pasha. The feet, as is usual with tailors when they sit at work, were bare; and the first object that caught Akaky Akakyevitch's eye was the big toe, with which he was already familiar, with a misshapen nail as thick and strong as the shell of a tortoise. Round Petrovitch's neck hung a skein of silk and another of thread and on his knees was a rag of some sort. He had for the last three minutes been trying to thread his needle, but could not get the thread into the eye and so was very angry with the darkness and indeed with the thread itself, muttering in an undertone: "It won't go in, the savage! You wear me out, you rascal." Akaky Akakyevitch was vexed that he had come just at the minute when Petrovitch was in a bad humor; he liked to give him an order when he was a little "elevated," or, as his wife expressed it, "had fortified himself with fizz, the one-eyed devil." In such circumstances Petrovitch was as a rule very ready to give way and agree, and invariably bowed and thanked him, indeed. Afterwards, it is true, his wife would come wailing that her husband had been drunk and so had asked too little, but adding a single ten-kopeck piece would settle that. But on this occasion Petrovitch was apparently sober and consequently curt, unwilling to bargain, and the devil knows what price he would be ready to lay on. Akaky Akakyevitch perceived this, and was, as the saying is, beating a retreat, but things had gone too far, for Petrovitch was screwing up his solitary eye very attentively at him and Akaky Akakyevitch involuntarily brought out: "Good day, Petrovitch!" "I wish you a good day, sir," said Petrovitch, and squinted at Akaky Akakyevitch's hands, trying to discover what sort of goods he had brought.

"Here I have come to you, Petrovitch, do you see . . . !"

It must be noticed that Akaky Akakyevitch for the most part explained himself by apologies, vague phrases, and particles which have absolutely no significance whatever. If the subject were a very difficult one, it was his habit indeed to leave his sentences quite unfinished, so that very often after a sentence hand begun with the words, "It really is, don't you know . . ." nothing at all would follow and he himself would be quite oblivious, supposing he had said all that was necessary.

"What is it?" said Petrovitch, and at the same time with his solitary eye he scrutinized his whole uniform from the collar to the sleeves, the back, the skirts, the buttonholes—with all of which he was very familiar, they were all his own work. Such scrutiny is habitual with tailors, it is the first thing they do on meeting one.

"It's like this, Petrovitch . . . the overcoat, the cloth . . . you see everywhere else it is quite strong; it's a little dusty and looks as though it were old, but it is new and it is only in one place just a little . . . on the back, and just a little worn on one shoulder and on this shoulder, too, a little . . . do you see? that's all, and it's not much work. . . . "

Petrovitch took the "dressing jacket," first spread it out over the table, examined it for a long time, shook his head and put his hand out to the window for a round snuffbox with a portrait on the lid of some general — which precisely I can't say, for a finger had been thrust through the spot where a face should have been, and the hole had been pasted up with a square bit of paper. After taking a pinch of snuff, Petrovitch held the "dressing jacket" up in his hands and looked at it against the light, and again he shook his head; then he turned it with the lining upwards and once more shook his head; again he took off the lid with the general pasted up with paper and stuffed a pinch into his nose, shut the box, put it away and at last said: "No, it can't be repaired; a wretched garment!"

"Why can't it, Petrovitch?" he said, almost in the imploring voice of a child. "Why, the only thing is it is a bit worn on the shoulders; why, you have got some little pieces. . . . "

"Yes, the pieces will be found all right," said Petrovitch, "but it can't be patched, the stuff is quite rotten; if you put a needle in it, it would give way."

"Let it give way, but you just put a patch on it."

"There is nothing to put a patch on. There is nothing for it to hold on to; there is a great strain on it, it is not worth calling cloth, it would fly away at a breath of wind."

"Well, then, strengthen it with something — upon my word, really, this is . . . !"

"No," said Petrovitch resolutely, "there is nothing to be done, the thing is no good at all. You had far better, when the cold winter weather comes, make yourself leg wrappings out of it, for there is no warmth in stockings, the Germans invented them just to make money." (Petrovitch was fond of a dig at the Germans occasionally.) "And as for the overcoat, it is clear that you will have to have a new one."

At the word "new" there was a mist before Akaky Akakyevitch's eyes, and everything in the room seemed blurred. He could see nothing clearly but the general with the piece of paper over his face on the lid of Petrovitch's snuffbox.

"A new one?" he said, still feeling as though he were in a dream; "why, I haven't the money for it."

"Yes, a new one," Petrovitch repeated with barbarous composure.

"Well, and if I did have a new one, how much would it . . . ?"

"You mean what will it cost?"

"Yes."

"Well, three fifty-rouble notes or more," said Petrovitch, and he compressed his lips significantly. He was very fond of making an effect, he was fond of suddenly disconcerting a man completely and then squinting sideways to see what sort of a face he made.

"A hundred and fifty roubles for an overcoat," screamed poor Akaky Akakyevitch—it was perhaps the first time he had screamed in his life, for he was always distinguished by the softness of his voice.

"Yes," said Petrovitch, "and even then it's according to the coat. If I were to put marten on the collar, and add a hood with silk linings, it would come to two hundred."

"Petrovitch, please," said Akaky Akakyevitch in an imploring voice, not hearing and not trying to hear what Petrovitch said, and missing all his effects, "do repair it somehow, so that it will serve a little longer."

"No, that would be wasting work and spending money for nothing," said Petrovitch, and after that Akaky Akakyevitch went away completely crushed, and when he had gone Petrovitch remained standing for a long time with his lips pursed up significantly before he took up his work again, feeling pleased that he had not demeaned himself nor lowered the dignity of the tailor's art.

When he got into the street, Akaky Akakyevitch was as though in a dream. "So that is how it is," he said to himself. "I really did not think it would be so . . ." and then after a pause he added, "So there it is! so that's how it is at last! and I really could never have supposed it would have been so. And there . . ." There followed another long silence, after which he brought out: "So there it is! well, it really is so utterly unexpected . . . who would have thought . . . what a circumstance . . . ." Saying this, instead of going home he walked off in quite the opposite direction without suspecting what he was doing. On the way a clumsy sweep brushed the whole of his sooty side against him and blackened all his shoulder; a regular hatful of plaster scattered upon him from the top of a house that was being built. He noticed nothing of this, and only after he had jostled against a sentry who had set his halberd down beside him and was shaking some snuff out of his horn into his rough fist, he came to himself a little and then only because the sentry said: "Why are you poking yourself right in one's face, haven't you the pavement to yourself?" This made him look round and turn homeward; only there he began to collect his thoughts, to see his position in a clear and true light and began talking to himself no longer incoherently but reasonably and openly as with a sensible friend with whom one can discuss the most intimate and vital matters. "No, indeed," said Akaky Akakyevitch, "it is no use talking to Petrovitch now; just now he really is . . . his wife must have been giving it to him. I had better go to him on Sunday morning; after the Saturday evening he will be squinting and sleepy, so he'll want a little drink to carry it off and his wife won't give him a penny. I'll slip ten kopecks into his hand and then he will be more accommodating and maybe take the overcoat . . . ."

So reasoning with himself, Akaky Akakyevitch cheered up and waited until the next Sunday; then, seeing from a distance Petrovitch's wife leaving the house, he went straight in. Petrovitch certainly was very tipsy after the Saturday. He could hardly hold his head up and was very drowsy: but, for all that, as soon as he heard what he was speaking about, it seemed as though the devil had nudged him. "I can't," he said, "you must kindly order a new one." Akaky Akakyevitch at once slipped a ten-kopeck piece into his hand. "I thank you, sir, I will have just a drop to your health, but don't trouble yourself about the overcoat; it is not a bit of good for anything. I'll make you a fine new coat, you can trust me for that."

Akaky Akakyevitch would have said more about repairs, but Petrovitch, without listening, said: "A new one now I'll make you without fail; you can rely upon that, I'll do my best. It could even be like the fashion that has come in with the collar to button with silver claws under appliqué."

Then Akaky Akakyevitch saw that there was no escape from a new overcoat and he was utterly depressed. How indeed, for what, with what money could he get it? Of course he could to some extent rely on the bonus for the coming holiday, but that money had long ago been appropriated and its use determined beforehand. It was needed for new trousers and to pay the cobbler an old debt for putting some new tops to some old bootlegs, and he had to order three shirts from a seamstress as well as two specimens of an undergarment which it is improper to mention in print; in short, all that money absolutely must be spent, and even if the director were to be so gracious as to assign him a gratuity of forty-five or even fifty, instead of forty roubles, there would be still left a mere trifle, which would be but as a drop in the ocean beside the fortune needed for an overcoat. Though, of course, he knew that Petrovitch had a strange craze for suddenly putting on the devil knows what enormous price, so that at times his own wife could not help crying out: "Why, you are out of your wits, you idiot! Another time he'll undertake a job for nothing, and here the devil has bewitched him to ask more than he is worth himself." Though, of course, he knew that Petrovitch would undertake to make it for eighty roubles, still where would he get those eighty roubles? He might manage half of that sum; half of it could be found, perhaps even a little more; but where could he get the other half? . . . But, first of all, the reader ought to know where that first half was to be found. Akaky Akakyevitch had the habit every time he spent a rouble of putting aside two kopecks in a little locked-up box with a slit in the lid for slipping the money in. At the end of every half-year he would inspect the pile of coppers there and change them for small silver. He had done this for a long time, and in the course of many years the sum had mounted up to forty roubles and so he had half the money in his hands, but where was he to get the other half, where was he to get another forty roubles? Akaky Akakyevitch pondered and pondered and decided at last that he would have to diminish his ordinary expenses, at least for a year; give up burning candles in the evening, and if he had to do anything he must go into the landlady's room and work by her candle; that as he walked along the streets he must walk as lightly and carefully as possible, almost on tiptoe, on the cobbles and flag-stones, so that his soles might last a little longer than usual; that he must send his linen to the wash less frequently, and that, to preserve it from being worn, he must take it off every day when he came home and sit in a thin cotton-shoddy dressing-gown, a very ancient garment which Time itself had spared. To tell the truth, he found it at first rather hard to get used to these privations, but after a while it became a habit and went smoothly enough—he even became quite accustomed to being hungry in the evening; on the other hand, he had spiritual nourishment, for he carried ever in his thoughts the idea of his future overcoat. His whole existence had in a sense become fuller, as though he had married, as though some other person were present with him, as though he were no longer alone, but an agreeable companion had consented to walk the path of life hand in hand with him, and that companion was no other than the new overcoat with its thick wadding and its strong, durable lining. He became, as it were, more alive, even more strong-willed, like a man who has set before himself a definite aim. Uncertainty, indecision, in fact all the hesitating and vague characteristics vanished from his face and his manners. At times there was a gleam in his eyes, indeed, the most bold and audacious ideas flashed through his mind. Why not really have marten on the collar? Meditation on the subject always made him absent-minded. On one occasion when he was copying a document, he very nearly made a mistake, so that he almost cried out "ough" aloud and crossed himself. At least once every month he went to Petrovitch to talk about the overcoat, where it would be best to buy the cloth, and what color it should be, and what price, and, though he returned home a little anxious, he was always pleased at the thought that at last the time was at hand when everything would be bought and the overcoat would be made. Things moved even faster than he had anticipated. Contrary to all expectations, the director bestowed on Akaky Akakyevitch a gratuity of no less than sixty roubles. Whether it was that he had an inkling that Akaky Akakyevitch needed a greatcoat, or whether it happened so by chance, owing to this he found he had twenty roubles extra. This circumstance hastened the course of affairs. Another two or three months of partial fasting and Akaky Akakyevitch had actually saved up nearly eighty roubles. His heart, as a rule very tranquil, began to throb. The very first day he set off in company with Petrovitch to the shops. They bought some very good cloth, and no wonder, since they had been thinking of it for more than six months before, and scarcely a month had passed without their going to the shop to compare prices; now Petrovitch himself declared that there was no better cloth to be had. For the lining they chose calico, but of a stout quality, which in Petrovich's words was even better than silk, and actually as strong and handsome to look at. Marten they did not buy, because it certainly was dear, but instead they chose cat fur, the best to be found in the shop—cat which in the distance might almost be taken for marten. Petrovitch was busy over the coat for a whole fortnight, because there were a great many buttonholes, otherwise it would have been ready sooner. Petrovitch asked twelve roubles for the work; less than that it hardly could have been, everything was sewn with silk, with fine double seams, and Petrovitch went over every seam afterwards with his own teeth imprinting various figures with them. It was ... it is hard to say precisely on what day, but probably on the most triumphant day of the life of Akaky Akakyevitch that Petrovitch at last brought the overcoat. He brought it in the morning, just before it was time to set off for the department. The overcoat could not have arrived more in the nick of time, for rather sharp frosts were just beginning and seemed threatening to be even more severe. Petrovitch brought the greatcoat himself as a good tailor should. There was an expression of importance on his face, such as Akaky Akakyevitch had never seen there before. He seemed fully conscious of having completed a work of no little moment and of having shown in his own person the gulf that separates tailors who only put in linings and do repairs from those who make up new materials. He took the greatcoat out of the bandana in which he had brought it (the bandana had just come home from the wash), he then folded it up and put it in his pocket for future use. After taking out the overcoat, he looked at it with much pride and, holding it in both hands, threw it very deftly over Akaky Akakyevitch's shoulders, then pulled it down and smoothed it out behind with his hands; then draped it about Akaky Akakyevitch with somewhat jaunty carelessness. The latter, as a man advanced in years, wished to try it with his arms in the sleeves. Petrovitch helped him to put it on, and it appeared that it looked splendid too with his arms in the sleeves. In fact it turned out that the overcoat was completely and entirely successful. Petrovitch did not let slip the occasion for observing that it was only because he lived in a small street and had no signboard, and because he had known Akaky Akakyevitch so long, that he had done it so cheaply, but on the Nevsky Prospect they would have asked him seventy-five roubles for the work alone. Akaky Akakyevitch had no inclination to discuss this with Petrovitch, besides he was frightened of the big sums that Petrovitch was fond of flinging airily about in conversation. He paid him, thanked him, and went off on the spot, with his new overcoat on, to the department. Petrovitch followed him out and stopped in the street, staring for a good time at the coat from a distance and then purposely turned off and, taking a short cut by a side street, came back into the street and got another view of the coat from the other side, that is, from the front.

Meanwhile Akaky Akakyevitch walked along with every emotion in its most holiday mood. He felt every second that he had a new overcoat on his shoulders, and several times he actually laughed from inward satisfaction. Indeed, it had two advantages, one that it was warm and the other that it was good. He did not notice the way at all and found himself all at once at the department; in the porter's room he took off the overcoat, looked it over and put it in the porter's special care. I cannot tell how it happened, but all at once every one in the department learned that Akaky Akakyevitch had a new overcoat and that the "dressing jacket" no longer existed. They all ran out at once into the porter's room to look at Akaky Akakyevitch's new overcoat, they began welcoming him and congratulating him so that at first he could do nothing but smile and afterwards felt positively abashed. When, coming up to him, they all began saying that he must "sprinkle" the new overcoat and that he ought at least to stand them all a supper, Akaky Akakyevitch lost his head completely and did not know what to do, how to get out of it, nor what to answer. A few minutes later, flushing crimson, he even began assuring them with great simplicity that it was not a new overcoat at all, that it was just nothing, that it was an old overcoat. At last one of the clerks, indeed the assistant of the head clerk of the room, probably in order to show that he was not proud and was able to get on with those beneath him, said: "So be it, I'll give a party instead of Akaky Akakyevitch and invite you all to tea with me this evening; as luck would have it, it is my name-day." The clerks naturally congratulated the assistant head clerk and eagerly accepted the invitation. Akaky Akakyevitch was beginning to make excuses, but they all declared that it was uncivil of him, that it was simply a shame and a disgrace and that he could not possibly refuse. However, he felt pleased about it afterwards when he remembered that through this he would have the opportunity of going out in the evening, too, in his new overcoat. That whole day was for Akaky Akakyevitch the most triumphant and festive day in his life. He returned home in the happiest frame of mind, took off the overcoat and hung it carefully on the wall, admiring the cloth and lining once more, and then pulled out his old "dressing jacket," now completely coming to pieces, on purpose to compare them. He glanced at it and positively laughed, the difference was so immense! And long afterwards he went on laughing at dinner, as the position in which the "dressing jacket" was placed recurred to his mind. He dined in excellent spirits and after dinner wrote nothing, no papers at all, but just took his ease for a little while on his bed, till it got dark, then, without putting things off, he dressed, put on his overcoat, and went out into the street. Where precisely the clerk who had invited him lived we regret to say that we cannot tell; our memory is beginning to fail sadly, and everything there is in Petersburg, all the streets and houses, are so blurred and muddled in our head that it is a very difficult business to put anything in orderly fashion. However that may have been, there is no doubt that the clerk lived in the better part of the town and consequently a very long distance from Akaky Akakyevitch. At first the latter had to walk through deserted streets, scantily lighted, but as he approached his destination the streets became more lively, more full of people, and more brightly lighted; passers-by began to be more frequent, ladies began to appear, here and there, beautifully dressed, beaver collars were to be seen on the men. Cabmen with wooden trellis-work sledges, studded with gilt nails, were less frequently to be met; on the other hand, jaunty drivers in raspberry colored velvet caps with varnished sledges and bearskin rugs appeared, and carriages with decorated boxes dashed along the streets, their wheels crunching through the snow.

Akaky Akakyevitch looked at all this as a novelty; for several years he had not gone out into the streets in the evening. He stopped with curiosity before a lighted shop window to look at a picture in which a beautiful woman was represented in the act of taking off her shoe and displaying as she did so the whole of a very shapely leg, while behind her back a gentleman with whiskers and a handsome imperial on his chin was putting his head in at the door. Akaky Akakyevitch shook his head and smiled and then went on his way. Why did he smile? Was it because he had come across something quite unfamiliar to him, though every man retains some instinctive feeling on the subject, or was it that he reflected, like many other clerks, as follows: "Well, upon my soul, those Frenchmen! it's beyond anything! if they try anything of the sort, it really is . . . !" Though possibly he did not even think that; there is no creeping into a man's soul and finding out all that he thinks. At last he reached the house in which the assistant head clerk lived in fine style; there was a lamp burning on the stairs, and the flat was on the second floor. As he went into the entry Akaky Akakyevitch saw whole rows of goloshes. Amongst them in the middle of the room stood a samovar hissing and letting off clouds of steam. On the walls hung coats and cloaks, among which some actually had beaver collars or velvet revers. The other side of the wall there was noise and talk, which suddenly became clear and loud when the door opened and the footman came out with a tray full of empty glasses, a jug of cream, and a basket of biscuits. It was evident that the clerks had arrived long before and had already drunk their first glass of tea. Akaky Akakyevitch, after hanging up his coat with his own hands, went into the room, and at the same moment there flashed before his eyes a vision of candles, clerks, pipes, and card tables, together with the confused sounds of conversation rising up on all sides and the noise of moving chairs. He stopped very awkwardly in the middle of the room, looking about and trying to think what to do, but he was observed and received with a shout and they all went at once into the entry and again took a look at his overcoat. Though Akaky Akakyevitch was somewhat embarrassed, yet, being a simple-hearted man, he could not help being pleased at seeing how they all admired his coat. Then of course they all abandoned him and his coat, and turned their attention as usual to the tables set for whist. All this—the noise, the talk, and the crowd of people—was strange and wonderful to Akaky Akakyevitch. He simply did not know how to behave, what to do with his arms and legs and his whole figure; at last he sat down beside the players, looked at the cards, stared first at one and then at another of the faces, and in a little while began to yawn and felt that he was bored—especially as it was long past the time at which he usually went to bed. He tried to take leave of his hosts, but they would not let him go, saying that he absolutely must have a glass of champagne in honor of the new coat. An hour later supper was served, consisting of salad, cold veal, a pasty, pies, and tarts from the confectioner's, and champagne. They made Akaky Akakyevitch drink two glasses, after which he felt that things were much more cheerful, though he could not forget that it was twelve o'clock and that he ought to have been home long ago. That his host might not take it into his head to detain him, he slipped out of the room, hunted in the entry for his greatcoat, which he found, not without regret, lying on the floor, shook it, removed some fluff from it, put it on, and went down the stairs into the street. It was still light in the streets. Some little general shops, those perpetual clubs for house-serfs and all sorts of people, were open; others which were closed showed, however, a long streak of light at every crack of the door, proving that they were not yet deserted, and probably maids and men-servants were still finishing their conversation and discussion, driving their masters to utter perplexity as to their whereabouts. Akaky Akakyevitch walked along in a cheerful state of mind; he was even on the point of running, goodness knows why, after a lady of some sort who passed by like lightning with every part of her frame in violent motion. He checked himself at once, however, and again walked along very gently, feeling positively surprised himself at the inexplicable impulse that had seized him. Soon the deserted streets, which are not particularly cheerful by day and even less so in the evening, stretched before him. Now they were still more dead and deserted; the light of street lamps was scantier, the oil was evidently running low; then came wooden houses and fences; not a soul anywhere; only the snow gleamed on the streets and the low-pitched slumbering hovels looked black and gloomy with their closed shutters. He approached the spot where the street was intersected by an endless square, which looked like a fearful desert with its houses scarcely visible on the further side.

In the distance, goodness knows where, there was a gleam of light from some sentry box which seemed to be standing at the end of the world. Akaky Akakyevitch's lightheartedness grew somehow sensibly less at this place. He stepped into the square, not without an involuntary uneasiness, as though his heart had a foreboding of evil. He looked behind him and to both sides—it was as though the sea were all around him. "No, better not look," he thought, and walked on, shutting his eyes, and when he opened them to see whether the end of the square were near, he suddenly saw standing before him, almost under his very nose, some men with moustaches; just what they were like he could not even distinguish. There was a mist before his eyes and a throbbing in his chest. "I say the overcoat is mine!" said one of them in a voice like a clap of thunder, seizing him by the collar. Akaky Akakyevitch was on the point of shouting "Help" when another put a fist the size of a clerk's head against his very lips, saying: "You just shout now." Akaky Akakyevitch felt only that they took the overcoat off, and gave him a kick with their knees, and he fell on his face in the snow and was conscious of nothing more. A few minutes later he came to himself and got on to his feet, but there was no one there. He felt that it was cold on the ground and that he had no overcoat, and began screaming, but it seemed as though his voice could not carry to the end of the square. Overwhelmed with despair and continuing to scream, he ran across the square straight to the sentry box, beside which stood a sentry leaning on his halberd and, so it seemed, looking with curiosity to see who the devil the man was who was screaming and running towards him from the distance. As Akaky Akakyevitch reached him, he began breathlessly shouting that he was asleep and not looking after his duty not to see that a man was being robbed. The sentry answered that he had seen nothing, that he had only seen him stopped in the middle of the square by two men, and supposed that they were his friends, and that, instead of abusing him for nothing, he had better go the next day to the superintendent and that he would find out who had taken the overcoat. Akaky Akakyevitch ran home in a terrible state: his hair, which was still comparatively abundant on his temples and the back of his head, was completely dishevelled; his sides and chest and his trousers were all covered with snow. When his old landlady heard a fearful knock at the door she jumped hurriedly out of bed and, with only one slipper on, ran to open it, modestly holding her shift across her bosom; but when she opened it she stepped back, seeing what a state Akaky Akakyevitch was in. When he told her what had happened, she clasped her hands in horror and said that he must go straight to the superintendent, that the police constable of the quarter would deceive him, make promises and lead him a dance; that it would be best of all to go to the superintendent, and that she knew him indeed, because Anna the Finnish girl who was once her cook was now in service as a nurse at the superintendent's; and that she often saw him himself when he passed by their house, and that he used to be every Sunday at church too, saying his prayers and at the same time looking good-humoredly at every one, and that therefore by every token he must be a kindhearted man. After listening to this advice, Akaky Akakyevitch made his way very gloomily to his room, and how he spent that night I leave to the imagination of those who are in the least able to picture the position of others. Early in the morning he set off to the police superintendent's, but was told that he was asleep. He came at ten o'clock, he was told again that he was asleep; he came at eleven and was told that the superintendent was not at home; he came at dinner time, but the clerks in the anteroom would not let him in, and insisted on knowing what was the matter and what business had brought him and exactly what had happened; so that at last Akaky Akakyevitch for the first time in his life tried to show the strength of his character and said curtly that he must see the superintendent himself, that they dare not refuse to admit him, that he had come from the department on government business, and that if he made complaint of them they would see. The clerks dared say nothing to this, and one of them went to summon the superintendent. The latter received his story of being robbed of his overcoat in an extremely strange way. Instead of attending to the main point, he began asking Akaky Akakyevitch questions, why had he been coming home so late? wasn't he going, or hadn't he been, to some house of ill-fame? so that Akaky Akakyevitch was overwhelmed with confusion, and went away without knowing whether or not the proper measures would be taken in regard to his overcoat. He was absent from the office all that day (the only time that it had happened in his life). Next day he appeared with a pale face, wearing his old "dressing jacket" which had become a still more pitiful sight. The tidings of the theft of the overcoat—though there were clerks who did not let even this chance slip of jeering at Akaky Akakyevitch—touched many of them. They decided on the spot to get up a subscription for him, but collected only a very trifling sum, because the clerks had already spent a good deal on subscribing to the director's portrait and on the purchase of a book, at the suggestion of the head of their department, who was a friend of the author, and so the total realized was very insignificant. One of the clerks, moved by compassion, ventured at any rate to assist Akaky Akakyevitch with good advice, telling him not to go to the district police inspector, because, though it might happen that the latter might be sufficiently zealous of gaining the approval of his superiors to succeed in finding the overcoat, it would remain in the possession of the police unless he presented legal proofs that it belonged to him; he urged that far the best thing would be to appeal to a Person of Consequence; that the Person of Consequence, by writing and getting into communication with the proper authorities, could push the matter through more successfully. There was nothing else for it. Akaky Akakyevitch made up his mind to go to the Person of Consequence. What precisely was the nature of the functions of the Person of Consequence has remained a matter of uncertainty. It must be noted that this Person of Consequence had only lately become a person of consequence, and until recently had been a person of no consequence. Though, indeed, his position even now was not reckoned of consequence in comparison with others of still greater consequence. But there is always to be found a circle of persons to whom a person of little consequence in the eyes of others is a person of consequence. It is true that he did his utmost to increase the consequence of his position in various ways, for instance by insisting that his subordinates should come out on to the stairs to meet him when he arrived at his office; that no one should venture to approach him directly but all proceedings should be by the strictest order of precedence, that a collegiate registration clerk should report the matter to the provincial secretary, and the provincial secretary to the titular councillor or whomsoever it might be, and that business should only reach him by this channel. Everyone in Holy Russia has a craze for imitation, everyone apes and mimics his superiors. I have actually been told that a titular councillor who was put in charge of a small separate office, immediately partitioned off a special room for himself, calling it the head office, and set special porters at the door with red collars and gold lace, who took hold of the handle of the door and opened it for everyone who went in, though the "head office" was so tiny that it was with difficulty that an ordinary writing table could be put into it. The manners and habits of the Person of Consequence were dignified and majestic, but not complex. The chief foundation of his system was strictness, "strictness, strictness, and—strictness!" he used to say, and at the last word he would look very significantly at the person he was addressing, though, indeed, he had no reason to do so, for the dozen clerks who made up the whole administrative mechanism of his office stood in befitting awe of him; any clerk who saw him in the distance would leave his work and remain standing at attention till his superior had left the room. His conversation with his subordinates was usually marked by severity and almost confined to three phrases: "How dare you? Do you know to whom you are speaking? Do you understand who I am?" He was, however, at heart a good-natured man, pleasant and obliging with his colleagues; but the grade of general had completely turned his head. When he received it, he was perplexed, thrown off his balance, and quite at a loss how to behave. If he chanced to be with his equals, he was still quite a decent man, a very gentlemanly man, in fact, and in many ways even an intelligent man, but as soon as he was in company with men who were even one grade below him, there was simply no doing anything with him: he sat silent and his position excited compassion, the more so as he himself felt that he might have been spending his time to incomparably more advantage. At times there could be seen in his eyes an intense desire to join in some interesting conversation, but he was restrained by the doubt whether it would not be too much on his part, whether it would not be too great a familiarity and lowering of his dignity, and in consequence of these reflections he remained everlastingly in the same mute condition, only uttering from time to time monosyllabic sounds, and in this way he gained the reputation of being a very tiresome man.

So this was the Person of Consequence to whom our friend Akaky Akakyevitch appealed, and he appealed to him at a most unpropitious moment, very unfortunate for himself, though fortunate, indeed, for the Person of Consequence. The latter happened to be in his study, talking in the very best of spirits with an old friend of his childhood who had only just arrived and whom he had not seen for several years. It was at this moment that he was informed that a man called Bashmatchkin was asking to see him. He asked abruptly, "What sort of man is he?" and received the answer, "A government clerk." "Ah! he can wait, I haven't time now," said the Person of Consequence. Here I must observe that this was a complete lie on the part of the Person of Consequence: he had time; his friend and he had long ago said all they had to say to each other and their conversation had begun to be broken by very long pauses during which they merely slapped each other on the knee, saying, "So that's how things are, Ivan Abramovitch!"—"There it is, Stepan Varlamovitch!" but, for all that, he told the clerk to wait in order to show his friend, who had left the service years before and was living at home in the country, how long clerks had to wait in his anteroom. At last after they had talked, or rather been silent to their heart's content and had smoked a cigar in very comfortable armchairs with sloping backs, he seemed suddenly to recollect, and said to the secretary, who was standing at the door with papers for his signature: "Oh, by the way, there is a clerk waiting, isn't there? tell him he can come in." When he saw Akaky Akakyevitch's meek appearance and old uniform, he turned to him at once and said: "What do you want?" in a firm and abrupt voice, which he had purposely practiced in his own room in solitude before the looking-glass for a week before receiving his present post and the grade of a general. Akaky Akakyevitch, who was overwhelmed with befitting awe beforehand, was somewhat confused and, as far as his tongue would allow him, explained to the best of his powers, with even more frequent "ers" than usual, that he had had a perfectly new overcoat and now he had been robbed of it in the most inhuman way, and that now he had come to beg him by his intervention either to correspond with his honor the head policemaster or anybody else, and find the overcoat. This mode of proceeding struck the general for some reason as taking a great liberty. "What next, sir," he went on as abruptly, "don't you know the way to proceed? To whom are you addressing yourself? Don't you know how things are done? You ought first to have handed in a petition to the office; it would have gone to the head clerk of the room, and to the head clerk of the section, then it would have been handed to the secretary and the secretary would have brought it to me . . . ."

"But, your Excellency," said Akaky Akakyevitch, trying to collect all the small allowance of presence of mind he possessed and feeling at the same time that he was getting into a terrible perspiration, "I ventured, your Excellency, to trouble you because secretaries . . . er . . . are people you can't depend on . . . ."

"What? what? what?" said the Person of Consequence, "where did you get hold of that spirit? where did you pick up such ideas? What insubordination is spreading among young men against their superiors and betters." The Person of Consequence did not apparently observe that Akaky Akakyevitch was well over fifty, and therefore if he could have been called a young man it would only have been in comparison with a man of seventy. "Do you know to whom you are speaking? do you understand who I am? do you understand that, I ask you?" At this point he stamped, and raised his voice to such a powerful note that Akaky Akakyevitch was not the only one to be terrified. Akaky Akakyevitch was positively petrified; he staggered, trembling all over, and could not stand; if the porters had not run up to support him, he would have flopped upon the floor; he was led out almost unconscious. The Person of Consequence, pleased that the effect had surpassed his expectations and enchanted at the idea that his words could even deprive a man of consciousness, stole a sideway glance at his friend to see how he was taking it, and perceived not without satisfaction that his friend was feeling very uncertain and even beginning to be a little terrified himself.

How he got downstairs, how he went out into the street—of all that Akaky Akakyevitch remembered nothing, he had no feeling in his arms or his legs. In all his life he had never been so severely reprimanded by a general, and this was by one of another department, too. He went out into the snowstorm, that was whistling through the streets, with his mouth open, and as he went he stumbled off the pavement; the wind, as its way is in Petersburg, blew upon him from all points of the compass and from every side street. In an instant it had blown a quinsy into his throat, and when he got home he was not able to utter a word; with a swollen face and throat he went to bed. So violent is sometimes the effect of a suitable reprimand!

Next day he was in a high fever. Thanks to the gracious assistance of the Petersburg climate, the disease made more rapid progress than could have been expected, and when the doctor came, after feeling his pulse he could find nothing to do but prescribe a fomentation, and that simply that the patient might not be left without the benefit of medical assistance; however, two days later he informed him that his end was at hand, after which he turned to his landlady and said: "And you had better lose no time, my good woman, but order him now a deal coffin—an oak one will be too dear for him." Whether Akaky Akakyevitch heard these fateful words or not, whether they produced a shattering effect upon him, and whether he regretted his pitiful life, no one can tell, for he was all the time in delirium and fever. Apparitions, each stranger than the one before, were continually haunting him: first, he saw Petrovitch and was ordering him to make a greatcoat trimmed with some sort of traps for robbers, who were, he fancied, continually under the bed, and he was calling his landlady every minute to pull out a thief who had even got under the quilt; then he kept asking why his old "dressing jacket" was hanging before him when he had a new overcoat, then he fancied he was standing before the general listening to the appropriate reprimand and saying "I am sorry, your Excellency," then finally he became abusive, uttering the most awful language, so that his old landlady positively crossed herself, having never heard anything of the kind from him before, and the more horrified because these dreadful words followed immediately upon the phrase "your Excellency." Later on, his talk was a mere medley of nonsense, so that it was quite unintelligible; all that could be seen was that his incoherent words and thoughts were concerned with nothing but the overcoat. At last poor Akaky Akakyevitch gave up the ghost. No seal was put upon his room nor upon his things, because, in the first place, he had no heirs and, in the second, the property left was very small, to wit, a bundle of goose feathers, a quire of white government paper, three pairs of socks, two or three buttons that had come off his trousers, and the "dressing jacket" with which the reader is already familiar. Who came into all this wealth God only knows, even I who tell the tale must own that I have not troubled to inquire. And Petersburg remained without Akaky Akakyevitch, as though, indeed, he had never been in the city. A creature had vanished and departed whose cause no one had championed, who was dear to no one, of interest to no one, who never even attracted the attention of the student of natural history, though the latter does not disdain to fix a common fly upon a pin and look at him under the microscope — a creature who bore patiently the jeers of the office and for no particular reason went to his grave, though even he at the very end of his life was visited by a gleam of brightness in the form of an overcoat that for one instant brought color into his poor life — a creature on whom calamity broke as insufferably as it breaks upon the heads of the mighty ones of this world . . . !

Several days after his death, the porter from the department was sent to his lodgings with instructions that he should go at once to the office, for his chief was asking for him; but the porter was obliged to return without him, explaining that he could not come, and to the inquiry "Why?" he added, "Well, you see: the fact is he is dead, he was buried three days ago." This was how they learned at the office of the death of Akaky Akakyevitch, and the next day there was sitting in his seat a new clerk who was very much taller and who wrote not in the same upright hand but made his letters more slanting and crooked.

But who could have imagined that this was not all there was to tell about Akaky Akakyevitch, that he was destined for a few days to make a noise in the world after his death, as though to make up for his life having been unnoticed by any one? But so it happened, and our poor story unexpectedly finishes with a fantastic ending. Rumors were suddenly floating about Petersburg that in the neighborhood of the Kalinkin Bridge and for a little distance beyond, a corpse had taken to appearing at night in the form of a clerk looking for a stolen overcoat, and stripping from the shoulders of all passers-by, regardless of grade and calling, overcoats of all descriptions—trimmed with cat fur or beaver or wadded, lined with raccoon, fox, and bear—made, in fact, of all sorts of skin which men have adapted for the covering of their own. One of the clerks of the department saw the corpse with his own eyes and at once recognized it as Akaky Akakyevitch; but it excited in him such terror, however, that he ran away as fast as his legs could carry him and so could not get a very clear view of him, and only saw him hold up his finger threateningly in the distance.

From all sides complaints were continually coming that backs and shoulders, not of mere titular councillors, but even of upper court councillors, had been exposed to taking chills, owing to being stripped of their greatcoats. Orders were given to the police to catch the corpse regardless of trouble or expense, alive or dead, and to punish him in the cruelest way, as an example to others, and, indeed, they very nearly succeeded in doing so. The sentry of one district police station in Kiryushkin Place snatched a corpse by the collar on the spot of the crime in the very act of attempting to snatch a frieze overcoat from a retired musician, who used in his day to play the flute. Having caught him by the collar, he shouted until he had brought two other comrades, whom he charged to hold him while he felt just a minute in his boot to get out a snuffbox in order to revive his nose which had six times in his life been frostbitten, but the snuff was probably so strong that not even a dead man could stand it. The sentry had hardly had time to put his finger over his right nostril and draw up some snuff in the left when the corpse sneezed violently right into the eyes of all three. While they were putting their fists up to wipe them, the corpse completely vanished, so that they were not even sure whether he had actually been in their hands. From that time forward, the sentries conceived such a horror of the dead that they were even afraid to seize the living and confined themselves to shouting from the distance: "Hi, you there, be off!" and the dead clerk began to appear even on the other side of the Kalinkin Bridge, rousing no little terror in all timid people.

We have, however, quite deserted the Person of Consequence, who may in reality almost be said to be the cause of the fantastic ending of this perfectly true story. To begin with, my duty requires me to do justice to the Person of Consequence by recording that soon after poor Akaky Akakyevitch had gone away crushed to powder, he felt something not unlike regret. Sympathy was a feeling not unknown to him; his heart was open to many kindly impulses, although his exalted grade very often prevented them from being shown. As soon as his friend had gone out of his study, he even began brooding over poor Akaky Akakyevitch, and from that time forward, he was almost every day haunted by the image of the poor clerk who had succumbed so completely to the befitting reprimand. The thought of the man so worried him that a week later he actually decided to send a clerk to find out how he was and whether he really could help him in any way. And when they brought him word that Akaky Akakyevitch had died suddenly in delirium and fever, it made a great impression on him, his conscience reproached him and he was depressed all day. Anxious to distract his mind and to forget the unpleasant impression, he went to spend the evening with one of his friends, where he found a genteel company and, what was best of all, almost every one was of the same grade so that he was able to be quite free from restraint. This had a wonderful effect on his spirits, he expanded, became affable and genial—in short, spent a very agreeable evening. At supper he drank a couple of glasses of champagne—a proceeding which we all know has a happy effect in inducing good humor. The champagne made him inclined to do something unusual, and he decided not to go home yet but to visit a lady of his acquaintance, one Karolina Ivanovna—a lady apparently of German extraction, for whom he entertained extremely friendly feelings. It must be noted that the Person of Consequence was a man no longer young, an excellent husband, and the respectable father of a family. He had two sons, one already serving in his office, and a nice-looking daughter of sixteen with a rather turned-up, pretty little nose, who used to come every morning to kiss his hand, saying: "*Bonjour, Papa.*" His wife, who was still blooming and decidedly good-looking, indeed, used first to give him her hand to kiss and then would kiss his hand, turning it the other side upwards. But though the Person of Consequence was perfectly satisfied with the kind amenities of his domestic life, he thought it proper to have a lady friend in another quarter of the town. This lady friend was not a bit better looking nor younger than his wife, but these mysterious facts exist in the world and it is not our business to criticize them. And so the Person of Consequence went downstairs, got into his sledge, and said to his coachman, "To Karolina Ivanovna," while luxuriously wrapped in his warm fur coat he remained in that agreeable frame of mind sweeter to a Russian than anything that could be invented, that is, when one thinks of nothing while thoughts come into the mind of themselves, one pleasanter than the other, without the labor of following them or looking for them. Full of satisfaction, he recalled all the amusing moments of the evening he had spent, all the phrases that had set the little circle laughing; many of them he repeated in an undertone and found them as amusing as before, and so, very naturally, laughed very heartily at them again. From time to time, however, he was disturbed by a gust of wind which, blowing suddenly, God knows whence and wherefore, cut him in the face, pelting him with flakes of snow, puffing out his coat collar like a sack, or suddenly flinging it with unnatural force over his head and giving him endless trouble to extricate himself from it. All at once, the Person of Consequence felt that someone had clutched him very tightly by the collar. Turning round he saw a short man in a shabby old uniform, and not without horror recognized him as Akaky Akakyevitch. The clerk's face was white as snow and looked like that of a corpse, but the horror of the Person of Consequence was beyond all bounds when he saw the mouth of the corpse distorted into speech and, breathing upon him the chill of the grave, it uttered the following words: "Ah, so here you are at last! At last I've ... er ... caught you by the collar. It's your overcoat I want, you refused to help me and abused me into the bargain! So now give me yours!" The poor Person of Consequence very nearly died. Resolute and determined as he was in his office and before subordinates in general, and though any one looking at his manly air and figure would have said: "Oh, what a man of character!" yet in this plight he felt, like very many persons of athletic appearance, such terror that not without reason he began to be afraid he would have some sort of fit. He actually flung his overcoat off his shoulders as fast as he could and shouted to his coachman in a voice unlike his own: "Drive home and make haste!" The coachman, hearing the tone which he had only heard in critical moments and then accompanied by something even more rousing, hunched his shoulders up to his ears in case of worse following, swung his whip and flew on like an arrow. In a little over six minutes the Person of Consequence was at the entrance of his own house. Pale, panic-stricken, and without his overcoat, he arrived home instead of at Karolina Ivanovna's, dragged himself to his own room and spent the night in great perturbation, so that next morning his daughter said to him at breakfast, "You look quite pale today, Papa": but her papa remained mute and said not a word to anyone of what had happened to him, where he had been, and where he had been going. The incident made a great impression upon him. Indeed, it happened far more rarely that he said to his subordinates, "How dare you? do you understand who I am?" and he never uttered those words at all until he had first heard all the rights of the case.

What was even more remarkable is that from that time the apparition of the dead clerk ceased entirely: apparently the general's overcoat had fitted him perfectly, anyway nothing more was heard of overcoats being snatched from any one. Many restless and anxious people refused, however, to be pacified, and still maintained that in remote parts of the town the ghost of the dead clerk went on appearing. One sentry in Kolomna, for instance, saw with his own eyes a ghost appear from behind a house; but, being by natural constitution somewhat feeble—so much so that on one occasion an ordinary, well-grown pig, making a sudden dash out of some building, knocked him off his feet to the vast entertainment of the cabmen standing round, from whom he exacted two kopecks each for snuff for such rudeness—he did not dare to stop it, and so followed it in the dark until the ghost suddenly looked round and, stopping, asked him: "What do you want?" displaying a fist such as you never see among the living. The sentry said: "Nothing," and turned back on the spot. This ghost, however, was considerably taller and adorned with immense moustaches, and, directing its steps apparently towards Obuhov Bridge, vanished into the darkness of the night.